GW01398039

DALEN PAX AND THE FOUNTAIN OF TRUTH

Dalen Pax
and the
Fountain of Truth

By Will Grey

To My Father

You taught me about the honor of putting everything on the

line to protect your country.

To fight for what I believe in.

And the truth about being both a warrior and a man.

Nothing but love.

Dalen Pax and the Fountain of Truth Dyslexic Edition

Text©2024 Will Grey (Simon)

The Way of Grey Publishing

All rights reserved, including the right to
reproduce this book or portions thereof
in any form whatsoever.
For information, e-mail the publisher at:

merlynsforge42@gmail.com

First Edition

ISBN
Hardcover: 978-1-64372-140-8
Softcover978-1-64372-142-2

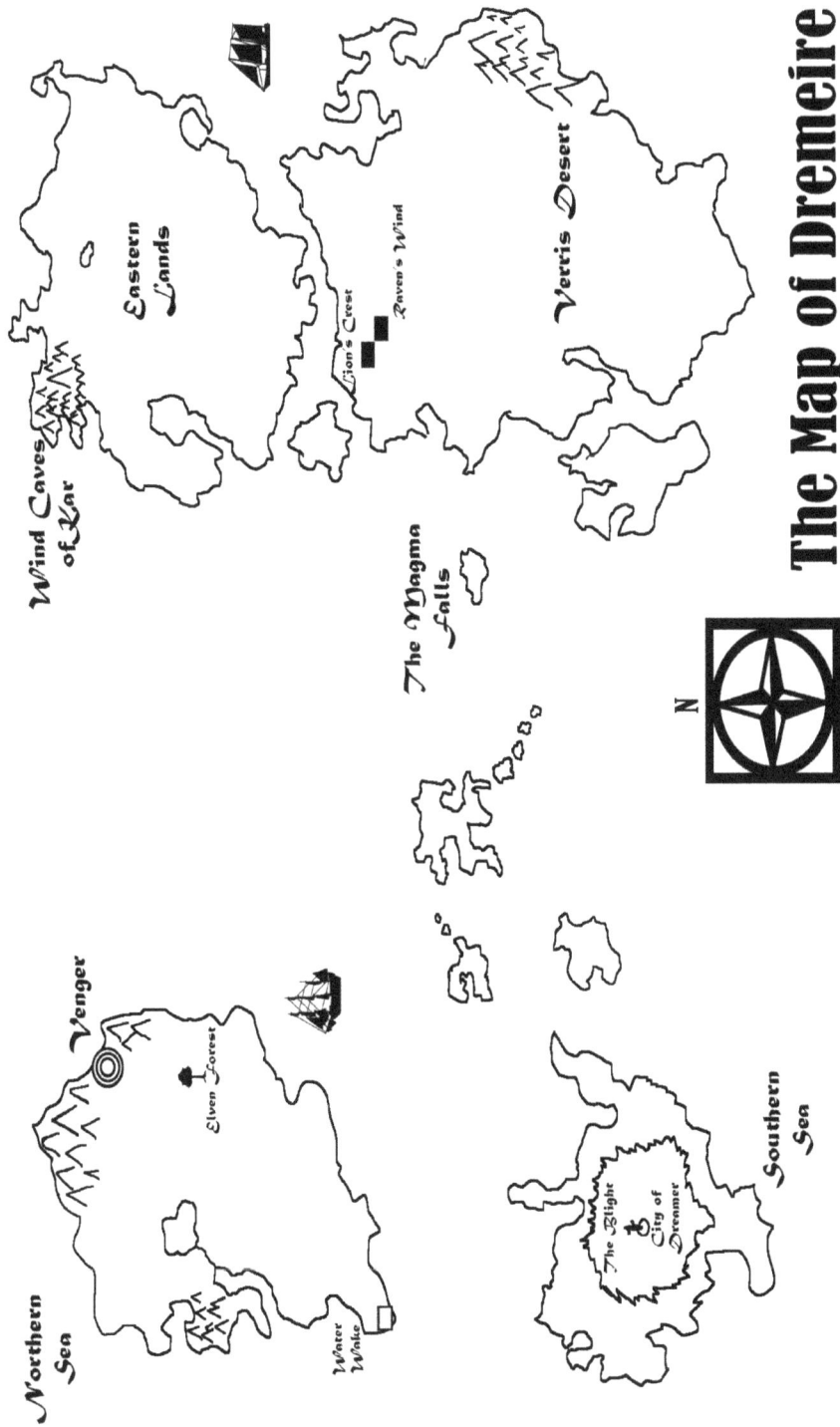

The Map of Dremeire

Northern Sea

Venger

Wind Caves of Kar

Eastern Lands

Elven Forest

Water Wake

The Magma Falls

Lion's Crest

Raven's Wind

Verris Desert

N

The Blight
City of
Dreamer

Southern Sea

TABLE OF CONTENTS

0

REFLECTION

There are some moments in time better left forgotten. Like an old pair of shoes, they have been worn out through miles of walking and have all but fallen apart. The only reason for keeping them is because of some emotional value placed upon them, and they no longer serve as they should. It would be best to discard them, but they are kept for sentimental reasons, in some dark back corner. From time to time, they will be walked in again, even though it is known they will only cause pain.

Most experience pain subjectively, and most would agree

that it is something to avoid, but nearly all have poked a bruise just to have it hurt as a child and were often told by someone older not to do that. That it was wrong, and one should not cause themselves to feel pain, and from one side of the coin that can be true. Courting pain – invites it. Inviting pain can, and often does, deliver. Most would not want to see another choose such a life and they would be coming from a place of wisdom and love when they suggest avoiding it unless it serves a useful purpose.

But what if the suggestion is heard by the minds of those who take a different understanding of that side of the coin? And what if what they hear is that they should always be afraid of pain? What if they understand that pain is bad, and one should never invite it? What if pain was something to be ashamed of? What if they had to hide their pain and live in fear that someone might see it?

Some people would say that not allowing yourself to process the pain is a great way to not recover from it, that in doing so that person would condemn themselves to a life of pain and fear. Not taking with them the intention of the lesson, the truth is, that pain should not be courted but should also not be shrouded. Pain is funny that way.

Constantly living a life of pain, the mind learns to adapt and even anticipate that hurt. Once it anticipates the suffering, it will become stressed if it doesn't get it, causing an anomaly within the mind where someone can become addicted to the pain, which brings me back to those shoes. Why do you keep them if they bring you nothing but agony?

Some moments in time should be saved and protected through time. Although sometimes those memories are of moments of pain, they are now a source of strength and determination. When those memories are thought of, they do not stir up the memory of the hurt, but instead, stir up the sensation of the strength it took to overcome it.

The difference between the two is how they are perceived.

Perception. It is the fundamental tool used to understand everything around us. It defines how we view things as they come into our understanding, and it is the lens we cast our field of intent through as we project outward. It makes us unique because each is different. Perception is both the thing that connects us all and that which keeps us separated, the notion that creates wars and decides who is a friend or foe.

Moving a layer in, each of us is a single being, but we carry many perspectives. The Tin Soldiers that we portray. An aunt and a sister. A father and a son. A friend and a foe. Being the individual that we are, we can shift from one to another as required. A woman and her sister can shift and become mommy or auntie the moment that the child walks into the room and perceives them as such, and they will shift perspective within themselves as they perceive the child.

Like the Divine field, always shifting and moving, with each God becoming a different version of themselves, as needed, depending on the individual perceiving them. Sometimes people must be more than one Tin Soldier at a time, and it can be confusing, not only to the people around them who only perceive them one

3

way, like a mother or an aunt, but to themselves as well. It's like being at a party with close friends, grandparents, and a few people from work, where it can feel overwhelming and stressful trying to be three different versions of yourself while shifting between them all to fit the persona known by everyone at the party.

What if someone could recognize that each perception was just an element of who they truly are? And what if they could see themselves as the person who is all of them at once? The element in the center of the circle. The thing that is greater than the sum of all its parts. Then there would be an understanding that they are already each of the respective perceptions. Whole. Changing not only the point of view of everyone who perceives them...but also themselves.

1

ARRIVING IN TIME

Dorn stared in disbelief as he watched the connection to the Elemental Blades in his children dissipate like fog in the morning sun. They were still connected to their elements and still held all their powers, but the connection to the keys that kept the nexus in balance was gone and the blades along with it.

Dorn and Venger had chosen this location because of the nexus. The energy it created was needed to sustain Venger, but her feeding on such nexuses made them unstable. When they chose this location, they knew that if they did not find a way to harmonize the nexus, there would be a possibility of creating a fissure in time and space. If that should happen, they knew the Chaos Dragon that destroyed the City of Dreams would tear its way into this world, with only one intention in its being. To kill Venger and destroy everything that Dorn held dear.

The answer they created was four Elemental Blades that when placed at the center of the nexus would stabilize the energy and keep the nexus harmonized. But there was a catch. Each of the Elemental Blades had to be owned by someone. They needed a wielder to activate their power. So, Venger, while in the form of a woman, and Dorn had four children before creating the foundation of Venger's true form, a living city. Each of their children was born directly tied to one of the four base elements of the natural field of reality. Earth, Air, Fire, and Water, each matching those of the Elemental Blades.

Dorn had sustained Venger during her pregnancy, but it was extremely hard on her to hold a human form for so long, so once the children had arrived, she let go of the form of a human, and returned to her natural state, which was a large crystal made of pure magic.

Dorn traveled with the children for many years. They explored the world and in time each of the children grew strong enough to wield their blades. Once they were ready, they returned to the location that they had long awaited to call home.

Dorn took them to the nexus and bound each elemental blade to one of his children. They were now the guardians of the nexus, and they would be this world's protectors for the rest of time. Once the nexus was harmonized Dorn placed the crystal in the center of it, and together the five of them made a wish.

Venger awoke from her slumber and began to draw power from the Nexus. As she did, she began to grow a new body. A body that her mind and soul would reside in, but it was not a body of flesh and blood, but a body of stone, and the City of Venger began to grow and take shape. Three concentric circles with the center point being the Nexus. The first ring was a representation of the Body Sphere of reality. Moving inward toward the center, the second ring was a representation of the Mind Sphere, and in the center of it all was the Soul Sphere.

The city was completed in a single day and once it was finished Venger created an avatar of the woman. The woman that Dorn had fallen in love with and for the first time in their lives her children got to feel their mother's loving embrace.

For a thousand years, they lived in harmony. Word spread of a magic city where your dreams and wishes could come true. Many people from many races and backgrounds flocked to Venger to begin their lives and there was great joy and peace. It was as if the mythical City of Dreams had been reborn. Thousands called Venger home, but there was a multitude of people who only visited, for many of them did not wish to find a home, but wished for adventure, fortune, or fame. They wished to find a piece of themselves, or a loved one gone missing. Venger would lend her support to help them, but often it would mean sending them forth to find their destinies.

Then one day, everything started to go wrong.

There was no doubt that there had been more that had happened before they noticed, but no matter how hard Dorn or Venger tried, they could not see anything from before the disappearance of a young boy named Kavlin. There had been no reason that anyone could guess that explained why Kavlin was taken. What is known is that Kavlin's disappearance was magical in nature. Someone or something had hidden their tracks, and no form of magic could divine what had happened to the boy. A city-wide search took place, and not only did they not find the boy, but another child went missing as well. A little girl named Xoxann, who was in the same class as Kavlin, disappeared the following day and the connection could not be ignored. Two days of intensive searching using every method available to Dorn and Lady Venger were used. They searched throughout the city and the outlying areas until all resources were depleted and neither child was found.

Venger sat on the crest of a cliff that was a few hundred feet high. At the bottom were a few small beaches but mainly just rocky shorelines and the northern sea. The concern was that they had somehow gotten out of the city and had possibly fallen from the cliffs. The shore was checked but nothing was found. They were thorough, but most people knew that if they had crossed the seal, Venger would have known about it, and everyone was convinced that the children must still be in Venger City.

Dorn became sure there were darker forces at work, and he was concerned what had happened before would happen again. So, Dorn set up garrisons of guards all over the city, waiting for the next move.

He didn't have to wait long.

Time itself was under attack. Reports began to come in of looping time and something akin to de ja vu, the difference being that once the event happened a second time, it was different from the previous memory, rather than happening exactly as before. Venger and Dorn used the reports to figure out where they believed the culprit was, and to their dismay, their hunch was proven right when the guards sent to investigate the area aged a thousand years instantly and were turned to dust. The Guardians of the Nexus were called for. It was believed that being a direct descendant of Dorn and Venger, they were immortal and wouldn't age. Dorn and Venger hoped that another time attack would not affect them. This was what the enemy had been waiting for. Whoever was attacking with time, incapacitated them and what could not be done was done. The Time Mage severed them from the Elemental Blades permanently.

Venger had been monitoring her children and the moment that there had been any sign of trouble they were teleported back to the castle. They had only been in the battle for all of three seconds, and yet in that time, they had sustained injuries to their bodies, minds, and souls.

Dorn was holding his daughter Jax in his arms. She was the only one who was still conscious as they appeared on the floor of the throne room. She normally had a rich mocha coloring to her skin but had now turned pale. He stroked her chestnut hair as she slipped in and out of consciousness. "What happened?" he pleaded.

"Time Mage." Her eyes rolled back for a moment.

"Stay with me, Jax." Dorn was holding her head up and began to vigorously rub her neck. He tried to heal her, but even with his greatest efforts, it only barely brought her back around. "Where are the Elemental Blades?"

"Gone." She grasped at Dorn's sleeve as if she were frightened that she would die if she let go. "Daddy. I'm scared."

She started to pass out, but Dorn shook her. "Look at me." She was no longer focusing. "Jax! Look at me!" Her eyes found him, and tears began to form. "Have I ever lied to you?"

Jax began to openly weep. "No Daddy."

"Look at me." He looked his daughter in her eyes and made a vow. "You are going to be ok. I promise." She closed her eyes and nodded. "Is there anything else you can tell me about the Time Mage?"

"She's a little girl." And with that, Jax passed out, and Dorn could feel her life fading from her. Her, and all his children.

"Do something!" Venger demanded. "Save our children!"

"What you ask of me, I cannot do." Dorn's words shook as he whispered. All he could do was hold his daughter and watch her die.

"You have the power to save them!" Venger was panicking and it surfaced as anger.

"You know I made a vow to never change the fate of another. What you ask of me, I cannot do." Tears rolled down his face as he held Jax close.

"Yes, you can. You choose not to!" Venger scolded.

"It goes against everything I stand for... Everything I have stood for since the beginning. I can't just break the laws to serve my own purpose. You know that."

"I know you have the power to save our children, and you would rather stand by and watch them die than lift a finger to save them because of some ideal you made a long, long time ago!" Venger's anger was growing as fear fueled her every word. "You made that damn law before you knew what would be at stake. Can't you break it just this once? You are above the law!"

Dorn held his dying daughter, and his pain dripped from his soul, but he matched her fury. "If anyone... even me... is above it, then it is not a law! I cannot do what you ask!" Dorn's heart tore in two and then in two again. Not only was he about to watch all four of his children die but he was breaking the heart of the love of his life, and the worst of it, she was right. The power to save them was within his ability. His heart was about to give in to grief, and he began to consider breaking his only 'real' truth to save them when a voice came from behind them and uttered two words.

"We can." The voice was calm but carried weight like a deep river. "We can do as you ask."

Dorn and Lady Venger turned around to see five individuals standing in the throne room with them. His mind tried to grasp what he was seeing because it should have been impossible to get this close without him or Lady Venger noticing them. He was in grief and not thinking clearly so his instincts chose before his mind had agreed.

"If you are the ones who did this to my children you have only moments to save them before you are destroyed." He set down Jax carefully and stood up to face the intruders. "I break no law if I kill you with my bare hands."

There was a jinn amongst them that wore the garb of the Brotherhood of Light. He was floating above the ground but made a deep bow and lowered himself to the floor. "We are not the ones who did this. We are the ones who have arrived in your time of need. We are from the future... sent by you."

"Prove it." Dorn could already feel the truth in his words, but they were all disjointed from time, and there was a real chance that if not the jinn, one of them could be the Time Mage.

The jinn rose from his bow and showed Dorn his right arm where a marking that looked like a tattoo, made of light, in the shape of three concentric circles was magically embedded in his skin. "I have the blessing of Lady Venger herself. We all do." Each of them bore the marking of the great seal of Venger, and when Dorn reached out with his heart and touched the mark with his soul, he knew it was true.

"Save them." Dorn's stance changed and he went to his

wife. "My love, they speak true."

Lady Venger nodded and took his hand. "I can feel the marks. It seems we have found a way to send ourselves the help we needed." She held him close and began to weep. "I am so sorry. I was scared. I should have known you would have found a way. I am so sorry for everything I said."

Dorn just held her and let her vent. As she cried, he watched the time travelers closely.

Another member of the Brotherhood of Light started checking vital signs. When Dorn looked over the monk asked permission to help. Both Lady Venger and Dorn looked at him confused and said yes. He smiled and said to them both, "You should always have permission, even when doing someone a favor."

Another came up to both Dorn and his wife and without fear or reservation said, "I wish for you both to read my mind to understand who we are and what we are doing here. I grant you permission." He reached out, took both of their hands, and closed his eyes. Venger allowed the wish to come true, and in only a moment, they knew who their sudden guests were. They were the Saviors of Venger.

Dalen looked over to Master Peace and tapped his pin. ‹Are you ready? This is going to get weird.›

Peace just grinned and shook his head. ‹So, like, same as always, eh?›

‹Yup. Here we go.› Dalen slowed down time to a point where

he could see between the frames. This was well within his ability, but he was taking Master Peace with him, so he had to focus, and it took him longer to find the exact speed he required.

‹This is amazingly beautiful that you can do this, and at the same time, terrifying.› Master Peace meant it as a compliment and Dalen took it as such. ‹I can slow it down, but nothing like this.›

Dalen looked around and nodded. ‹You know, I never thought about it, but I can see your point. If I were to attack you with magic from this state, it would... be...› Dalen's thought trailed off as he started to inspect one of Dorn's children, by the name of Jed. ‹I would do something like this. I activated the Eye of the Beholder on my Vengerian Pin. Look at this through my eyes.›

Master Peace allowed his vision to lose focus as he began to allow his mind to draw the picture rather than his eyes. As he did, he saw through Dalen's eyes instead.

Jed was more than human, that was for sure, but he didn't read like a jinn either. Somehow his very essence was magical and directly connected to the Element of Air. Dalen could get lost in trying to understand everything that was a part of his makeup, but he had to focus. It was much like focusing on a 3-D image that can only be seen when changing the focus of the eyes. As Dalen slowly changed his perspective it came into view. Jed was partly frozen in time while another part of him was moving normally in time, and another part was moving backward in time, and the entropy it was creating was tearing him apart like he was being dragged through time by wild horses going in different directions.

‹My guess is that this is not normal.› Master Peace said as he pulled out his weapon and tool, The Dragon Claw of Light, so named for the dragon claw at the end of the handle that created a ball of light with both terrible destructive power and miraculous healing abilities. ‹Just tell me how you want me to do this.›

‹They have been hit with some sort of time attack. We are going to have to realign them.› Dalen was still trying to find the source of the attack when Dorn began to move at the same speed they were.

"I will apologize for eavesdropping later, but for now, know that I can hear your thoughts Jinn, you said attacked by time. We sent them to stop a Time Mage." Dorn looked at them closely. "This should not be possible. The only thing that could do something like this would be..." Dorn stopped dead in his tracks and put his hand over his mouth. "It can't be."

"It can't be what? And please, they don't have time for secrets. You sent us because you trusted us. What am I up against?" Dalen's words were strong and to the point. He knew that Dorn had to focus if they were going to save them. Even in this state, time was running out for them.

"The Time Stone." Dorn looked at his children closely. "It's the only answer."

"Thank you for your trust." said Master Peace, "but what does that mean?"

Dorn knew the monks from the Brotherhood of Light were correct. If there was any chance of them saving his children, he had to give full disclosure. "The Time Stone is a single moment of time frozen into a solid state. It was created by Venger's mother, who was the mother of the Jinn. It was created to imprison a, beyond God-like being, that has the power to destroy this world."

"The Chaos Dragon?" asked Master Peace.

Dorn nodded. "While it was in its dormant state, it acted as a seal for the original hole that was ripped in time that had allowed the dragon to come through killing The City of Dreams. Now that it has been removed, it means the dragon has awakened from its slumber, turning the stone into a piece of pure time, powered by a Creator Being more powerful than the Gods. It literally controls time."

Now Dalen understood what he was looking at. The Time Stone was altering them through the Reality Spheres. Their Mind Sphere was being forced backward through time, but their Body Sphere was specifically untouched, so their bodies were still moving forward in time. This caused a disharmony that forced their souls, which were incorporeal, to separate from time completely, thus seemingly not moving through it at all. Any one of those would not be a problem on their own. The problem was that they were beings who lived in all three spheres and moving in all three directions at once was tearing them from reality.

"I can get them back, but there is nothing I can do about their sever from the Elemental Blades. Even in my time, that is a truth."

"But you can save them?" Dorn made no attempt to hide his

concern and fear for his children. Their lives were paramount.

Dalen smiled, "Yes, but I am going to have to play with time to do so."

Dorn looked over to Dalen and looked deep into his soul. "Of course. That's why I would have sent you. You are precisely built to do just that."

"You can see it?" Dalen asked with surprise.

"See what?" asked Peace.

"Sorry Peace. Just found out myself." Dalen shrugged. "Just before the tree. It's why I took so long."

"You are a time anomaly," Dorn said with certainty. "You shouldn't even exist. Time changed and somehow you are both the cause and the outcome of that change."

Dalen nodded. "Keep going."

"Well, first off everything you do since the moment of that time change, affects the entire timeline. How far forward did you come from?" Dorn asked, not wanting to know the answer.

"More than a thousand years," Dalen said, knowing the implications.

Dorn stared at him wide-eyed. "Sending an anomaly in time that far back would..."

"Change the whole thing. I know."

"I swore I would never do that."

"You didn't. We are here because of our choices, and you did nothing but point us in the right direction. You made sure of it. Your oath still stands."

Dorn took a deep breath of relief. "What gets changed?"

"I don't know," Dalen said honestly. "From our point of view, this is how it has always been."

"And why are you also disjointed from time?" Dorn asked.

"We took the Pillar of Time to get here," added Master Peace.

Dorn ran his fingers through his hair a couple of times and then stopped midway and just hung on to it and pulled ever so slightly. "You are an incorporeal divine being that is a time anomaly, which touched the Pillar of Time, disjointing you from it, and then moved out of your timeline? You pose a great threat to everything jinn."

"Ah yes..." Dalen shrugged, "But it does allow me the ability to do this." Dalen slowed time to the point that the frames were so separated that there was an obvious space between the frames of time. It flashed like a slow-moving strobe. Between the frames of reality, the bodies and minds of Dorn's children slipped into superposition in the Quantum field. As this happened each of their three spheres could be managed separately.

A frame of time flashed in, and everyone snapped back into reality for a moment.

"Peace!" Dalen was concentrating on holding time together.

"Light them up. Full strength!"

Master Peace lit up his Dragon Claw and poured himself into it. It ignited with a pure white light of healing energy. The frame disappeared and they all shifted into the quantum realm again. The light filled the room as it moved into superposition and engulfed every space at once.

This was the moment that Dalen was waiting for. He too let go of reality and as he slipped into superposition, he knelt by each of Dorn's four children. Bathed in the Light of Peace, Dalen could see their bodies healing rapidly. He touched their minds and inverted their fields so that they would reharmonize with the way their body's direction was moving in time.

Another frame hit and snapped them all back into reality. As it hit, Dalen let go of his control of time and in doing so it kicked Dorn's children's bodies into realignment and their souls attuned by themselves.

Blaze, Blizzard, Jed, and Jax took a deep gasp of air and sat up. Lady Venger fell to her knees and began to openly weep. Multiple versions of her took form from the very stones of the castle and each of them went to be by her children's side.

Dalen stood up just in time for Dorn to hug him, as another version of Lady Venger emerged from the floor directly in front of Master Peace and began to cry on his shoulder and thank him profusely.

As each of them showed signs that they were all right, they looked their mother in the eyes making sure she knew it. One by one, the other forms of Lady Venger began to meld back into the floor and walls of the castle. Eventually, the only one left was the one that was still holding onto Peace. "How can we repay you?" she asked.

Peace smiled at her and said, "The joy of creating good in the world is more valuable than diamonds or gold." Venger stared at him in awe. "You owe us nothing."

‹I am willing to bet anything I own, that you just did what she said you were going to do.› whispered Oubliette. ‹And on the very first thing you said to her.›

‹Peace.› added Travis. ‹My man.›

"These are the moments we live for Your Majesty," added Sir Adam.

Travis, who was the one who asked them to read their minds, gave both Dorn and Lady Venger a bow. I am hoping you read my mind deep enough to know that we are friends and that we are here to help. I am Travis, and this is my girlfriend Becky behind that shadow."

Becky pulled back her hood, gave a curtsy, and said, "How do you do?" But then she turned her attention back to Travis. ‹So, we are introducing each other to royalty as boyfriend and girlfriend?›

Travis didn't break eye contact with Lady Venger and gave a bow. ‹I think that you and I have gone through enough where I can refer to you as my girlfriend. I was your prince like, five minutes ago.›

‹Well, that was like two thousand years ago.› Becky huffed.

‹From now.› added Travis.

‹What?›

‹Two thousand years from now, not two thousand years ago.› He raised an eyebrow and smiled at her.

"Are you aware, that I can hear your thoughts?" asked Lady Venger.

Becky turned bright red.

Travis replied with a sheepish, "No Ma'am."

"I believe it has to do with this mark," Dalen said as he showed them again the illuminated tattoo on his arm.

Lady Venger saw that Peace had one too. She reached over to it and touched it softly. Master Peace watched as her eyes went slack. She was no longer focusing on what was around her and he guessed that she was magically gleaning information.

"I gave you this mark in recognition of our faith and trust in you. It stores great power and with this, you have full access to the city and all its secrets." She let go of his arm. "You most assuredly are from the future, because I have never made this mark before and I can feel it bypassing secrets and securities that we do not yet have in place."

Dorn clapped his hands together once just to get everyone's attention. "Alright. It's a tough sell, but you have convinced me you are from the future and have been sent by Venger and myself to help us in our time of need. The floor is yours. What do we do next?"

"Next," said Dalen, "Let's get everyone up to speed on both ends. And we need to find someone in your city by the name of Christoph. He is the only hope that any of us have."

2

THE PLAN TO MAKE A KING AND QUEEN

The search for Christoph was short-lived. Dorn had barely had enough time to explain that one of Lady Venger's personal protectors was a man by that name when he and his partner entered the room. They had heard Lady Venger crying and had come in to investigate.

"Dorn." Christoph's hand moved toward his sword as he saw the strangers in Venger's throne room. "We heard Venger weeping. I see we have guests. How would you like us to introduce ourselves?"

‹That may be the coolest way to say, 'You want me to kill them?' that I have ever heard.› Everyone connected to Travis's thoughts could feel respect in his tone.

Christoph's partner smiled with wild eyes as she slid her hand to the sword on her hip. With a practiced fluid motion, she grasped the scabbard just below the hilt and with her thumb, she pushed the blade from its sheath just far enough to unlock it for a faster draw. "If you have hurt my Lady, you will spend the rest of your life asking for forgiveness. Don't worry. It won't take long." She was beautiful and fierce and stared at them with piercing eyes that spoke of life and power. She seemed almost human but there were features about her that were unmistakably elven. Her hair was the color of sapphires with highlighted streaks of periwinkle and white that were braided along the sides to keep it out of her face, all of it came together in the back and cascaded down past her shoulders. She wore custom-fitted black leather armor accented in brilliant green.

‹Okay. She's terrifying.› thought Sir Adam.

‹I love her.› whispered Oubliette as Becky smiled.

"There will be no need for that Grelf." Venger gave her a nod, gesturing for her to stand down.

"Yes," said Dorn. "They are friends. Introduce yourself accordingly. They just saved our children's lives; they are to be trusted."

Christoph nodded and changed to a relaxed stance. Dalen had known Christoph before and recognized him immediately. He looked just as Dalen expected save for the fact that the Christoph he knew had a large burn on his right hand and arm, where this version did not. Dalen assumed that it was from an event that had not yet happened.

Grelf, with a simple move, relocked her sword into place and went to check on Blizzard who was closest to her. Blizzard confirmed the story and Grelf's demeanor changed as she breathed a sigh of relief. She smiled and gave Dalen and his friends a nod of respect.

"Greetings." Christoph walked over to Sir Adam who was closest to him and offered his arm. "I am Christoph of Venger. Thank you for saving them."

Sir Adam took his arm and grasped it tightly. "It is good to see you, Christoph. I am Sir Adam the Pure Heart. Thank you for your words but your thanks belong to those two." Adam gave a small squeeze and then let go of Christoph's arm. "May I introduce Brother Truth and Master Peace of the Brotherhood of Light. Brother Truth is also known as Dalen Pax, The Reality Bender, and Master of Time." It was what had been written on the plaques in the Saviors Garden, so he figured he might as well introduce them as such. Adam then gestured over to Becky and Travis. "This is my brother Travis, also known as the Celestium Arrow, and next to him is his partner Oubliette."

Becky smiled sheepishly and waved.

Grelf had gotten Blizzard to his feet and turned her attention to the team. "I am Grelf." She scanned their expressions for recognition and saw none. With a small hint of disappointment, she raised an eyebrow and said, "The Orc Slayer." Again, she scanned their faces and again found no recognition. She cocked her hip as she put her hand on it and with a tone of frustration she said, "You must have heard of me." The team looked at each other and shrugged. "Grelf? Grelf the Orc Slayer?"

"I am sorry." Travis was trying to be as soothing as he could. "I do not recognize the name, but we are from the future."

"No one has heard of me in the future?" Frustration gave way to despair and Grelf looked as if she could cry. She thought for a moment then a glimmer of hope came across her face. "Perhaps you may know the name the Stained-Glass Dragon?" She pointed to her hair and every lock changed to a new color.

"Yes!" Becky shouted.

‹That was nice of you Becky.› Travis had thought that Becky just said it to be kind.

‹No. I really did see her.› Becky walked over to her and gave a small curtsy. "Two thousand years from now there are portraits of the royal line and the greatest heroes who have ever protected Venger. It was the hair that reminded me. Your hair was like that in one of the large portraits hanging in that room. You are not only remembered but revered for thousands of years."

Oubliette had many skills and was powerful in many ways, but Becky's true gift was how to see into the hearts of others, and she knew how to speak past all their defenses. Grelf's hair changed to a single color. It was a beautiful dark brown and Becky guessed it was her real color. Grelf took her hand and fought her emotions as she said, "Thank you." Then she remembered that they were not alone, and her entire demeanor changed, as did her hair. It changed back to the blue and periwinkle that she had when she arrived.

‹Did you see that? She switched Tin Soldiers.› Master Peace was right, and the team silently agreed. Travis telepathically mentioned that he made a note in his notebook that the color of her hair may have a connection to being able to read her, much like an aura.

"Do you know me as well?" asked Venger.

Becky smiled and gave a deep bow. "The first time I met you, you had time on your side, now, time is on mine."

At that moment, Dalen felt a small blink in reality and stopped time to try and see what it was. Master Truth was waiting for him, sipping on his cup. Dalen knew this was just his mind talking to himself but was glad to see his old friend. *Come to see the anomaly?* Master Truth asked telepathically.

I saw something, but I don't know what I saw. Dalen sat next to his master. *What was it?*

Becky. Said Master Truth. Despite being made of smoke he smiled at Dalen and patted him on the head. *See for yourself.* He stuck out a finger and slowly moved it to his left. As he did, time began to move backward to the moment the anomaly happened. It was a small waver in time that happened as Becky spoke.

What am I looking at? Dalen asked. *I can see where time appears to be looping in on itself. But I don't understand why.*

It still amazes me that people do not understand how powerful they are. They are literally creating time with every frame they exist in. Master Truth floated around behind Dalen's right shoulder. Dalen could no longer see Master Truth but could hear him on his right side. *As you know, words are powerful things.*

Yes. Dalen agreed. *It's why incantations work. They are generated through the throat Chakra, a creating element, The Element of Arcane.*

Indeed. Master Truth was amused at the answer. *The anomaly happens as Becky says the exact same words that Venger will say to her thousands of years in the future.*

Dalen stared at the frame of time. Grand Master Truth was right. The anomaly was coming from Becky as she spoke. Her words were creating a loop spanning thousands of years in the future, and somehow at the same time looping in a matter of only a few days. *But why does that cause a loop in time?*

Because when Venger said it, she was quoting Becky from this meeting, answered Master Truth.

Okay. Dalen looked at the anomaly curiously, trying to figure out what had created it. *They are quoting each other, so what's the problem?*

Master Truth took a sip from his cup and very simply asked; *If they were both quoting each other, who was the person who decided to create the sentence first? Where did it come from?*

Dalen's eyes widened as he saw what Master Truth was saying. He understood that they were not just creating time, they were creating history. Their past tense was also their present tense, and they were creating eddies in time.

Is this going to be a problem? Dalen asked, hoping that Becky didn't just accidentally destroy the world.

Master Truth laughed with amusement. *Not today. This loop ties the present and the past together. See this as a stitch in the fabric of time.* Master Truth then chuckled to himself. *No, the real problem would have happened if Becky had not remembered what was said accurately therefore quoting it wrong. That would have caused a break in the stitch of time because then Venger would have remembered it wrong and said something different back to Becky. Then you have a paradox.*

If that happens then what do you do? Dalen loved learning from Master Truth and had already settled into the old roles of teacher and student.

Master Truth shrugged. *As the Jinn of Time, I would hope you would use the Quantum field to create the frame of reality where Becky then forgets the line again, accidentally says the original line correctly, and in doing so, resets the proper timeline.*

Wait. Are you suggesting that not only can I use the Quantum field to observe space but time as well? Dalen knew that Master Truth would not have lied to him, but this was more than he could have ever imagined.

Yes. Master Truth had a way of suggesting the impossible as if it were merely commonplace.

Then what happens to the timeline that the mistake began in?

asked Dalen trying to get the details of this concept.

Master Truth pointed at the anomaly. *Hey, look, an anomalous time loop.*

It becomes a stitch in the fabric of time. Dalen nodded. I understand now.

Watch for them. Learning the road signs of time will be important, and they happen more often than you might think, especially with your lot. Master Truth chuckled and then his form faded like fog and Dalen was again by himself. He took a moment to deeply examine the anomaly then brought himself back into the corporeal movement of linear time.

• • •

Dorn was speaking as Dalen blinked and refocused on what was at hand. "It's fortuitous that you are here Christoph, these people are here to see you specifically. I would request that you join us in a conversation."

Christoph nodded and then asked, "Will Grelf be joining us?"

Venger answered. "I would prefer it if she were there."

Dorn agreed.

Lady Venger raised her hand, and a table grew from the stones with thirteen seats, one for each. Christoph and Grelf sat next to each other, as did Dalen and his friends. Blaze, Blizzard, Jax, and Jed sat next to Venger, and Dorn sat directly across from her, starting the conversation.

"Okay. Ever since I took a corporeal form, I see time linearly. So, I find myself in an amazingly rare position. You have more knowledge than I do." Dorn's tone matched the amused look on his face. "What happens next?"

Instinctively the team looked at Dalen, the rest of the table took the cue and turned to Dalen too.

"Oh, right." Dalen stalled by clearing his throat. "That would be me." Dalen rose from his seat, once he was standing, he continued rising about three inches off the ground. It was too late to be timid, Dalen decided to be direct and tell them exactly what they needed to know. "In ten days, the Genie DeSalvo and a Time Mage under his control will awaken the Chaos Dragon that destroyed the City of Dreams."

"That's impossible!" Venger had already been through too much to be calm that morning and the idea of that monster being set free meant the end of everything. "Dreamer imprisoned it three thousand years ago, to ensure it would be trapped for all time. She enlisted the aid of three Gods to create that prison and neither she nor the three have ever been heard from again. They sacrificed everything to make sure that this would never happen."

"The only way this Time Mage could have affected our children the way they did, is if the mage possesses the Time Stone." Dorn's words were resolute and Venger knew he was speaking the truth.

"If they have the stone that means..." She trailed off because the thought was too much for her to say.

Dalen looked to Dorn and asked with concern, "What does, that mean?"

"It means that if they have the stone, they have taken it from where it has been for thousands of years and reopened the Breath of Time," Dorn said gravely.

Travis had been writing in his notebook, but when Dorn mentioned the Breath of Time, he raised his hand with a finger up. Dorn gave him a nod and allowed him to speak. "Alright. Breath of Time. Great name by the way. But you say it like it will kill us all. What is the Breath of Time?"

Now everyone was looking at Dorn. He glanced at Dalen and smiled. "Oh. Right." Dorn playfully raised one eyebrow. "That would be me." Everyone smiled but all were too serious to laugh. "The Breath of Time is a hole in time and space. The whole expands and contracts giving it the illusion of breathing, thus the name Breath of Time."

Travis was writing quickly to keep up. "Why does it expand and contract?"

Dorn spoke as if what he was saying was commonplace, even though everyone could feel the gravity of his words. "The hole starts as a singularity. Infinitely small, and in that state, it creates an infinite probability field, where absolutely anything is possible. Then it expands to a sphere roughly as large as two adult humans. As it does, the probability field diminishes until it reaches one-to-one against, what we recognize as reality. Then it shrinks again bringing the probability field back to infinite possibilities. The dragon in its creator-being state used this hole within reality to enter our world. It attached itself to the anomaly at the point of infinite probability when anything could happen, and then rode the wave of expansion all the way into the physical world."

Travis finished writing and pulled back half the pages in his notebook. He thumbed through the pulled-back section until he found the page he was looking for and made a small note, then went back to the page he had just been on and jotted a reference to the note he had just made. "Thank you, that may also solve another problem I am working on. So, why can't the dragon just come through now?"

Venger answered the question with an obvious expression of concern. "My mother used the power of three different gods in the last moment of her life to imprison the dragon in a single frame of time. She solidified the frame of reality into a solid tangible object and imprisoned the dragon within that moment forever."

"That stone..." Dorn continued, "Is the Stone of Time. That means that if they have it, all they need do is free the dragon from the stone and it can rip itself back into this world."

"Then what do we do to stop them from freeing the dragon?" Christoph asked.

"That's the thing." Dalen rubbed the back of his neck for a moment. "We haven't been sent back to keep it imprisoned."

"WHAT?" Venger rose from her chair. She rested both hands on the table and leaned forward like she was getting ready to pounce. "What exactly were you sent here to do?" Her tone was threatening, and everyone could feel that there was a real possibility of Venger becoming extremely dangerous.

"My Lady," Travis said as he rose to his feet. He reached out in both directions away from him leaving himself prone and vulnerable. It was a bold move, but it showed everyone at the table that Travis was ready to face whatever happened next with faith and trust in Lady Venger. "We are here to help you destroy the Chaos Dragon...once and for all."

Silence flooded the room. It washed over all of them and bathed them in the moment. Not even their minds challenged its power.

The mark made of light on Travis's arm was much like the others. He had received it at the same moment his friends had, and with it, a deep connection to Venger. She could feel their thoughts and knew their hearts, but with Travis, something else was given. Something that only Venger could have put there and only Venger would have been able to detect.

In Travis's mark, a memory was stored and kept safe through time. In these moments of silence, Venger watched an image of herself standing in front of a mirror and saying "This man will risk more than everything to protect this entire world. He deserves our respect and trust."

The silence was still engulfing the room as Venger blinked and tears fell from her eyes as she nodded and sat down, overwhelmed by the truth of the memory. The silence was finally broken by Dorn who was not as convinced.

"You don't understand what you are up against. This thing cannot be destroyed." Dorn was calm but insistent. "No weapon that exists can harm it. It's more powerful than the Gods."

"Except the Eye of the Dragon and the Horn of the Unicorn." Dalen's tone was just as calm as Dorn's.

Dorn scoffed. "Like I said. No weapon that exists."

"I was told by someone in this very room, thousands of years from now, that I will help bring them back into existence."

"Who?" asked Venger.

Travis smiled and as he spoke Dalen watched him create another stitch in time. "I was once told by you that it's better not to know your future. But I promise you this, we have the information needed to save this world, and to help create an amazing future for you all. So, if Dalen says he can make the Eye of the Dragon and the Horn of the Unicorn, he can."

"Alright." Dorn leaned back in his chair. "Even if he could, I could not wield it, the same way my children cannot wield their Elemental Blades, which were created from the weapons you speak of. Split into the four elemental states. Whatever DeSalvo did to them I can sense he has done to me as well."

Master Peace leaned back in his chair as well. "That is why you must have a surrogate."

Dorn closed his eyes and shook his head. "Impossible. It would take the power of thousands of people over thousands of years to collect enough raw power to be able to wield it."

Sir Adam raised a finger in the air. "It's funny that you should say that Dorn, because that is exactly what we brought with us."

Travis snickered to himself as he wrote something down in his notebook and then finally spoke aloud. "That makes so much sense. That's why they built the statues."

"Statues?" asked Dorn.

"Yes," said Sir Adam. "Very nice ones. Before we started on our quest to the Pillar of Time, we visited a garden with statues made of each of us. They had been there for thousands of years, and thousands of people made pilgrimages to it every year. There, they gave of themselves. Their courage, their joy. They gave their skills and their knowledge. For generations people came, kings and peasants alike. They gave honor, love, and respect to the saviors of their world, and they gave until the day that we arrived. Then all that power was instilled into us. We are here to give that power to the one man who will kill the Chaos Dragon of Destruction and become the first King of Venger, whose bloodline will be tasked... cursed and blessed to be the bearers of the Elemental Blades, including the time that we come from."

"And who is this first king?" Dorn had guessed before this moment, but as he asked, he watched all five of them look at Christoph then he knew.

"Me?" Christoph asked.

"I believe being infused with that much power eventually makes you immortal. I have had conversations with you, thousands of years from now." Travis answered. "It's you."

Christoph looked at Travis with doubt and asked, "But what if I can't do it?"

Grelf stood up and with conviction, she spoke with all her heart. "Even if it means my final breath, you will not fail."

"That must be why her portrait was in the hall." Sir Adam blurted out. "Grelf must be the first Vengerian Guardian."

"Why do you say that?" asked Christoph.

"We are all Vengerian Guardians." Explained Travis, flipping back through his notes on the subject. Each one of us has sworn on our lives that we will protect Venger and her current queen. Every member of the royal family must go forth and prove they are worthy of the throne. Each of them has two elemental challenges. When the prince comes of age the Water Blade vanishes, and he must go and retrieve it. When it is time for him to become king the Air Blade vanishes, and he must go through a second challenge to retrieve it. The Vengerian Guardians are the people who go with them to protect them on the journey, but they cannot interfere when it is time to perform the task of retrieving the blade. That is for the seeker alone."

"What of the other two?" asked Blaze.

The princess is tasked with the Fire Blade, and when she becomes queen, she retrieves the Earth Blade. Interestingly enough, just before the princess must retrieve the Fire Blade, the queen first must retrieve the Earth Blade again, proving that she is still worthy, even though there is an heir to the throne. If she fails, the princess must go forth and retrieve them both. I believe that's true for the king and prince as well."

"That's where I saw you!" squealed Becky. The Stained-Glass Dragon. First Queen of Venger."

Grelf just stood there with her mouth half open long enough to concern Christoph. "Grelf, my love?"

"But I don't want to be queen." She panicked a little and was starting to hyperventilate. "I mean, I am all down for you being king. You would make an amazing king, and I like the idea of trying to find the Elemental Blades with a ten-day death clock ticking. I mean... you know I live for that kind of thing."

Christoph rose and took her hands and held them close to his chest. "I know. It's your favorite."

"Right! Because I am Grelf! The Orc Slayer!" She wanted to get mad and pull away, but Christoph held her hands, keeping her calm. "I don't know how to be a queen."

"You will have me and Dorn as your advisors for as long as you want us." Lady Venger said in soothing tones.

"Yeah. You, see?" Christoph asked. "Can you imagine having a better pair of advisors?"

Grelf slipped her hands out of Christoph's. She grabbed him by his tunic and pulled him close. "Bloodline Christoph! They want the Orc Slayer to raise princesses!"

Christoph couldn't help but laugh. "I love you because we are all doomed. We only have a small window of chance where you and I must find all four Elemental Blades, and then kill a malevolent destroyer being that is more powerful than the gods, and what you are worried about is becoming queen and having children."

"But if I marry you, settle down, and have kids, my mother wins." Grelf punched him in the arm. "Why do you have to go and save the world and become king?"

Christoph laughed. "I hope one day, you will forgive me."

"Fine!" Grelf rolled her eyes and gave Christoph a kiss. "I'll be queen."

Becky cleared her throat and once she had their attention she said, "If it helps at all, I am a Vengerian Guardian of the queen of my time, and I can tell you there has never been a more of a bad-ass queen and I am sure it is because she walks in your footsteps."

Grelf looked at the other four who nodded in agreement.

Then Sir Adam smiled and said, "It has always been the queen who must retrieve the Fire and Earth Blades. Grelf, this should make you excited. Do you know why?"

Grelf matched his smile and asked, "Why?"

Sir Adam pointed to Grelf and said, "That means that the fate of the world hinges on you, Grelf the Orc Slayer, doing the impossible. Sir Adam waited for the promise of adventure to take her and as he saw the glint of excitement in her eyes he added, "Twice."

"I'm in," she said.

Sir Adam waited while Grelf savored the moment then walked around the table and stood directly in front of her. "I swore an oath to protect the current Queen of Venger. Today, that is you." Sir Adam knelt, looked up at her, and said, "Even if it means my final breath, you will not fail."

Becky and Travis nodded to each other and hand in hand walked around the table to stand next to Grelf. They both knelt and together they gave the oath.

"Then Master Peace and Dalen will come with me." Christoph looked at both. "Agreed?"

Master Peace nodded and together they took the oath to Christoph.

"I have something for the two of you," added Dalen. "A gift from our queen." Dalen retrieved the two Vengerian Pins that Hope had given him before they parted ways. "She said I would know who these belonged to when it was time, and I feel that time is now." He gave one to Christoph and the other to Grelf and taught them how to access the menu so they could learn how to use it.

"How do we find the Elemental Blades?" asked Christoph.

Dalen shrugged. "The queen instinctively knew where it was. She said that is the way it has always been."

"Okay." Travis was going over his notes. "Hey, Christoph. Grelf. Don't think, just answer. Even if it sounds stupid. Where are the Elemental Blades?"

"They were attached to Blaze, Blizzard, Jed, and Jax since the beginning, right?" asked Christoph.

"Yes," answered Dorn. "Tied to their very souls."

Christoph shrugged "Then when they vanished, they would go where they thought they would be found. A place that reminds them of their wielders."

"They went to their favorite places in the world," answered Grelf.

"The Magma Falls. The nesting grounds of the Phoenix" blurted Blaze.

"The Aquatic Maze of the Northern Sea. It's the home of a Water Dragon who is a seer," Replied Blizzard.

"In the Verris Desert, there is a permanent stone. It is an immovable object." Answered Jax.

"High in the Wind Caves of Kar is a shaft that will lead to the home of the Gold Dragon of the East. He is the wisest being in the corporeal world, and a good friend." Jed shrugged. "If the Air Blade is not there, he will know where it is."

"Then it is settled," Dorn said. "What you are about to attempt is impossible. But if I were to make a wager on the people who I think could make the impossible possible, you are the people who I would want."

"Anyone can accomplish the impossible," added Master Peace. "All they need is true belief and the will to take that leap."

3

THE CREATION OF

DORN'S

It was well past midday and unlike their Vengerian Guardians, Christoph and Grelf were not yet packed for the journey ahead of them. They quickly left their new friends to prepare for what was in front of them, which left their guardians with little to do for a bit. Each of them knew where they wanted to go even before they checked with each other telepathically.

It was Sir Adam who approached Dorn and asked him, "We were thinking of going to Dorn's, but with Jax, Jed, Blizzard, and Blaze taking it easy, we were wondering if it would even be open?"

Dorn scrunched his eyebrows inquisitively. "Dorn's?"

Sir Adam looked defeated. "I guess that you have no idea what I am talking about. Do you?"

"I am sorry Sir Adam." Dorn put his hand on Sir Adam's shoulder. "I do not." He grinned and raised an eyebrow. "But I would love to hear about it."

"Well, first of all, It's amazing!" blurted Sir Adam.

"It has the best food," added Becky.

"Yeah, and all four of your kids work there," added Travis.

"They do?" Dorn was completely intrigued.

Dalen had had the most experience there and instead of blurting out his answer, he calmly raised a finger for initiative. The rest of his friends saw it, stopped talking, and allowed him to speak. "Not just them, but you as well." Dalen smiled. "I imagine it's your retirement plan. You wanted to be close to people and still help in your own way, yet at the same time keep your promise you were talking about when we first arrived."

"How do you know that was my plan?" Dorn asked with a sincere desire to understand.

"Because you helped me." Dalen smiled.

One by one, each of the Vengerian Guardians added, "And me."

"You even built it into the world with purpose." Dalen laughed at a private joke and then grinned with a clever plan in mind. "Yes, or No? Venger can build and rebuild the city as needed in the same way that I can make a fist with my hand?"

"It is different and way more complicated than that, but the principal is sound."

Dorn nodded.

"Yes, or No? Venger is much like a jinn and can create what is wished for?" Dalen asked with certainty, but he needed to hear Dorn's answer to be sure.

Dorn smiled and nodded. "It is only known by a few why, but yes, like the City of Dreams, Venger does have the ability to make wishes come true."

"Come with me Dorn," Dalen smiled and the stones in his body began to glow. "I have something to show you." Dalen walked briskly toward the exit but turned back and smiled. "Come on."

"There is nowhere in this town I have not seen," Dorn added as he got up and followed. The other Vengerians fell in line behind Dorn.

"I am taking you somewhere that is not in the city." Dalen chuckled to himself. "I was told by the queen of my time that you never would say where it was, but she knew that it wasn't really in the city."

"What do we need to do?" asked Dorn.

"We need to get Christoph and Grelf." Dalen was now floating down the hallway that led to Grelf and Christoph's quarters. Everyone else had moved into a jog. He stopped only long enough to get Christoph and Grelf and then set off again at an even faster pace.

They left the castle and were now running through the city's streets. Making a direct line toward the outer ring, but once he got there, he began making the turns every time there was the option.

Dalen activated his Spheres of Magic and allowed his mind to connect to his physical surroundings. He was no longer looking with his eyes but sensing everything with his entire being and feeling his way with his soul. He kept his speed and movement but turned around to face the group as they ran through the streets of Venger. "Tell me." He said to Christoph and Grelf. "Out of the two of you, who knows the city the least?"

"Grelf does," Christoph answered. Grelf shot him a dirty look. "It's true. I know you hate to admit weakness, but I grew up in Venger, not too far from here, and you have only been here a few years."

"I know that," Grelf said sharply as she scowled. "And I can admit weakness." Her scowl turned into a mischievous grin as she shrugged and added, "I just don't have any."

"In this case, it is not a weakness, it is a requirement." Dalen was still flying backward along the ground. He swung around and out of the way of people walking along the city streets all the while holding his conversation as if he were standing still. "I want to show you a place that you could really use right now. I remember how you said that the idea for you to change certain aspects of your life would be difficult, changing from being the guardian of a ruler to being the ruler herself, getting married, having kids, and being queen. It's all very big and it's a hard choice that you must make."

"The choice is to save the world and everything I hold dear. I will absolutely make it." Grelf's words were strong and there was no question of her determination.

Dalen slowed to a stop quickly, but slow enough that those running would not crash into each other by the sudden stop. He peered into her eyes and said, "Of course, but be honest. Have you?"

"Are you questioning my resolve?" Grelf's hair turned black with flares of red.

Dalen could feel her emotion. He could feel her anger and indignation. When he heard her thoughts, he could tell she was deciding whether to attack him, and beyond all of that he could sense fear.

"Never would I suggest, that when the time comes, you wouldn't make the choice. I know it in my heart as a truth." Dalen looked deep into her soul, and as he did, she sensed he meant it. He could see the recognition in her eyes. He humbly added, "I am only suggesting that time has not yet come."

It struck her in a way she was not expecting. There was nothing to attack or defend against, leaving her with nothing but understanding. Her emotions were still high, so she still responded with strength. "What does that have to do with anything?"

Dalen smiled and started moving at his quick pace. Being

connected to the Body Sphere, he was in complete flow and harmony with his surroundings and could feel his way. Besides, he had to keep moving, she needed to be good and lost.

"It means that you are at a fork in the path of your life," Dalen turned another corner and had to raise his feet to avoid a cat then ducked under a canopy connected to the shop along the road. "When I first went to where we are going, it was explained to me that one of the most beautiful things about it is that it is, in a way, an oasis. A place where you can gather your thoughts and learn what is needed before you head back into the world."

He turned another corner and kept his speed. He was watching them closely, and they were watching him. It was what he had been waiting for. He had remembered many times on long trips how he would be looking out the window of his foster folk's car, but his eyes were not paying attention to what was happening outside the window. He would be lost in thought and his mind would be looking at what he was thinking about, and not what his eyes were perceiving directly, then randomly, his mind would refocus on the physical world, and he would realize that he had not noticed miles of road. Maybe even pass through a town and not even notice it. This was the state of mind that he was trying to get them to, not only were they busy watching him fly backward, which itself was a spectacle, but they then had to run to keep up. They were beginning to watch him for movement clues and not the environment directly. They were there, even Dorn. The speech was just another layer of distraction, and he used a bit of Grey Speak to allow their minds to see what he was saying.

"I learned about magic in one of the rooms upstairs, but the more I think about it, I feel that the room I was in was someplace other than where the actual tavern was. Like the door was a portal or something, I believe that every person who goes there can find a room to help them learn what they need to know. Do you want to know why I think this place will not only help you Grelf but will help Christoph and Dorn as well?"

Grelf was now completely locked onto him, nearly stalking him like prey. "No. Why is that?"

Dalen stopped quickly, right where the road split in two different directions. He took a deep breath, and a tear welled up as he knew the wish had been granted. He stepped aside and gestured with his hand toward a small tavern that sat right at the fork of the road. "Because the only people who can find it are those at the fork in their lives." With reverence that Father Light would have been proud of, he let the tear fall. "The people who truly need it."

"Dalen?" Dorn looked at him baffled. "What did you do?"

Dorn looked over to Lady Venger who shrugged. "Yeah, it's here, and I felt its creation, but it was not created by my conscious thought. Sometimes the wishes of others are reflex, and this one was strong."

Dalen took a deep bow. "Consider it a gift from the Jinn of Time." Dalen studied the stunned looks on Lady Venger and Dorn. "I'm sorry. Have I somehow stepped out of line? Like is this the jinn equivalent of inappropriate behavior?"

Dorn could tell by Dalen's words and tone that he didn't

understand how truly amazing of a thing he had accomplished. "No." Dorn paused for a moment to think of an equivalent idea. "You didn't sleep with my wife or anything like that. More like you discovered a secret that nobody knew."

Dalen let out a sigh of relief. "Because I didn't even think about it until afterward, but I can see from one point of view how I may have gotten Venger to change her form to my will."

"I see your concern," said Lady Venger. "Your intentions are pure and your actions noble. You have done nothing wrong."

"Dalen put his hand over his Heartstone, and the light glowed a little brighter. "Thank you." The feeling of relief and respect was felt by all who could hear him.

"Actually, you did something very right." Dorn was still wide-eyed staring at the building. "I ask you again Dalen. What have you done?"

Dalen turned around and looked at Dorn's. Then he took a deep breath and stopped using his eyes. Instead, he looked at it through the eyes of magic and what he saw was more than he could have imagined.

Dalen slowed time down past where things virtually stood still. And the frames of reality began to flicker. Now he had time to look at the tavern carefully. Dorn moved with him, and they marveled at it together.

"I have very rarely seen what it looks like when two Jinn make a wish together," Dorn said with admiration at the sight of it.

"Is that what I am looking at?" Dalen was still trying to read the creation spell. "I recognize myself in it. I have a specific resonance, but I do not recognize the other. If I had to, I would guess it's Venger."

"You are right. And this combination is more powerful than anything else I have seen in this world." Dorn caressed the magic as if it were alive. "Venger is the direct offspring of Dreamer. Their greatest ability is to take the dreams, and wishes of others, and make them real in the physical plain. Like her mother, Venger is the Jinn of Physical Reality." He put his hands directly in the magic and let it move around his fingers like water. "This is the merging of time and space itself."

"It's beautiful," Dalen said.

"Every child of hers is," Dorn said with tears in his eyes but a smile on his face.

"Child?" Dalen asked.

"For lack of a better term... yes," Dorn said as he wiped his eyes. Dorn once again saw the look of concern on Dalen's face. "Don't worry. Like I said, it's not like you slept with my wife. You just had a child together." Dorn's words had the exact reaction he was hoping for, and it made him laugh. Jinn do not mate like humans; they create like gods. You are divine beings after all. The same way that Venger is a sentient city, this tavern is alive." He read the magic at a skill level far beyond Dalen's. "Dorn's will be a focus point of the abilities of Venger. Those who need our help will find their way here."

"Do you want to see the inside?" asked Dalen. They got right up to the door and Dorn pointed out the runes that made every window and door a portal to a location that was not there. When Dalen asked what that meant he simply said that all the portals led to a place that was not in corporeal space and that stood outside of the flow of time. Dalen wanted to ask him more about it, but Dorn had moved back into the flow of normal time. Dalen joined him long enough for Dorn to ask everyone to give Dalen and him a minute. Everyone nodded and Dorn and Dalen walked in together. The moment he walked in Dalen again slowed time to a flicker and Dorn followed him in. They gazed at the sheer wonder of it all.

The room was much larger than the building suggested, but Dalen understood that had no relevance because they had stepped through a portal to another dimension of being, it looked just like he remembered it. There was an empty stage to the right with golden cords partitioning off an area for the audience. There were circular booths along the outside walls, a large stairway going up to a second level, and in the back a traditional bar. As Dalen moved Dorn toward the bar area, he told the story of his first arrival at Dorn's. He explained how a Tea Faerie had performed that night whose magic would not pass the golden cords.

Dalen brought Dorn up to the bar and said, "It was right here, where I met you for the first time. Normally you do the night shift, but the performer was a friend of yours, so you had decided to stay that morning and watch the show, but now that I look at it in hindsight, I think you were waiting for me."

Dorn smiled at that and nodded. "That sounds like me."

Dalen got behind the counter and said, "I want you to know that I consider this to be an amazingly huge honor that I get to be the first person to serve you a drink in this place." Dorn gave him a nod of permission. "Name it, anything you want."

"Anything?" Dorn began to read the magic field of the bar. "This is ridiculously brilliant. The bar itself is a receptacle for wishing, what a magnificent element this being can produce." He shook his head in near disbelief. "There is a wine that was only made in the City of Dreams, and in three thousand years it has never been replicated nor have I ever found better."

Dalen reached underneath the bar and felt a goblet materialize in his hand. He brought it up and set it in front of Dorn. "As you wish."

Dorn took a small taste that didn't end. Instead, it quickly turned into him drinking the entire glass with a single pour into his mouth, gulping as the tasty liquid coated his throat. "That was delicious and exactly correct! He created it from my memory perfectly."

"He?" asked Dalen.

"Yes," Dorn said plainly. "Dorn's...your son."

With a jolt, Dalen fell back into the standard time flow. It was sharp and it made him nauseous. Vertigo set in and the room began to spin. It turned out it was Dalen who was spinning as he lost his balance and fell toward the floor.

Dorn caught him before he landed, and he helped Dalen catch his breath. "Together, Venger and you created this sentient being. So, in truth, it is yours and Venger's but look here." He touched the bar, and a piece of the magic began to glow. "This is me. You and her together made it for me. I am connected to it at its origin." Dorn had Dalen refocus and set his mind's eye to be the one that could see magic. Dorn touched Dalen's shoulder and all at once, Dalen could see more than he knew was possible.

Dalen witnessed the very fabric of creation. He saw how it was woven and designed within the realm of magic itself. The very foundation of matter and the dance that takes place in all the empty places within it. Like the space between the frames of reality, so too, was there space between the things that called themselves real. Dalen recognized how both were reflections of each other. "What am I looking at Dorn?"

"Reality is reality. No matter how you look at it." Dorn said with amusement. "Just as there is more than one way to see the Elements of Magic. Each of them is an aspect of the same reality, but they completely change depending on which perception you use to observe it. Right?"

"Right," Dalen said almost like a question, still trying to read the whisps of magic creating the walls and floor of Dorn's.

"This place is a joining of time and space. Which, by the way, are Elements of Existence."

Dalen had to fight for a moment to keep his connection to this incredible vision. The magic began to fade but Dalen relaxed his mind and allowed his thoughts to flow freely with it, and his body, mind, and soul refocused. As he did everything realigned, and he was able to see again. He absorbed what this felt like and could feel his violet eye memorize how to see this perception. Dalen only had one question left. "There is something past the Elements of Reality?"

Dorn's smile was that of amusement, but when he spoke Dalen could feel that he was quite serious about such things. "Oh yes, Dalen Pax. Reality is just an element to something else."

Dalen was excited. "What is it?"

"When you master reality, I will tell you." Dorn turned back to the streams of magic and said, "Look here." He was pointing to part of the counter near the kitchen. "This is Christoph. This place was made for him as well, and here is Grelf." Dorn glanced around a bit. "Actually, she is kind of everywhere."

"She was directly involved with this being's creation." Dalen looked along the walls. "Like I said, it's for people at the fork in their journey."

"What are you suggesting?" Dorn asked.

"You and your family have ruled this world for a long time, but now the time has come for the world to rule itself. You have your heroes and your bloodline. They are at the fork in their path for sure, but there is another to consider. It is time for you and your family to step down, and that means that you are at the fork in your journey too."

"You believe that this is the path I should take?"

Dorn asked.

"It is the path that you will eventually find. You and your children. I suspect that if you check the kitchen, you will find the essence of your daughter Jax." Dalen pointed toward the kitchen.

Dorn glanced in that direction and did a double-take. "And a ridiculous amount of Time Magic."

"Read it. It gets better." Dalen said and reached under the bar and produced a small cup of mint tea. He raised the cup to the counter and said, "Thank you." As he did, he watched the light that made up the fabric of reality pulse a bit brighter for a moment and Dalen knew in his heart that Dorn's had responded.

Dorn had finished reading the kitchen and was excited about what it had suggested. "You were right. She will have to find new ways to create. What a beautiful gift. Thank you."

"When I first met you, I can say you were happy. I have no idea what happens between now and then, but I do know that you and your children consider this more of a home than the castle." Dalen patted him on the back and then after a moment went back to trying to read the bar. "I think Dorn's said hello. Will he be able to manifest a form like his mother?"

Dorn shrugged. "I think that will be up to him." He looked around. "Do me a favor. I need a moment in here. If I am going to be working with this place, then I must know it inside and out."

"How long do you need?" asked Dalen.

Dorn grinned and then gave a quick exhale out of his nose.

"Leave me here in a space where time nearly stands still. By the time you reconnect with the normal speed of time, get out the door, and get them in, I will be ready."

"Fair enough." Dalen looked back at the bar. "Okay. I'm going to leave you with Uncle Dorn." He shrugged at Dorn. "Be good, and I'll be right back."

As Dalen moved himself back into normal space and time his eyes readjusted, and he could no longer see the fabric of magic. For a moment he felt the loss of not being able to observe the beauty of it, but he was sure that if he concentrated, he would be able to do it again. A truth that Dalen had recently noticed was that he was able to recreate any bit of magic that he had witnessed, he felt that this would be no different.

"Goals," Dalen told himself and walked to the door that led outside.

When he got outside, Grelf let out a small chuckle, "Well that didn't take long. Are we ready or what?"

Dalen stepped out completely and allowed the door to close. As it clicked, he thought to himself the possibilities of how much time could have already passed for Dorn.

"Yeah. I'm ready. The question is whether or not, you are ready." Dalen scoffed.

Grelf crossed her arms in front of her and brazenly replied, "I am always ready."

It was Master Peace who responded. "Going into Dorn's is

like bending over at the waist and taking a drink from a geyser as it goes off." Everyone looked over at him while the image of what he said played out in their minds. "The only way you can be ready is to understand there is no way to be ready."

Christoph laughed and pushed Master Peace playfully. "I think I could use a drink." and headed into Dorn's.

4

A BARD OF THE GREY CONTINUUM

It had been a millennium since Dorn had come directly to the Grey Continuum. The Grey Continuum itself is more like a thought than a place, but much like many things in this world, it can manifest into something... tangible, if observed directly. More often than not when this occurs it takes the shape of no more than what is required. In this case a floor no more than twenty feet from the center point. Everything beyond faded into a field of obscuring haze, as if the entire meeting took place in a cloud. Past what could be perceived, was the edge of reality, so as

Dorn entered, it was as if he had walked into this place from a fog.

We assumed it meant trouble, and since The Grey Continuum had only one avatar, he was met by Angel of Grey who has had many names throughout time, through different lore, myths, legends, and religions. You will know him through his work. He is the one angel you want standing next to you while walking through Hell... because nothing there would ever dare face him.

He stood before Dorn in a white tunic made of angelic cloth that radiated light. His pants were gray, and his knee-high boots matched his tunic. His sleeves had been cuffed so that the Celestium plated glove on his left hand, and a large burn scar that ran the length of his right hand and halfway up his arm, could be seen. Each had been received because of the terrible burden that he once carried.

He had been charged with carrying the deadliest weapon ever created by Dorn during the First Dynasty. It was known as the Sword of Dorn's Promise. Named so, because it was created with the promise that the world could defend itself against anything it needed to, even himself. It was so powerful that seeing the blade could mean your end. People have been known to turn to stone or salt just by looking at the blade directly, and there is nothing in creation that can withstand even a single blow from it. Not even Dorn.

Dorn believed that the blade would only be safe with Angel of Grey because only Angel was strong enough to withstand the blade for any real amount of time, and if it came down to it while wielding the Sword of Dorn's Promise, Angel would be the only person strong enough to protect this world.

During the fall of the First Dynasty, the Old Gods had become corrupt and were demanding the impossible from their followers. When Dorn told them that they had to change their ways they rebelled and tried to destroy him. The Old Gods fell to Angel of Grey that day, but commanding the sword left a mark on his soul the same way it made a scar on the hand and arm that wielded it. Angel, by his very nature, is a protector. An angelic guardian, not a killer and destroyer. So, after the fall of the First Dynasty, Angel requested to be freed of the sword. Controlling that much power had taken a toll on him and he felt that he could no longer bear the weight of wielding it again. Dorn understood and relieved him of the responsibility. Hundreds of years went by, then suddenly The City of Dreams fell. Angel considered it a failure on his part because there was no one to stop the Chaos Dragon and swore to Dorn that if it were ever needed again, he would pick up the mantle. But Dorn had other plans.

Instead of keeping the most powerful and deadliest sword ever created whole, Dorn split it into two pieces. The Horn of the Unicorn and the Eye of the Dragon. Then split each in half again into the four Elemental Blades of Power. In this new form, they would be bound to four instead of the burden being placed on one. Angel offered to be one of the four but again, Dorn had other plans. He embraced Angel and swore an oath that he would never have to wield the blade again. Instead, Dorn blessed Angel of Grey with the Hand of Redemption, an artifact that not only identifies the need for redemption but can grant it through its divine power.

From that point on he would be an Angel of Mercy. He accepted the gift, placed the Hand of Redemption on his left hand, and began to smile like his old self. He has been smiling ever since.

The four Elemental Blades would go to Dorn's children. Being of direct bloodline to Dorn made them incredibly powerful and well-suited for the task. He asked another of our continuum, the Grey Bard, Hip-Gnosis, to connect their souls to the blades. Once the connection was made each of them took on characteristics of the element they were then tied to.

More than two thousand years had passed since that day and Dorn had not directly contacted the Grey Continuum more than once or twice. He finally had found his peace, and for the first time in a long time, he was at rest. We were happy to see him, but the thing that caused us alarm was how quickly he was moving through time.

"This state you are in, is it intentional?" Angel's concern was clear in his tone. "What is going on? If you can, I pray thee, speak."

"Everything is fine, Angel. I thank you for your concern, but I am not here for your services." Dorn took Angel's left hand in his, and as he did, he closed his eyes and took a deep breath smiling as he let out all the air slowly. "You see? Nothing to redeem. Everything is fine."

Over the years Angel had seen what the face of someone looked like who was trying to hide from what he had come to redeem them of. He recognized the look. Dorn was hiding something, whether he needed to be redeemed from it or not, and Angel could tell. "So, everything is well then?"

"Well, there is the whole business of a mysterious Time Mage, who almost killed the kids, while stripping their abilities to wield the Elemental Blades," Dorn said as if he were explaining the daily gossip.

"What!?" Angel's ability to Grey Speak allows him to comprehend anything that is said to him, but his first response was shock and that was all he could get out.

Dorn didn't skip a beat and continued with the same manner of explanation. "Not to mention, all of this is in an attempt to free the Chaos Dragon, and the fate of everything now lies in the hands of two humans who will become the wielders of the Elemental Blades and kill said Chaos Dragon if she does so happen to emerge from her frozen imprisonment. But you know, that's how things go."

Images kept coming as flashes of what had occurred. They filled Angel's memory as if he had been there and was just now remembering the event. Still, surprise won out and all he could say was, "What?"

"I know," Dorn said almost giddy. "But don't worry, it is all being handled. It looks like there is a real chance that things are going to work out better than originally believed." Dorn took Angel's right hand this time and held it with meaning. Dorn opened his heart and mind to the Knight of Grey and spoke from his soul. *There is a chance that we can both finally rest.*

At that moment there was only that one single thought. It

brought them together in mourning because Dorn and Angel had shared the loss of The City of Dreams and neither of them had ever forgiven themselves. It was a bond between them as both had watched the final moments of Dreamer and both were powerless to stop the Chaos Dragon.

But there is hope, there is a prophecy that one will come and herald the end of the vile beast once and for all. The chance that one will come and help bring her to her well-deserved end. This news brought with it hope and the idea that everything that happened had happened for a reason, that the purpose of it meant that all was not lost in vain, and the great villainy that occurred that day would be avenged. They would finally find redemption and both of them could be at peace. It moved Angel in ways he had all but forgotten he could be moved, and a tear fell from his eye. Dorn manifested a celestium vial and caught it halfway down Angel's cheek. And then he caught the one from his own eyes and placed the vial in Angel of Grey's left hand.

Angel knew what the tears of the Angel of Redemption could do, but a tear from Dorn... With the essence of the intent from both beings... It was beyond what Angel had ever imagined. "For the one who must wield it?" Dorn nodded. "No, Brother. It's for the one who will do what neither of us could."

"I thought he was lost to us."

"I believe he may have found his way home."

They touched their foreheads together and took in the moment. "Even gods must make a leap of faith from time to time."

Angel of Grey tightened his grip on Dorn's hand. "Let me take this one with you."

"That's why I am here." Dorn took a breath of hope and let it saturate his being. "But I need your brother. I need to make sure. I need to speak with the will of this world... The Will of the Continuum." Dorn took another deep breath in and then let it out slowly as he regained his center. "I need The Narrator. I need Will of Grey."

When Dorn looked up the avatar of the Grey Continuum had changed, and it was me who was pressing his forehead against Dorn's. I smiled politely and asked, "Sup?"

Dorn smiled to see me and stepped back to allow his eyes to adjust so we weren't looking at each other cross-eyed. I was dressed in my best. As always, I wore one black shoe and one that was white. A remembrance that in the path you walk, every step is a choice. My pants and shirt were made of angelic cloth, as was the inlay of my sleeveless black long coat. Down my right side was a stripe as wide as the length of my hand from wrist to fingertips that ran the entire coat length from shoulder to hem in both the front and back. Looking at the stripe was like staring through a window into space. As I moved, the pattern did not, as if I were only moving the window not what was being seen within it. Staring into the mark of Grey is like looking into the void. Pinned to it I wore a brooch of a recognized universal symbol of balance, the yin-yang and that was wreathed in silver fire. The symbol itself has been used to represent this world and the true magic that has governed it since the First Dynasty. As the only beings having been there since the beginning, The Grey have adopted it as their own.

With unremarkable brown hair, average height and build, and a face that can easily be lost in a crowd, it could be said that there was nothing special about my appearance. My eyes are one of the only things ever noticed about me. That and... my voice. Both are due to who and what I am. I have spoken the collapse of nations and the fall of gods. I have spoken life into worlds and with my words have made them cease to exist. I speak... therefore it exists, yet I am bound by one law. As the speaker and narrator of this existence, I am to observe and report, only when the avatar of the Grey Continuum is controlled by myself am I able to act. In my true state, I can only observe.

The eyes of my avatar give away that I have seen too much. I have watched heroes rise to glorious victory and I have seen the best soldier a world can provide crumble and become corrupt. I have seen art from a thousand cultures that none remembers, and I have watched as cultures were wiped out, all of their artifacts destroyed by those who want to conquer the world. I have witnessed the power of true love, and I have witnessed the torture, pain, and suffering, of loss. Because of all I've seen my eyes appear different from those born into the physical realm. Much like the stripe that goes down my long coat, looking directly into my eyes is like gazing directly into the infinite expansion of space.

Dorn looked me directly in the eyes and said, "I am glad you could be here. I have something to ask you."

"I'm always here, you know, for you." I said, "I mean, you know...there is a part of me that is still telling the story." I rolled my eyes and added, "Probably in perfect grammar, being all omnipotent being the storyteller." I re-centered my thoughts and focused on the brighter side of the coin. "I love it when I get to be this instead." I looked at my hands and wiggled my fingers at myself. Since the dawn of this world, being corporeal was something I had not been too often, and I always had found it amusing. I laughed and said, "I can say things like, 'I am he, who is the one, that you are to be speaking with' and it is very refreshing." I hugged him and when I let go, I said, "Thank you for summoning me. How can I be of service?"

"You know what is going on with my children and the Elemental Blades, right?" Dorn asked.

I put up my hand and said, "Let me stop you right there Dorn ol' boy. My very first mandate, directly proclaimed by you, and never to be broken no matter what tactic was used, was to never tell you the future if it led to changed events. I can't tell you how it all goes down, besides, this avatar doesn't know the infinite. You know this, man."

"I know. I also know how it goes down because I sent a team of five kids back in time from two thousand years in the future." Dorn was no longer gossiping; he was practically accusing.

I nodded and said, "Yes. I am aware of them."

"They are instilled with levels of power that were cultivated over thousands of years." Dorn's words were excited now.

"Why are you here Dorn?" I folded my arms in front of my chest. "If you want to break your own rules, you don't need me, you can just reinstate your powers."

Dorn looked me right in the eyes without flinching and said, "One of them is a Jinn, who can not only manipulate time and even heal with it, but he can create with time itself."

I smiled. "You speak of the prophecy."

"There is more." Dorn was sure of it now. "He is a walking time anomaly. Not only that, but I knew he was one before I sent him back two thousand years, by telling him to touch the Pillar of Time, which disjointed him further from time."

"You must have had a good reason. Have you considered speaking with the Brotherhood of Light? I do believe their Grand Master was the one who made the prophecy in the first place." I said with a slightly dismissive intent.

Dorn smiled and said, "That is the second time you spoke of the prophecy, and I have not mentioned it once to you. Thank you for confirming my suspicions."

I smiled and bowed. "I am honored to serve."

A glint flickered in Dorn's eyes. It was the same glint I had seen before when Dorn was being creative. To many, it was a terrifying look to see because it usually meant trouble, a bad idea was brewing. But Dorn smiled at me and said, "I may be in need of your services again."

"Oh?" I asked.

"You say you like experiencing the corporeal world and I have a need for a bard," Dorn said as he put his hand on my back and began to walk me toward the edge of the Grey Continuum.

"You require a Grey Bard? What are your terms?" I asked.

"I will give you exclusive rights to the greatest stories ever told." I looked at him as if to ask what else. "Free room and board."

I stopped only a step away from the edge of the gray nothingness that surrounds the creation of the Grey Continuum and asked, "When you say the greatest stories ever told, what level of great are we talking about?"

"You know the guy in the prophecy you can't tell me about?" Dorn asked.

"Yeah," I said blankly.

Dorn nodded and said, "Well, if it's him, his story will be your first."

I clapped my hands together and decided to take the step that would carry my avatar into the real world. "I'm not saying he is, but I'm in. Let's go." And together we moved into the corporeal realm.

• • •

I found myself standing in Dorn's, moving so fast in time that the frames of reality were almost flickering. I looked around and noticed I was standing in a group with Dorn and his children. We all looked at each other and nodded hello.

Dorn politely waited until we had all greeted one another

and then got down to business. "We have a little bit of time before everyone else gets here. And we have a lot of work to do." The group were all moving with the same quickness, harmonized in the speed that Dalen had left Dorn in. By his account, Dorn figured we would have about two years before Dalen and the rest of the team showed up.

For two years we prepared. Each of us got to know Dorn's well. A year in, Dorn's figured out how to make itself an avatar. When it did, the avatar that was created was a young boy who looked to be only about twelve or so. Now that he was his own being, the avatar wanted to be called something other than Dorn's. Lady Venger chose the name Aiden, and by the time the grand opening was ready, Aiden too was ready, to meet his father for the first time. For Dalen, it had only been the few moments it had taken to walk over to his friends and then walk back to the door, but for Aiden, it had been a lifetime.

5

THE FIRST CUSTOMERS

OF DORN'S

As the door swung open, I readied my lute and began
to play. Master Peace, Becky, and Travis were the first inside,
followed by Sir Adam, Christoph then Grelf. Dalen had held the
door for everyone, so he was the last in and did not get to see the
surprised look on the others' faces as small magical fireworks went
off as they walked in, they were still going off as he joined the
group. Using her natural ability to manipulate fire, Blaze controlled
the fireworks as she danced to the music in the center of the room,
small explosions of light created the beat of the song.

"Welcome," said Blizzard. He gave a small bow and asked, "Before my brother seats you, can I get anyone something from the bar?"

"Mint tea please." requested Dalen as he memorized how to create the miniature fireworks.

"Make that two," added Master Peace.

"Monks." Grelf rolled her eyes and asked for their house ale.

"Make that two," repeated Christoph. He said it in the same tone to match Ben's request. The two of them gave each other a look and then nodded to Master Peace, who returned it openly. Dalen could watch their bond grow stronger, but he wasn't completely sure why. When Master Peace was still the boy he used to be, he was a guy's guy and never had trouble making friends of the same type. It was something that Dalen was never good at, and it was part of the reason he was ostracized and teased. Dalen forced his eyes to see the fabric of reality as he had seen earlier with Dorn and laughed to himself as he watched their bonds grow in the Body Sphere. Dalen could wield amazing universal energy, but just being one of the guys and making friends was a mystery whose answer he had still not gleaned from his universal understandings.

"Elven wine." Becky paused for a moment and then added, "Oh, and please, with it I would like the supplement, so I don't trip my ever-living mind out."

"Make that two." Travis only got about halfway through his words before he began laughing at the running gag as he spoke.

71

They all laughed together and just as it was dying down Sir Adam pointed at Christoph and Grelf and held up three fingers.

Blizzard nodded and headed toward the bar. As he stepped out of his place in front of them Jed stepped in gracefully with a smile.

"Hello. It is good to see you again." Jed said with joy. He turned to face Master Peace and Dalen directly. "Also, we wish to give you both our thanks. We were pretty out of it at the time, and we never thanked you properly. Thank you for saving our lives. We are all in your debt."

Master Peace smiled and gave him a formal bow of the Brotherhood. "It was our honor and pleasure. It would have been a terribly sad day to lose your light in this world."

Jed blushed a little and returned the bow with his own and then said, "Right this way." He led the group to one of the booths that were built directly into the wall. The area inside was big enough for ten people to sit around the circular bench lining the alcove but had no table. Right in the center of the space was a small crystal cone that could fit in your hand sitting on its base, its point about six inches tall from the floor. When everyone was seated Jed reached over and pulled the cone upward. It was connected to a long pole the width of the cone base and rose from the ground. When he reached about table height, he twisted the cone, and a circular table extended from the center leaving the crystal cone as a centerpiece.

Jed stepped out of the way and like clockwork Blizzard

stepped into position with their drinks. Becky took her supplement right away blushing when she did as if she were embarrassed to have to take it. Travis was trying to ask her if she was all right when he was asked a question. He waited until she nodded in approval, and then looked up to pay attention to what was being asked.

It was Grelf who had asked the question. They stared at each other for a moment until Grelf realized that he had not heard her at all. "I asked if you had eaten here before. During your time."

Travis just stared at her for a moment. The question had taken him off guard and it took him a moment to process what she was saying. Dalen could also feel him trying to decide if answering the question would give too much information. He decided the question was safe and only then did he respond.

Travis nodded at first and then said, "Yes. Everything was more than amazing. Truly magnificent. I have no doubt, whatever you order will be delicious."

"Then this will be our first exercise in trust. If we are going to make it, I am going to have to learn to trust you, as you lead me through my peril." She raised her cup. "To new journeys." She gave Travis a wink. "Here's to new perils and experiences."

Everyone raised their glass and drank. When they did, Grelf cracked a smile.

Menus were given, but on the recommendation of Jed, everyone decided to order the special. The special was something called the Quantum Special. It was served on an enchanted silver tray with a matching cover. One was set in front of each of them with instructions to imagine the meal they wanted the most. Imagine every detail, from the mashed potatoes' texture, to how crispy they wanted the skin of their chicken to be. As each person made their choice, they lifted the silver cover to find the exact meal they had imagined before them.

"There is nothing like getting exactly what you want when you order something," mentioned Becky as she looked at Travis and smiled.

Travis smiled back and said, "After 'it' received half a dozen awards, my German friend and I ate his 'No'."

Becky just stared at him confused. "What did you say?" Travis repeated it, which only concerned her. "What are you talking about?"

"The musketeers twice, plus D'Artagnan, really were there for one another," Travis said as if that would explain everything.

Becky was now directly worried. "What's happening?"

Grelf couldn't take it any longer. She began to giggle and couldn't stop.

"What did you do my love?" asked Christoph.

She looked at him doe-eyed and said as innocently as she could, "I did nothing."

Christoph's demeanor changed and he was now very serious. "Grelf?"

Grelf couldn't hold back her smile, let alone her giddiness. She raised her hands as if to show she was not holding anything. "As I said, I did nothing." She frowned and shrugged her shoulders. "I just find it amusing that Travis forgot to take the elven supplement before he joined in the toast and drank his wine."

"What!?" Becky looked down at the small paper coaster next to Travis's glass and sure enough, his supplement was still there.

"I did say here is to new experiences." She began to laugh as she added, "And he is definitely having an experience right now."

Everyone looked back to Travis who was smiling at everyone with a dopey grin. He raised his hand to the table and said, "Five?" Sir Adam, who was directly next to Travis, reached out and gave his brother a high five. Travis laughed and gave a fist pump then completely zoned out into his thoughts.

Becky spun her attention to Grelf. "You did that on purpose!" she accused.

Grelf's hair turned green with highlights of brilliant yellow. It was a color pattern that Christoph had seen before, and he suggested that she take a breath. Grelf smiled at him and nodded, yet the table could read how she fought against saying something she would regret. She took a deep breath, and her hair changed into a beautiful warm chestnut, but her tips were brilliant blue.

"Tell me, little one, which part have I done on purpose?" Her eyes glinted as she smiled. She reached into a pouch she had on her belt, and when she brought her hand out, she had something in her closed fist. "Was it the part where you ordered Elven drinks and then he followed suit? Or was it the point that he knew what he was ordering and so did you, but when you took your supplement, he was too busy taking care of you to remember to take his own?"

Becky scowled at her, "That is not what I am talking about."

Grelf cut her off but spoke with a calm tone. "Yet, it is what I am talking about." Grelf's tips turned red, and orange as her demeanor warmed. "Wherever and whenever you are from, I am sure they have a saying that is close to the idea of; if you play with fire you will end up with burns?"

Becky nodded. "We do, and I see your point."

"I am not sure you do little one." Her tone was now kind and caring. "In this world, there are some beautiful things that are good and kind. Lady Venger for example, and there are terrible things in this world that are as ugly as the black heart that beats within them." She scooted closer to Becky and leaned in. "Now this is important, so I need you to hear me. The greatest man I have ever known was my father. He was noble and true, and he was a farmer and not a beautiful man to look at. Because of his work, he was always dirty and smelled of hard labor, but there has never been a kinder more beautiful man, and in the same respect, it is the brilliant-colored creatures of this world that are the most poisonous. The deadliest. You will find that the most beautiful things in this world are the deadliest. I mean..." she shook her head and as her hair shook and tossed it changed color and became black with beautiful streaks of blue and purple. "Look at me." She smiled and winked at Becky. "I am the deadliest thing here."

"The Orchid Mantis." For as far back as Becky could remember, she had loved the Orchid Mantis. From time to time, she still had dreams about them. This outstanding predatorial insect that hunted by looking like a flower, making the orchid more beautiful to its prey. Becky instantly knew what Grelf was saying and quietly whispered, "I let the romance and beauty of it being Elven blind me. So caught up in it... I didn't respect what it could do."

Grelf smiled and said, "The only thing I did on purpose was to point it out in a harmless joke. If you weren't in the middle of it, you would think it was hilarious. I promise you a year from now you will tell this story and laugh."

Becky looked over to Travis who burped followed by a look of shock, like he had no idea what had just happened to him, then he looked at Becky for help. He opened his mouth like he was going to speak, but then he clapped both hands over his mouth as if he were afraid the burp would happen again if he tried to talk. "You call this harmless?"

Grelf chuckled. "You guys are the ones who ordered the intoxicants. Besides, it won't kill him. If he flows with it correctly, he could even expand his mind." Becky tried to get him to take down his hands long enough to get him to take the supplement. "Oh, you're well past that. He has already started to metabolize it. The supplement would only slow it down at this point."

"Then what do we do?" Becky asked in a panic. "We have never done any drugs before." She began to get scared and Grelf could see it in her eyes.

Grelf sternly said, "Becky." to get her attention and then said with a soothing voice. "Then don't play with this fire. You aren't prepared for it. The good news is that I am prepared and would never let you fall to any real harm." She extended her closed hand to Becky and when she opened it, she was holding a glass vile that held a thick yellow liquid. It was only Christoph between them, so she was close enough to place the vile in Becky's hand. "This will clear him of any toxins within seconds."

Becky took it and helped Travis drink it. Grelf was right and within seconds Travis had regained all his mental faculties.

"You just happen to have one of those on you?" asked Becky.

Grelf smiled and shrugged. She looked Becky truthfully in the eyes and said, "I am only half Elven and I am not immune to all the things a full-blooded elf might be, so I stay prepared. It's why I'm alive."

Everyone around the table held their breath to see if he was all right. Travis began to laugh. "That was amazing!"

Sir Adam asked, "You alright brother?"

"Better than all right. I was completely aware of everything that was going on here, but there were also so many other things happening. That was an amazing experience." He looked at Grelf. "Thank you for that amazing experience and what a fantastic lesson."

"You're not mad?" asked Becky.

"No." He kissed her. This was one of the first times he ever kissed her in front of people, and it surprised her, but she welcomed it. "Neither should you. I bet, somewhere down the line, she just saved our lives." He looked back to Grelf again. "Thank you." Then he turned back to Becky. "I am okay. I promise you, but I needed that reality check." He then turned to Grelf once again. "You are going to be an amazing queen. I mean... I pity the fool who faces you, but you are wiser than you let on, and you fooled me. I mean, no, really. I am usually on top of catching things like that, but you knew the exact second to distract me, and then to offer up a toast. Damn, way to go."

"Ha!" proclaimed Becky, as she turned her attention to Grelf. "Yes! That's what you did on purpose."

Grelf just smiled and said, "You're welcome."

Becky gasped, but Travis smiled and gave the best small bow that seated at a table would allow. He then reached into his bag and pulled out his notebook and cup. He activated the cup, began to sip on his drink, and started writing in his book.

"What are you writing?" asked Master Peace.

"Like I said, I could see all the things that were happening, but there was a lot more going on. I must write it all down before I forget." Then Travis began to write furiously.

Christoph cleared his throat. "Well, that was an adventure, and only three bites into lunch. I see that we are in for quite a journey." His words broke the tension in the air and within minutes they were all laughing about everything that had just happened. Grelf even switched seats with Christoph so she could sit next to Becky, and they spent the better part of the meal quietly chatting back and forth in hushed tones. By the time they were done eating, they were well on their way to being excellent friends.

After they had finished their meal, a young boy came up and asked if he could take any plates. He was carrying a good-sized bin with him, and he began to clear the table. Dalen recognized him and began to chat with him while he picked up the plates.

"I have seen you before," Dalen said. It took him a moment to put together where he had seen him, for Dalen, it had been years ago. "When I first came to Dorn's, years from now, in my time, I met you. You were working as a busser then as well. You would think after a couple of thousands of years they would have given you a promotion."

The boy laughed. "No. I am happy right where I am. My name is Aiden."

"Nice to meet you Aiden. I am Dalen Pax." Dalen shook his hand.

Aiden smiled and said, "Yeah. I know. You made this place."

Dalen looked at him closely. He had coffee-colored skin slightly darker than his own. As he looked closer, he could see that some features about him seemed familiar, but it was his eyes that gave it away.

"Your eyes." One of them is blue while the other is violet. "You don't see that often," Dalen said as the truth of it began to swell.

"They are like my father's." It was all that Aiden needed to say. Dalen knew who he was.

"Everyone," Dalen said without looking away from Aiden. "You know how Venger is alive and can manifest the avatar Lady Venger to communicate directly with us?" Everyone nodded. "I would like to introduce you to the living avatar that is Dorn's. My son. Aiden."

Sir Adam responded by spraying his mouthful of ale across the table. None seemed to notice, for at that moment they were all as dumbfounded as Sir Adam. Travis turned the page in his notebook slowly, still staring at Dalen, and raised his finger, to ask a question.

Dalen knew what the question was, so he just nodded to Travis and answered. "It is different than what your mind is trying to piece together. Together with the City of Venger, we created Dorn's. Half her creation, half mine. This place... Dorn's itself... I created with her, and because it is part of her, it can also create an avatar." Dalen just stared at him for a moment and a tear fell from his violet eye. "And this is him. Dorn's incarnate." Dalen's mind began to fill with dreams and questions as everyone picked their jaws up off the floor and said hello. "Aiden?" The boy turned and smiled. "Why Aiden?"

Aiden cocked his head and said, "Dorn's is fine for the storefront, but it was odd having me be addressed as Dorn's, so my mother named me. I have waited my whole life to meet you."

"I'm sorry I wasn't there but know this..." Tears fell from both eyes now as Dalen spoke. "Now that I am here. I want to get to know you and I want you to get to know me."

Aiden nodded and began to tear as well. "I have only heard stories about you my whole life. I would really like to get to know the person for real."

Dalen stood up and opened his arms. Aiden stood there for a moment. It was a lot to take in, but in the end, he wanted to know the man who made him, so he quickly stepped forward and embraced him. They stayed that way for a moment or two. It was too much for either of them to fully take in all at once. Dalen slowed time and stretched the moment. To his surprise, Aiden followed suit.

Aiden smiled at his father's expression of surprise. "I am the creation of the Jinn of Time and Space." He stepped back and wiped his eyes, and then with a grin Dalen had seen a thousand times in the mirror, he raised an eyebrow and said, "Guess what I can do?"

Time began to move again at a normal pace. Dalen had done nothing, and it was Aiden who was now controlling the flow of time.

"Well done," Dalen said impressed.

Aiden nodded with pride but then turned his attention to Grelf and Christoph. "You are here because you are at the crossroads of your lives. I would like the opportunity to help you understand why you are here. If you would, please follow my brother, Jed, we would like to show you something." The table retracted slowly enough for people to grab the drinks that were still there, and Grelf and Christoph got up from the table to follow Jed. "As for the rest of you, I am sure that you can understand that Dalen and I really should talk." Still slightly stunned, the team nodded. "So, to keep you entertained I present to you the greatest storyteller that Dorn could find for his opening day. Will of Grey."

I knew my cue. I had worked with Aiden a few hours prior and was ready to make my entrance. I walked up and said hello. Dalen grasped my arm and looked me in the eyes. I smiled and nodded, and then he did something that I wasn't expecting. He spoke in Grey Speak.

Dalen smiled and said, *Dude.*

My mind opened like an iris and his memories of me, including the moment I had taught him how to Grey Speak came flooding into my mind as if they were my own.

I am a being that transcends time. I am in every moment that exists. But while my avatar is in a corporeal state, I am only aware of what could be known in corporeal or linear time. Getting the flash of memories from Dalen, now knowing who he was and the stories we had already experienced, I remembered him. I remembered the first time he walked into Dorn's, and I remember what he had to go through to become the Reality Bender, and then I remembered his journey to become the Jinn of Time.

With a new understanding, I rolled my eyes and jokingly scoffed. "Time travelers." Then I laughed and gave him a hug. "You are still an amazing dude. Keep up the good work."

Dalen and Aiden went to another booth to have a private chat, and I began to regale the rest of the group with one of my favorite stories from the Second Dynasty about an evil wizard who created a mansion filled with deadly traps that would steal members of royalty and keep them as his... guest. He would take great amusement in heroes rushing to their deaths trying to save them. Until one day a group of adventurers foiled his plans and ended his reign of terror.

In the back of my mind, I was more interested in the story that was about to unfold. Christoph and Grelf were about to get the inspiration and understanding needed to get them prepared to take a step that, at the moment, they still didn't believe they could take.

6

WHY ARE WE FIGHTING

Christoph and Grelf had been taken to a door in the back of Dorn's. Jed gave a small bow and respectfully said as he held the door for them, "Your Majesties." Christoph and Grelf had known him for many years while being in the employment of the City of Venger. It was odd for him to address them as such, but they knew that they would eventually have to get used to it. They had begun to walk through the door when they were caught off guard by a second Jed who was standing on the other side of the door. "Your Majesties." echoed this new version of Jed.

Christoph looked at both and asked, "There are two of you?"

"Not a bit of it." said the first.

"The world couldn't handle two of us." replied the second, and then they both gave a wink to each other and in unison said, "Chair, monkey, hinge, door, biscuit."

The first Jed smiled and said, "You remembered."

The second Jed nodded, happy with himself. "I repeated it every day for a year." Then he turned his attention to Christoph and Grelf. "There is only one of me, but now you are a couple of thousand years from the other side of that door."

They turned around in time to watch the first Jed grab the door handle. "See you when you're ready." Then he waved as he closed the door.

"Jed," Christoph said with confusion in his eyes. "We have been friends a long time. Be straight with me. What's going on?"

Jed pretended to lock his mouth shut and then he mimed throwing away the key. When Grelf asked as well, he replied with, "What? And ruin the surprise?" Both frowned disapprovingly at his lack of forthcoming answers. "I will tell you this." He leaned in and waved them close. "You are going to head out the door and get in the carriage. Then we are going to take you for a little ride to the place where you will have to decide if what you'll be fighting for is worth it. Then, you make your choice and choose your path." Jed smiled and nodded at them, and instinctively they nodded back. "Alright then, but first our day manager would like to tell you something. He is over near the bar."

Still a little confused about what had all transpired, they walked over to the bar. As they approached a hand came up from behind the counter and they heard a somewhat familiar voice say, "Be right with you." They were expecting Dorn, but who they saw could not have been anticipated.

Christoph stood up from behind the bar took a look at both of them and cracked a playful smile. "I may have to go speak with the brothers at the Temple of Light. It seems I've just found myself."

Grelf and the Christoph standing next to her just stood there and stared. Neither of them could process what they were looking at.

The Christoph that still had control of his faculties smiled and said, "I remember the feeling that you are having right now. After all this time it has stayed with me, as it will you. This is one of the main reasons it's not suggested to meet yourself anywhere in time."

Being the more focused one of their partnership, Grelf was able to clear her thoughts enough to speak first. "How is it, that you are not so affected?"

The Christoph that was standing next to her was only a moment behind her, but as he regained his ability to speak, so did he gain his ability to think. He chuckled and said, "He had time to prepare." The Christoph behind the bar smiled and pointed at the other. When he did the scar that ran up his right hand and halfway up his arm caught their attention and Christoph pointed it out with humor. "I see you hurt yourself shaving." It was an old joke from his childhood and if this were really himself, he would get the reference.

The Christoph behind the bar looked at his hand, shrugged, and said, "Yeah, never shave by candlelight." They both looked at Grelf who was still lost and together they said, "Old Dwarven proverb." Then they both laughed and shook hands. Then the Christoph behind the bar gestured at his scar and said, "Epic moments leave epic scars my man."

Grelf just blinked in disbelief and said, "Dear gods and goddesses help me, there are two of them." Both men watched as she processed this information. It went from concern to fear, to amusement, and then with a wicked grin, she looked at both of them like her next meal. "There are two of you."

The Christoph behind the bar laughed and said, "We don't have time for such shenanigans right now, and besides, you would have to get past my wife."

"Wife?" Grelf's hair turned green with streaks of yellow and red. "Who is she? I can take her."

Christoph who was standing next to her leaned in and said, "I think he means you."

"Oh." Her hair turned white while the tips filled in with blue.

The Christoph next to her hugged her as he chuckled. "Oh, my love, don't be embarrassed.

"The other Christoph was chuckling too. He said, "I forgot you said that. I am so, going to remind you of that tonight."

Grelf popped her head up and looked around. "Oh Bibitz! Am I here too?"

"No, no. Not a bit of it. You are elsewhere." Christoph said from behind the bar.

"Where am I? And why are we immortal?" Grelf asked.

Christoph reached under the bar and produced their favorite drinks. He smiled and then explained, "There are some rules that I have to follow to have this conversation, and one of them is being very careful about not giving you certain information about the future."

Grelf didn't like the answer, but she nodded and said, "Then, what is it you wanted to tell us?"

Still behind the bar, Christoph folded his arms and proudly said, "I wanted to say, that I regret nothing." The two on the other side of the bar looked at each other and then back to him. "What you are about to do, is the hardest thing I have ever done, and I can say without a doubt it tested me past what I thought possible, but standing on this side of it, I would do it again."

Christoph let go of Grelf and shook the hand of the version of himself that was behind the bar. "You have no idea how much I needed to hear that."

The other Christoph gripped his hand tightly and simply said, "Actually. I do."

Their conversation was cut short when Jed interrupted to tell them that their coach was ready. They said their goodbyes and stepped outside of Dorn's where they found the coach was waiting for them.

On board, they were greeted by me who had been given the honor to tour them through the highlights of Venger on their way to the castle. From my point of view, these two people had been dear and close friends for about two thousand years, and Christoph and I still shared stories every time I came to Dorn's. It was fun to meet them again for the first time. As we rode through the city, I pointed out to them some of the amazing things that had been added since their time. Such as The Vengerian Forge and the School of Magic, but the thing I pointed out more than anything else was the look of peace and joy on the faces of all we passed. The people did not know who was riding in the coach, but they recognized it as the official coach of the city and waved at whoever might be inside with smiles and cheers.

I looked at them earnestly and asked them both. "Do you see the love and admiration?" I looked to Christoph and said, "Do you see the honor?" I looked at Grelf and added, "Do you see the respect?" After that, it was all they could see. I could have driven past miraculous events, and they would have missed them. All they could see was the truth in the eyes of the people of the City of Venger. As we reached the castle, I leaned in one more time and offered them one more piece of truth they needed to understand. "This is all your doing." Both of their hearts swelled as did their eyes.

They were met by the Captain of Castle Security as we arrived. She was dressed in full parade uniform; she wore a black shirt and pants under half-plate steel armor beautifully inlaid with celestium, consisting of a chest plate, arm and leg guards, and a helmet with face and nose guards. Over that, a tabard, blue on the right half and red on the left that bore a silver Vengerian Seal on the chest, sinched with a belt that carried a sword featuring celestium inlay and a glowing blue stone on each side of its hilt.

I introduced them and she gave a proper bow and spoke with an almost reverent whisper. "Your Majesties. If you will follow me, please." She turned and gave the courtyard a good scan and then walked them into the castle. She led them through the main hall and paused for a moment so that they had the opportunity to look at the portraits of all of the kings and queens who had come before. Grelf let out a small yelp of surprise when the Captain of the Guard pointed out the portrait in the center of the back wall. Directly between the two staircases that wrapped around either side of the room was a portrait of them.

Their minds were adapting to the shock as they stood there for a few moments before Grelf spoke up. "I look fantastic." She nudged Christoph. "You look terrible."

Christoph knew she was joking and grunted at her with amusement. "Are you wearing a dress?" he asked.

Grelf slapped him on the shoulder and said, "Hush, you."

They were led up the staircase to the right and made a left at the top of the stairs before being ushered into the first door on their left. They knew the castle well and knew that they were being taken to the Main Throne Room. They braced themselves as they walked in and bowed.

Neither the King nor Queen were sitting on their thrones, nor were they dressed in robes or crowns. Both had Long Swords strapped across their backs. Neither of them was wearing armor, but Grelf and Christoph could tell that they were dressed for a fight. Their clothes were well-fitted, but they had enough give to allow them both complete movement. They both gave their bows. Christoph recognized that the King's bow was a traditional bow of the Brotherhood of Light.

"What is this?" asked Christoph as his well-tuned instincts registered them both as threats.

"We know you well." responded the Queen. "I am Her Royal Majesty Queen Hope of Venger, but I know that the title will mean nothing to you until I can show you, I am worthy of your respect."

Grelf smiled and said, "You got that right sister."

It was the King who spoke next. "It's the man who makes the king. Not the title that makes the man."

Christoph nodded in agreement, "Good idea. Who are you quoting?"

The King pulled his sword. It was a standard blade that didn't even look sharp. The only thing that made it exceptional was a glint nearly undetectable to the human eye which seemed to pull light along its surface as the blade was moved. "Roughly sixty-five generations ago those words were spoken by the greatest king who has ever sat on this throne." He pointed his sword directly at Christoph. "His Royal Majesty King Christoph of Venger." The truth of it hit Christoph like being slapped with a fish. It was hard and uncomfortable and left a presence that lingered. "I am Gavin. The direct descendant of the bloodline of Venger, and I stand before you now to be tested."

The Queen drew her sword. Like Gavin, she was not wielding an Elemental Blade, instead, she was using what looked to be a practice sword with a hint of a glow along its blade. She looked deep into Grelf's eyes and said, "If you hold back even a little, I will know."

I was still standing in the doorway with the Captain of the Guard. I leaned sideways toward her and said, "You trained her well."

The Captain of the Guard's chest swelled with pride. She gave a simple nod and said, "Without question, out of all of them, Hope has been the greatest queen I have ever had the privilege to train."

She meant it. My ability to Grey Speak is not a one-way flow. I can hear the thoughts of others and even deeper than mere thought, I can feel the moments in their life that created those thoughts. So, as she spoke, I could feel her sincerity and see the memories of training Hope that had been burned into her mind.

"Damn, she's that good? Who do you think is going to win?" I meant it more rhetorically, but the Captain of the Guard answered without hesitation. "Hope wins." She removed her helmet and allowed her dark hair with blue streaks to fall out of its binding. "I thought of myself as the great and powerful Orc-Slayer. I had no real knowledge of power or greatness. I didn't even know myself."

I smiled at them both and said, "Look how far you have come."

She smiled at me and allowed one tear to race down her cheek. "Thank you, Master Grey."

Our conversation was happening behind Grelf's back, so she had no idea what she had just missed. She often carried two blades. One was her father's blade, and she never pulled it unless she was sure her goal was to kill the target in front of her. This was not the case. She was going to fight with all her ability, but the goal was not to kill this upstart queen who thought she could best her. Instead, she drew the sword from her hip and was preparing to show this little whelp the mistake she was making by choosing to face the great and powerful, Grelf the Orc-Slayer.

Grelf was the first to attack out of the four of them. She had been still for a moment looking Hope up and down and then without a word she propelled herself from a standstill to a full run within two steps as her hair changed to a brilliant fiery orange with tips of yellow that faded to white. Within three more steps, she was at her target, and she attacked Hope with a diagonal strike starting from the upper right. As she came down with her strike Hope stopped it with an inverted block so that the point of her sword was facing down. Their swords crashed together and once contact had been made the momentum stopped, leaving Grelf in a vulnerable pose and putting Hope in position to complete an overhead strike on her right-hand side from the block position. As Hope brought down her strike Grelf matched her using the same block and returned with another strike. While Grelf made her second attack Hope stepped forward and to the left with quickness, effectively dodging the attack and placing them side by side facing opposite directions. They both turned their heads and locked eyes.

Grelf cocked her head to one side and said, "Not bad."

Hope nodded as she accepted the compliment. "I was trained by the best."

Grelf scoffed. "Yeah?" She went at Hope with a volley of five blows. Hope blocked them with skill and grace. "And who was that?" she asked with another volley of strikes. Hope looked over to her mentor and Captain of her Royal Guard. Grelf followed Hope's line of sight and for a moment forgot the fight altogether. She watched as the other version of herself smiled and gave a small bow. Grelf had almost no time to process what she was seeing when the Captain of the Guard pointed back toward Hope.

Grelf had multiple thoughts running through her head at that moment. Her first thought was a sharp reminder that she was in the middle of battle. The second thought was reminding and berating herself that she shouldn't allow herself to take her eyes off the prize. She was half-elven and possessed very accurate hearing. Her ears perked up as she heard three steps get taken and then nothing. Hope had leaped, she was sure of it. She contemplated the first moves that Hope had used as her mind simultaneously sent messages to her limbs to stay in the battle. She remembered Hope was right-handed. The strike could come from the right or left, or even directly overhead. But because she was right-handed there was more than a good chance that the blow would come from either directly overhead or from the right. There was a slight chance that she could go left, but Grelf decided to risk it. She dropped to one knee, brought both hands up and over her head, and allowed her blade to rest flat over her right arm. As the strike landed Hope's blade glanced off the block and slid sideways down Grelf's blade and away from her body.

...

Christoph and Gavin had been watching Grelf and Hope fight when Christoph remembered that he had a fight of his own to contend with. He smiled at Gavin and gestured with his head toward the girls. "She has skill."

Gavin sheathed his sword. "She can hold her own."

Christoph read Gavin's stance and could tell that even though his sword was strapped across his back, he had not relaxed. Every movement was intentional, and he was ready to act. Ready or not, Christoph believed that sheathing his weapon was a mistake and he intended to use any advantage his opponent would give him. He began a volley of attacks but as each swing came, Gavin stepped just out of the way. Sometimes he would simply duck or sway but strike after strike Christoph cut through nothing but air.

"What is this?" Christoph questioned as another strike missed its mark.

"This..." Gavin said as he spun around, ducked under another strike, and drew his blade again, "... is a Blade of Intent." Gavin showed it to Christoph, holding it out horizontally with one hand on the hilt letting the tip of the blade rest in his other outstretched hand. Gavin quickly pulled back to dodge Cristoph's next blow and then returned the sword to the same position as before, resting in both hands.

Christoph was studying Gavin's movements. It was obvious that he had been trained by the Brotherhood of Light and was amazingly agile on his feet, but Christoph had watched Gavin long enough to start to anticipate his movements. Christoph feigned a maneuver and as Gavin began to respond to the perceived attack Christoph swiftly changed his stance and was able to send the blade in a new direction. It surprised him. Christoph saw it in Gavin's eyes, but even surprised, Gavin caught the change and moved his blade into a blocking position barely in time.

Still holding the handle with one hand and allowing his other to guide the tip Gavin changed his tactics and began to fend off each blow with a clean cross block. If the attack came directly overhead Gavin's block was directly horizontal. As he now deflected strike after strike, he began to explain his blade to Christoph as if it were a book report.

"You see," Gavin said as Christoph thrust forward. Gavin parried his attack. "A Blade of Intent..." Gavin blocked another strike coming from his left. "... is a special type of blade." Gavin defended two more blows. Each one was stronger than the last as Christoph, now breathing heavily, attempted to break his defensive line. Christoph tried to disengage after his volley, but Gavin, still gripping his blade with the tip and hilt stepped forward and pushed both hands toward Christoph, who instinctively blocked it as if it were a strike. Gavin quickly followed with another, and then another, each time stepping forward, always keeping both hands in the same position but aggressively changing the tilt on the blade. Christoph landed a large blow against Gavin's sword in hopes of pushing him back. "As the name suggests..." Gavin quickly changed to a different block position and advanced half a step. "It does the bidding of the wielder's intent."

Christoph realized he was no longer choosing the targets. Each time Gavin took another blocking stance Christoph instinctively attacked that location. As if Gavin had some type of control over Christoph's blade. For the last few hits, Gavin was just making targets, almost playing with Christoph who began weakly hitting Gavin's weapon instead of aggressively attacking his opponent. "What are you doing?" Christoph asked with exasperation.

"I am intentionally wearing you out." Gavin changed tactics again and switched to a standard one-handed fighting stance. "It worked too. You are getting tired from all those power swings. I'd say you have slowed down by at least a third of your reaction time."

Gavin came at Christoph with blinding speed. He had been right, with all the over swings and power hits one after another, Christoph was running out of energy. All that Gavin had done in this fight was take a few side steps and sustain the absorption of pressure on his hands that came with every one of Christophs hits. He was still at full strength.

Christoph tried his best, but Gavin moved like the wind and eventually got past his guard. At the last moment just before the strike hit, Gavin turned his blade so it would hit Christoph with the flat edge, and as it struck Christoph's left arm, searing pain as if his arm had been cut off, shot through his body and everything below where the blade had touched went numb. Christoph screamed through his clenched teeth and did his best to push through it. He dared not look at his arm. He was sure it had been cut off and he had no time for the horror of it. He swung a kill shot at Gavin's neck, but Gavin easily ducked under it, and with the flat of his blade slapped Christoph's right arm. The mind-altering pain of having a second arm amputated shot through Christoph's body. His body went into shock, and he fell to his knees.

Gavin had the point of his sword an inch away from Christoph's neck. Gavin looked him in the eyes and asked with respect, "Am I worthy?"

Christoph could no longer feel the pain, his body was now in complete shock. He couldn't move and could barely speak, but his mind was sharp. He nodded. "Tactics. Knowledge. Skill." He nodded again. "You are worthy."

"Gavin grinned and said, "Thank you. That means everything coming from you." Gavin closed his eyes for a moment and touched the top of Christoph's head with the tip of his blade. The second he did Christoph was released from his pain.

He could breathe again, and when he looked at his arms, he was surprised to see them still there, and even more surprising than that, he could move them. "Neat Trick," Christoph said as he got up from the floor.

"Blade of Intent." He held it out for Christoph to inspect once more. "A fantastic tool to allow new fighters the opportunity to understand the true nature of being a warrior and being wounded, without all the messiness of actually harming someone."

"This is a practice tool for novices?" Christoph said with disbelief after being utterly beaten by it.

"Oh, yeah." Gavin looked it up and down, "But like I said, it does what you intend." Without warning Gavin sent the blade into Christoph's mid-section and it made him double over.

The sensation was instant, and Christoph had no defense against it. It was torturous and again it brought him to his knees. The sensation of being tickled was too much to ignore and Christoph found himself on the floor in a fit of laughter. His muscles convulsed and seized as he lay writhing on the floor. With every breath, all he could do was squeal for mercy and beg Gavin to make it stop.

...

Grelf had just made her glancing block and was still on one knee. She used that position to launch herself into an arial spinning heel kick. Hope had to step back to get out of the way, which is right where Grelf believed she should be. Backing up and in retreat.

Grelf glanced at herself from the future and then back at Hope. "No wonder you have talent. You were trained by the best." Her hair went blond with highlights of red and orange. Grelf pushed her advance and took a few swings at Hope. Hope matched her movements and continued her retreat. Grelf wasn't really trying to hit her, she was just trying to move her. Keep her back peddling until she had moved her back far enough to trip her on her throne. It worked perfectly. Hope moved back as if they had choreographed it, every one of Grelf's swings causing Hope to inch closer and closer until she finally hit the throne with the back of her knees, forcing her to sit down.

Grelf went in for a thrust, but Hope's legs were longer than Grelf's arms, she kicked up and caught Grelf's upper arm with the niche between the ball and heel of her boot. With that, Hope had leverage, and even though she was in a position to block Grelf's weapon, Grelf could not thrust forward to make the attack. Hope put her other foot into Grelf's chest and pushed her back.

Grelf used the momentum of being pushed to tuck into a ball and rolled backward. As she landed the somersault and her feet touched the ground, she allowed her muscles to absorb all the energy of the motion and used it to propel herself forward, sending it back at Hope, sword first, like an arrow.

With one fluid motion, Hope kicked at the blade about halfway down the hilt as Grelf came in, effectively moving it far enough outward that the strike wouldn't hit her. Hope steadied her other foot on the ground, used her hips to pivot her body, and thrust all of her strength and body weight through her fist as she caught Grelf in the jaw with a powerful right hook, which sent Grelf careening into Hope, toppling both of them and the throne over and onto the floor.

Each of them had lost their weapons in the tumble and

were now both wrestling for position. Grelf got the upper hand but chose to use it to push Hope away and retrieve her weapon. Right then Grelf heard Christoph scream. She looked over to see him get struck in his right arm. He dropped his sword and fell to his knees. Gavin moved his blade to Christoph's neck and said something that she couldn't make out.

"That's the last thing you will ever say." She pulled her dagger and flipped it around in her hand so that she was holding the blade. She raised her hand and reached back ready to throw it.

Hope was behind her and just took ahold of the handle and slid it out of her hand. "He is in no danger," Hope said. I promise you.

Grelf was tired of this queen, and no one took her dagger from her like that. She gripped her sword tightly and as fast as she could spun and attacked Hope across the chest.

Hope's body had turned into metal, which looked like Damascus with layers of steel and celestium. This was shocking, but it was dismissed as Grelf watched her blade shatter against Hope's skin.

Grelf backed away in confusion. She looked over and saw that Christoph was getting back up. She looked back at Hope, but she had reverted to her fleshier form. "You, see?" she asked. "Everything is fine." They both looked over to Gavin and Christoph just in time to watch Gavin take a free swing into Christoph's gut. "Oh, Gods and Goddesses, that was bad timing my love." Hope said as she rested her forehead with her fingers.

Grelf was at Christoph's side in a moment and was trying to search his body for wounds when he gasped for air and bellowed, "I'm going to pee!"

Out of all the things that Christoph could have said as he lay there dying, that was the last thing Grelf was expecting him to say. Gavin tapped Christoph's boot with the end of his sword and Christoph regained his senses. "What did you do to him!" she demanded.

"This," Gavin said and tapped her shoulder with his blade. In all her life she never laughed so hard. Gavin was kind and did not leave her there long and when he released her Hope and Gavin helped them both up.

After that, Gavin and Hope earned their respect. Once they explained that the only reason they were as powerful as they were, was because they had been trained by the two of them, they became friends. After all, they had known each other for quite some time. Christoph had been playing wooden swords with Gavin since he could walk and the Grelf that was standing by my side spoke with great pride about how she had never trained a stronger queen.

"The city. The people. Gavin and Hope. They are all here because of what you chose to do, you both chose to fight an unbeatable foe." I moved past the thrones to the large crystal window that filled the wall behind them. "All of this is because you chose to save us all."

"And what happens if we choose not to fight?" asked Grelf.

There was fear in her voice as she spoke. Afraid of what the answer would be.

The Grey Continuum has many aspects but there is only one avatar. It changes to match the characteristics needed at the time, the same way a person changes to match their surroundings. When speaking to your child, you're a different person than when speaking to your lover, or your boss, each is still a true aspect of who you are, but one truth can have many faces. Thus, when it was Hip-Gnosis who answered her question, it was he who stood before them.

"Then the Chaos Dragon wins." A bright light flashed outside, so bright that Grelf and Christoph had to shield their eyes. As they looked back blinking, they stared in horror as they watched a ball of fire rip apart all of Venger. Through the fire, they caught a flash of the Chaos Dragon. It burst from the ground and tore itself from the earth. Venger sat at the top of the cliffs, but as the Chaos Dragon emerged from the mountainside, the void it created made the land give way and the entire city of Venger fell to the sea. In that moment, the earth moved but Grelf and Christoph did not. They hung in the air, paralyzed, as they watched the City of Venger fall to the sea. Hip-Gnosis had cleared the distance and now stood directly in front of them. "This is if no one comes. This is if the choice not to choose is made." The earth below fell to even greater depths, creating a birds-eye view of the entire kingdom. They could see past the mountain range to the Northern Sea, and they could see the Elven Forest to the south. "Here is where no one stops this, from happening."

The dragon was much larger than they had guessed. It was the size of a mountain and dwarfed the City of Venger as it now lay broken along the shore. The Chaos Dragon took only a moment to gloat and then with all its might it sent a destructive blast from its mouth that vaporized Venger instantaneously. The blast sent out a powerful shock wave that traveled further than they could see in every direction.

Grelf and Christoph watched in horror as everything they knew was burned in seconds. They heard the screams when the wave went out and killed thousands upon thousands as the blast rippled in every direction. It was more than either of them could bear as they not only watched their world be destroyed but could also feel it in their hearts. Hip-Gnosis was gone, and Angel stood before them. He wrapped his comforting wings around them and shed a tear for them both.

7

A CONVERSATION BETWEEN KINGS AND QUEENS

Grelf and Christoph found themselves standing in the throne room. They blinked at each other as the haze wore off and then together, they glanced out the window and were happy to see that Venger still existed. Gavin and Hope were there, but each had an air about them that suggested that they too had experienced the terror that had been shown. Hope held Grelf and let her shake while Gavin stepped in to take Christoph to the side. Partly to talk him down, but also because Gavin knew that Grelf would never want to let Christoph see her cry. Not yet.

Christoph pushed against Gavin at first, wanting to be there for Grelf. The event they had witnessed had greatly affected them, but he relented knowing that Grelf was proud. Her specific pet peeve was to be perceived as needing a man for her to be all right. He knew that if he tried to comfort her right now, it would only upset her further. "You've got this," he told her and only eased back from Gavin once she looked up at him and nodded. He looked her in the eyes, made sure she kept his gaze, and said to her, "I'll be all right, but I am going to need a minute to walk it off. If I need you, you'll be close by, right?"

She understood that he wasn't talking about himself. He had meant it with roles reversed but was ready to look weak so she could feel strong. This was one of the moments where Grelf knew in her heart, that, besides her father, Christoph was the greatest man she had ever met. She could see that even though he was reeling as hard as she was, he was there for her, and was letting her know in a way that didn't play down to her or treat her like she was a child who needed someone to take care of her. She smiled, nodded, and followed his lead. And even though her mind was reeling she got out, "If you need me, I'll be close."

It was all Christoph needed to hear from her. He nodded and then let Gavin take him into another room that was on the right-hand side of the throne room.

"I don't believe in a world where I would sit by and let that happen." Christoph's emotions were not in check and pouring out of him.

"Nor do I." Gavin took his right hand and looked him deep

107

in the eyes. "That reality is not what happens as far as I am concerned. I wouldn't have ever existed, I could not have existed if it weren't for what lies in front of you, and now that you have seen what the other option is, I am quite sure that if it does happen, it will not be because of you."

"But it can still happen?" Christoph's mind began to refocus. "That is impossible. This reality proves what happens. I can just look in a history book and know exactly what to do. At this point, it's a fact. Right?"

"At this point, yes." Gavin's gaze didn't let go, he continued to stare into Christoph's soul as he spoke. "To us it is history, but to you, it will be the present, and traveling with you, will be the one threat to what we know as fact."

It froze Christoph in his tracks. Gavin was trying to tell him something. Something important. "I'm listening."

"Dalen Pax." Gavin's words were filled with concern but equally filled with certainty.

Christoph was not expecting that answer. He broke eye contact and let go of Gavin's hand. "I thought he was a Vengerian protector...sent by you, and now you tell me he is the only thing that can bring about that destruction? Why would you send him?"

"Because he is the only one who can prevent it as well." Gavin had brought him into a waiting room near the main throne room. There were refreshments there and Gavin poured them a drink. "Dalen is more unique than even he realizes at this point." Gavin clinked his glass against Christoph's, gave it a slight raise in respect, and then took a sip before he continued. "All of time is fixed in a single position. It is what it is, and it will always be what it is."

"So, what you are saying is that it can't happen any differently. Yes?" Christoph glanced at a small table and gestured for Gavin to sit. Christoph, minding his manners and respecting etiquette, remembered he was still in the presence of royalty, and he wasn't about to sit down before the King did.

Gavin took a seat and then leaned in like he was telling a secret or a good bit of gossip and Christoph returned the gesture. "Yes, except there are two individuals who have the ability to rewrite time as they move through it, literally changing reality and history in a way that ripples out in both directions from the beginning through the end of time."

"That sounds dangerous." Christoph took a sip of his drink. It was a brandy unlike any other he had ever tasted but it somehow reminded him of home.

"It can be devastating." Gavin took another sip and then continued. "For a long time, there was only one. He was an insane genie by the name of DeSalvo. He has been known as a scourge, a... plague of time. Every genie has had a master, but no one has ever known who his master was. I only know that he sent DeSalvo through time again and again to destroy key moments in history."

"If he changed time, how would you ever be the wiser?" asked Christoph.

"Now you are thinking like a king." Gavin clinked his glass

against Christoph's again and then finished his drink. While he continued, he got up and brought back the bottle. "The City of Venger was visited by two seers. Fae in nature. They lived away from most people at the far end of the Elvish Forrest. They traveled here to warn me of something I needed to know."

"What was it?" Christoph finished his drink and offered the empty glass to Gavin who refilled it and his own. "What did they have to tell you?"

"The Oracles told me of DeSalvo. They warned me that he was just one part of something much larger." Gavin took a drink. "They said that there would be another that could bend reality and create with time. There is a prophecy about the God of Time, and how there would be two who would precede him. One would bring the world into chaos and the other would have the chance to set right what the first had done. Both would be able to wield time." Gavin took another long pull on his drink and then got to the meat of his point. "The seers said that one day the timeline completely changed and suddenly there were miracles everywhere. Events that had once gone wrong in both our past and our future were now changed, and in their place were life and light. I listened but from my point of view, all the things she told me were history. I had studied them as a child, and I knew them to be the greatest moments in the history of our world. The moments that genuinely made a difference in our lifetime. I had grown up knowing that one day I would have to live up to those moments as I wrote my page in the history of this world."

"So, these destroyed histories that you are talking about...

this DeSalvo, never happened?" Christoph asked, trying to understand what Gavin was explaining.

"For me, never happened. I had never even heard of this DeSalvo until they mentioned him, but they staked their reputations on the point that the day before had been vastly different. And that the world I had known my whole life was not as it seemed. Then they said that this change in the timeline was a marker of this prophecy and that the second predecessor would soon make his presence known."

Christoph took another pull as well. "And?"

Gavin smiled and gave a quick salute with his glass, "That very day Dalen Pax strolls right past the Great Seal and straight into Dorn's." Gavin finished his second glass. "You, in part, are the one who slays the Chaos Dragon. Dalen Pax is the one who makes it possible. That is why I sent him. Well, that, and the seers specifically told me when he showed up to make sure that he found his way to them. Which I did, and he did. It's history for both of us now."

"So, what is the variable that decides which way this goes?" Christoph finished his second glass as well, but neither man seemed to want a third.

"When they face the Time Mage, somehow DeSalvo is there. We don't know what happens there. No one does. It's like that part of history was erased, forgotten, or both. All we know is the outcome. But the truth of it is, that with both of them there at the same time and knowing what each of them can do... what they are capable of, there is a chance that it could go differently. If DeSalvo wins that fight, then just like his timeline, everything that we have come to know can be wiped from reality."

Christoph stood up. He had heard what he needed to and only had one more question. "So, Dalen Pax is only a threat if he fails?"

Gavin shrugged. "Only if he fails. If he succeeds...you and Grelf will have a chance to save us all." Gavin stood up and took him by the forearm.

Christoph laughed and said, "In that case, I better do all that I can to make sure he succeeds."

...

"That was some bibitz, right?" asked Hope.

"Indeed." Replied Grelf. Her hair had returned to her standard chestnut, but when realizing what Hope had said, the highlights turned from blue to orange as she asked slightly surprised, "That's my personal swear word, how do you know it?"

Hope smiled and shrugged. "It's commonplace now. One of the first gifts from our first queen."

Grelf glanced over to the Captain of the Guard. Her highlights turned blue again. "This is your doing?" She was pointing at Hope.

"You won't find better." answered the Captain of the Guard. "I taught her more than everything you know." She smirked and added, "I taught her everything I know."

Grelf looked Hope up and down again, but this time with different eyes. "You fought well. I'm impressed."

"Thank you," said Hope with a small bow. She was on the verge of tears. "That means a lot."

Grelf returned her gaze to the Captain of the Guard. "You taught her everything?"

"All but one thing."

Grelf raised an eyebrow. "Yeah, what was that?"

"I haven't told her about Father, or Mother."

"I would imagine not."

"You would be right, but you would be wrong about why." This older version of Grelf walked up to her younger self, took her by both shoulders and looked her in the eyes. "There was a time long ago when I felt the same way as you do now. But centuries have passed, and time and knowledge have rewritten all that I know on the subject. I want you to tell her the story as you remember it. I want you to tell her everything, and then I want you to do something that I know is hard for you."

"Yeah?" asked Grelf. "What is that?"

"I want you to listen." The elder version of Grelf hugged her younger self and kissed her on the forehead, which came as a great shock to the Orc Slayer. "Tell her about Father and tell her about Mother. Tell her about the woman who sang to us, and then just listen. Because what Hope says, is exactly what you need to hear."

"How do you know?" asked Grelf.

"Because it was exactly what I needed to hear when I did it. It changed everything and it's why you are here." The older Grelf let the younger one go. "Now, I must go. Being me is a full-time job of continuously being the bibitz and I am the only one who can do it, so...." She smiled and gave her younger self a wink and her hair turned prismatic. It was a color that Grelf had never seen before.

"That's new." Grelf had gotten the enchantment bestowed upon her the day she was considered an adult. It was her birthday gift to herself and a direct attack against her mother's sensibilities. The enchantment made her hair change color with her thoughts and emotions, and she had paid extra to have it permanent, knowing her mother would hate it. Seeing herself with this beautiful prismatic coloring told Grelf something more. That version was feeling something...something more than Grelf had the ability to feel in her specific place in time.

"Nice to meet you!" Grelf called out as she watched the other version of herself make her way to the door. Her hair in a continuous state of changing color.

The older of the two turned back around quickly and with a devilish smile exclaimed, "Go get it! Go Dragons!" and then she was gone.

Grelf slowly looked back over to Hope. "How is it that you could have known me, and trained with me, and have never heard this story? How could you possibly know me, understand me, without knowing the very thing that makes me, me?"

"I believe the answer is because, by the time we first meet, it no longer is the thing that makes you who you are." Hope smiled, shrugged quickly, and continued, "You had already embraced hundreds of years of new life experiences, they reshaped you." Hope led Grelf to a room that was on the opposite wall from where Christoph had been taken.

Grelf was still trying to glue pieces of herself together as they walked toward the door. There had been no filter in the vision that Hip-Gnosis had given them. No offer of protection for the mind. As far as she was concerned, they had been there, and it was terribly traumatic on her mind and soul, but she was not going to let herself break. She was the Orc Slayer, and she could handle this.

The room that Grelf was led to was used for guests to freshen up in before being let into court. There was a large fireplace with marble statues of a dragon and a unicorn on each side. It wasn't lit at the time but was well over fifteen feet long and would have no problem keeping this room warm in the colder months. Two long couches came out perpendicular from the fireplace with a third one just past, and between them forming a U-shape that faced inwards toward the hearth. Along one of the walls was a fully stocked wet bar so the Queen poured both her and Grelf a drink. She sat right next to Grelf on one of the couches, handed her one of the glasses, and tucked her feet under herself.

Grelf took a sip of it and let its warmth move through her. "This is wonderful. What is it?"

"It's a magically preserved Brandy. Incredibly old. You collected it on your journeys and drank it at your wedding. I believe it was distilled by Star Folk. You had the decanter enchanted to never be empty. It has been the Royal brandy ever since." Hope took a sip. "Now, please, I have waited a long time to hear the tale of how a young half-elven girl became Grelf, The Orc Slayer."

Grelf took another sip of her brandy. It was quite good. She took another sip just to stall one last time before she told Hope the story of her father's death at the hands of a vicious orc and how her mother's lack of love and faith in her, drove her to become the woman she became.

. . .

It started when she was still young. She was part elven, so she had aged slowly. She was nearly fifty by the time she was starting to become a woman. Her father, Gregor, had been an amazing adventurer in his prime and had won the heart of Dandillion, Grelf's mother, who was an elf from the Woodland Realms south of Venger. They had gotten married and had a daughter. Five decades passed with them knowing nothing but peace and joy, but that all changed the day Iron-Tusk, an orc from the Northern Mountains, made his way from the Orcish Lands and began terrorizing any settlement that he came across. Shortly after word began to spread about the orcish fiend, Iron-Tusk found his way into Grelf's quiet village.

It broke through the gate while Gregor and his family were in the market. There was no time for him to go home to retrieve his sword. It was enchanted and he had relied on its strength many times throughout his career, but this day Gregor knew that he would have to face this foe without it.

"It will kill you, Gregor! Please, don't face it." Grelf's mother pleaded with him. "Please! Think of us. If you die, how will we survive? Think of your daughter!"

Gregor looked at Grelf and smiled. "I am thinking of her. What am I teaching her if I run and hide, while this monster walks around and kills everyone we know?"

Dandillion scoffed. "You would be teaching her that your daughter and your wife are more important than your ego." Gregor was obviously wounded but she didn't stop there. Her tone changed and she began to scold him, "I love you. You know that, but you are human. You have grown old and are not the man you once were." She took Gregor by the hand. "You don't even have your sword. Be realistic. You can't win." Dandillion had loved Gregor for many years but had lost faith in him and his strength.

"Mother! How could you!" Grelf had tears running down her cheeks as she screamed at her mother over the noise of the carnage that was drawing ever closer. She turned her gaze to her father. "I believe in you. Don't listen to her. You're the bibitz!"

"Shut up you stupid child!" Dandillion spun around with a backhand that caught Grelf across the face. "How many times have I told you not to use your foul, made-up words?" Dandillion stood over Grelf and raised her hand as if she were going to strike her again. Fear and anger had blinded her as she stared at her daughter with malice and hatred. "If he goes now, it will be your fault he dies!"

Grelf held her cheek, but it was her heart that broke. She lay there on the ground and began to cry.

Gregor's heart was broken too. He couldn't even look at his wife but spoke to her as he searched the general area for anything he could use as a weapon. "You have lost faith in me. I am going to remind you who you married and have spent the better part of sixty years with." He found a shovel along the side of a shop that was close. "And if you ever lay a hand on Grelf again, we will be done, and I will take her, and you will truly be alone." She began to protest but Gregor raised his voice with power and certainty. "Do you understand?"

Dandillion shrank back, "Yes. Of course. I, don't know what came over me."

Gregor turned his attention to his daughter. His smile and tone were loving as he scooped her up in his arms. "I love you, daughter. It is you who are the bibitz and never let anyone, especially your mother tell you any different." He smiled at her and caressed her wounded cheek. "Now I must go. Do you understand why?"

"Yes, Father." She pressed his hand firmly to her face. It hurt, but she held it close until he slid it away.

"Stay down," Gregor said to his family. "Stay quiet. I'll be right back." He smiled and slipped out of the back of the small booth that they had hidden in when the attack began.

Gregor moved quickly past a few more booths and stopped

only long enough to assess the orc. He was a young male orc in his prime. He stood nearly ten feet tall and was pale with dark eyes that were set deep in his skull. He was partly bent over as he growled and took random swings with his blade at anyone who was near, and he squinted as he rummaged through the baskets of fruit he was initially after.

"I'm in luck," Gregor said to himself. "It's a Moon Orc." Gregor knew that meant it had poor peripheral vision, and Moon Orcs were built for low-light surroundings. Caves and deep forests were where they usually made their home. Being in direct bright sunlight as it was, meant that it could barely see, which was the reason it was bending down to see the baskets on the ground. "This may not be a complete disaster."

Gregor moved in toward the Moon Orc from a sharp perpendicular angle. The Moon Orc didn't even know he was there until the first blow of the shovel cracked him at the base of its skull. It roared with pain and lashed out trying to protect itself. It got lucky, and its hand crashed into Gregor and sent him flying back. Gregor did his best to roll with the impact as he landed but his age was felt in his knees and back. He was barely on his feet as the Moon Orc attacked him head-on. Gregor did his best to deflect the blow, knowing that there was no way that he was strong enough to take the direct force of the Moon Orc's strength. But on the third swing, the vile creature made an overhand attack, Gregor blocked it, but the power behind the hit dropped him to his knees.

Dandillion screamed, "Gregor!" in a moment of panic. The Moon Orc heard her and smiled at his would-be victim.

"You must be Gregor." The Moon Orc had sustained his last attack and was using his strength to push Gregor further toward the ground. "I am going to make you pay for attacking me." Iron-Tusk leaned in and pushed Gregor to the ground. "I am going to do terrible things to whoever just screamed for you, and I am going to make you watch old man." Then he turned and started to make his way toward the stand that Dandillion and Grelf were hiding in. As he approached, Dandillion screamed for Gregor to save her. "That old man can't save you now!' laughed Iron-Tusk. He ripped and tore at the awning, and as he looked in and saw Dandillion and Grelf he stood up and laughed. "Oh look. Two." His smile made Dandillion's heart skip a beat and go cold with fear. "I am going to hurt you... a lot, and I am going to make the old man watch."

Dandillion screamed in horror. But it only encouraged the Moon Orc. Grelf, gripped by panic, just sat there on the floor, staring in horror as the orc loomed over them. She was sure that her father, the only man who ever meant anything to her was either just killed or only going to be alive long enough to watch whatever torture Iron-Tusk had planned for her and her mother. Fear won and she froze.

"Oh good. A screamer. I'll kill you last. Last and slow. I will bath in your suffering." Whatever else was going to be said was hushed by a loud clang that rang out like a bell and Iron-Tusk fell limp to the floor.

Gregor was standing behind him with the shaft of the broken shovel. Gregor had cracked the Moon Orc so hard that the shovel had shattered on contact. Gregor quickly moved to a position that put him between the Moon Orc and his family, but before Gregor could say a word, Dandillion was in his arms. She kissed him again and again as she spoke. "I thought you were dead. I thought we were all dead." She tried to hold both sides of his face and kiss him, but Gregor pushed her away and fought for room.

He finally got a good push and made her take a step back. "Stop!" Gregor cried. "He's not dead." It was the last thing that Gregor ever said. The Orcish blade exploded from his chest, covering Grelf in his blood. Iron-Tusk was badly wounded and barely conscious. He chose to run so he pulled the Blade from Gregor's back and fled.

Grelf still, just knelt there, unable to think or feel. She could hear her mother screaming but it sounded muffled or as if it were far away. As did much of the next few days. Grelf had to be carried home, and then bathed and dressed in clean clothes, but it didn't take the memory away. She was lost to the world and slipped into a catatonic state while her mind struggled to process the horrific event.

Her world had been destroyed, one of the only things in her entire life that made it worth living had been killed right in front of her. With nothing to hold on to she fell deep within her broken mind and shattered heart. The whole time hearing her mother's words repeatedly. "If he goes now, it will be your fault he dies!"

It was there, lost in the depths of her despair, that she first heard the woman singing. Grelf didn't know if it was a trick in her mind or if there was really someone there, but they were lying in bed next to her gently singing. She was a young woman, but pale and gaunt. Her eyes were darkened as if she were starving and anemic. Grelf turned her head to look closer at her and although she had never seen this woman before, she felt that she knew her.

"Why are you here?" Grelf asked. The woman continued to sing but it wasn't until that moment that Grelf realized that she could hear the sound of the woman's voice as clear as day but could not make out a single word she was saying.

The woman continued singing to her in her incomprehensible but beautiful voice. It was a terrifying visage, and although she was frightening, Grelf only found strength in her voice. It bid her to rise from her darkness, step back into the world, and leave her doubts and fears behind. It moved her and she began to hear her heartbeat within her chest. She began to hear people talking in the next room, and then all at once she sat straight up and screamed.

The first person through the door was a local woman who was familiar with medicine, followed by her mother, who was honestly glad to see she was at least moving again. She threw herself on the bed with her daughter and held her close. "I thought I had lost you both!" she cried, as she rocked her back and forth.

The singing woman was gone, and it would be two days before Grelf saw and heard her again. That day her mother had come home in good spirits and called Grelf into the main room. She had news that she wanted to share.

"I have found you a husband," Dandillion said with the first smile Grelf had seen on her mother since the day she awoke.

"A husband?" Grelf saw no reason to be happy about this.

"Why would I marry someone whom I have never even met?" Grelf stopped for a moment to think about the men who lived in the same town as she, and panic began to set in. "Wait! Do I know him? Because this is getting worse by the moment."

"No dear, you don't know him." Dandillion took Grelf by the hands. "Now that your father is dead, we can finally move out of this human town and head toward a better elven community." She stopped for a moment and swung Grelf around. "I found a good elven man for you, and he is even willing to overlook that you are a half-breed as long as we also give him Gregor's sword, and with his name and prestige we might even get you to be accepted in polite elven society."

"You are going to give him Father's sword?" Grelf asked with confusion and concern. "That is the only thing I have of his, Mother. He left it to me. Please don't take that from me too. It's all I have left."

"What are you going to do with it?" Dandillion scoffed at her daughter. "You're no warrior, you are just a little girl, and if you keep going down this path, you are just going to end up dead, just like your father."

Grelf sank into herself and began to weep. "Don't do this Mother. I don't want to marry someone I don't know."

Dandillion's mood swung on a pivot, and she was now yelling at her, not only that, but she began to mock her. "This is your only chance Grelf. Do you think you can find someone who will take care of you? I know you think that you are a woman, but you are still just a little girl, and you will never be anything without a husband."

From behind Grelf and to her right the mysterious woman stepped into Grelf's sight and began to sing. Dandillion didn't seem to notice her. Grelf stared at her with disbelief and fear. Was this woman even real? Had she been broken in ways that she didn't yet understand, was the death of her father causing her to hallucinate? The woman seemed stronger than before. She was still pale, but her eyes weren't as dark and sunken, and she was beginning to look less gaunt. She was singing with more power and strength, but Grelf still could not make out what was being said, she could hear and feel the music, and it began to drive her as her mother continued.

"And yes! I am going to give him Gregor's sword. He is no longer using it, and you never will either. You just sat there and froze as your father was killed. You drove him to fight that monster that I knew he could not defeat and then when he needed you, you just stood there and let him die. It's your fault that he is dead! And now this is our only chance to be taken care of. So, you will do as I say, you ungrateful half-breed!"

The music was so loud in Grelf's mind she had to yell to speak over it, and as she did the woman cheered her on as she continued to sing in the incomprehensible yet beautiful song.

"No Mother! This is your last chance! You are the one who needs this." Grelf was right up in her mother's face. "You are wrong! You are wrong about everything." Dandillion could feel the heat of her daughter's breath as she stood toe to toe with her for the first time. "It was you who got Father killed. You failed him so many times that day and so many days before it!"

"How dare you!" Her mother reached back and with her full force struck Grelf, but Grelf did not budge.

Instead, she looked her mother in the eyes, and with tears rolling down her face, she said, "I am the keeper of my father's final promise." She turned and began to walk towards the door. "I am leaving you, Mother. You are wrong about me. I am going to find that Moon Orc and I am going to kill him." Grelf said as she packed a few belongings and clothes and headed for the door.

"You will never make it out there alone," Dandillion said in hopes of detouring Grelf, but by this point, all Grelf could hear was the woman's song. "That monster will not care that you are a girl."

Grelf stopped in the doorway, knowing that she may never see her mother again. She reached up with her hand to the magical sword perched above the door. "Then I better take Father's sword with me."

She took it from over the door as she walked out of her childhood, and didn't look back, she could hear her mother crying and screaming at her about being a stupid girl, but Grelf no longer cared about what her mother thought. There was an orc out there and it needed to be slain.

As she walked toward her future the woman followed her, encouraging her with her song. She kept walking until her home was far from her sight. She turned to try to speak to the woman but as she did the song stopped and she was nowhere to be seen.

Iron-Tusk had been fleeing and had not covered his tracks at all. They were a few days old, but Grelf's father had taught her tracking as a child, and she had no problems following his trail. It took a few days, but the trail led to a small canyon in the earth, some forgotten dead river that had cut deep into the ground. She could tell by the erosion of the sides of the riverbed that it had been an old river that had worn away the ground for many years before it dried up. She climbed in and followed the footprints, moving along the curves of the dry bed that ended in a dark cave. The entrance to the mouth of the cave lay between two walls that were at least twenty-five feet long on either side of her and rose more than twenty feet high. It was a death box. Nowhere to go, and no means of escape except back the way she came, and it would be a long run to get back to a place where she could scale the walls and get out of this death trap.

Her fear began to grip her and for a moment her doubt began to ask whether her mother had possibly been right, when suddenly a low but familiar voice came from the darkness.

"If you have come from the human town to seek revenge, you are slow. I have had time to recover." Iron-Tusk stepped out of the cave and looked around. He roared with laughter. "The humans seek me out and the only person they send is a little girl." He stepped right up in front of her and leaned in to be eye-to-eye. "I can smell the fear on you. I am going to kill you slow."

Grelf froze for a moment as the image of this monster killing her father played in her head. But behind it, she could hear the music again. She strained to hear it as it came into focus and as the music filled her mind, she was able to move. Fight or flight took over and her body prepared to run. The woman was behind her still singing, and she grabbed Grelf by both of her arms. Grelf somehow understood that if she ran the Moon Orc would kill her before she could get two feet from him.

Instead, she chose to fight. This was why she was here, and there was no turning back. Grelf looked this monster in the eyes and said, "I was not sent by the humans. I am here because of one man. My father was the man who wounded you, and I am here to avenge him."

Iron-Tusk smiled at her mockingly and asked, "What are you going to do about it, little girl?"

"You know. That's exactly what my mother said, but do you know what?" asked Grelf as she found her groove to the music that was filling her mind.

"What?" said the Moon Orc as he leaned in close enough to have their foreheads almost touch.

"I'm not just, a little girl." Grelf's hand moved like lightning and with one single motion drew her father's sword from her hip and slashed it across Iron-Tusk's throat.

He grabbed his neck with one hand as blood poured from it and with the other hand, he backhanded her so hard that it flung her across the dry riverbed. She hit hard and was sure she broke a rib or two, but she had no time to cry about it. The Moon Orc was only paying attention to his wound. Her cut had caused him to begin to bleed out, but it wasn't deep enough to kill him. The woman continued to sing as the Moon Orc in desperation came at Grelf.

The woman danced to her song and Grelf followed her steps. As she did, she dodged and blocked attack after attack as if the whole fight had been choreographed to fit the song. Iron-Tusk took hit after hit as Grelf swung her sword, dancing around him continuing to dodge his every attack.

Still following the woman's movements, she spun around him and used all her momentum to throw herself forward at the Moon Orc. When she hit him at full force she toppled him to the ground, face first. She jumped on his back and screamed. "I am not some weak little girl who needs to be saved! Do you hear me?!" She raised her father's sword high into the air and claimed her destiny. "I am Grelf! The Orc Slayer!" and plunged her father's blade into Iron-Tusk's back as hard as she could, and it sunk into the Moon Orc's flesh until the hilt stopped its motion. Iron-Tusk's body went rigid for a moment, and he gurgled and spit up blood. Grelf grabbed both sides of the guard of the sword and with all of her strength twisted the sword and the music stopped. The Moon Orc's body went limp as he exhaled for the last time.

Grelf looked up to where she expected the woman to be, but she was gone. Grelf looked for her but could not find her, nor had she seen her ever again. She had wondered if she had always been a dream but preferred to see her as some guardian angel who had watched over her in her greatest moments of need.

Grelf had done what she had set out to do. She took its head and carried it back home to show her mother, but by the time she arrived home, her mother had already left. Grelf's neighbors told her that she left the same day that Grelf had, believing Grelf to be surely dead, she went home to the Elven Lands.

Grelf decided that she was not going to seek Dandillion out. If she wanted to believe she was dead, then her mother was dead to her as well. They never spoke again. Some years later she heard that Dandillion had died. She set it out of her mind and accepted her new life. The life of Grelf the Orc Slayer. And she swore then and there that she would never accept that she wasn't enough, and with that she decided that she would never be a little girl who needed to be saved, especially by a man, and she would never need to be tied to a man to fulfill her destiny.

...

After Hope had heard the story in its entirety, she wept tears of respect and compassion. "She never got to see what you became?"

"No, but this is the reason I falter now. I can't accept that my destiny is still tied to my getting married and having kids. That my connection to a man will decide my fate."

Hope began to smile at a joke that was going off in her head. "You can't stand to be the storybook princess who is saved by the prince."

"Why is that funny?" asked Grelf. She thought that Hope was somehow making fun of her, and because this was a core truth, she felt attacked, so she stood up and lashed out as her hair turned fire-orange with streaks of red. "What would you know about it? You have been a princess your whole life!"

Hope stood and matched her in tone. "A princess who just kicked your butt into next week!" Hope regained herself quickly. She continued but with a calmer tone. "I am not laughing at you. I am laughing at the truth of it. I respect you and the choices you have made. I have made many of them myself, and I have earned the right to follow in your footsteps."

That stopped Grelf in her tracks. 'She had earned the right to follow in her footsteps.' That one sentence put things in a new perspective. Grelf took a breath and remembered the advice that she had just given herself. "I am sorry. The wound is still very real."

Hope hugged Grelf and it only took about ten seconds before Hope told her that she wasn't letting go until Grelf hugged her back. They embraced and became friends once more. "I know what I am supposed to tell you," Hope said with a look of amusement still riding the corners of her smile.

"And I will honestly try to hear you." Grelf didn't know if she was ready, but she knew she had to trust whatever was going to be said.

"You aren't the storybook princess," Hope said with glee. "Christoph is."

Grelf wasn't ready at all. "I don't understand."

"Christoph. He is the one who was born of noble blood right?"

"His father was a Duke in Lions Crest, the kingdom across the sea."

Hope took Grelf by the hands, she was so overjoyed she was about to pop. "We are so alike it hurts right now. I am going to have an amazing conversation with you two thousand years from now later this evening. To me, it will be about ten minutes after you leave but I do understand you better my dear friend." She hugged Grelf again and then stood back and explained. I had this same problem when I was first betrothed to a man I had never met. Some prince from another kingdom, and once it was set, I had to go out and do the quest that every Princess of Venger has to do to prove we are worthy of your throne." She hopped up and down. "This is what I figured out. I didn't want to be a storybook princess either, but here is the joke. It was Gavin who was the prince born into this, and he could not do it alone. He had to be saved... by me. I was the hero. You are the hero who saves Christoph."

Grelf's hair turned back to its natural state of a beautiful chestnut, but the tips of her hair were pure white, signifying a peacefulness as her mind accepted the truth of the situation. It was a new reality that changed everything. "Why is it funny?"

Hope refilled Grelf's drink and held hers up to toast. "It's funny because you still call him Princess to this day."

8

TOOMBA

Dalen had returned before Grelf and Christoph had come back. His conversation with Aiden had gone well, though he was quiet, he was in a good place. I had just finished my story about the Evil Wizard and his Castle of Death when Christoph and Grelf returned. They said hello, and that was all I needed. My fluency with Grey Speak allowed me to experience all they had just been through with the simple sound of one word from their mouths. My brother, Hip-Gnosis tends to leave an impression. I too witnessed the dragon lay waste to all; saw the end of the world and felt it as intensely as they had. When I looked at them, I could see the intensity of the effects on their faces. The knowledge that they now possessed had prepared them and they were ready to face what they must. They were different now. They had a new purpose. I gave them a bow and said, "Your Majesties."

Christoph cracked a smile and replied, "Not yet. Let's go fix that, shall we?"

Grelf leaned her head on his shoulder as they approached. "We shall indeed, Princess."

"Oh no. Hey. Wait a minute." Christoph stopped in his tracks. "I get the story, and I am glad you found whatever truth makes you smile again but I'm not sure about this whole calling me Princess, thing."

Grelf had a spring in her step that she hadn't had since all of this started and a smile on her face to match. "You know that world we are fighting for?"

Christoph looked worried. "Yeah."

"In it, I call you Princess your whole life." Grelf stopped for a moment, gave him a kiss, and said, "You're just going to have to get used to it, Princess." Grelf looked as if the words tasted odd. "Okay, I see your point. Not in front of people." She smiled, "All the time."

Christoph looked lost. He turned to the group to be his council, hoping they would side with him. "Master Peace. What do you think?"

Christoph had no idea that just three years ago, Master Peace was a bully who would have loved the idea of the brand-new king being tagged with that name, but what was worse and even more of a surprise was that his answer was so on-point that Christoph could not argue his wisdom.

"Does it help her?" Master Peace looked deep into Christoph. When he found what he was looking for he smiled and raised an eyebrow. "Then what do you care?" Master Peace shrugged. "If your ego or manhood cannot handle being called a cute silly name, you are not worthy to be king."

Christoph stood there for a moment stunned. He stared at Master Peace, who winked at him, and to his credit, Christoph grinned and nodded. "Fair enough. It does help, and she can call me whatever she wants." He smirked. "That does not give you all free reign! Please... guys?"

Master Peace held up his glass to Christoph. "My training at the brotherhood has taught me that one should be called by what it means to be them. Thus, Princess, I shall from here on in refer to you as Christoph, or Your Majesty." Christoph glared at him jovially. "Oh. I had to get one in. I am sure you understand."

Defeated Christoph waved his hand to shoo him away. "Fine." He said reluctantly. "Just this once."

"Excellent!" Master Peace held up his glass to all and said, "To the Princess!"

Everyone, Grelf being the loudest, held up their glass and said, "To the Princess!" Then they drank and laughed. They knew this would be the last time they would get a chance to do this together until either they succeeded, or all died trying because that was what was on the line. If they failed in even one of the challenges, it meant the death of all. Christoph and Grelf told the rest of the group about what Hip-Gnosis had shown them and before they headed out everyone fully understood what was at stake.

Christoph requested the two monks say their goodbyes and go with him. Dalen put out his hand to his friends who all responded in kind, they interlocked their fists and formed their galaxy. Adam requested a few words, he glanced between them as he spoke from his heart. "Remember Rule 16. This is your adventure. Don't forget to act like it." He paused as the joke became real and Sir Adam continued. "Never give up. Always believe in the quest...these are the moments we live for."

Dalen still carried a magical brooch that I had given him at the beginning of his journey with Queen Hope that allowed me to experience all that he would see, hear, and feel, so I decided to travel with Grelf and the rest of the team.

"From what I understand," mentioned Master Peace, "You will be required to obtain the Water Blade first."

Christoph was gathering his things and preparing to head out. "Why is that, Master Peace?" he asked. "What is the difference?"

"When a young prince comes of age or is betrothed to the princess who is the next in line, they must first earn the right as prince by claiming the Water Blade, thus proving that he is 'worthy' of the throne." Dalen looked to Master Peace to see if he agreed with his assessment, and when Master Peace gave him a nod, he continued. "When he is old enough to take the throne and must now become a king, he will go forth and claim the Air Blade. Earning the right to claim the Vengerian Throne."

"I have to earn the right, to earn the right. Understood." Christoph rechecked the supplies and equipment he had stored in his Vengerian Pin. "Alright, anything else?"

Dalen shrugged, but Master Peace spoke up slightly amused. "Yeah. It also turns out that once the prince is of age, the king must first reclaim the Air Blade to prove that even though the prince is of age, he is still worthy to rule."

"He's right," Dalen added. "When we helped Hope get the Earth Blade, it was because her daughter was about to come of age and so Hope and to reclaim the Earth Blade to prove that she was still worthy to be queen."

As they left Dorn's, Dalen hugged Aiden and told him to be good and listen to Uncle Dorn. Aiden rolled his eyes as he hugged him back and told Dalen to be careful. Just because he was a jinn, didn't mean that he was invulnerable. They set out past the edge of town and along the open plain, where there was a white tree standing by itself in a field.

"You know. In our time this is a valley." Dalen looked out over the plains of grass that stretched out for miles, all the way to Venger, and the cliffs that overlooked the sea the magical city was nestled next to.

"I was shown a scene of the future. The Chaos Dragon emerges from underground and all of Venger falls to the sea." As Christoph spoke Dalen remembered a flash of the future that he saw at the beginning of his quest. A huge dragon ripping itself from the earth.

"If it helps at all, Venger is in one piece, even though it's now a harbor city." Dalen looked at Venger in the distance. "She is resilient. As long as the Chaos Dragon is stopped in time, Venger continues to thrive."

"You know what?" Christoph looked across the field to Venger. The memory of everything he saw played again in his mind. "It does help."

Dalen could feel Christoph's hope for the future. It rippled off him and with every ripple it gave Dalen strength, he started to believe that Christoph had it in him to fight this fight. He only needed to find it.

Christoph looked at the tree. "I have never tried this without a compass. Dalen, I am guessing that you understand how the tree works by now?" Dalen nodded. "Alright. The location that you want is a fishing village on the shores of the northern sea. Looking from the location of the tree, you will see some buildings close to the water's edge and behind them multiple small boats, possibly one or two larger ones because it is the last harbor before you hit big water."

Dalen instructed both Master Peace and Christoph to

hang on to him so both reached out and put a hand on each of his shoulders. Dalen touched the tree and as he did, he opened the Mind Sphere and connected to every location the tree was at. He scanned the warbling images of each location until he found one that was located near a small fishing village constructed at the edges of the Northern Sea. Dalen decided that out of everywhere he and the tree were, this must be the place they needed to be. He focused his mind on the village, forcing the image to become clear, and let go of his grip on the tree.

The three of them stood just outside the small village. It was exactly how Christoph had described. "Christoph, do you know this place?" Master Peace's eyes were darting from building to building, taking in their new surroundings.

‹Everything all right?› Dalen asked using the Vengerian Pin to telepathically communicate with Master Peace.

Master Peace reached up and activated his Vengerian Pin as well. ‹Yeah, just keeping an active account of how many people and how many of them are armed.›

"This is Kels, It's about two days' travel from Venger by boat." Christoph walked toward the village. "Worry not. I know this place and I'm sure I can get one of them to talk if needed. They are not a threat."

Master Peace was not completely convinced and asked, "Have you seen it on a map, or have you been here?"

Christoph patted Master Peace on the back and strolled toward the village. The first merchant he passed he waved to and said, "Hey, Zeke."

Zeke was an older gent. He appeared salty and grizzled as the years of living on the sea could be seen in his weathered smile. He waved as he came around his stall and excitedly shook Christoph's hand. "It's so good to see you. How's Grelf? Is she with you?"

‹I have been here. So many times.› Christoph returned Zeke's handshake. "No, today she is on a completely different mission."

Zeke stepped back and put his hand over his mouth for a moment and then asked, "How bad is it if they had to separate you two?"

Christoph put his other hand on Zeke's shoulder. "You know us well, and you know what it would take to separate us. So, you can imagine that I don't have time to stay and chat."

Zeke shook the cobwebs from his mind and nodded with enthusiasm. "Right! What do you need?"

Christoph pointed out to the sea. "The Northern Sea is the home of many things. One of them is a dragon who is a seer. Can you take me to someone who can get me there?"

"That would be Toomba. He is Star-Folk and knows the Northern Sea better than any five of us in the village." Zeke pointed Toomba's boat out to Christoph, it was noticeably different than the rest of the boats in the harbor, and twice the size.

Star-Folk were amazing sailors. It is estimated that they

were sailing and mapping the world hundreds of years before the other races took to the sea using anything other than a small craft for fishing. They learned not only to map the land but also the sky. All the constellations that are used today amongst any races that share astronomical commonalities, use the Star-Folk constellations, which is the chief reason they were called Star-Folk. Their boats were vessels of luxury and beauty, often twice the size of the human equivalent, and three times as fast.

Their homelands were in the southern hemisphere and most of their kind have dark hair and olive skin. Half the size of their human counterparts but they are fearsome and quick and never let their height stop them.

As they approached his yacht Dalen opened the Mind Shere to reach out and connect to the thoughts of Toomba. He could tell he was a good man. The sea had given him a hard exterior, but he was a decent enough fellow. They stopped just outside his vessel and Zeke called to him a few times before he appeared.

"What do they want Zeke?" Toomba's accent was thick as he spoke and Master Peace and Dalen both agreed he sounded Italian.

"Do you remember how we told you the story about how that sea monster almost destroyed the whole village, but this guy and a crazy half-elf killed it?"

"Yeah," Toomba said with a wince on his face like he knew where the conversation was going. "What of it?"

"This is the guy," Zeke said and presented Christoph with

both hands.

"Oh." He waved and said, "You did a good job man. Way to save the village."

He began to turn toward the way he had come but Zeke called out to him again. "Wait! He needs to talk to you."

Toomba muttered something under his breath in Star-Folk and rolled his eyes. "What? I hope this isn't one of those, 'now I have to pay you money because I'm using part of the dock you saved' conversations, is it? Because I am going to be honest with you man, it will change my whole opinion of you, and not for the better my friend."

Both Dalen and Master Peace touched their pins and tapped out the sequence that would allow them to understand whatever language was spoken to them. Reversely, it translates their words into their fellow conversationalists' native tongue, making it easy to maintain a friendly dialogue.

"Not a bit of it." Christoph smiled. "Your first impression was correct. You owe me nothing. Matter of fact. I may have some business for you."

"Business?" Dalen could immediately feel that Toomba was used to doing business. He could sense what Toomba's thoughts were about the group, he believed they wished for passage somewhere and he thought he could make some easy coin. "What kind of business?"

Christoph gestured back to Dalen and Master Peace and said, "My friends and I need you to take us to the Aquatic Maze in the Northern Sea, and we were hoping that on the way there you could give us whatever information you have about the maze and the dragon who guards it."

Dalen felt Toomba's amusement. "You wish me, to take some village hero and two members of the Brotherhood of Light, to the Aquatic Maze in the Northern Sea, because you are going up against the All-Seeing Dragon?"

Christoph nodded and said, "Overall." As if the task he asked were simple.

"Did Gerky put you up to this?" Toomba laughed. "It's quite good. Especially using the lore of the city." He stopped laughing and looked at Christoph almost mockingly. "How much did you pay those nice villagers to tell me the tale? It must have been Gerky."

Christoph began to try to explain. "You don't understand..."

"No sir! It is you who does not understand!" Toomba's mood shifted from jovial to angry and afraid. "You must be a joke from my cousin Gerky, because if you are not, you are insane, and I have no desire to get mixed up with crazy people. So, I am going to go."

"At least tell me why I am insane! Come on man!" Christoph called out to him. "Save our lives."

Toomba turned and walked close enough to the railing of his ship that he could be seen again. "You hurt my heart man." He lowered a rope down. "Okay. I will tell you why you are all dead, and why you are all insane, over a drink. I mean...it's the decent thing to do, to have one last drink with good people who are doomed."

142

Christoph thanked Zeke and climbed up the rope, followed by Master Peace. Dalen had barely touched the ground since his arrival and found floating to be his preferred means of travel. He would only land if floating made the folks around him feel awkward. So, instead of climbing the rope he just floated alongside Master Peace who was startled at first but eventually just shook his head at his brother and friend and began to hum to himself the song that had become their private joke.

Master Peace reached the top and climbed onto the boat, while Dalen hovered over the edge. Toomba looked at him sideways and pointed. "Neat trick man. You learn that at your fancy temple?"

Dalen stepped down and planted himself on the floor. His legs were unsure for a moment, and he realized that if he weren't careful, his legs could become weak if not used. "Partly Toomba, yes, but I also wield this power because I am a jinn."

"That would explain the sacred stones through your body." Toomba turned to point at Christoph. "Just because you have a jinn it doesn't mean it's not too late for you. No matter what you bring man, Crystal will be ready and waiting.

"Her name is Crystal?" asked Christoph.

"See how very little you know, man?" Toomba rolled his eyes again and then under his breath and in Star-Folk he said, "Goddess protect me from the fate of my passengers and cargo." Dalen sensed from Toomba that the prayer had been used by his people, it was more of a phrase than a prayer really, but today he meant it.

"Her real name is Draconic and very hard to pronounce. But like a crystal ball, she can see clearly, man. And much how a crystal can take apart the light and split it into different colors man, she can take time and see it in many ways. Because of these abilities and gifts, she became known as Crystal, man."

Dalen saw a potential problem. "During our training at the Brotherhood of Light, Master Peace and I were both taught that one of the strongest positions in an altercation is to know exactly what the opponent is going to do. The dragon has an advantage that we can't anticipate."

"Agreed." Master Peace gave a small nod. "Brother Truth is right. We are taught to try to find an understanding of our opponent. If you can anticipate what they are going to do, before they do it, you can win a fight before it ever begins. I learned this from my teacher Master Sight. Blind, except for her continuous state of having visions. It was Crystal who taught her. She is my master's master."

‹That is what you did with the goblins, isn't it?› Dalen remembered just a few days back when they had been faced with that challenge.

‹I knew I had won before the fight ever started.› Master Peace smiled slightly but showed no other sign of the telepathic conversation that was happening.

"Wait?" Toomba turned his attention to Dalen. "You are Master Truth of the Brotherhood of Light?" There was a look of shock and amazement on his face. "I heard he was a jinn. Why did he call you Brother Truth?"

Dalen had to carefully choose how to give his answer. Time slowed to almost nothing and Grand Master Truth appeared floating next to him. He looked the way he did while Dalen had been training at the Brotherhood of Light. He seemed to be made from mist or smoke. His eyes, which looked like someone had captured a lightning storm in them, matched the stones that were placed throughout his body and in his hands and feet. Master Truth reached out with his hand and the smoke formed a small cup. "That's a good question. How are you going to answer it?" He took a sip from his cup and waited for Dalen to respond.

"Do you mean, how do I explain that yes, I am you, but I am not you yet, and you are eventually something that I become, or do you mean, how do I explain to him that Master Truth is actually just an aspect of myself, as seen through the Mind Sphere?"

Master Truth laughed. "Don't forget if you go with the first, from his point of view I have been Master Truth since before the beginning of this dynasty, so thousands of years, and you would be saying that from your perspective that is a future event." Master Truth took a sip from his cup. "You could go with option two. You will have to admit you are talking to yourself right now and I don't know how he will respond to the idea of a jinn that does that."

"Oh, you have jokes," Dalen said with a slight hint of frustration.

"I have jokes." Master Truth said. "You are going to have to learn to find some humor in all of this."

"I am still trying to get a handle on all of it." Dalen began to pace. "I know that I am supposed to remember my training and breath. I know that I am supposed to be able to keep my emotions in check and not just..." Dalen let his emotion build for a moment and then he yelled, "Freak out!" time shuttered for a moment. It surprised Dalen and took all the wind out of his sails.

As Master Truth took another sip from his cup, he glanced around at the world to see if the shutter was going to stop. When it did, he looked at Dalen and smiled. "That would be one of the options. Yes, but it would not be the only option you have."

Dalen was frustrated. He was concerned that he had made time do something weird and he didn't like it at all. Now Master Truth was talking in riddles again. He looked at Dalen plainly and said, "Hey Dalen, just talk to me."

Dalen dropped to his knees and pleaded. "I know you are me. I know that this is just happening in my mind, and I am just talking to myself in a way, but don't you understand that scares the hell out of me? I mean, am I crazy? Are you real? Am I?"

"Yes, on all accounts," said Master Truth.

Dalen remembered that he asked if he was crazy. "Wait what?"

"I got jokes." Master Truth changed his form so that the smoke flowed and moved and when it reformed Master Truth was sitting next to Dalen. "I am you. I am your mind. Your... subconscious mind, in the same way the Fire Jinn can be seen as your higher self. People of many worlds have conversations with their subconscious all the time. It is something that makes us connected as one because we all do it. When someone gives themselves a pep talk, who are they talking to? For you, the difference is that because of who and what you are, the individuals in your subconscious are more real and pronounced, but I guarantee you, you are no crazier than I am."

"Well, that's a relief." They both laughed. "So, are you really here?"

"I am here because you are here. This version of me is just in your mind. The version of me who trained you was the real version of you much further ahead in your path. I am just the imprint you made during your time at the Fountain of Truth." He took another sip from his cup.

"If you are just me, then why do I still see you like this?" Dalen had begun to calm down, and he was trying hard to understand. He smiled at Master Truth and although he was still on his knees, he bowed to the Air Jinn and said, "Help me understand more."

Master Truth remembered that this was the phrase Dalen had used during his training. Dalen had heard another master use it and had adopted it as his own. "I am Master Truth. You do not see yourself as a master, which is why you still have people call you Brother Truth, such as Master Peace over there." Master Truth pointed to Master Peace. "He earned that title and from then on, was always referred to as Master Peace. You don't feel you have reached your mastery yet, so you see yourself as someone who is not yet Master Truth. Thus, you cannot see yourself in

147

the position."

"Okay, damn. That makes sense." Dalen said.

"It all makes sense if you get a couple thousand years to stare at it and make sense of it all." Master Truth smiled. "You okay now?"

"You already know that answer, don't you?" asked Dalen teasingly.

"Yes." Master Truth changed his form back to a standing position. "But you need to hear yourself say it, so I ask again."

Dalen got up off his knees and wiped his face. "I'm okay. Just needed a minute to not be okay."

"Good. That's healthy." Master Truth pointed at Toomba. "So how are you going to handle the question?"

Dalen took a deep breath and allowed time to move normally again. As he did Master Truth faded into nothing. "When Master Truth began the Brotherhood of Light, he was already Master Truth, but what good is a Master who had never been a beginner? So, Master Truth went back to the beginning. I am Brother Truth, and during my experience, I have not yet earned the title of Master."

Toomba just stared at him for a moment trying to process what Dalen said. "I have heard of tales of the Brotherhood of Light for many years man, and I am going to have to say you don't disappoint. That is deep man. Demoting yourself so that you can experience the struggle." Toomba just stared at Dalen for a few moments and then nodded and continued. "So, I guess that you at least understand the problem?"

"In part," answered Christoph. "They are here as protectors and advisors, but it is me who must do this. Teach me what I don't understand."

"You must have been getting some training from these guys. Most hero types, act like they know everything. You don't. That will take you far man, but the problem is too big to solve."

"Please. Teach me." Christoph's tone was sincere, and Toomba pointed to a seat.

While Christoph sat down Toomba got four glasses and a large bottle made of blue glass. He poured each of them a drink from it and sat the rest on a small table in his galley. When he returned, he sat down with them and took a swig from his glass. He looked at it with admiration and slowly let out a deep breath. "This is the best I have man. Understand that I am only sharing it with you because you are all going to die. With all respect, cheers."

Christoph leaned in on his chair. "Why?"

"If you are going to see her, she already knows you are coming. She knows we are having this conversation." He waved at nothing. "Hello. Do you see that I am trying to convince them to go away? See that I am on your side and have no intention of harming you in any way. Okay? Okay."

To Dalen, this was just another Tuesday, and it made not just sense, but it seemed normal. Master Peace got it. Dalen could hear him think *oh bibitz* in his head. He didn't send it through the Vengerian Pin, but Dalen was connected to him within the Mind

Sphere and could hear his surface thoughts. Christoph was used to dealing with the here and now and never had to consider thoughts like this.

"What do you mean? Do you mean she can see us now?" He began to look around.

"Yeah man! That's what I am trying to tell you, and it's not like she can just see a couple of moments into the future or past, she can see all the way into the past." Toomba's voice had a hint of fear in it.

"We can all see into the past. It's called remembering things." Christoph said jovially.

Toomba closed his eyes and took a deep breath in. "I am sure you weren't trying to be insulting, and your words are based on aggravation and ignorance. What I am saying is that she can remember your memories. See your past. She is so all-seeing that she was aware of your attempt to reach her days ago."

"My apologies. I am not intending to be rude. But it was rude, and I meant no offense. I'm on edge and it was meant to be funny." Christoph said earnestly. "Everything that I was sure about in this world has fallen. The line of Venger was broken..."

"It was broken?" Toomba's attention had been stoked. "What do you mean?"

"My name is Christoph, and I was one of two Vengerian Guardians who had dedicated our lives to defend Venger, her children, and the safety of the entire world. Yesterday, I failed."

Toomba finished his drink and rose from his seat. "I have heard of you Christoph of Venger." Toomba seemed almost scared. "What happened?"

Christoph spoke with the same fear in his heart. "A time mage and an evil genie from another timeline, broke the connection to the Elemental Blades, effectively severing the line." Toomba dropped to his knees with his hand over his mouth. Christoph took a hard breath in like he had just been punched in his gut. "And I couldn't stop them."

It was at this moment that Dalen understood how much Christoph cared for Venger and how personally he took their failure.

Toomba was in shock. "What is to be done?"

Dalen could feel the intensity of Christoph's emotions and could see that he was barely holding it together and decided to answer Toomba's question himself. "It was decided by the powers that be that Christoph and his partner Grelf are to become the new line. Someone must reclaim the Elemental Blades, and it has to be done in the next nine days. We are here because we believe that the Water Blade is with Crystal, and so it matters not what you say, we are going, and Christoph will find the Water Blade."

All of it began to register and Toomba's face hid nothing. "So, you are going to be King?"

Still, and with a heavy heart, Christoph nodded and simply said, "Yes."

Toomba's shock and surprise made way for his swagger. "You should have started with that man. You just said you were a hero of a village, man. You said nothing about you asking me as a king." He poured himself another drink and offered more to everybody, but all their glasses were still full. "Doesn't matter. King or not, you can't defeat her."

"We are not asking you to help us attack her. We are asking for directions. We need to find the Aquatic Maze." Dalen calmed Toomba the best that he could without overpowering his mind with magic. Dalen knew that he could, but he knew that there were prices to pay for pushing past someone's free will. Prices he was not willing to pay, so Toomba's mind and free will remained his own.

Still...there were a lot of things Dalen could do. For instance, he could lock him in a time state where the world seems to stop. And then threaten to leave him that way if he doesn't do as they say. There were so many other methods too, but Dalen knew that he couldn't execute them, even as he thought the words. It brought him despair to know that he could think of terrible plans to break people's free will and had the skills to carry them out.

Dalen felt the Fire Jinn to his right as she flew into view. Dalen knew he was looking at an aspect of his own soul. "You would be hurting us. You and me." No one could see her or hear her. She only lived in his mind's eye, but to him, she was here and very real. "There have been a few moments since you finally started listening to me where I have told you that the main difference between you and DeSalvo is the choices you make. This is one of them. This choice is the difference between being on the team to stop great evil and becoming great evil that must be stopped." She flew right in front of him. She was still beautiful and the fire that engulfed her did not burn but felt more like a warm beam of light in his very being. "You're not going to let me down, are you?"

Dalen closed his eyes and inwardly he smiled to himself and swore he never would. When he opened his eyes again, she was gone. "Toomba, if you can't help us, can you at least tell us where we can charter another boat from someone else?"

"They would never make it." Toomba rubbed his neck. "Human boats are fragile and would never survive the voyage man."

"So, that leaves you." I am not asking you to do anything to harm Crystal, and if what you say is true, she will know that you helped us knowing that ahead of time." Christoph took a knee. "The entire world is at stake, even if the odds are impossible against me, I must try. As future King of Venger, I ask you, beg you. Help me save the world."

"I don't know man." Toomba was on the fence. Dalen could feel his thoughts sway. He was glad that Christoph had convinced him. He understood what was on the line, but he still thought it was impossible. Dalen could feel him making the choice, but he was going to need one more push. "I want to help you, man. You say the world is at risk? But we are all at risk if you think you can get one over on Crystal. I don't think I can help. Not even for a king."

Christoph stood up and in an unshakeable tone without wavering or stuttering he told him, "I will fill this boat with gold until it sinks."

Toomba rubbed his neck once more. "Well, maybe for a king."

9

TAKING THE TREE
FOR A SPIN

"It goes completely against rule five, never split the team, but since we have to, I am glad to have my brother and my love." Travis gave his brother a nod and Sir Adam returned the favor. Travis flashed a smile at Becky that made her cheeks flush with heat. He turned to Venger's protector and soon-to-be queen and added, "You are in good hands."

"I believe you, Travis." Grelf got up from the booth and checked her Vengerian Pin to ensure she had everything she needed. "How about you Master Bard? You asked to join, but are you ready for what awaits us?"

I closed my eyes and focused on creating one deeply saturating thought. A thought derived by pulling from the different intentions of a phrase and choosing just the right ones to blend into a singular new intention. Giving new meaning to a familiar phrase that once spoken, would carry an understanding meant just for Grelf. I focused my energy and in my mind's eye, I composed a special message for her. A message that even though others would audibly hear me say, only she would fully comprehend. As I uttered the words to her, she could feel in her soul that my presence would be required on their journey and that I would be prepared for anything.

I wouldn't miss it for the world. The Grey Speak flowed off my tongue sending an empathic, telepathic message through my voice, that Grelf not only comprehended in her mind but felt deeply in her heart.

Grelf shook her head and tried to pull her mind from the fog it was in. It's often jarring the first time someone hears me use Grey Speak. People are usually not prepared to receive such an intense wave of emotional understanding and mental comprehension at once. It can take them a moment to focus and process their own thoughts again. The entire system has to readjust, like the mental equivalent of being unexpectedly flashed in the eyes by a bright light.

She finally began to blink again and took a deep breath. She bobbed her head in understanding and quietly spoke as she watched the rest of her world come back into crystal-clear focus. "Very

155

well. Glad to have you with us."

I dipped my head in recognition and then turned my attention to her Vengerian Guardians. "You understand that only Grelf can retrieve the Blades of Fire and Earth?" Travis, Sir Adam, and Becky all responded with a nod. "Do you understand that it's in your hands to make sure she gets there?" They nodded again. "Do you know what that means?"

Sir Adam raised his finger. "It means we are to protect her and keep her safe."

I acknowledged his answer and said, "Partly. What else?"

Travis had been holding up two and Becky was holding three. Both of them dropped a finger and then Travis answered, "The fate of this world lies in her hands, it is our job to protect those hands with our very lives."

"This is true." I looked over to Becky who put down another finger and was ready at one. "What else?"

"I have been trying to see it from her side, and I think there is going to be more to this than just guard duty." Becky got up and stood next to Grelf. "This is the craziest thing anyone has ever had to do. I was there when Queen Hope of Venger ran with the trees. We all saw how much she had to go through before she was even given that opportunity. This will be a difficult journey. You have to recover the Earth Blade, but before you do that, you must first retrieve the Fire Blade. This will push you far beyond what you believe you're capable of. You will have to reach deep into yourself, into your soul. You will face your fears, fight your demons, and become a queen. But you will not have to do it alone."

Sir Adam and Travis were now on their feet. They remembered the time they had spent with Hope, how they were all together when they had to ask to be seen in the Elven Forest, and how they stood by her as she faced the Elven Queen. They were with her when she met Gnomon and her family. And as they used her eyes to witness her courageous run through the trees, they encouraged her to overcome all. The twins stepped over to Becky and Grelf and formed a circle.

"One of the last things Hope said to me after I returned her home, safe to Castle Venger, was that she would have never done what she did if it wasn't for us." Adam was almost in tears but did his best to keep himself together. "I didn't fully understand it until just now." He looked Grelf in the eyes and spoke from his heart. "I give you my word, you will not have to face this alone."

Travis echoed his brother. "You will not have to face this alone."

"With you all the way," Becky added.

I couldn't help myself. I had seen and talked about this so many times, I had to experience one for myself. I stepped in and closed the circle, putting out my right hand as I did, my thumb facing upward. The three Guardians had done this before and added their hands the same way, touching their fingertips to mine. We all looked at Grelf who caught on and followed suit. Then in one motion, we all began to bend our fingers together, cradling the hand of the next person until all hands were tucked in a spiral, creating what looked like a multi-armed galaxy. We all felt the connection much like the calming of a group hug. We looked back and forth to each other and then I said, "Family on three." I quickly prepared my thoughts, creating a deep and thoughtful understanding of what that word meant, and what it could mean. I amplified the connection and as they spoke with me, in Grey Speak I sent it out.

Family.

They were still feeling the effects an hour later while making their trek to the White Tree of Travel. A tree that allowed someone with the means to use it, to instantly travel to multiple locations. Grelf had used the tree to do Venger's bidding for years and had the proper tool to use it.

It was a talisman that she kept in a small pouch in her belt. At first glance, it looked as if she carried a palm-sized golden bowl. The object was a circular disc of silver that had a notch carved out for each location. In the center of it was a raised circle of celestium that you could use to turn the disc like a knob. This piece rested in a concave vessel made of gold with a rim that folded up over the silver disc creating a brilliant golden edge while maintaining enough space for the disc to spin. On this outer golden circle, there was a beautiful etching of a dragon on one side and a unicorn on the other. When looking at it from a bird's eye view, you can see the three concentric circles that make the Seal of Venger.

The object could shift quantumly and anyone who was holding it could enable the teleporting properties and phase with the tree. The location is chosen by using the spinning silver disc, setting the destination by placing the correct notch in a small window cut out of the golden rim. Then you simply touch the tree for a moment and let go. It's called the Quantum Compass, and it's required to use the Tree of Travel if you don't have any other magical means to do so.

Grelf placed the Quantum Compass in her hand and turned the center knob until the location she wanted was in the viewing window. "Alright, you three. Each of you are going to need to take hold of my shoulder or something." She grinned at the boys and gave Becky a wink. "You can grab on to whatever you want to, just remember, grab wisely or you will have Christoph to answer to."

Travis and Adam looked at each other for a moment and in unison they shrugged and said, "Fair."

I told them that I would be making my own way there. They agreed and prepared themselves for their jump, which was not specifically difficult, but the last time they were teleported to an unknown location, they appeared next to a cursed tree radiating sadness, so they had no idea what to expect when they got to the other side this time. Once ready, both Sir Adam and Travis placed their hand on one of her shoulders while Becky took the upper arm directly below Travis. Grelf looked at the compass one more time to make sure she had the right setting and placed her other hand on the white tree. Her eyes began to dart back and forth as they tried to look at the hundreds of locations that were appearing in front of her and flashing in her mind. Her eyes finally locked onto a single thing, and she took a quick breath in. By the time she finished it, the four of them had faded into nothing.

The place they had left was daytime, the temperature was

mild, and they hadn't felt uncomfortable in their armor. Where they were now was much different. It was sometime in the deep of night and the air hung hot and humid. The lush dense forest was tropical with large leafy plants and tall palm trees. There was no moon, so the group had to rely on the stars for light. Fortunately, they had arrived on a clear night and the stars were abundant.

Each of the guardians used their Vengerian Pins to change into the clothes they had packed from their home world on the night of the dance. They were lighter and their bodies could breathe making it more comfortable to travel through the thick vegetation. All three kept their weapons about them. Grelf looked them over for a few moments then asked, "Is this what people are wearing in the future?"

"Funny enough no," answered Travis. "Not only are we from what you consider the future, but we are also from another world. This is clothing from that culture."

Grelf didn't seem surprised as much as intrigued. "I have heard stories of other worlds, which one are you from?"

"Have you heard of Earth or maybe Terra?" Travis asked hopefully.

Grelf began to look around as they spoke. She knew this location was inhabited by wild beasts. "Yes. They are words in the common tongue for one of the elements."

"It's the names we use for our planet." Sir Adam took his cue from Grelf and watched the tree line for movement. Cautious, he started warming his hand.

Grelf seemed amused by the idea. "You named your planet Earth?"

"Yeah. Have you heard of it?" Sir Adam asked while he continued to scan.

"That's a little on the nose, don't you think?" Grelf stopped scanning and looked at him. "I mean, that would be like naming your dog, Dog."

Sir Adam scrunched up his nose. "Never thought about that." His face began to twist into an expression of deep thought. "Huh."

"Wait!" Becky smiled the way she always did when she thought that she had a good idea. "You said they are words in the common tongue, right?"

Grelf had gone back to scanning the terrain. "Yeah."

Becky was getting excited. "Why is that the 'common' language?"

"I can answer that," I said as I popped out of the foliage. Grelf drew her sword, but I held up my hands, "It's just me."

"You almost got yourself killed," Grelf said gruffly.

"It would have been messy, and quick, I am sure." I put my arms down. "I told you I had other means to get here. Next time I'll try to make my entrance more obvious."

"What other means?" Travis asked while writing in his notebook.

"I can be wherever the story is taking place." They looked at me with blank faces. "Never mind." I took a second to check out my surroundings and then focused my attention on the first question that had been asked. "A long time ago many different races of creatures could move between worlds, and they found one that was inhabited by humans. After discovering the humans, who would become known as 'people,' they reached out and tried to befriend them. For a short time in their history, the humans welcomed the creatures, and they began to share their worlds. But humankind was a young race and very violent and power-hungry. Eventually, they discovered the magic that came with all the different types of folk from this world and used it to do horrible things in their quest for power. The humans tried to kill or drive out anything they thought might be stronger than them, attacking all other races, and killing innocent beasts. All so that they could reign supreme over their world. Violence became a nightmare for every being who was not human, so they fled, closing the doorway between their worlds, and cutting humans off from magic."

"There were some people who proved that they had evolved past such a violent and primal stage, yet compared to the other species of this world, they were still savages and they were considered less intelligent by most of the residents here. One difference that the elves found particularly peculiar, was that the human race considered a hundred years long enough to develop a culture. Whereas for the elves you have to be at least a century old to even be considered an adult. For them, culture happens over thousands of years. Humans had a lot to learn and for that, they were seen like children by many other species."

"A lot of the different cultures knew the languages of each other, but the humans only knew their own. It was understood that the ones we let stay were out of place and far from their home. A home that they would never see again. Collectively, everyone began to use the language of the humans as a common dialect so they could become a part of society while they adapted to life here."

There was a chance that any of them could have taken what was said as an insult, suggesting that humans were inferior, but Becky didn't care about that. What she did care about was that the language they spoke was the same language that had become known as common in this world. "I'm sure Travis could undoubtedly tell you what the chances are, that two different worlds created the same language randomly."

"It's a statistical impossibility," added Travis.

Becky smiled at him and blew him a kiss that he caught with his hand. "I guess that unless we are dealing with the impossible, the world we came from is the origin world of the humans."

"Only humans? No magic?" inquired Grelf.

"That's home." Sir Adam shrugged and smiled. "Things have gotten a little better." He held up his fingers to show his index and thumb barely separated in a pinching pose, indicating just   how little.

Grelf looked at them one by one and then asked, "How did you get here?"

All three of them answered in unison, "Dalen."

Travis flipped through a couple of pages in his notebook and said, "I'm sure Dalen mentioned that he was cast to Earth when he was a baby. Lived amongst us until magic awoke in him and blah blah blah..." He put his notebook away, pulled an arrow from his quiver, and readied his bow. "Should we talk and move?"

Grelf led the way as she explained where they were. They were on an island known by locals as Fire Stone Island, which was home to the Magma Falls. It was said to be one of the most breathtaking sceneries in this world to see. It was considered a natural wonder and the legendary nesting grounds of a cluster of phoenixes who went there periodically to die and be reborn. The island was volcanic, and the volcano was still very much alive and active. At one point the island had gone dormant for a short while and a cap cooled and hardened in the main shaft. The next time the pressure changed, instead of pushing through the top, the magma exploded through the side, creating the Magma Falls. Somewhere within the falls, there is supposed to be a cave that leads to the place where the phoenix has a nesting ground. There was a small village of about two hundred people who lived on the island. The village was nestled next to the mountain right along the coast. They were protectors and caretakers of the nesting grounds, as were generations of their ancestors. The hard part wasn't going to be finding someone in the village who knew where the cave was. It was common knowledge. The problem was going to be finding someone willing to tell them.

"Why can't we just explain that if we don't find the caves and get the Fire Blade, the whole world will be destroyed?

Shouldn't that be enough to make anyone want to help?" Sir Adam had a good point, they thought about it as they traversed the thick flora. Who in their right mind would stand in their way?

Travis was always the tactician. "Well, I can see a possibility where this can go bad." They were moving through the lush tropical jungle at a good pace, but they were still moving slower than full walking speed. Keeping an eye out for wildlife and not specifically on the path ahead contributed to their slower speed. Travis still had his bow at the ready as he spoke. "What if the village is full of zealots who worship the phoenix and believe in the rebirth principle of burning to ash, and have no problem with the idea of ending life in a giant ball of fire? And even worse, what if they want to come after us thinking we want to put a stop to their fiery end?" Travis continued to keep a vigilant eye on the terrain. They were moving quietly but had no idea what was out there, and it was impossible not to be downwind to everything. "The larger problem that we have to keep in mind is that we don't want word getting out that the blades have gone missing, and that right now Venger is actually very vulnerable. We will have to explain it to someone so they are willing to help us get to the caves, but we should also not advertise it and generally follow a clear understanding of 'stranger danger'."

"Stranger danger?" asked Grelf. Adam began to explain where the term came from, but Grelf stopped him. "Oh, I get it. It just caught me off guard."

We traveled for about an hour heading east and when we finally emerged from the dense jungle, we were on a beautiful coastline with crystal clear waters and a beach made of white sand. There was phosphorus in the sand that made their footsteps glow as they stepped onto the beach. Shimmering greenish light came off the crest of the waves and they lit up as they crashed along its shore.

"It's beautiful," Becky said under her breath.

Further up the shore, the village could just barely be seen. The glowing sand was an appreciated addition to their source of light.

Sir Adam reached down and raked the sand with his hand producing a light where he did so. "This place is magical."

How little Sir Adam understood the truth in his words. I decided to keep to myself how powerful this island really was, and that what they were walking into was more than they had bargained for. I could have told them that they were in one of the original locations where Magic was born, dating back to the First Dynasty. I could have told them that the phoenix did not just nest here by coincidence. I could have told them that they weren't here by accident, but I didn't. Instead, I looked up at the stars and quietly spoke to the spirit of this place. "Goddess of Life, Death, and Rebirth. We come here and ask for your blessing. I bring you four who are worthy. Each of them will hold the fate of this world in their hands."

We traveled for a while and finally made it within near sight of the village. There was a large sailing ship that didn't match the aesthetic or construction of the village just far enough out from shore to avoid running aground. It had anchored and five long boats took over a large area of the small dock.

"We aren't alone." Grelf was back to business. "Everyone on your guard and..." ‹Everyone, keep unneeded chatter silent.›

They each activated their Vengerian Pins, remembering that I didn't have one they looked over at me, and I smiled and said, "Don't worry about me. I can hear you anyway."

‹You can?› asked Grelf.

"Yes, I can. As a Grey Bard, I am fluent in every form of telepathy." I spoke it with just enough Grey Speak so that they would understand and move forward.

Which is exactly what Travis did. ‹I say we walk in like nothing is wrong. We have no idea who this ship belongs to, so be on the lookout.›

‹Agreed› Answered Grelf. ‹Here we go.› She began to walk into the village and the four of us followed close behind her.

10

THE DRAGON AT THE BOTTOM OF THE SEA

Christoph awoke to the biting wind of the Northern Sea. It was just dawn, and the sun had not yet cleared the horizon. For two days and two nights, they traveled, trying to reach the Aquatic Maze hidden deep in the depths of the water. The abyss that was home to the All-Seeing Dragon. The sea had been unkind, and no part of their travels could be described as smooth sailing, but they had pushed through and made it to the coordinates that Toomba had provided.

"How long until we arrive?" Christoph asked even before he

moved or opened his eyes.

"We are already here man." Toomba was at the helm and had been circling for about an hour.

"Why haven't we stopped?" Christoph rolled out of his hammock and made his way to the railing to get a better view of where he was. The sky was dim and the clouds on the horizon suggested that a storm was close at hand. The sea was dark and looked more black than blue in the early morning light.

"I can't drop anchor here. We're directly above the maze." Toomba gave some slack to the main sail and allowed it to catch the wind. "The maze is a coral reef, and it is huge man. It would take me three or four hours at strong wind to clear it, and if I dropped anchor here, we would never get it back man. Best to keep moving until you're ready to do whatever it is you think you're going to do man."

Christoph looked around until he spotted Master Peace and Dalen having breakfast. "Any chance there is more?" Answering Christoph's question, Toomba gestured with his head to the table. Christoph gave a quick bow and said, "Thank you."

"It's pretty good for a last meal man," Toomba suggested again, trying to remind him of his folly.

"Toomba. My man. I didn't come here with an army; I came with two of the wisest people I could get. Do you really think that Brother Truth and Master Peace, of the Brotherhood of Light, would give council to the idea of attacking a being that would know every strike, hours before the fight ever started? Days?

Weeks even?"

"There are other answers to a problem, rather than beating the opposition into compliance." Master Peace took a sip from his mug and ate another bite of grilled fish. "The greatest loss to an enemy I have ever suffered was at the hands of someone half my size and he never threw a single punch."

Toomba thought about it for a moment. "Your greatest loss was at the hands of someone smaller than you. I can appreciate that. But he beat you without ever throwing a single punch?"

"Utter defeat." Master Peace flashed Dalen a smile, but quickly returned his attention to Toomba.

"Then how did he beat you?" asked Toomba. He was now invested in the tale.

"Do you know the greatest way to defeat an enemy?" Dalen asked, returning the smile to Master Peace.

Toomba took a piece of grilled fish from the breakfast table. "How?"

"You make them your ally." Master Peace said and held up his mug to Dalen, who clinked his mug against his.

It only took a moment to understand that it was Dalen that Master Peace had spoken of and that somehow, out of that defeat, a friendship was born. He looked back and forth at them for a moment, contemplating this concept, then finally put thoughts together into something that could be used as words. "So, you are going to try and make friends with Crystal?"

Christoph just shrugged and asked, "Why not?" as he took a couple of pieces of fish.

"Because..." Toomba couldn't think of a good reason. "What if she doesn't want to be your friend?"

Dalen got up and began to cast a magic spell on Christoph, who just smiled at Toomba and said, "Impossible. Everyone wants to be my friend."

Toomba scoffed. "I don't want to be your friend."

"It's way too late for that Toomba. We are already friends." Christoph looked like he was going to say something else, but Dalen grabbed his attention and asked him to focus. Any other conversation was cut short as Dalen finished casting his magic on Christoph.

"This spell will allow you to adapt to your environment. While under water you will grow gills, and your system will adjust to the building pressure." Dalen grabbed both sides of Christoph's face and looked directly into his eyes. "This spell will go against your nature. Your subconscious mind will try to fight the spell and return you to a state that it recognizes as true." Dalen jostled Christoph's head and made sure he was listening. "Listen to me because this is important. The first chance that your free will has to reverse the spell, it will, so it's only temporary. Your time is limited to how long you can go without consciously thinking about how you shouldn't be able to do this."

Christoph nodded and looked Dalen in his silvery eyes. "I understand." He walked over to the railing and tapped at his

Vengerian Pin.

Toomba rubbed his eyes for a moment and made sure that what he saw was real. Christoph was now wearing full-plate armor. "I would be careful man. If you go overboard all that metal will drag you straight down."

Christoph smiled and said, "I'm counting on it." He gave Toomba a wink, nodded to Dalen then leaped overboard and sank like a stone.

Christoph's mind flew into a tizzy after only twenty feet. He made the mistake of looking up and watching his only source of light move further and further from his reach. The light gave him perspective, and he could watch as he sunk deeper and deeper into the darkness.

‹I can feel your panic.› Dalen's words were a godsend at that moment, and Christoph stopped feeling like he was utterly alone in the inky blackness. ‹Calm yourself and remember what's happening. Remind yourself that you have my spell on you, and you can breathe just fine.›

Christoph did as Dalen suggested, then noticed an itch on the side of his neck. He reached up and touched it and found that gills had begun to sprout there.

‹There, you see, nothing to be afraid of. Remember, it's okay that you are where you are. It's where you wanted to be› Dalen's words in his mind continued to help Christoph gain his composure as he sank further into the darkness.

‹I can't see anything.› Christoph thought louder than he needed to.

‹It's alright. Your eyes will adjust, there is nothing but water to see right now.› Dalen said. But he was wrong.

As Christoph sunk lower and lower, he could feel the current move around him. There was something else in the water, he was sure that he wasn't alone. Christoph peered into the darkness, and at first, he saw nothing. He had sunk well past where the light could reach, and even though he was not in pain, he could feel the water pressing in on him from every angle. He did his best to stay calm with all that was happening and instead of trying to force his eyes to see, he allowed them to take in what they could.

Christoph knew what he had to do, but he was terrified, and his mind was trying desperately to get him to quit, but everything depended on him seeing this through. He fought his urges to flee and instead, he let his mind drift to Grelf as he sensed the dragon was close. ‹I made it to my first challenge. I am with the dragon now,› he thought to her.

Her voice filled his mind and his heart. ‹I am with you always, even now. You may not be able to see me, but wherever your heart is I will be with you. I am about to face my trial as well. Knowing that we are doing this together at the same time fills my heart with light. Let my heart be a light for you in your darkness.›

At first, it was nothing, he merely felt a presence as if an invisible phantom had manifested against the blackness. Then Christoph began to detect motion. His eyes began to track whatever it was as it moved closer and then further from his position. It was bioluminescent and each time it came near Christoph could make out more of its shape and color. The scales were different shades of blue and purple and it was much larger than he had anticipated. Now that his eyes had something to focus on, they began to create images in his mind and Christoph marveled at its size and beauty. As he sunk deeper, the maze started to come into focus. It looked as if it were intentionally created to mirror the one Christoph had seen made from hedges at the castle, except this one was all made from coral, and it too was bioluminescent. It glowed in the darkness in brilliant blues and greens and with breathtaking reds and oranges that contrasted against each other in a luminous menagerie of colors.

The dragon moved in and there was little Christoph could do to stop it from grabbing him, so Christoph relented. ‹Now we get to see how wise you two really are. It has me, there is no turning back.›

‹Remember.› Master Peace's voice echoed in Christoph's mind. ‹You didn't come all this way to fail.›

As the dragon took Christoph to the center of the maze, he had a moment to take in how absolutely beautiful it was. The coral maze and the dragon were not the only things alive with bioluminescence and now that his eyes had completely adjusted to his environment, before him he could see a strange land of colored light teaming with life.

At the center of the maze, there was a large mass of coral that arched in the center to create a dome. At the top of the dome, there was an opening that the dragon swam down into. ‹I think it's taking me to its lair.› Christoph sent out to Dalen and Master Peace.

‹Activate the Vengerian Pin's ability to show us what is happening.› Dalen made sure his tone was easy and unstressed.

‹And don't forget,› Master Peace's voice was light and playful in Christoph's mind, ‹Every moment that thing isn't eating you on the spot...is good and means everything is going to plan.›

Somehow that helped and Christoph found his courage. He looked around as the dragon gently sat him down. The mass of coral had been almost completely hollowed out. Inside was large and spacious. Christoph saw a nest of coral and kelp along the inner wall to his right, and to his left, a large hoard of gold and treasure. Except for the Royal Vault in Venger, Christoph had never seen this much treasure in one location before.

The dragon sat Christoph down in what was relatively the center of the room. Taking a few steps back, she moved away from him, giving him some space. She uttered some vocalizations that Christoph didn't understand but when she was finished all of the water drained from the room. His mind took a deep sigh of relief as he felt the air begin to fill his lungs and the gills vanish one by one from his neck as they released all the water that was still in them. The sensation of breathing had the same gratification of finally being able to scratch an itch that had been out of reach.

The scales on the dragon began to glow brighter until the room was filled with indigo light. Her body transformed into a mass of concentrated light that started to change its shape and size. The mass continued to shrink and morph until it was roughly the same size as Christoph. As the light faded Christoph could see that the dragon had taken the shape of a young woman. She had blue hair that still held indigo bioluminescence, and she looked to be human. Christoph could tell it was out of kindness she chose that form and to him it made sense. If you were going to change shape to communicate with someone, it would be wise to take the form of the same race as the person you are dealing with.

Christoph took a knee and bowed his head. "I am Christoph of Venger." She raised an eyebrow at him in amusement. "Blizzard, son of Dorn, said that in all his travels, this was his favorite place in the entire world."

"Such a kind boy." Her voice echoed in the chamber and resonated as if she were in a cave and speaking at twice the volume she was. It made her voice come from everywhere all at once. Yet, after she spoke, Christoph was not sure that she had actually spoken at all.

"The world is in great peril." Christoph pleaded. "Please, the world needs your help."

"The world needs my help, whether or not it is in peril." Again, as she spoke it echoed and resonated within the confines of the chamber, and once she spoke, he was not sure she had spoken at all. She had her eyes closed and could not see the quizzical expression on his face, but she responded to him as if she had. "The world is in less peril than you might think, and in a grave deal more." She put out her hand and when Christoph took it, she pulled at him to stand. "Please, stand up. There is much you have to say so that I can give you the responses that you came for."

"So, you do know why I'm here?" As Christoph got up, he casually glanced at the giant pile of treasure, silently scanning for the Water Blade.

"You won't find it over there. It's not with my belongings." Her tone was still magical, and every time she spoke the same sensations continued.

"Don't worry. I am not here for your treasure."

"I know." She smiled. "I know what intentions you came with, and I know what objects you leave with. If it were any different, I would be different, but I know you are here for the one thing that I don't want."

"Christoph sighed a breath of relief. "Then it is here?" She nodded. "We were unsure. This was a long shot at best, and we didn't know if we would find it here or not." He sent a thought through his Vengerian Pin, ‹Confirmed, it's here.›

‹We are both watching the whole thing. You are doing amazing! Keep going.› Dalen's tone was joyful and full of hope.

The moment that Dalen's thoughts connected with Christoph, the young woman stood in front of her visitor. She waited for Dalen's thoughts to finish and then said, "Brother Truth. I see that you are watching. One day a young girl will be taken to the Temple of Light. Blind to the world around her but in a constant state of seeing, having visions from a third eye that never closes. When she arrives bring her to me. I will help her see. See that she is not cursed but blessed. I will teach her to have true sight with an eye that will not deceive her, and Master Sight, as she will become known, will train Ben one day and help him find peace."

Christoph put up a finger for a moment while he listened, and then said, "Brother Truth gives his word as a Jinn and a Brother of Light that it will be done. Master Peace has asked me to tell you that he gives his highest regard and respect to the master who taught Master Sight. One of the women who saved his heart and soul."

"Thank you both and hear me when I say this. If you can hold this line of thinking and keep this truth, then on the day you return to your own time, I will be waiting for both of you in Dorn's, but for now..." Crystal cracked a playful one-sided grin. "You know how each has to face their challenge on their own?" She didn't wait for them to respond. She simply reached over and removed the Vengerian Pin from Christoph's chest. "You can have this back when you have retrieved what I have lost."

Christoph was suddenly hit with the feeling of being alone. It did unnerve him for a moment, but he knew from the start that he was going to have to do this alone, and he reminded himself that this was all a part of the plan. Instead of dwelling on a feeling of dread and loneliness, he decided to focus on the task at hand. "I have to help you find something you lost?"

"You won't be helping me, my friend." Her words held truth that Christoph could not yet see. "As I have told you, it is Venger who needs my help."

"Then help me, please. Help me save the world and give me the Water Blade." Christoph's request was heartfelt as he put out his hand in a gesture of receiving.

Crystal simply said, "I will do no such thing."

Christoph's hopes that this was going to be easy had been dashed. "Why not?"

"I have seen it, I know exactly what I do, and I do not give you the Water Blade." Crystal rested her face in her palm for a moment.

"Okay. Yes. I am not arguing that. I am asking why you don't" asked Christoph, trying not to get mad and yell at a dragon.

"Because to do that I would have to retrieve it and I don't want to be Queen of Venger, now do I?" Crystal said bopping Christoph on the nose with an index finger, making a little "boop" sound. When she could tell that he understood, she said, "I don't want the whole world to end by a nightmare that hides under the guise of a dragon. I know exactly where I lost the object that you seek, and I intend to help you."

"I don't understand. If you know exactly where something is, and where you lost it, how is it lost?" Christoph was still unsure of what he had to do and began to doubt her sanity.

Crystal smiled, she stood in front of him again as if she were looking him in the eye, but still held her eyes shut. "Let's say for a moment, I lost my love, and I knew who that love was when I lost them, and I knew the exact place and moment I lost them, would you be able to find my love? Are you sure you would find them in the same place or time, or as the same person for that matter?"

Christoph nodded slowly and said, "The thing that I need to find, that you lost, is not the Water Blade."

"Yes and no, but you will require what I lost to find it," Crystal said as she took a deep breath in. "A long time ago, I made a deal with someone immensely powerful. I was granted the gift of sight." She held up her right hand. On her ring finger, she wore a ring with a band made of celestium that was adorned with a piercing indigo-colored eye. "I was granted the ability to see into the future." Then she held up her left. On her ring finger was a ring made of a material so black that it looked like a void wrapped around her finger. It too was adorned with an indigo eye. "I was granted the ability to see the past. It came at a price, of course, as such things do."

Christoph began to understand, and he knew that for such an ability, the price would be steep. "What did you lose, Crystal?"

She opened her eyes, and Christoph had to brace himself not to react. Her eyes were dead. Gray and lifeless as if she had died. "My ability to see the present."

"You're blind, I had no idea that you could not see." Christoph was trying to be apologetic but the surprise in his voice cut through.

"I can see more than most." She closed her eyes again.

"Your eyes lie to you all the time, where my visions are always honest." Crystal walked over to her hoard and grabbed a coin. She flipped it in the air and caught it deftly. "I use my vision of the future at one-sixteenth of a second away from the present." She flipped the coin in the air and this time plucked it from the air with two fingers. "It's almost like cheating to know exactly where it will be." She flipped Christoph the coin. "Hold on to that. One day soon you will need it."

Christoph caught it and examined it for a moment. It was gold on one side with an image of a dragon's head and on the other side was silver with an image of an eye. He tucked it away into a little hidden pocket just inside his boot and as he put it away, he asked, "Do you know when I will need it?"

"Yes," answered Crystal, then a devious smile crept across her face. "And when the time is right, so will you."

"Well, now isn't the time, because at this moment I am not sure what to do." Christoph looked around the room he was in, taking in as much as he could. Besides the opening at the top that he and Crystal first came through, there was a large opening along one side. "My instincts say that whatever I am to do, it's through there, but I just have my regular eye so the present is the only thing I can see."

"You have eyes, but you cannot see." Crystal walked Christoph over to the other opening in the room where just on the other side of the coral there was a wall of water, and beyond that, a glowing maze that stretched for miles. "To be worthy of the throne you must demonstrate nobility, wisdom, bravery, the ability to connect, and in this case, the ability to flow with your environment and be able to see more than a narrow perspective." Crystal paused and took in the moment, as her visions of what was to come filled her mind. "Anyone with power can force their will on others. That is what the blasphemous creature of chaos, who tarnishes the name of 'Dragon' intends to do. Not at all noble in my mind. A true king would have the ability to feel the moment. He should be able to not just see his truth, but the truth of his kingdom. He should be able to see both truths together as a whole. A king must be able to see more than his eyes allow him to see."

"That is why I must find what you have lost." Christoph hugged Crystal as the relief of understanding came to him. "I need to be able to see past myself. I need to be attuned to the present and be able to see it for the truth of it, and not just what I think or wish it to be."

Crystal hugged him back. "You will have to do it quickly as well." Christoph let her go and stepped back. "The spell that Dalen Pax put on you has long since ended. When you are ready you must take a deep breath because you will not get another until you reach the Eye of the Present, and you will only have until you run out of breath to do it. Once you have the Eye of the Present, you will be able to find what you came here for. With the Water Blade in hand, you will be able to breathe underwater, and you will be immune to the change of pressure when you return to the surface."

Christoph looked at the opening and began to take deep breaths quickly to get as much oxygen in his blood as possible. "Any hints?" he asked and went back to his breathing.

182

"I have already told you all you need to know to survive, save this. The Northern Sea pulls a deep current through the maze and the coral is like razors. Be wise about how you choose to move through it."

Christoph told himself this was it. This was the moment that he had spent his life getting ready for. He allowed his breathing to become rhythmic and deep. He needed to be in the present. He needed to see past his own perspective. He took a long deep breath and with intent, he stepped forward as a king.

11

GIVE ME A COUNT

Grelf and her Vengerian Guardians had made it into the village without noticing anyone. Until they reached the dock. The long boats docked at the harbor had two men guarding them who were quietly chatting to themselves and Grelf suggested that someone should get close enough to hear what they were saying. She suggested that it would be better to know what was going on before they walked up to them in the middle of the night and said hello.

"I got this," Becky said as she tapped her Vengerian Pin

and changed back into the uniform of Oubliette. It was completely non-reflective and when she was in a shadow she could disappear completely. "I'll be right back," Becky said as she pulled up her hood. Her face went dark and over the communication of the Vengerian Pin, Oubliette whispered, ‹They will never even know I was there.›

Oubliette retrieved her weapons from her belt. She refrained from extending the blades but used the hilts as virtual monkey bars. With just the switch of a button, Oubliette could suspend the hilts in midair anywhere she chose. She was an amazing gymnast and began to swing hand over hand to a location near enough for her to hear the two men guarding the boats. Then she swung up a little higher to get above them. Once she found the spot she wanted to observe from, she used one hilt to swing her body around putting herself in position to set the other hilt under her butt as she completed the swing. Leaving her sitting about five feet in the air hidden under the dark cover of night. She activated the Eye of the Beholder so that the rest of her team could see and hear what she could.

"They will never give up them bloody phoenix feathers." said the first one. His clothes were dirty, and his odor could be smelled from where Oubliette was sitting. He looked strong and capable, but he was barefoot, and his clothes had not properly fit since about thirty pounds ago.

His friend was not much better. At least he had shoes. He had an unkempt beard and wore a sword at his hip. "That's why the captain is going to have to kill a couple of them before they start talking." They both laughed. "Then once we get our hands on one of them birds, we are going to be rich!"

‹Pirates!› Sir Adam's voice came out of nowhere and was filled with a magnitude of excitement. It took Oubliette by surprise, and she lost her balance. Luckily, she was quick to respond and caught the hilt with her knee leaving her dangling over the men.

‹Travis.› Oubliette spoke with a whisper, ‹I may have to kill your brother.›

‹I'm sorry Oubliette. They're my first real pirates. I got excited.› Oubliette couldn't see whatever face Travis was giving his brother but whatever it was Sir Adam's tone let her know that it was disapproving. ‹Are you alright?›

‹Oh yeah.› She looked around to get her bearings while she dangled there upside down. ‹Just hanging around.› She reached up and grabbed the hilt that she was holding herself up with then placed the other hilt straight down underneath her and locked it in place. Once she had her balance, she straightened her legs, unlocked the first one, and brought it parallel to the other, leaving her in a handstand, looking down over the two men. She began to move hand over hand in the direction her back was facing, giving the appearance of walking on her hands while suspended in the air. When she was far enough away, she allowed her weight to fall forward, using the momentum to swing herself around, she released the hilts on the downswing and allowed her whole body to move freely as she was launched into the air with breathtaking hang time. With a backflip that seemed to drift in the air, she landed next to her friends without making a sound.

Travis held up his notebook. On one of the pages, he had just written a big ten on it. "That was impressive."

Oubliette gave a little bow and took down her hood. "Thank you. Thank you." Becky said, and then she turned her attention to the leader of this party. "Grelf. What do you want to do with them?"

Grelf thought about it for a moment. She considered her options carefully before finally coming to her conclusion. "Leave them for now. The Orc Slayer says to kill them and burn their ships, but I have to start thinking like a queen, right?" She looked toward the ship offshore with a look on her face that showed how much she really wanted to burn it into the sea but instead said, "Let's try to talk to them first. Maybe they can see reason. Who knows? And if they won't listen to reason, then we can burn their ships into the sea and leave the burnt wreckage as a warning to any who think that they would be so foolish as to ever attack this town again."

"Hey." Travis put one hand on Grelf's shoulder. "I like the plan but let's not get ahead of ourselves about leaving messages. For now, let's try the whole reasonable route."

Grelf smiled. "Was that out loud?" she shrugged. "At least I want to give them a chance first."

"It's a start," Becky said with the same shrug. "Don't worry." Becky pulled her hood back up and went dark once again. "You're doing great," whispered Oubliette who then faded away as she and the shadows merged into one.

I told them that I was going to keep back and out of sight, but not to worry, because I would always be watching and if they needed me, I would be there.

Travis took point in front while Sir Adam was watching the rear, and the three of them moved slowly into the village, out of the sight of the two men at the docks. The village itself was a beautiful place, filled with impressive obsidian statues that littered the area and brilliantly colored paintings of phoenixes on almost every wall. Each piece of art was masterfully crafted into something more than just beautiful. It looked like art that should have taken lifetimes to master.

As they moved through the streets that were surprisingly bare, Adam began asking questions telepathically through his Vengerian Pin. ‹These statues would have to be worth a fortune, but the pirates are only here for the feathers. What makes them so important?›

‹Phoenix feathers have some very powerful properties.› Grelf stopped as Travis stopped, and with a hand gesture, he told them to stay back and peered around the corner for a moment. Grelf looked back at Sir Adam. ‹They can heal you, even if you are on the brink of death. They can even bring someone back from death if it is done right away. When someone dies, there is a window between when the body dies and the spirit leaves. If you can burn a phoenix feather and have the ash fall on someone during that window, then you can save them.›

Travis swung back around, pulled out his notebook, and asked, ‹What happens if you miss the window?›

‹Necromancy. I don't suggest it. Once you miss that window the spirit is gone. All you are doing is reanimating the body. Nobody's home.›

‹ Straight-up zombies?› Sir Adam asked with just a hint of too much glee.

‹Yes. Now hush you.› Grelf turned back around just as Travis was putting away his notebook and readying his bow. ‹What's happening?›

Travis gave one more quick look. ‹It seems that they have gathered a bunch, maybe all, of the villagers into the town square. I count twenty heavily armed guards at the ready.›

‹There are ten more wandering the streets looking for anyone hiding.› Oubliette whispered through the Vengerian Pin. She had been scouting ahead of them, swinging from rooftop to rooftop, and had a clear understanding of how many others there were and where they were patrolling.

‹Me and Travis got this.› Sir Adam said and stood up.

‹We do?› asked his brother with more than a hint of concern.

‹Absolutely. Just give me a countdown.› Sir Adam gave his brother a playful slap on his cheek. ‹It's going to be fun.›

Oubliette whispered her objections. ‹You are not going to stake the lives of all of them and all of us, including Grelf, on a game tactic that you only got to work once, are you?›

‹I have only tried it once. That means it works every time.› Adam snorted. ‹Rule sixteen.›

Travis looked over to Grelf and thought, ‹You are on an adventure. Act like it.›

Grelf smiled. She shooed Travis to move and both caught up to Sir Adam. ‹I am beginning to like you more and more Sir Adam. Do you have any more rules?›

‹Yes.› Sir Adam started warming up his right hand by stretching his fingers and then making a tight fist a few times. ‹Rule eighteen: All bullies are cowards. Even Pirates.› Sir Adam gestured with his hand for both of them to stay back. ‹Keep her safe.› Then Sir Adam strolled into the village square as if he lived there and waved at the pirates as they noticed him. The pirates had all the villagers sitting, pressed together, and in the center of the square. The pirates themselves were standing around the edge of the village square in tactical positions. "Excuse me." He started looking around. "Who's in charge here?" One of the armed guards approached Sir Adam who put up his hands. "Hi there. Are you the man in charge?"

The pirate seemed confused about Sir Adams's apparent lack of concern or worry. He looked him up and down trying to believe what he was seeing. This bold young man was wearing his sword on his back, but besides that, he was wearing a pair of blue board shorts and a sleeveless white shirt with matching slip-on sandals.

"Hey, buddy." Sir Adam waved at him. As the pirate looked him up and down, he pointed to his face and said, "I'm up here big boy. Are you in charge?"

Sir Adam turned as a voice from his left said, "I'm in

charge." The man was in a gorgeous long coat and was the only one of the crew, who was clean.

"Yeah, you look it." Sir Adam began to walk around the captives who were sitting, and toward their leader, but the guard tightened his grip on his sword and pointed it at him. Sir Adam regarded his threatening stance with the same concern as if his assailant were a toddler with a wooden sword. "Hey, big guy. If it's okay with you I am going to talk to the guy in charge. Okay?" Sir Adam didn't wait for a response he just sauntered over. It was so bizarre to the pirate that it stunned him, and he just stood there in disbelief letting Sir Adam walk by.

"Who do you think you are?" asked their leader.

"Me?" Sir Adam pointed to himself almost questioningly. "I am Sir Adam the Pure Heart, but that is not what is important right now." Sir Adam began to stretch and clench his fingers again. "What is important right now, is that I am the people person in my team, and instead of just killing you before you knew we were even here, I wanted to allow you to surrender."

Their leader laughed in Sir Adam's face. "I am Markus Jolee. Captain of the Jagged Fin, and why would I ever surrender to the likes of you?"

"You, see?" Sir Adam smiled and took a breath. "Captain Jolee. You are somebody. A person." Sir Adam pointed to Travis. "That's my brother, and he isn't like me. He is tactical. Where I see people, all he sees are numbers. Here, let me show you what I mean." Then Sir Adam called out to Travis, "Give me a count!"

"Counting the Captain, you will have to drop seven of them, while I pluck off half a dozen before they will retreat. That's not counting the ten wandering the village, that Oubliette has subdued by now."

"So." Sir Adam let out a slow sigh. "Not counting the ten, that's still thirteen of you who have to die before we reach a place where whoever is left surrenders. Now, I don't want that, and I don't think you want that either."

Captain Markus couldn't help but check the rooftops and alleyways. "Not counting the ten." He rubbed his neck trying to stall while he tried to figure out whether Sir Adam was bluffing or not. He pointed to Grelf who was still standing by Travis. "I am guessing this is your Oubliette."

Sir Adam smiled. "No," he said with a slight hint of whimsy that he hoped hid the truth that he was risking everyone's lives, and he was far past the point of no return. "Nothing but the best for you. I present to you the legendary, Grelf the Orc Slayer." She smiled and her hair turned brilliant shades of red and orange like fire. Murmurs of 'Grelf' and 'Orc Slayer' began to be whispered amongst the pirates. "Give me a count!"

"It helped but I still need to drop four and you still have five." Travis smiled. "Counting the Captain."

Captain Marcus was furious and pointed his sword at Sir Adam. "You're outnumbered almost seven to one. How dare you think you can intimidate us?"

Sir Adam didn't flinch. He forcibly controlled the expression on his face. Although his adrenaline pounded through his system and made his pulse race, he refused to offer the pirate captain anything but utter control. He just shook his head and with a strong voice said, "Give me a count."

Travis's tone was cold and methodical. "His men can tell he is scared. Kill him and then the first two. Grelf and I will only have to take care of one each."

Sir Adam nodded. Then he looked at Captain Jolee and said, "We are down to five. Look how many lives we have already saved today, but you can save them all, Mark. All you have to do is calm down and see that you are already beaten."

Captain Jolee did his best to stand his ground. He yelled and beat his chest. I am Captain Marcus Jolee! Captain of the Jagged Fin and I will not be intimidated by this boy in sandals!"

Travis interrupted Captain Jolee's rant and called out, "If you just kill the captain with one strike, the rest of the men will surrender."

Sir Adam shrugged and said, "That, I can live with." He reached up and pulled his sword from his back. As he did all of the light from the torches, and even the stars were pulled to his blade, which, made of pure celestium, began to brilliantly glow. It was as if all the ambient light were stolen to create this impressive radiance. By the light of his blade, Sir Adam could be seen in his full armor. It shined in the glow of the blade that was now humming with power. Captain Jolee stood there in fear and disbelief. Sir Adam took a single swing and cut the pirates' sword in half, and then pointed his blade at Captain Jolee's chest. "Now, come on Captain Jo-Jo, give me a reason to save your life."

Captain Marcus Jolee of the Jagged Fin dropped his broken sword and demanded that his men do the same. As they did, the villagers got up and detained them while Travis and Grelf collected their weapons.

Once the villagers detained the Captain, Sir Adam said to him, "Captain Jolee, I leave you in the hands of those who you had captured. May they be forgiving." Then he sheathed his blade, and the light of the torches and stars were visible once again. He gave a nod to the villagers who had Captain Jolee in custody and said, "Citizens." Then turned and walked over to join Grelf, Travis, and Oubliette, who had just joined them. ‹Works every time.›

"You are full of surprises Sir Adam." Grelf gave a small clap. "I don't impress easily, but the three of you continue to do so."

"We were lucky," Travis said modestly.

"You were brilliant," I said standing next to them.

All four of them reacted with surprise when I spoke. From their point of view, I was just suddenly standing with them as if I had always been there. Which I was, but as much as I enjoy being corporeal, I do my best work behind the curtain.

Becky pulled back her hood and said, "You were both." She hugged Sir Adam and then kissed Travis. "You are both crazy to try to pull that little stunt off, but you were both brilliant. You can't imagine how proud I am of you both." She took Sir Adam's hand in hers and looked him dead in the eye. "I know your title, but I am talking to you. Adam. That was the bravest thing I have ever seen you do, and I am proud to know you."

Adam teared up. "It was good?"

"It was the bibitz." Becky caught Adam as he hugged her.

Adam's favorite part about Becky was she always understood him, and he knew in his heart he could let his guard down. "I'm so glad I didn't have to hurt anyone."

"In my travels with Christoph, we have been faced with some difficult choices to make. After doing this for years and all the experiences I've had, I can tell you this as a truth." Grelf turned Sir Adam toward her. Becky stepped back, took Travis's hand, and leaned her head against his shoulder. "A good man will try to save the villagers. Only a hero will also try to save the pirates." Grelf looked around and realized that the whole village was watching them. "Tonight, Sir Adam, you were a hero."

The villagers erupted in applause. Grelf pushed Sir Adam forward and then gestured to Becky who pushed Travis next to his brother. The twins smiled and waved as the villagers showered them with their appreciation.

"You know what, brother?" Travis asked his twin as he wrapped one arm around his shoulders, squeezed him, and looked around at the people... the people they had just saved. Smiling he said, "These are the moments we live for."

12

THE MAZE AND THE WATER BLADE

As soon as Christoph stepped into the maze he had to compensate for the current because it was much stronger than he expected. He turned his back to it and had to lean back with most of his strength just to keep his feet. The heavy armor that he was wearing was giving him extra weight, which was good because it helped anchor him against the strength of the current, but it hindered his movement and encumbered him further with every step.

He had been in the maze for only thirty seconds, but to Christoph, it had felt like hours. He had only managed to take three steps. Each time he took a step he had to fight the current from sweeping his other leg out from underneath him, and then use his strength to rebalance. Although he was wearing metal armor that would protect him for a while, his concerns were that the weight of the armor, if he fell, would cause him to tumble and get slammed into every wall in this maze. He feared he would never have the strength to get back up, so he had to keep his feet. Yet, three steps in, and he was exhausted. He didn't think he could hold his breath for more than two minutes, perhaps three, but that number diminished quickly with all the effort that he had to put into every step.

Flashes of light came from the opening where he had entered the maze. He looked over and saw both Dalen Pax and Master Peace standing on the other side of the water wall, and behind them was Crystal. He couldn't hear them, partly due to the water distorting their voices, but also because the current was rushing over him and around his armor, making it impossible to make out anything that they said. He could only see them and could make out their actions. Crystal stood there calm... just watching, but the two monks of the Brotherhood of Light were anything but still. Christoph recognized their movements. Movements he had seen hundreds of times in the Adventure Ball stadium. They were cheering him on. They were jumping up and down and throwing their fists in the air. Both of them waved to him to keep going. They knew something about this that he did not, because they were rooting for him as if they believed that there was hope. There was another answer other than what he was doing, and they were screaming it at him. There was a way. He was sure of it.

It was then Christoph's mind began to work on solving this full contact word problem. "Crystal said that everything I needed to know, she already told me. What did she tell me?" He took another step. "This can't be the answer. I will never make it like this. I missed something and because of it, I am going to die. Drown right here." Christoph stopped trying to move. He put his strength into holding his ground against the current and concentrated on the answer. "What did she actually say? I knew everything I needed to know except that the Northern Sea pulls a current through the maze and that the coral is razor sharp." Christoph looked forward toward where the current was moving. Before him was a corridor of beautiful green bioluminescent coral that went out another twenty feet and then turned right and out of his field of vision. "Check, and check. What else did she say?"

The current seemed to be getting stronger and more of Christoph's attention and strength had to be focused on not being shoved forward into a sprawling tumble as the armor anchored him to the sea floor.

"That was close." Christoph thought to himself. "If this gets much stronger, I don't think I'll be able to hold myself up." Christoph drove the thought from his mind. He reminded himself that now was not the time to think about what would happen if he failed. Now was the time to put all his thoughts into what he needed to do to succeed. "What else did she say? I had to find the thing that she had lost." He remembered the ring on her right and left hand that allowed her to see the future and past. Perhaps what he was looking for was another eye of sorts, but it was speculation, and Crystal never specifically said what the item he came for looked like. He was sure he would know what it was when he saw it, but for the moment, that was not what he needed to understand.

Christoph was beginning to feel the pull in his chest. He no longer had any idea how long he had not been breathing, but it had been long enough that his system was beginning to give him signs that he was running out of time.

Christoph looked back at his companions. They were no longer cheering him on, but instead, they were facing Crystal. She handed something to Dalen and then a light came from his hands. Then Christoph felt a warm sensation in his palm, he looked down and noticed that in his right hand, there was an object. He felt it with his fingers and knew that it was his Vengerian Pin. He attached it to his belt immediately.

‹We got here as fast as we could, but Crystal has explained that you have begun the challenge, and we aren't allowed to help you.› Christoph was so glad to hear Dalen's voice. ‹Crystal did say that I could give you back your Vengerian Pin.›

Then Master Peace's voice spoke in Christoph's mind and simply said, ‹Use it wisely.› and then communication was cut. Crystal and Master Peace seemed to be arguing but Dalen just stood there staring at Christoph.

Christoph could feel in the back of his thoughts a push. As if someone or something were rooting for him from the inside, and he knew he had to think fast while he could. Soon his air would run out and his ability to think sharply would be the first to go. "The eye itself is an item that does something. It's that something that matters. What I am looking for is the ability to see the present."

The pressure from the current was getting stronger, and it forced Christoph to take a knee.

Christoph tried to see this moment for all that it was. "What am I looking for? How do you see the thing you can't?" Christoph tried to remember what else Crystal had said. "The only way I am going to see more is to look beyond my own point of view, but also see the point of view of what? The maze?" Christoph looked back over to Dalen. "And why would Dalen make sure I have my Vengerian Pin even though he isn't allowed to give me advice or help me? But he did. He helped me in a way, but how? And Master Peace. He tried to help me too; it's probably why Crystal and he argued. He said, "Use it wisely" but what could that mean?"

The answer was staring him in the face, and he still couldn't see it, the frustration of that was echoing in his heart and thoughts, but Christoph knew that he had to find the answer. If he failed, he would die, and not only would he die, but most of the world. Then it was his heart that spoke. "If I fail, Grelf dies too."

Christoph decided to use that motivation and as his lungs began to ache, he gave it his all. "What I am looking for is somewhere in a maze I cannot move through. Even moving with the current is impossible. How do I move through the maze? Try to see it from the point of view of the maze." Christoph closed his eyes and remembered the view of the maze he had while he was being carried to it by Crystal. He pictured himself above it looking down. He imagined moving through it and tried to see how it was possible. "The Northern Sea pushes a current through the maze. The current." Christoph thought. "The current moves through the entire maze."

Christoph opened his eyes and looked over at Dalen who was standing right up against the edge of the water and staring at him. He smiled and nodded. "Why did you give me my Vengerian Pin back, and why did Master Peace say to use it wisely?"

He reached up and tapped the pin to allow him to see what he could use it for. When he did both Master Peace and Crystal stopped their conversation and once again, all eyes were on Christoph.

Most of the abilities for the Vengerian Pins were for communication with the team, and Christoph knew that he had to do this alone, so that wasn't it. He knew that the teleportation was only effective while in Venger City so that couldn't be the answer. All that was left was the ability to save an outfit or to change into another. "Could that be the answer, but if it were, how would it help? My armor is the only thing that will protect me from the coral, and right now it is the only thing that is keeping me from being swept away because this current is getting stronger and stronger."

Christoph was running out of air, and he knew if he didn't act now, he was going to drown. His mind was getting foggy and thought was getting harder to maintain.

"See it from the point of view of the maze." He thought to

himself. "The current moves through the entire maze." Christoph grabbed onto a thought that frightened him. "The only thing that is keeping me from being swept away is the armor." Christoph decided what he was going to do. "First. If I am going to die, it's not going to be on my knees." With all his strength he fought against the current and stood back up. "Second. If this kills me... It should be one hell of a ride." Christoph tapped his Vengerian Pin and instantly was wearing just his leather boots and pants with a light linen shirt. The current swiftly took him.

On the first turn, he hit some of the coral with his arm and the pain of it almost made him scream. He knew that he would be cut to pieces if he didn't do something, but what could he do? He was at the mercy of the current now. He decided to turn his body horizontally and try to move with the flow of the current. No longer fighting the current Christoph relaxed his body and allowed his movements to match the flow of the current and put all his strength into holding his breath. His lungs ached and burned as the current began to pull him faster and faster through the maze. To his surprise, the current would pull him in a new direction when the corridors changed and if he bent his body to move with the current, he never came in contact with the coral.

Through twists and turns, he flew through the maze. Most of it was open to the Northern Sea but the current pulled him into a tunnel and now he was surrounded by coral with nowhere to go but where the current took him. Up ahead of him, Christoph could see that the main corridor bent hard to the right and he was about to move with it when he noticed that there was another hole in the coral that went through it directly in front of him. He saw a light coming from within it. The hole was too small for him to pass without hitting the edges, but he felt it was the way to go.

Christoph put both hands in front of him and when the current turned, Christoph put his head down and didn't change his direction. Like an arrow, he shot straight forward into and through the coral. It lacerated his back deeply in three places as he went through and his arms that had protected his face and head had taken multiple deep cuts as well. Still holding his breath, it took every ounce of energy to hold back screams as he also sustained more than a few broken bones in his left hand and wrist.

He was in a lot of pain and bleeding badly, in fact, he knew that he was now bleeding out quickly and there was a possibility of bleeding to death before his air ran out, which was only moments away. The tunnel of coral that he had passed through had emptied into a larger coral chamber that the current was not directly affecting, and it was large enough to swim and move around in. The light was coming from above him, but he was beginning to black out. Christoph swam with all that he had, even though every movement was excruciating, and felt like he must still have coral deeply embedded in him.

Christoph broke the surface of the water as he swam up into a chamber that although underwater, a pocket of air had been trapped within the coral. Christoph gasped for air and his body began to tingle. While he kept his head above water and caught his breath Christoph fought through the pain and swam toward the light.

There was a shelf of coral that Christoph swam over to and climbed up on, effectively giving him a floor to stand on with only his feet and ankles still in the water. He was getting sleepy and cold. He had to shake off the sensation and forced himself to keep walking. "You're fine," Christoph said aloud. "You're just bleeding to death." He took a breath. "Walk it off." Christoph continued to stagger toward the light.

When he got to it, he could barely keep his eyes open, and he blinked a couple of times to try and correct the blurriness of his vision. At the far wall, was a small alcove behind a curtain of water where the light was coming from. Beyond the water, Christoph could see an indigo reptilian eye staring back at him.

"Please be it," Christoph said, almost prayer-like, as he reached into the alcove. He grabbed the eye and pulled it from the water and as he did, he saw that the eye itself was the center jewel in the hilt of the Water Blade and the rest of it was made of water.

Christoph had run out of strength and fell to his knees. He was tired and wanted to sleep. He stared at the eye and said, "Can you see that I'm dying."

The eye lit up into a beautiful indigo light and as it did the alcove behind the small waterfall disappeared and in front of him were Dalen Pax and Master Peace as if they were just on the other side of the curtain of water in front of him. His time was up. He had achieved his goal but at the cost of everything and had nothing left to give to get back to his friends. Christoph fell forward and as he did, he landed on the floor of Crystal's room at the center of the maze, right in front of them.

Master Peace pulled out his Dragon Claw. When he activated it, a small sun made of divine healing light appeared at the end of a mace. He placed it against Christoph's back, his wounds began to close, bones pushed themselves back into place and mended and color began to come back to his flesh, but he still wasn't breathing. Master Peace reached out with his other hand and placed two fingers over the artery in Christoph's neck, searching for a pulse. "He's going to make it. He must." He closed his eyes and the ball on his Dragon Claw grew larger and the light began to fill the room. He breathed slowly, and with his third breath, Christoph matched him.

Dalen had been connected as much as he could to Christoph's mind without interfering. The moment that Crystal had taken off his Vengerian Pin, he and Master Peace acted. They told Toomba to wait for them and then using his magic, Dalen and Master Peace were quantumly moved to where the dragon was and arrived just as Christoph stepped into the maze. Dalen slowed time to almost nothing and took Master Peace and Crystal with him, but before he could ask a question Crystal began talking to them as if she already knew how to answer. She explained that he had already started and that they could not interfere. Both Master Peace and Dalen agreed. They had been with Queen Hope when she was seeking the Earth Blade, and they knew as Vengerian Guardians they were allowed to help get Christoph to the challenge, but once the trial had started, it was up to him.

She then explained that this was a test of perspective, so in this case, they could not give advice, the same way they could not help Queen Hope run. Both Dalen and Master Peace understood, but Master Peace had a question for her. "Why did you take away his Vengerian Pin?"

Crystal's answers came quickly like this was all a play and her lines were memorized. "Christoph shouldn't have the ability to ask either of you for guidance. It's easy to see the answer when you aren't in the thick of it. Succeed or fail, this has to be on his own terms. He will not always have you for council when he is king." Time began to move normally and the three of them walked to the edge of the water. The magic that Crystal used to create an air pocket in the room they were in created an odd effect because the edge of the spell was smooth. Although they could walk through it, it was like watching Christoph in an aquarium. Watching Christoph fight so hard against the flow of the current, both monks knew what he had to do. Then they saw him look over at them. It was then when Crystal said, "But the reason I took it from him, is so that you can give it back to him now. It was the only way I could help him. Giving it to him will give him a clue to the point that he is acting like an anchor during a water test." She shook her head. "I know this is what is done, but I do not know if it is helping too much." She handed it to Dalen who used the Mind Sphere to quantumly place it in Christoph's hand.

Master Peace told him to use it wisely but was interrupted because Crystal said he was walking a narrow line of cheating the rules of the challenge. They began to debate about what counted as cheating, but Dalen was fixed on Christoph. When he put it on and touched it, Dalen thought he had figured it out, he had reached out with his mind and was trying to help keep him focused without telling him what to do. As Christoph reached for the pin, Dalen called the other two over so that the three of them could watch as Christoph let go and allowed the flow of the maze and the energy within it to move him.

Time moved in ways that were not conscious choices and each of them held their breath and waited. After what seemed a lifetime Crystal grinned and said, "You are going to love this." As she spoke the water wall in front of them began to glow with an indigo light.

Dalen didn't see Christoph until his body broke the wall. Master Peace was taking care of him, so Dalen turned his focus to the dragon and asked, "What just happened?"

Crystal nodded to the Water Blade that was still in Christoph's hand. "Christoph passed his trial."

"I know you know what I mean," Dalen said as he floated over to her. He realized that there was little point because she couldn't make eye contact, but it was a habit to stand in front of the person he was talking to.

"Do you remember the answer you found when trying to answer whether you can step on the same piece of water twice?" Crystal's question to Dalen caught him off guard and he had to think about it for a moment.

Dalen closed his eyes and returned to the moment of the memory. He played it in his head and quoted back what his teacher had said. "The water continues to change its shape as anything disturbs it, so the water your foot touches will move when you do, and as you set your foot down again the part of the water you are touching will be a different part of the water than you had been touching before. But from another point of view, all of the water in that pool is connected. One water, if you will, and any place you stand in that pool, you would be standing on the same piece of water. So, I would have to say the opposite is true as well."

"Well done," Crystal said joyfully. "You remember your past well. In this case, we will be looking at the latter truth and not the first."

"Alright, all of the water is one." Dalen clarified.

"How much of it?" asked Crystal with the same tone that Master Faith or Master Ki would use when asking questions they weren't seeking answers to themselves, but wanted Dalen to find the answers to on his own.

Dalen thought for a moment and then answered, "All of the water in the maze."

Crystal raised an eyebrow and said, "Think bigger."

Dalen thought about it. He tried to remove his thoughts and tried to see it for what it was. "All of the Northern Sea."

Crystal folded her arms and asked, "Are you sure?"

Dalen looked at it again and tried to see it from an even larger perspective. "All of it. Every creek that touches every river that lets out to every ocean is all connected."

Crystal nodded, "With the Water Blade Christoph can be at any place the water he is touching is connected to. Much the same as how you use the Tree of Travel. But instead of just a few locations, he can be anywhere the water touches."

"I think I understand." was all that Dalen got out before Crystal interrupted him.

"I hope you do." She said with concern on her lips. "Time Jinn." The eyes on her rings began to glow. "You are burdened with much the same power, but the waters you swim in are the oceans of time, and you will have to eventually decide where in those oceans you actually are, and that will lead you to the truth about yourself."

"You can see it. Can't you?" As Dalen spoke Crystal nodded. "What is that truth?"

Crystal laughed so hard she snorted. "You want your fortune told Time Jinn?" She fanned herself with her hand for a moment. "Okay. You will know the answer to the second truth when you know why the first one is irrelevant."

13

THE PHOENIX

"We seek council with the phoenix." Grelf's words were strong, but you could hear the need in them.

The village elder raised an eyebrow and looked her over with judgmental eyes. "So, like the men you just saved us from, you have come for the phoenix? Who will save us from you, I wonder?"

Sir Adam put up a finger and stepped forward, but Grelf politely waved him back. ‹I got this Sir Adam. You have been amazing, but I feel in my heart, this is something I must do.› Sir

Adam sensed it. This was a part of her trial, and if Grelf said she had it, he was going to let her, so he put down his finger, gave her a bow, and stepped back.

"No one will come and save you because you will not need to be saved." Grelf gestured to the pirates. "These men came to rob you. Steal the phoenix, or at least her feathers, for their own immoral desires." She kneeled before the village elder and said, "We come before you to request your help because of something we need."

The village elder smiled. "I have lived enough years to be able to understand the difference." She looked Grelf over and finally let out a sigh once she was satisfied. "Very well, get up girl. I will hear you out, for three reasons. The first is that you and your people rescued us from what would have been an unpleasant night. The second is because of something you said."

Grelf got back to her feet. "Something I said?"

The village elder nodded. She put her hand to her heart and said, "A good man will try to save the villagers, A hero will also try to save the pirates."

Grelf cocked her head and asked, "Why is that one of the reasons?"

The village elder smiled and said, "Takes one, to know one."

"Fair enough. I'll take it." Grelf liked this old lady. Even at her age, she had spirit.

"The third reason I am going to hear you out is that my

son, who is now the keeper of the phoenix caves, said that when he last spoke with the phoenix, she told him that the next time he visited her, he would bring with him a friend of an old friend." The village elder started looking for someone in the crowd. When she found who she was looking for she waved to them to join the conversation. "It was very confusing to him at the time, which is why he came to me for counsel about it."

Just then one of the islanders approached. Most of the villagers were wearing not much more than a sarong but he wore loose-fitting, white knee-length shorts that were trimmed with red and a white vest that had a beautifully embroidered phoenix on the back. He smiled, nodded to Grelf and the group, and asked, "Yes Mother?"

The village elder pointed to Grelf and said, "I want you to listen as this half-elven hero explains why you should take her to Magma Falls to have a council with the Phoenix."

His eyes widened with surprise as he understood what his mother was saying. He bobbed his head slowly as he began to take in Grelf for who she was or might be. "That is a very serious request, Mother. No outsider has had council with the Phoenix in many life cycles."

"My son." She hugged him dearly and when she let him go, she said, "I know what she asks for is rare, but I want you to consider what the Phoenix said, and if that is not enough for you, I am asking it as my final request."

Her son bowed his head and said, "As you wish Mother. I

will listen." He then turned to Grelf. "First, I want to say thank you for saving this village. We could have lost everything, and for that, I cannot thank you enough. I am Getu. Why are you here?"

Grelf stood there for a moment still looking at the village elder pondering what she meant as a 'last request', but a small cough from Travis brought her back to the matter at hand. "Have you heard of Blaze of Venger?"

The question openly amused Getu. "Yes. She is known."

Grelf was relieved that they already knew her. "We were sent here on her suggestion."

Getu looked puzzled at first and then as his mind tried to answer his first question of why, his face became concerned as all the reasons that she might send people here filled his mind, for none of the reasons were joyous. "What has happened?"

Grelf confirmed his worst fears as she explained. "Blaze of Venger has been separated from the Fire Blade by terrible magic. The connection has been severed."

Getu's eyes widened as he asked slowly, "Does...she...live?"

"She does." Grelf could see that this relieved Getu. "There is more. Blaze and her siblings have all been severed from the Elemental Blades and Venger is in peril."

"That could mean the destruction of Venger City." Getu's words were direct and there was a sense of fear in his tone. "Is that why you are here? To ask the Phoenix to rebuild her bond?"

"I wish it were that simple," Grelf replied. "I am Grelf the

Orc-Slayer. My partner is Christoph of Venger."

"I have heard of you both." Getu gave a small nod of respect. "The sacred defenders of Lady Venger."

Grelf glanced over to her Vengerian Guardians and lingered for a moment. "It was told to us by a trusted source, that as the Protectors of Venger, the mantle of wielding the Elemental Blades has to be reforged."

Getu covered his mouth in shock. "The line was broken?"

"Yes." As Grelf spoke, Becky, who was naturally empathic, could feel shame in Grelf's tone. Becky had never noticed it before, because Grelf's wall of strength was hard to see through, but Becky could tell that Grelf was still suffering from the weight of all of this and in some ways blamed herself for not being able to protect Venger.

"That means..." Getu stopped himself and let the truth of it wash over him. "I know why you are here."

"The Fire Blade is here then?" Grelf breathed a sigh of relief. "We weren't sure if it would be here or not. We came to seek counsel with the phoenix. If it weren't here, we were hoping that she would know where it was."

Getu laughed. "Oh, the Fire Blade isn't here yet. It will only appear for the royal line of Venger, but that is just the exhaust. An afterthought to the reason you are here."

Grelf cocked her head and put her hands on her hips. "I am pretty sure I am here for the Fire Blade. What else are you talking about?"

"Seeking council with the Phoenix is seeking death and rebirth." Getu looked over to his mother and said, "I see why you had me speak with her. How did you see it when I did not?"

"I have taught you everything that I can teach you, my son." The village elder hugged Getu and then held his face in her hands. "But there are some things that you can only be taught with time and life experience itself."

"Yes." Getu held her hands against his face and said, "I look forward to telling Atula and Tongo's child about how your wisdom and joy were the greatest things I remember about you."

The village elder let go of her son to wipe tears from her eyes. "I will miss you too."

Grelf did not want to interrupt this moment. Her heart ached for her father, and she wished that he could see who she had become before he was taken from her, but once they were done and both looked back at her, she only had one question. "See what?"

The village elder then took Grelf's face in her hands and said, "The Fire Blade will only present itself to the future Queen of Venger. My dear sweet child..." She looked deep into Grelf's eyes and said, "Grelf the Orc-Slayer has to die."

Grelf was surprised by this revelation and pulled away. "I have no intention of dying today."

Getu could see that Grelf didn't understand, and her stance was becoming aggressive. "Even if it means the destruction of everything you hold dear?" Getu could tell that Grelf did not like his answer, but it got her to listen again. "The Orc-Slayer has to die so that Grelf, the Queen of Venger, can be born."

‹This is your trial Grelf.› Becky was sincere and supportive. ‹I know that you still hold yourself responsible, but retrieving the Elemental Blades has always been a part of your redemption.›

‹Becky's right.› Always the strategist, Travis had been listening to not only what was said, but the implications of what was meant. ‹So is Getu. Your greatest fight has been accepting this role.›

Grelf interrupted him and argued, ‹I have already agreed to this.›

‹You have, and I am not suggesting that.› Travis took a moment to look up from his notebook, which he was currently writing in, to see what Getu and the village elder were doing. They were watching Grelf, and patiently giving her time to understand and come to grips with what she had just been told. ‹You have already moved from knowing the path to walking the path, but what they are suggesting is, that there is a difference between walking the path and being the path.›

Sir Adam didn't bother with telepathy. He wanted his words to be heard. "A hero who dies in the service of what they believe in is the dream of any who would pick up that mantle."

"Damn right," Grelf said with a newfound strength. The words of her Vengerian Guardians and friends had given her the courage that she needed. "And well said. All of you." She stood up straight and with conviction said, "What is it I must do?"

Grelf, her guardians, and I were led to the cave that was the nesting ground of the phoenix. Besides us, Getu, and his mother, two others came along. They were introduced as Atula and Tongo, a young couple who continued to talk about the baby they would soon have. They filled the village elder's ear with stories of how they would play with their child and teach them everything they knew, and how their child would be happy with them in their family. When speaking to the village elder, they referred to her as Popotu but kept referring to their child as Popotu as well.

On the way up to the cave, Grelf received a connection from Christoph. He had reached his trial. Grelf didn't mention that she was on her way to be killed and reborn; she wanted him focused on his task. But all of us who knew her knew that at that moment, she needed to hear his voice, to give her strength to go forward in her trial.

When we finally reached the cave, the villagers showed us the way in and once inside we could feel the intensity of the heat. The cave itself had been a lava tube at one point and led into a chamber-like area inside the volcano. This chamber was behind the Magma Falls so along the entire right side molten rock poured like a curtain from the ceiling to the ground. The ground itself was solid rock for only a short distance and then it was just molten rock and fire. Lava also poured from other places in the ceiling creating multiple waterfall effects scattered throughout the cave.

"What kind of magic is protecting us?" Travis was taking in the splendor of it. "Between super-heated air frying our lungs, and heat levels that should make us combust instantly, we should all be dead already."

Popotu raised her head, lifted her chin, and outstretched her arms as if she were in worship or prayer and said, "It is 'The Phoenix' who protects us and keeps us safe, so that we may commune with her." She raised her voice louder than they expected a woman of her age could muster. "I call to you now Phoenix! Come forth! I am ready."

The high-pitched screech of a bird echoed throughout the cave. From the wall of lava itself, something came flying out. It looked like a peacock made of fire and light and it flew towards them.

This was a special treat for me. Phinix was and is from the Grey Continuum. The aspect of life, death, and rebirth... incarnate. Phinix has been seen as the Mother of all Things in one culture and has been seen as the Angel of Death in many others. Somewhere in the beginning of this dynasty, a small tribe of islanders began to worship the spirit of life and death as a goddess. When they had believed long enough and given their own free will hard enough, they created an image of The Phoenix in their minds, hearts, and souls and when they did that, they allowed her to manifest here in these caves. She was not using the avatar of the Grey Continuum as I was but rather using the avatar of the goddess that they had created. Because of this, it granted me an opportunity to physically speak to another of my kind corporeally. We are always in perfect communication together as one in the continuum, because we are all aspects of the same thing, just from different points of view, but since there is only one avatar for all the Grey Continuum to share, we never have a chance to sit down together and talk.

As Phoenix arrived, she burned into a large ball of fire, and out of the fire stepped my sister, Phinix of Grey as Phoenix, Goddess of Life and Death and Rebirth. She looked like she was from the same island as the folk who lived here, which Travis wrote down in his notebook as looking akin to Polynesian. Her chest was wrapped with black silk that matched her sarong, and she was adorned with golden rings at her ankles and wrists with matching bangles on her upper arms and around her neck. Her beautiful black hair draped about her shoulders, and when she turned you could see the tattoo of a phoenix made of light on her back.

She greeted Getu first and then Tongo and Atula. After a few moments, she took Popotu into a loving embrace and told her she had truly lived an amazing life. Then she turned her attention to me, "Hello Brother." Which did get the attention of everyone in the room.

"Hello, Sister." I hugged her and we both allowed it to linger for a moment. "May I say you're absolutely stunning as a Polynesian goddess. You wear it well."

She acted shy and said, "Stop, you will make me blush, and look at you, walking around all corporeal and whatnot. I thought you said you were done with such trivial things."

I shrugged and said, "I was asked for."

"Asked for?"

"By Dorn."

"Well, aren't you fancy?"

I looked at my corporeal self and said, "More like slumming it."

Phoenix slapped me on the shoulder and jokingly said, "Manners." Then turned to look at the quartet I had with me. "I have been dying to meet you in the flesh. I have heard so many great things about all of you through Will here." Becky, Sir Adam, and then Travis were introduced and each of them gave a bow of respect. Phoenix was kind and took the time to meet each one separately. Then she turned her attention to Grelf and presented her with a single phoenix feather. "To be used when all is lost." Grelf thanked her and tapped her Vengerian Pin so that the outfit changed to one that had a pack on her back. She slid it off and placed the feather in it. She pulled it back on and reset her Vengerian Pin to what she had just been wearing. "And now..." Phoenix held Grelf's forearm in a warrior's stance. "Are you ready to be braver than you have ever been? Braver than your mother and Iron-Tusk combined.

Grelf laughed. "You are trying to kill me?"

Phoenix chuckled back. "Not yet. You're second in line." She returned to Atula. "Are you ovulating?"

Atula smiled and held both of her hands over her uterus. "Yes. It is time."

Then Phoenix looked at Tongo. She put her fists on her hips and raised her chin so she could jokingly look down her nose at him. "And you Tongo. Have you been doing your part?"

Tongo blushed and smiled. "Yes. Many times. Twice just today."

Atula blushed too. It was plain to see she was embarrassed as she spoke "Tongo."

Phoenix smiled and reassured them. "Don't be embarrassed." She took Atula's hand and placed it in Tongo's. He was taller than her by a foot and her hand seemed so small in his. She waited until he looked Atula in the eyes and then she spoke in Grey Speak, *I don't need much attention. She is the goddess you should worship every day. Love her, protect her, and remind her she is the goddess of your world so often, she has no choice but to believe it.*

Tongo was overwhelmed with emotion. Tears flowed from his heart as he shared his soul with Atula and told her how much she truly meant to him.

Phoenix didn't let up for a moment. *Atula, this is your god. Hear him as he speaks his love.* She took Atula's other hand and placed it over Tongo's Heart. *Open yourself to the love he is showering you with.* She closed her eyes and felt his heart. Their love began to build and strengthen until it started to affect everyone in the room.

‹I love you.› Neither Travis nor Becky knew who thought it first. They had found their own new religion, with each other as the pantheon, and both were ready to be devout worshipers.

"Are you ready?" Phoenix's voice had returned to normal, but the effects remained.

Popotu was staring at Tongo and Atula. "I couldn't imagine

221

being conceived in a more perfect moment of love. I'm ready."

Phoenix opened her arms and said joyously, "Then do not run from me, but embrace me."

Popotu pulled her eyes away from the two of them as their love resonated throughout the chamber and embraced Phoenix as the Goddess of Death. Fire began to consume her and as it did, she screamed as the flames overtook her.

Travis held Becky close. His reaction was just a fraction faster than Becky's as she tried to rush forward to stop what was happening. Getu stood in front of Adam, placed his hand on his chest, and said, "You couldn't save her if you tried, and it would be considered blasphemous."

"But she is in pain!" Sir Adam shouted and tried to push past him.

Getu matched his moves and held his ground. "I know you feel a connection to her, but I promise you she means more to me than she does to you." He looked into Sir Adam's eyes. "Pain is one of the things life and death have in common." He looked back at his mother. "She knew what was coming. She has witnessed it hundreds of times as have I." Then he turned the rest of the way and said goodbye as he watched his mother be flash-burned to ash. Once the fire had burned, the only thing left, other than ash, was a small ball of light that sat in the heart chakra of the goddess and lit up from within her.

"Reflex. Sorry." Sir Adam said with regret. When he had a second to think about it, he realized this was to be expected from people who worship a phoenix. "Can you explain what is happening?"

Getu explained that their village had been the guardians of the phoenix since the beginning of the Third Dynasty. The tribe was two hundred and thirty-four, which was fifteen more than the number of people who were inhabiting the island now.

All of them were unable to conceive normally. Neither man nor woman could produce life until it was time for one of the elders to pass. When an elder knew it was their time, a family would be chosen to have a child, which was considered a great honor. Then the elder and the couple would come to this place and the elder would give up their life to reincarnate as the couple's child.

In the beginning, the villagers would just repeat the same life with the same jobs over and over, but that tradition was broken, and they began to create new lives with new experiences. After lifetimes of experiencing all that they could, every person in the entire village had the knowledge and wisdom of every walk of life. They had all been artists and farmers or healers and even keepers of the nesting grounds of the phoenix.

After generations of experiencing all that life had to offer, education became more about remembering than learning something new. Like remembering an old skill that hasn't been used in a long while. Each villager kept journals of their lives. They recorded everything about their life, capturing the knowledge, feelings, and memories of who they were in their present lifetime. When each villager is taught to read, they are given the journals of the elder they were born from, for generations back. These journals allowed them to take in a deep understanding of what drove their hearts and fed their soul for thousands of years. This is how they learned the best.

They weren't born with knowledge of who they were but they, from time to time, would recognize familiar things and people, or even pick up old habits, but they were always different people. Just the same soul.

It was their way and had been for some time. As guardians of The Phoenix, they had been granted the favor of the Goddess of Life and Death. Their reward was hard to grasp at first, but Getu took the time to explain as they watched Phoenix take the ash and spread it over Atula's lower abdomen then placed her hand directly over her uterus. They watched in miraculous awe as the small ball of light began to move from Phoenix's heart. It moved through her into her outstretched hand, then from the goddess into Atula.

"You see? That little girl will be told stories of my mother. She will read her private journals and learn everything that my mother was able to share with her. She will read them all... back to the beginning and know every past life she has ever had. As have I. As have we all." Getu looked at them with a deep connection and they could feel his sincerity. "We have lost a few. If we die in any other way than this ceremony, no new child is born." As much as he did his best to not let it affect him, it was written all over his face. It screamed silently in his calm words. The loss of those few was devastating to him. "There have been rare occasions where with enough prayer and faith a woman will give birth to twins, and one of them will be a lost soul, but it's rare. If it weren't for you, we could have lost more than you can imagine. You didn't just save our lives tonight. You saved the memories of our entire tribe, our entire history."

"What would have happened if I had gotten to her?" Sir Adam asked, almost afraid to hear the answer that he had already guessed.

"We could have lost her." As Getu said it he got choked up and tears welled up in his eyes. "We could have lost her."

Sir Adam hugged Getu and said, "Thank you for stopping me. I feel so foolish."

Getu patted Sir Adam on the back and told him it was going to be all right. "You have to prepare yourselves for what is coming next. I am going to check on them and help them find their way out." He shook Grelf's hand. "If you have other gods, now would be a good time to pray to them."

In that moment there was only one being in this world that she wanted to give herself over to in worship. She had been affected more than she had thought by what she had just witnessed and the only thing in the whole world she wanted was to be in Christoph's arms. "Don't move."

"Where are you going?" asked Becky.

"You heard the man. I am going to go pray." She reached up and touched her pin. ‹Dalen, I need this. I wish to be with Christoph now.› Her guardians began to protest but before they could, Dalen granted her wish, and she was gone.

14

YOU'RE MORE THAN THE ORC-SLAYER

"She let you keep it man?" Toomba was exhilarated to get the three of them back on his boat. "I figured you wouldn't have a chance to live, but she handed over her ability to see the present. That's crazy!"

Christoph was still wet from his experience but in good health. Master Peace had learned the art of healing from Master Love, the greatest healer in the Brotherhood of Light, and he had done her proud. "It was no longer hers." He looked at the Water Blade in his hand. "She told me I needed to find something that she had lost. The price she paid to be given the ability to see the past and future was to give up the ability to see the present. It was the cost, and she gave it away willingly. It was no longer hers to keep. Chances are, if she tried to keep it, she may lose the very thing she bought with it."

Just then Grelf appeared before Christoph and embraced him so hard it almost knocked them both to the ground. Grelf didn't say a word, but her breathing was deep as she pressed herself close to him and lost herself in his embrace.

Dalen decided to break the silence, so he cleared his throat so that Toomba looked over to him. "May I present to you the one and only... Grelf the Orc-Slayer."

"The Orc-Slayer? I've heard of you man."

Dalen shrugged. "She is Christoph's partner and is the soon-to-be Queen of Venger. Umm. Permission to come aboard?"

"Yes. Of course. I like you man; you show me and my ship respect man." Toomba looked at the two of them for a moment and then said, "I am going to get some glasses and something worthy to drink for such a great victory." Then headed to his galley.

Grelf looked up from where she had her face buried in Christoph's chest and asked, "Victory? You, did it?"

Christoph kissed her and held her close with a gentle but powerful strength. "Guess why I'm only holding you with one arm." Grelf took a step back and Christoph brought it around between them so she could see it.

"You, did it?" Grelf stared at the Water Blade for a moment and then squealed, "You did it!" She ran her finger across the flat end of the blade. It was made of water, and she giggled as her touch sent out a ripple along the length of it. This time her tone was soft and endearing. "You did it."

Christoph gave her a moment to look closely at it. "I have seen the Water Blade of Venger. This is it for sure, yet it seems different."

"When we were helping Queen Hope, she said that the Earth Blade had changed as well." Dalen rubbed the stone that was over his third eye as he speculated. "It might be that they change depending on the challenge."

"Or perhaps they change because of the wielder." Master Peace thought about it for another moment. "It would make sense for the Water Blade. Water is known for its ability to change form to match its containment while keeping its essence, but I think there is more to this than that. Each king and queen will rule differently. Sure, they could be trained the same, but every king and queen will be unique, and the Elemental Blades change to match."

"I like it." Christoph looked at the Water Blade carefully. "Alright, Master Peace. I am willing to entertain that as a possible truth. What makes you think so?"

"When we helped Queen Hope she said that the Earth Blade had changed. Now, it is possible the blade changes every time, with every challenge, because the challenge is different each time, and that may very well be the truth of it. But I feel it had changed for her for a different reason." Master Peace closed his eyes and watched Hope running with the trees. "The trial is meant to test you, but it is meant to temper you as well. Perhaps the reason it changed was because she was no longer the same woman she had been when she first became Queen. She had claimed it once before, to become Queen, but this was to see if she could keep it because her daughter was coming of age. She was now a seasoned queen, and I have no doubt a different woman from when she first obtained it."

"Oh, Master Peace, how I needed to hear those words." Grelf's eyes welled up, but she fought against them, and no tears fell. "I am about to face my trial, and to achieve it I must be tempered, and who I am will be no more."

"What are you talking about?" Christoph sounded concerned. "What is your trial?"

"I don't know the details, but I have seen enough to know that it will be a trial by fire, and I have already been told that to achieve what I must, Grelf the Orc-Slayer has to die so that the Queen of Venger can be reborn in me." Grelf looked deep into Christoph's eyes and as her hair turned dark blue with highlights of white, she said, "I'm terrified."

Christoph looked at her hair and said, "That may be the first time I have ever heard you say that." He ran his fingers through it and everywhere he touched turned to warm colors of yellow and orange. "You and I have faced death more than once and you have never been this afraid."

"Grelf plunged herself back into Christoph's embrace. "That's because I had you." She held him close and finally spoke her truth. "I have spent my entire adult life being the Orc-Slayer. Sure, I wanted to prove to my mother that I was more than just some girl to be sold off and forgotten. I was the daughter of one of the greatest heroes of his time, and I have spent my life trying to bring honor to his name. I didn't just do it to make him proud or to show Mother that she was wrong. It was a choice that I made about who I am. When I faced death I faced it as the Orc-Slayer. Even if I died, I knew who I was, and now I have to let go of..." She swallowed hard and fought back tears. "I have to let go of me."

Christoph sheathed the Water Blade on his back "You are so much more than what you imagine My Love." He held her tight but then pulled back so he could look her in the eyes. "The Orc-Slayer is only a part of who you are. I have said it for years and it is about time that you heard me. Your mother was never able to see herself as anything more than what she was told she was. She believed that a woman was supposed to be a wife and a homemaker, so that was all she could see for you." Grelf shrugged and looked away but with a gentle hand, Christoph lifted her chin so that she was looking at him again. "You are more than that."

Grelf nodded. "I know."

Christoph smiled. "I know you know but, you are also not just the daughter of Gregor, one of the greatest warriors of his time. You are Grelf, the greatest warrior of your time." Christoph teared up for both of them. "And even still, you are more than that."

"Then what am I? Who am I?" Grelf asked unsure.

"You are the woman who is powerful enough to be the Orc-Slayer. You are the woman who is stronger than that. You are the woman who carved a name for herself. No one remembers you for the deeds of your father. They remember you for the deeds that you, yourself have done."

"But who am I beyond that?" Grelf was almost in tears.

Christoph's chest swelled. "You are the woman who has captured my heart, and you are the woman who is so powerful and fearless, that you are going to give Hell to whatever challenges this world has for you and never fail to be the amazing person you are while doing it. You say the Orc-Slayer must die. I say good!"

Grelf's surprise was written in her eyes. "Why would you say that?"

"Because, My Love, she is holding you back." Christoph stepped forward and placed his forehead against Grelf's "You are greater than the best she could ever be."

Phoenix's words resonated in her mind. This was her god, and he was worshiping her. She had to open herself up to it and hear his love. She kissed him long and deeply. "Remember me. Remember who I am in this moment, because I fear by the time we are done, neither of us will be who we were."

"Without growth, there is only stagnation." Master Peace was in tears. In all the time that Dalen had known him, he had watched him change and grow from the mean bully to the man of peace he had become. Dalen could feel the heart of Master Peace and knew that at his core, Ben Watts understood what Christoph was trying to tell Grelf better than most.

"Then remember me, because I go to face my death." She kissed Christoph one more time and then gave a warm hug to Master Peace who embraced her and said, "There is no question in my mind that your father is proud of you."

She then turned to Dalen and hugged him too. "Grant me a wish?"

Dalen knew that there were rules that he would have to abide by, like not messing with free will. "If I am able."

Grelf took both of Dalen's hands and took a deep breath. "I wish for you to tell me the one thing that I need to hear."

Dalen connected to her through the Natural field and allowed them to meld into one. From there he slowed down time until it stopped, although the boat still bobbed on the water. A wave crashed up and over the railing and as the water came crashing onto the deck it formed a person. Master Ki was standing beside them. Grelf looked directly at him and asked who he was. It was surprising to Dalen at first that anyone could see Master Ki, but without words, Master Ki reminded him that they were now connected, and she was seeing him through Dalen's eyes.

"This is Master Ki of the Brotherhood of Light." Dalen nodded to him. "I would give you a hug but..."

"Then you would break the connection with Grelf. I feel the hug anyway," said Master Ki. He touched both of them on the shoulder at the same time and pushed his ki into them. They both felt great love come from him and the safety and warmth of an embrace.

Grelf was still looking at Master Ki but spoke to Dalen, "I can tell that he is here, but also he is not, it's as if you are creating him, but I also feel that he is very real."

"Both are true," Dalen explained. "Master Ki is very real, but he is also how I perceive a part of myself. The same way that you can perceive yourself as Grelf the Orc-Slayer. I call it a Tin Soldier. An aspect of the truth of who I am, but in no way the only truth about me."

"Are you saying that you hear voices in your head?" asked Grelf.

"And you do not?" responded Dalen dryly. "When you tell yourself to keep fighting, who are you talking to, and if the answer is yourself, who is asking?"

"But I don't see them as another person," replied Grelf.

"I guess I do have more skill in it than most." Dalen's shrug suggested the matter was of little importance. "It had to do with my training." Dalen cocked his head to one side as he gave a minor grimace of admittance and nodded. "Being a Jinn may have had something to do with it as well."

Being connected to him at that moment, Grelf understood not only what he was saying, but she understood it as if she were Dalen.

The world changed. She was standing in the center of

a magic circle. Around her were glowing glyphs on the floor. She recognized them as the Elements of Reality, and she also recognized the individuals standing on each. Master Ki was standing on the Natural Element, the source of truth that all things are one. Master Truth was hovering on the Quantum Element, the source of truth that all possibilities are one. The Fire Jinn floated above the Divine Element, the source of truth that all power is one, including Grelf's soul.

On the Kinetic Element stood Brother Truth, an aspect of Dalen from when he became adept at channeling his ki and found himself mastering the four Natural Elements by understanding he was one with all of them. On the element of Arcane stood Father Light. Dalen had spent years in the temple of All-Faith learning the spells and rituals of the gods. He had become an expert in them the day he realized that all of it came from the same source. He was a master sorcerer, and a priest, of the source where all gods derive their power. Standing on the Element of Imagination, of the Observer, was Dalen the Reality Bender. He was an aspect of how Dalen saw himself when he had first come into his power and was able to create his magic through all of the elements as a whole. He had become able to see himself as not only Father Light but Brother Truth. The monk and the sorcerer. The warrior and the priest. Standing directly in front of Grelf, was the Jinn, closer than the rest. He was standing in an Element of Existence, the Element of Time. Together, they said in unison, "I am all of this and so much more."

The lights went out save for the place where she was

standing in the middle of the circle, and everything went black. The kinetic glyph began to glow and, in its place, Grelf saw a vision of herself the day she killed Iron-Tusk. The moment she became the Orc-Slayer. Then the Arcane Element lit up and Grelf saw herself as Queen of Venger. She wore leather armor that had been dyed royal purple over a black and red blouse and wore two blades on her back. The Element of Imagination lit up and Grelf saw the Vengerian Captain of the Guard.

She heard a voice that she didn't recognize at first but as its words hung in the air, she knew for certain it was her own. "You are the being in the center. You are the person who can be all of them."

She then heard Christoph's words in her mind. "You are more than all of it. You are the being who is powerful enough to be all of it."

Time came crashing in like an unwanted guest. Grelf stepped back and found herself standing on Toomba's boat still holding on to Dalen's hands. All of his stones were glowing, and at that moment, she believed it was the light of his soul pouring out of him. She looked around trying to regain her bearings, not sure if where she was, was real.

"Thank you, Master Dalen." She embraced him as a brother. "I understand what I have to do." She kissed him which was very surprising to Dalen. She smiled and shrugged with a nonchalant swagger. "You earned it."

Dalen looked to Christoph and still in shock shrugged and

asked him, "Are we good?"

Christoph laughed and gave a wink to Master Peace. "If I can't handle Grelf giving a nonromantic kiss to someone who deserves it, I am not worthy of being King."

She walked directly over to Christoph and said, "Damn right." And then gave him a kiss that would remove any doubt of where her love and loyalties were.

Christoph smiled and agreed. "Damn right." He paused for a moment and then asked, "Do you want me to come with you?"

Toomba had made it back in time for Grelf to take a glass of whatever he had poured and slam it back. She recognized it instantly as the Star Folk Brandy that she had enjoyed with Queen Hope.

Dalen was still connected with her, and he watched her create a stitch in time, as she chose to have that drink be the remembrance for the moment when she finally chose the path she was now on.

"Thank you. I needed that, but I am going to be honest with you, My Love. I am not sure what is to happen next, but I know that I need to do it without you there. I don't know if it's because I don't want you to see what I am about to face or if it's because I think you would distract me by thinking about you instead of what I needed to be focused on. It's not that I don't want you. I will undoubtedly be right by your side once it is done."

Christoph held her close for a moment. "I understand. You have to do this without me there to support you. If you are going to be Queen it will be because of you, not because I stood next to you and held your hand. You know, I feel the same. Grelf the Orc-Slayer has always had my back, and I have never had to face my greatest deeds alone. You were always there. Maybe it should be like this. I will be there with you shortly. Get the Fire Blade and I will celebrate with you afterward. You need to do this on your own and so do I. Deal?"

Grelf smiled. "Deal."

Christoph gave her one last kiss and said, "Well then. You have a step to take. Tell me how amazing you were when it's done."

Grelf took a couple of steps back and began to think about her Vengerian Guardians. "Time to take that step." She looked deep into Christoph's eyes and in them, once again, she found peace and hope. "I love you."

Christoph put his hand over his heart. "May my love give you strength." And then he waved to her as she gave Dalen a nod and quietly wished to be back with her Vengerians.

"As you wish," Dalen replied. As he touched his heart, she faded from the boat, then his third eye blew her a kiss, and he wished her away.

15

REFLECTIONS OF GRELF

"Now that you have prayed, are you ready for what comes next?" Getu had kind eyes, and the hand that he offered reminded Grelf of her father, so she instinctively took it. "I myself do not know what is to come. In my lifetime, something like this has never happened. I am very excited to see what comes next."

"You don't know?" Grelf had guessed that in all the years of tending The Phoenix, something like this must have happened already.

"No." Getu let his eyes wander about the cave trying to imagine something that had never been seen. "Isn't it marvelous? The Fire Blade has never been severed from Blaze before, nor has anyone ever tried to obtain it other than her. I have no idea what will be." Getu squeezed her hand. "Don't worry. It will be fine."

It bothered Grelf for a moment. She was about to be offended that he was treating her like a child, but as she sized up her opponent, all she could see was a man who had just lost his mother and was trying to be brave. She took a breath as she understood and allowed him to guide her to Phoenix. She made sure she had a good grip on his hand and said, "Yes."

Getu was more focused on getting Grelf to where Phoenix was and had only partly heard her. "Yes, what?"

Grelf gripped Getu's hand and pulled just hard enough for him to turn around and look at her. "Yes... It will be fine."

Getu empathized and paused for a moment to listen intently to her, showing an expression of understanding on his face—a mixture of a tear and a smile all at once. "Yes. It will." With a new strength, he turned back toward the Goddess, and together, they approached Phoenix.

"Are you ready?" Phoenix's voice was calm and soothing like slipping into a warm bath.

Grelf nodded and said, "What is it that I have to do?"

Phoenix turned and faced one of the places where molten lava poured down from above like a glowing waterfall. As she spread her arms out, fiery wings appeared on her back and a rock path wide enough for at least three people to stand side by side, rose out of the pool of lava on the floor, spanning from near where they stood to the waterfall of molten rock.

She took a deep breath in and as she let it out, she brought her hands forward and clapped. As she did her wings gave a mighty flap and all the molten lava that was still on the path blew off. The blast of wind momentarily split the curtain of lava and as it did, Grelf could see that the Fire Blade was just a few steps beyond it.

"My magic can keep you from the heat until you reach the end of your path, but it stops at the curtain of fire." Phoenix walked Grelf right to the edge of the path and said, "If you want to be Queen, you now have to be brave enough to walk through fire to earn it."

"That will kill me!" Grelf said with more than a little surprise.

Phoenix lowered her head but maintained eye contact, her stance changed and Grelf could tell that she was being aggressively direct. "A true queen will have to face that often during her rule. What are you going to do? Cower back and let Christoph handle things?"

That was too far and Grelf had had enough. She screamed in Phoenix's face. "I would never!"

Phoenix didn't back down an inch. She didn't scream or yell but with all the power of her fury and might she calmly demanded, "Prove it."

Her Vengerian Guardians and I had been standing to the side watching this entire thing take place and I was content to allow things to progress, but I felt a calling and knew that one of my sisters had something to say.

I began to step forward cautiously. "Are we still in a place to offer help?"

Phoenix nodded. "Until she reaches the curtain of fire."

I nodded. "Okay. Good. In that case, there is someone who wishes to say hello."

"Who wishes to say hello?" Grelf was willing to entertain any who might be able to offer help at that moment.

It was myself whom Grelf had asked, but it was my sister who answered her. The avatar of the Grey Continuum physically shifted into a new being that was speaking. "I am Reflection of Grey. It is a pleasure to meet you."

Grelf had to look twice. She stared and still her mind would not accept the truth of it. The woman from her childhood, who was with her when she was too broken to move. The woman who stood by her not only as she faced her mother for the first time, but also faced the orc who slayed her father. She was now standing before her, more powerful and beautiful than Grelf remembered her.

She was a pale woman with no freckles or marks save one, a scar or birthmark on the left side of her face that came down her forehead and stopped about the center of her eyebrow, continuing an inch under her eye and halfway down her cheek. She was wearing laced black patent leather boots that looked closer to a military style of Sir Adam, Travis, and Becky's world than Grelf's, they had steel toes that had been brought to a reflective polish. She wore tight black leather pants with matching gloves and a silver halter top, under a black leather long coat. The inside lining was designed to look like a window out into the stars, a standard custom for those connected to the Grey Continuum. Her black hair was cut short into an A-frame, and she had perched a pair of mirrored eyeglasses on her head. The only other visible adornment was a necklace she wore with a chain long enough to come together at her sternum, the pendant was a gold-edged shard of shattered mirror.

"It's you," Grelf said in shock. "You're here."

"It is me. I am here." Reflection hugged her. "This will always be true, but I am curious as to who you think I am. This is the first time I have ever laid eyes on you."

"No," Grelf argued. "You were there when I faced Iron-Tusk. When I faced..." Grelf didn't finish the sentence, instead, she just trailed off in thought and stared at the woman who she had spent years wondering if she was real or just a figment of her imagination.

"Both really." Reflection replied to Grelf's thoughts as if she could hear them. "I am a figment of imagination, but that doesn't mean I am not real."

"You are a figment of my imagination?" Grelf had faced many things in her life, some had been planned and some had been a surprise. She had spent years learning to be prepared for the unexpected, but there was no preparation for this and Grelf was having trouble processing.

"I said I was a figment of imagination." Reflection folded her arms in front of her and cocked her head to the side. "I never said I was a figment of yours." She turned to face Grelf's Vengerian Guardians and asked, "Am I in her head, or am I standing here?"

"I can see you," Becky answered as did Sir Adam.

"When you are here, where is Will?" Travis asked as he scribbled something in his notebook.

"The same place he always is. Nowhere, and everywhere all at once as if two sides of a coin." Reflection laughed. "He, more than most, is always present." She closed her eyes and tilted her head as if she were listening to something extremely faint. She gave a sly half-smile, nodded, and looked at Becky. "He was with you as you celebrated with Ben that he had made it to tomorrow." Shifting her attention, she continued, "Travis, always the tactician, you did your best to talk Biff down from the fight at school. While your fearless twin was ready to face off against the other two goons that were with Ben the day this all started."

Becky shook her head. "This must be some kind of trick. That was an entirely different world."

Reflection just winked at her, then turned her attention back to Grelf. "You said that you have seen me, but I have not met you before. I can hear though, in your words, the memories of me, and I believe you. Which means, from my point of view, we have reached the nexus of our meeting."

Grelf had had a moment to regain her ability to think but her head was still a little foggy. In her memories of the woman, she could never understand her. Although she could now make out the words, it generated no help. Grelf still had no idea what she was saying. "What does that mean?"

"It means, that there is certain proof that suggests you are going to ask me for help, which I will give. And that my help will involve making a journey through your timeline, to actively help you, with the aspect of that which I represent." Reflection raised an eyebrow and waited for Grelf's response.

Grelf looked over to the Goddess of Death and Rebirth and remembered that Will referred to her as a sister. She had heard of Followers of the Grey and had assumed that he was one of them. She had never considered the idea that he was a member of the Continuum. To her, it was preposterous to think of it. "He's one of the Original Gods?" It was a common phrase used to recognize The All-Father, The Goddess Tune, and the God Allegro. "The Song, The Reason You Can Hear It, and The Reason You Dance, Original Gods?" Grelf asked.

"Ahh, the new names. Haven't heard those in a while. I have heard them called The Word, Atonement or her darker side Distain, and her brother Narrator God, whose very words create the world. He speaks; therefore, the world exists. To me, you speak of Omni, Peace, and Will of the Grey Continuum, but we have little time, and I am not the one for explanations, speak to my brother about such things. Let's use the names you know, but even so, let's not forget the fourth in that collection." Reflection added. "The Song,

Reason You Can Hear It, Reason You Dance, and The Grey... the bards that sing the song."

Travis was busy writing, and Becky was looking over his shoulder as he furiously scribed. Sir Adam had taken a knee and was honestly surprised that the others were not doing the same while in the presence of two goddesses.

Grelf knew that she was supposed to attempt her trial, but there was a part of her that needed answers before she could move on, as well, when a goddess asks for an audience... You make time. "They are all of those gods?"

"Since the beginning of the Second Dynasty. But we were witness to the first, and only asked to..." Reflection searched for a word that would be understood, "help, with the Second Dynasty after the First Dynasties gods tried to rebel and overthrow everything."

"But you have been different gods in both dynasties?" It was Travis who spoke, but it was both Travis and Becky who looked up from his notebook with expectant eyes of curiosity.

"The term 'God' is a profession, not a species." Reflection shrugged. "It's what we do, not who we are. Each of us with a facet or aspect that we are primordially a part of."

Grelf had to let go of any concept of what she thought was true. Her understanding of the world and how it works had been wiped clean and she had to start from scratch. In many ways, this helped her because she was no longer fettered by her own opinions. "Each of you has aspects. Aspects of what?"

Reflection smiled. "That was a good question." Grelf smiled because she had asked a good question and hadn't failed this test by losing her mind and hiding from her imaginary friend who had now shown up from whatever corner of the world she'd been hiding in, to explain to her that she was a goddess, who was about to go back through Grelf's life, and do all the things that Grelf already had a memory of, because they hadn't actually happened yet.

"I am an aspect of a single concept that can be perceived in many ways, but when you get right down to it, there is still only one concept."

"How can that be?" As Becky spoke it slightly startled Grelf, but it was just the little jolt she needed to help refocus.

Reflection looked over to Becky and simply said, "Our shape may change, but who we are in essence remains. The same way you are both Becky and Oubliette. They are both very different people, no? You speak aloud and Oubliette only whispers, but even though I could list all the differences between you two, the fundamental truth of it is, that you are many people. As am I." Reflection then turned back to Grelf. "As are we all."

"Just a few moments before I returned here, I wished for Dalen Pax to give me some advice. It is hard to explain everything I experienced, but in the end, the message was that I am more than just one version of myself." The pieces were beginning to fall into place and Grelf started to believe. "It couldn't just be coincidence. It can't be." Images of the last few days began to dance in her mind. She had met herself in the future, she knew that she survived this moment, and she remembered that the older version of herself had learned so much and had become so much more than her present version. "The thing that must die is the part of me that clings to my past instead of looking to my future. I can no longer be just the Orc-Slayer." Echoes of the past began to fill the cave and Grelf, along with everyone else, heard Grelf on the day she killed Iron-Tusk say, "I am not just a little girl." Grelf had been lost in her thoughts but hearing her primordial self, she remembered that was the last time she had seen Reflection. "Out of the entire Grey Continuum, it is you who is standing in front of me. What is the aspect that you are connected to?"

"I am Reflection of Grey." She stood tall and proud as she spoke. "Most often I am perceived in four stages. First is Plague, that moment of pure weakness where there are no defenses left and all you can do is reflect on pain and suffering and be swallowed by it." As she spoke, she touched the piece of broken mirror around her neck and began to wither, she became so pale she looked almost dead with dark circles around her eyes and the mark over her left eye now appeared more like a festering wound. "The greatest hits of your pain reflected at you." As her body began to take on mass again the color returned to her skin and the wound over her eye closed up.

"The second is that of Introspect, or inner reflection. The place where one begins to decide who they are, and the boundaries they keep." She smiled as she fiddled with the shard of mirror. "A lot of work is done here. A lot of deciding who you believe you are." Her body continued to gain color and mass and when it stopped, she looked healthy and strong. "The third stage is a stronger form of inner reflection, Insight. This is where one must come to understand one thing."

Grelf had experienced different stages during moments in her life and knew that this was the stage that she was at now. "What is the one thing I have to know?"

Reflection stood toe to toe with Grelf and peered deep into her soul as she spoke from her own. *That the boundaries that limit you are only the limits you place upon yourself.*

Grelf stood there in the grip of her consciousness trying to comprehend what had just happened. Grey Speak tends to bring pause to the mind and soul of those who get to experience it.

"What is the fourth?" Reflection turned to look at Travis who still had his pencil in one hand and his notebook in the other. "You said there were four, correct?" She was impressed that he showed no sign of difficulty with Grey Speech.

"The fourth form is the ability to withstand and adapt to anything, Reflection. To be able to reflect anything that comes." Again, she spoke with Grey Speak and said, *when in the face of an unstoppable force, the ability to become an immovable object.*

Something happened that they could not explain. A ripple of energy came from Reflection and neither Travis, Sir Adam, nor Becky could move. They could feel that the connection between their Vengerian Pins was broken, and they all went dormant. This was Grelf's moment, and she had to face it alone.

"Now that you know who I am, do you know what you are

going to ask me?" Reflection lowered the mirrored glasses over her eyes. "I'm ready."

Grelf looked at the path that was before her, and not just of stone and fire. "Help me let go of my self-limitations. Help me take the steps to become the Queen of Venger."

"I will not change who you are," answered Reflection.

Grelf stared at the curtain of molten lava that she had to walk through. "Okay. Yet I know for a fact I have seen you. You can't change it now, those steps are mine, but you can go back and instill it in me, during the moments where it really mattered."

"That is possible." Reflection put her hands on her hips and cocked her head to the side once more. "What do you have in mind?"

"I already know exactly what you will need to do." All the pieces of this moment started to not just fall into place but stack in ways she couldn't have seen coming. "You will have to appear to me in all four forms." Grelf was excited and almost giddy. "Send Plague to the moment I was trapped in my suffering after my father died. Give me Introspect the day I stood up for myself and chose not to let my mother dictate my life. The third version I will need in two places. The first is when I face Iron-Tusk." Grelf closed her eyes and did her best to remember those moments. "Those are the ones I know for sure because I remember them. The second time is now, right now. Then at your fullest strength, the moment I become who I choose to be in my near future, as I face the Earth Trial. If Jax is correct, it will take place in the desert and if it is anything like this, it is going to involve an immovable stone." Grelf took Reflection's hands and asked, "Can you do this for me? It is hard for me to ever admit that I need anyone, but in these moments, I need you. I have needed you, and I will need you again."

"If what you say is true, then it has already happened." Reflection grasped the shard of mirror around her neck and held it up so Grelf could see herself looking back at her. "Do you remember?"

As Grelf stared into her own eyes she could hear the music. At first, it was just a memory of the events that had unfolded in her past, but now she could hear the music so much more distinctly. She was lying on her bed, lost in her pain and grief. Plague was lying there with her. The picture was clear in her mind and now Grelf could see that the way Plague had looked was just the reflection of Grelf's own pain.

Plague had no defenses against Grelf's pain and loss, she felt it all. In that moment she knew Grelf completely, as if Grelf's life and memories were her own. There was a part of her who wanted to die, but instead, she pushed through it and looked into Grelf's eyes as she opened them. Plague drew hope from an experience where Grelf had first encouraged herself to be empowered. She wanted to start with something that would remind her of something special about this lost kid who had just lost her dad. She found the memory of when Grelf imagined the word 'Bibitz'. Her mother had told her to stop using foul language so instead, she created a word that could be anything that she wanted it to be. It was the first time Grelf ever tried to empower herself.

Plague used the power of this memory and began her song. The song was filled with words, but the words were secondary to the magnitude of the feelings the song invoked. The words were spoken in Grey Speak, so they carried with them a weight and intensity far beyond their standard meaning. The words created deep and meaningful thoughts, no matter what was spoken, the intention was what was heard. *You can be amazing. You have had the power all along. See how you are creating your strength and power, even at such a young age.*

Plague continued to sing, *there was never weakness here on your part. The weakness came from those who were afraid of the thoughts of others. You can choose to take the role they give you, filled with the backlash of their guilt and lack of love.* Plague squeezed Grelf's hands and said, *"Or you could choose to live your truth."* It was enough to jumpstart Grelf's heart and mind again and she pulled herself out of her self-imposed coma.

Reflection began to rub Grelf's hands in hers as she delved deeper into her memories. There, she found hopelessness. Grelf's father was the only person who had not treated Grelf like a half-breed. Even her mother often spoke about how they were living in a human community because Grelf would not be accepted in the elven.

So, Plague shifted... not just through time to Grelf's next moment, but she now reflected the strength that Grelf already possessed and became the visage of Introspect. Grelf's mother had just told her that she was going to be married off and her father's sword, which was the only thing left of Gregor in the house, and Grelf's birthright, was going to be used to sell her off because no one wanted a half-breed. She could sense Grelf's pain and her feeling that what she wanted didn't matter, nor did she. Introspect took a deep breath and sang to Grelf; *Nothing hurts more than the words of those you love, when what they say harms you, if you let them fester within. Locked away from the light, sometimes sadness and pain win.* Introspect saw that Grelf could see her so she added, *But I wonder what would happen if you found that power within you and chose to live and not just exist. Instead of their truth, what if you spoke yours?* The music kept building and Grelf moved to it. She spoke out and stood her ground against her mother's demands.

Introspect could feel Grelf's power beginning to build. She encouraged her to continue and sang from her heart as Grelf let go of her fears and began to make her choices about whose truths dictated who she was. Introspect was now feeding on Grelf as was Grelf feeding on her and together they began to grow stronger with every step she took.

Grelf was now accomplishing more than she thought possible. She had had many arguments with her mother over the years, but she had always had her father to fall back on or protect her if her mother got too angry. Now she had to do it alone, blaming her mother for her father's death, she stood her ground.

Introspect moved with Grelf toward the front door. *Have faith.* The sound of her voice held strength and power, but she could have been humming for all Grelf knew. The words were just the vehicle in which a perfect connection of mind, heart, and soul could be established. It was the pure encouragement and support of the thoughts and emotions behind the words that Grelf was hearing and feeling in her soul. *Don't try to be brave. Be the person you were meant to be. You have always been brave enough.* Grelf reached up over the doorway, reclaimed her birthright, and walked away from being her mother's dutiful daughter. Introspect's song burst with triumph and power as the song moved into the chorus and together, they walked away from Grelf's childhood and stepped into being an adult. Introspect was singing the truth that was pouring from Grelf's heart.

There was time to shift and Introspect moved forward from that moment and took her place as Insight standing next to Grelf as Iron-Tusk emerged from his cave. She could feel the fear and doubt in Grelf's heart as the Orc that killed her father advanced toward her.

Insight reminded Grelf; *everybody feels fear when stared down by the enemy.* She moved behind Grelf while she sang, *everyone has that moment of fight, flight, or fawn when the only thing you want to do is shrink away from the moment and the fear, and just relent to it.* Grelf quickly surveyed her surroundings, which was the dry riverbed with high walls all around her, leaving nowhere to run. If Grelf was going to survive this moment she was going to have to fight. Insight reached out and held Grelf in place singing, *there are some moments when you can't run.*

Grey Bards can connect to anyone who has relented to the music. We call it the Dance Floor and it works like an area effect spell. Anyone who relents to the Grey Bard's song can be compelled to dance in a style that would suggest that they are backup dancers for the performance. It's usually all good fun.

There have been large events where one Grey Bard got twelve hundred people to do the same dance in unison. It is often used in dance parties or even to teach individuals how to dance when they normally have two left feet. Insight used the Grey Bard's ability to create a connection through her song to tap into Grelf's mind and link the two of them so that they could move in harmony together. As she did, she sang, *maybe there's a way out of this cage. Maybe this is not as hopeless as it looks.*

Insight smiled as the connection to the future queen was created, but now it was up to Grelf. She had to make the first move to complete the connection. As a scare tactic, Iron-Tusk moved right up to Grelf and leaned in so that he could be nose-to-nose with her. *Show me,* Insight sang, and then with power crooned louder, *how brave you can be!*

In a single swift motion, she drew her father's sword which surprised not only Grelf but Iron-Tusk when it cut through his neck. There wasn't a lot of power, but it was deep enough to panic the giant Moon-Orc who backhanded Grelf flinging her away from him.

The connection was now complete and as Insight entered the second chorus she began to dance to the music, using her ability to match the reflection of any force and every attack that the Moon Orc used, Insight and Grelf parried and dodged strike after strike, the entire time Insight continued to sing and tell her that she wanted Grelf to not just speak her truth but live it.

Among the Continuum, we have a phrase, yes, there is a difference between knowing the path and walking the path, as well, there is a difference between walking the path and being it. She had walked her path, and it had brought her to this event. Now that she was there at the moment, it was time to be it. Insight and Grelf spun around Iron-Tusk and knocked him to the ground. Grelf leaped up as Insight and lyrics burst from her mouth, *I want to see you be your path!* As she did, Grelf declared herself the Orc-Slayer and plunged her father's sword into the Moon-Orc.

Insight shifted again and now Grelf and Reflection were standing in the cave of the Phoenix. She turned Grelf toward the path and as she did, The Goddess of Death and Life made a gesture with her hand and the ghosts of Grelf's mother and father appeared on each side of the curtain of molten magma that she now had to face.

Reflection could feel Grelf's hesitance as if the idea of speaking to her long-dead parents was more frightening than walking through a wall of lava. The song became gentle as she turned toward Grelf, *you have spent years in silence. Holding your pain locked away, with no chance of escape that its only choice is to rot and fester. Has your silence helped you in any way?* Grelf looked to Reflection with tears in her eyes. *Did you think it would?*

Grelf shook her head and as tears rolled down her face she said, "But I have no idea what to say to them."

Reflection had gotten Grelf to the edge of being strong enough to do what she had to do, but once again, it was up to Grelf to take the first step. *Tell them anything...everything. Speak with the weight of the truth in your heart.* Reflection hugged her from behind and then let her go. *Why don't you tell them the truth?*

After that Grelf didn't hear what Reflection was saying. She knew the words now and as the final chorus started Grelf began walking toward her destiny.

"Mother. For years I have blamed you for everything. Father's death and your image of who I was and was supposed to be. I understand now that you were just reflecting on the image you had of yourself, and the only reason you never wanted more for me was because you could not imagine more, even for yourself. You did the best you could."

The ghost of her mother could not speak. It was still in pain from her mortal life, but flashes began to appear in Grelf's mind. She saw a terrified woman in fear for her family. Flashes of fear as the orc knocked down the love of her life whom she was sure she was about to lose. The fear turned to crippling regret as she blamed her daughter, then it tripled as she watched the man she loved die, and in her heart, she knew it was her fault. Fueled by guilt and shame until she could no longer admit to it... even to herself. Then Grelf felt the years of shame as she tried to live with the knowledge that she had killed not only her husband but also believed she was to blame for her daughter's assured death. She eventually took her own life due to the grief and it was only after death she learned that her daughter still lived, by Gregor who had waited for her.

"I forgive you." Grelf meant it and could feel her soul let go of the pain and anger that she had held on to for so many years. "I want you to know I have found my way, and I have become more than you could possibly have imagined."

Her mother teared up at hearing those words, and for the last time, spoke to her daughter. "From this side of life and death, know that I see you. I have watched you grow, and I understand all that I could not when I was alive. I am proud of you, my daughter."

Grelf was already halfway there as she turned her attention away from her mother and gave it to her father who smiled and said she was the bibitz. "I have spent my whole life trying to live up to being your daughter. I have worked so hard so that you would be proud of me."

Gregor blew her a kiss and said, "I am with you always Grelf, and am so proud of you."

Grelf acted like she caught his kiss with both hands and then placed them both over her heart. "This is what I must let go of, isn't it? Living my life in the shadow of what you both expected of me. I understand that now. Know that I love you both, but now I must stop living my life through your eyes and start seeing it through my own." She was close enough that she was almost parallel with them, at the edge of the curtain of lava but she never slowed down.

"I am so proud of you," Gregor said as tears rolled down his face.

Grelf turned her head and gave her attention to her estranged mother. "Mother... Father." She looked at the curtain of lava that was directly in front of her. Her last words were "I'm ready."

...

The only saving grace was that the moment that Grelf hit the lava, all her nerves were instantly burned away and at first it only felt like extreme cold, but as she took her second step everything changed. She tried to scream but as she breathed in to do so, she flash-fried her lungs and started burning from the inside as well.

The lava itself was thick and didn't act like water. As it poured from Grelf's head like sludge, her hair caught fire, burning to nothing before she completed her second step. She had tilted her head down, so she was able to see for about three seconds once she cleared the curtain of fire and molten rock. Her face was burned but it was her head and back that took the worst of it. Her clothes ignited and began to burn her entire body.

The last thing Grelf saw before her eyes went cloudy and began to melt out of her skull was the Fire Blade just two steps past where she was. The lava that was still on her was burning the top half of her, but her legs were still functioning. Everything was getting hazy and she all but forgot what was happening. The pain was intense, but the heat was also cooking her brain, and everything was going dark. The pain was more than her body could take, she was past shock and was shutting down completely.

Yet, she could still hear the music and Reflection singing. She took another step, and her life flashed before her mind's eye ending with Grelf the mighty Orc-Slayer dying for something she believed in. Something greater than herself. She died the hero she had always strove to become and her death was a death that all true heroes wish for. Grelf the Orc-Slayer died saving the world.

Then from somewhere deep within her soul, the Fire Princess of Venger took one more step and claimed The Fire Blade.

...

Meanwhile, her Vengerian Guardians were freed from their frozen state. Becky screamed and tried to run to Grelf, but the pathway sunk back into the glowing pool of lava that covered the floor. She reached for her Vengerian Pin and opened a telepathic connection, but Grelf did not connect from the other side.

Becky's face grew stern, and she grabbed her sky-blades as she headed toward the edge, intending to try and get to Grelf, but Travis held her back while he pleaded with her. "Oubliette, think it through. Either she made it, and everything is fine or she's dead." She pulled at his arm trying to get him to let go. "Becky please!" He paused for a moment as he let her make her choice. "I can't lose you like this." Becky turned back to Travis and threw herself into his arms in tears.

Sir Adam just stood on the shore of fire, staring at the place where Grelf went in. "Come on." He muttered to himself under his breath. "Come on. You got this. These are the moments... these are the moments." As Grelf emerged back through the lava he leaped into the air, threw both fists up, and screamed, "These are the moments we live for!"

As Grelf emerged she was whole. All her burns and wounds were gone, and she wore red and purple armor made of the finest leather. Her hair looked as if it were made of living fire which matched the blade of the weapon she carried. They both flickered and danced with her movements as she walked. She wore a gold tiara that was encrusted with rubies that matched the hilt of the flame blade that she wielded in her right hand. As she walked to them, she walked on top of the lava as if it were a solid floor.

Reflection finished her song and as the music stopped, I was standing there once again. I looked at Phoenix and said, "That was a nice thing you did, letting her folks see that moment." She gave me a small grin and a nod. And then I turned back to the team and began to hoot and holler with them as they cheered and celebrated Grelf's victory. As she reached the shore, I gave her a bow and said, "Your Highness." And for the first time, Grelf didn't shrink from it.

Sir Adam turned to me and asked, "Don't you mean Your Majesty?"

It was Travis who answered him. "No, Will is right, the Fire Blade is retrieved by the Princess of Venger. She won't officially be queen until she claims the Earth Blade."

"That may be so," said Sir Adam, "but that was the bravest thing I have ever seen anyone do and you are more a queen than anyone I have ever met."

Grelf smiled and said, "Thank you, Sir Adam. I take that as a compliment of the highest caliber."

Sir Adam took a knee. "I meant every word." Grelf asked him to get up and when he did, he said, "Ready to go for the Earth Blade?"

Grelf's eyes widened a bit, and she put her hand on

Sir Adam's shoulder. "Sir Adam. I know without question that throughout my time as Queen, I will never find another like you, and your faith in me gives me the strength to continue. That said, I have just saved the world tonight." She patted him on the shoulder and looked at the Fire Blade. "I will save it again tomorrow."

Getu found them all places to sleep that night. Grelf contacted Christoph to share the news of her victory. The evening ended with a visit from Christoph, and Grelf asked not to be disturbed for the night. Sir Adam understood and took the opportunity to get some well-earned rest.

...

Becky and Travis said that they were going for a walk, after everything they had experienced, they needed to be alone. They walked together hand in hand and strolled along the shore, bathed in starlight. They found the beach they had passed when they first arrived and decided to use their pins to change into their swimwear and took a swim in the water that sparkled and shined like the stars that watched over them from above.

Travis was standing chest-deep when Becky swam up to him and clung to him in the water. They held each other as the waves rocked them back and forth with their motion, taking each other in. Becky pressed closer against Travis as the next wave hit them, and she could feel his intent was the same as hers.

"Are you with me?" Her lips were so close to his that they brushed them as she spoke. She kissed him and although they were in the ocean the only thing Travis noticed was how wet her mouth was as she kissed him, and the sensation of the air on his moist lips once the kiss was over.

With one arm he held her close by her lower back, and with his other, he supported her head. He closed his hand around her hair firmly as he peered into her eyes and spoke. "You are my goddess."

"And you are mine." She kissed him again. "Let me worship you at my temple."

He held her close as the next wave hit them, and he was sure what she meant by how she held him back. "I love you, Becky. All of you."

"I love you too." No more words were said nor were they needed. They made love that night. They let go of their worry and doubt and gave of themselves as they had seen Atula and Tongo do and poured their souls into every motion. The universe moved. True love was created and when they were done, they held each other close and laughed as they lay there together under the stars.

16

BROTHERS OF PEACE AND TRUTH

Christoph had been gone for a few hours before Dalen Pax and Master Peace arrived at the shore of the Northern Sea. Toomba had brought them back to the same village he had met them in because it was the closest location to one of the White Trees of Travel. Dalen thought about moving on from there, but something Christoph said had stuck with him.

Master Peace and Dalen were there to ensure his safety and support him so he could reach the trial, knowing that the trial itself would be solely for him. Supporting someone on their journey and making the journey for them were two different things so Master Peace and Dalen had agreed to wait for him. They said their goodbyes to Toomba and told him he should make his way to Venger sometime, but not until all this was over. They told him that an event was going to happen in eight days and that it wouldn't be safe until afterward. Then they waved goodbye and made their way to the White Tree.

Dalen used his magic and created a couple of benches with a table between them filled with food and drink and the two of them sat down to talk while they waited for Christoph.

They talked for hours about their experiences at the Brotherhood of Light. They laughed and reminisced about what they had learned and how they had learned it. While both had been trained in the kinetic field and both were accomplished martial artists, they were trained by different teachers toward different goals. Dalen had been trained to truly harness the physical elements of Earth, Air, Water, and Fire, and how to flow with each as a foundation for understanding how magic can flow through a practitioner. Master Peace had a different path. He was trained in the same disciplines of flow but also taught how to move his energy or ki, not to create spells but to be used in the mystic arts of healing.

Their conversations covered much, and both were open vessels for knowledge. Neither of them argued with the other trying to explain why their way was different or better. Rather, both accepted each other's truth as a new way to see their own. By the time Christoph arrived, they had decided to become each other's pupils. They believed that with time and effort, they could learn from each other, both growing because of it. Dalen suggested that each night before bed he bring time to a near standstill so that they could spend hours on their training. While at the Brotherhood of Light, they had become accustomed to the hours of training, and both missed it. They knew there would be a learning curve but also knew that once each of them understood how their styles were the same, they would be able to overcome how their styles were different.

Christoph smiled at them in a way that suggested that his night went well with Grelf but never mentioned where he had been all that time or what he had been doing. Instead, he put one hand on each of their shoulders and simply said, "She did it."

They cheered and celebrated. Dalen had always believed that she would pass but it was good to hear. Master Peace asked what her trial was, and Christoph regaled them with his version of what had happened.

They could tell that he was tired, from his perspective he had spent the night with Grelf, but here it was still a few hours before dusk. "One of the problems with teleporting all over the world," Christoph mentioned. "It's why we decided to make some rules."

"Rules?" Dalen could see a stitch in time forming and he was fascinated. He allowed his eyes to see the way Dorn had shown him. It was hard to see it at first but then the weavings of the fabric of time and magic appeared before him.

"Yeah." Christoph yawned. "We initially split because we only had so much time and had to get to each place, but with the abilities of our friend Dalen Pax, we can teleport to each other when we want to. I know that it was not your plan, but I overheard you talking. You did not sever your connection with me before the two of you had your conversation about why you were waiting here for me, and how this was my journey and not yours." Both monks began to try and explain but Christoph held up his hand and said, "You were absolutely right. This is going to be how it is for thousands of years right?" Dalen and Master Peace nodded. "Each time someone has to do this, which no doubt will be hundreds of times, the individual goes with their Vengerian Guardians, but is never accompanied by their other half, right?"

Dalen started to see the stitch form deeper into time. "Gavin showed no sign that he was planning on going when we took Hope, but I assumed it was because someone had to stay behind and watch the throne."

"We also met the Vengerian Guardians who were going to protect Princess Joanna, and there was no talk of one of her parents going with her." Master Peace added.

Christoph seemed to be amused at their answers. "Now why would you suppose that is?" He folded his arms and leaned in. "If my daughter were about to do anything like what I just did and Grelf went through, you can bet your bibitz that I would want to come with her. Especially since I know what they would face. I met Gavin. I like him. I respect him. He would never willingly 'let' harm come to his wife or daughter, so why? Why wouldn't he go?"

Master Peace closed his eyes and nodded, as Dalen spoke the words that he was thinking. "Tradition."

"Exactly!" Christoph clapped his hands. "I was alone during my first trial and so was Grelf. We know this to be part of it, but the other blade bearers never go with them. It must be for a reason. Then I overheard your conversation about waiting for me because it was my quest and not yours and it hit me."

"You realize you are creating the reason as we speak, right?" Dalen asked as he watched the stitch become real.

Christoph thought about it for a moment and then chuckled to himself. "I guess you're right, but that doesn't mean I am wrong. From here on in, the only contact and communications that can be made will be with the Vengerian Guardians who are with us on 'our' quest. Grelf and I decided together." Christoph smiled and almost got misty-eyed. "It was our first decision together as the Royal Bloodline of Venger."

Dalen watched as the stitch in time became permanent. "Congratulations, you just made history." Nobody got the joke except Dalen, both Master Peace and Christoph took it as the statement suggested, that he and Grelf had created the first Vengerian decree together, but Dalen understood how much more profound that moment was.

"So, no more bouncing back and forth? You and Grelf are not going to know the fate of each other until you meet back up in Venger eight days from now?" Master Peace had worded it to make sure that Christoph understood what he was setting in motion.

"That's right," Christoph said with a swagger. "We already said our goodbyes and we know there is a chance that we will never see each other again, but we will have to act on faith that the other person is succeeding."

"You have to have faith in your partner if you are going to trust them to rule your world." Master Peace's words found their mark in Christoph's core as a truth, and he was sure the monk was right.

"Well said Master Peace." Christoph blinked at him a few times. "That might be your best one yet."

Dalen remembered that the day they first arrived in Venger, Lady Venger told Master Peace that he was responsible for many of the philosophies that the city lived by. He had watched as that stitch in time formed around him. He also recalled how afterward Brother Peace confessed to his friends that the idea of it frightened him. At the time, he could not see himself as someone who could provide such wisdom. Then Dalen's memory moved forward past the Tree of Sorrow where Brother Peace became Master Peace and then thought about the moment when they first arrived in Venger's throne room. Almost everything that Master Peace had uttered since then was something that the team took with them.

"Master Peace. I want to tell you something and I hope that you will hear me." Master Peace turned to Dalen who watched as Peace took a breath and eagerly listened. "You have my respect, Ben. You continue to be someone who I am proud to stand by. We are fortunate to have you with us brother."

Dalen stood up and began the Bow of Respect. Master Peace was honored by Dalen's words and knew the bow that Dalen was performing. Master Peace slowly and with purpose gave the Bow of Thanks, also from the Brotherhood of Light. He stood with his feet shoulder-width apart. With both hands, he reached out and then focused his ki. He pulled in with his arms and hands and as he did, he pulled with all his might, drawing inward to the core of his being.

As Master Peace pulled in with his ki, Dalen used his focus and ki to build a charge. He moved his hands around as if they were on opposite sides of a ball. The ball itself was the energy of his ki building. Dalen focused his ki deeper and stronger, which gave it more power, causing it to visibly illuminate. As Master Peace began to pull his arms inward and open himself to an inward flow, Dalen connected his thoughts and emotions to his energy ball and made it harmonize with the vibrations of his heart, giving it a brighter glow. Now that the energy matched the thoughts of respect and admiration flowing from his heart, he sent it outward toward Master Peace.

The light touched Master Peace, he pulled it into his Heart Chakra and held it close to his soul. It filled him with the respect that Dalen had offered him, which was almost overwhelming. Together Master Peace and Dalen breathed, taking alternate turns with their breaths. As Dalen breathed out Master Peace breathed in, switching back and forth effortlessly. They both inhaled and exhaled deeply and slowly and on the next breath, Master Peace harmonized the energy with his own thoughts and feelings of gratitude and thanks. He understood all that Dalen had meant. To have the boy that he had bullied and tortured be able to stand and say all that he did, and to truly feel the respect, somewhere deep inside of Master Peace, Ben found something more than peace. He found closure and resolution. He had no words, so instead of creating a thought, he just focused on the feeling of perfect peace and harmony, with all his demons at rest.

Dalen was still projecting his ki and was holding nothing back, allowing his soul to push into this connection with the same amount of heart that Queen Hope gave to the Mother Tree. He felt Master Peace's energy change, so he released all his energy and at the end of his breath was left feeling spent.

Master Peace had built up the energy with his ki until it began to glow and at the end of his breath, he pushed from the center of his being and returned his thanks, gratitude, and love. As he did Dalen breathed in and pulled with all his strength. The connection was strong, and the light began to fill Dalen in all the same ways he had given.

This did not deplete Master Peace, no more than a candle taking light from another as it is lit by the first. Together they just stood in the light of each other. They stared with warm grins on their faces locked into each other's eyes. Now and then one of them would widen their smile and then they would both nod.

"Should I leave you two alone?" Both Master Peace and Dalen remembered that Christoph was there. "I don't mean that to come out the way it sounds, and I apologize for that."

Master Peace was still in the glow of everything and with no defensiveness or malice he asked, "Then what is it that you mean to say? Brother Truth and I will do our best to understand."

"It's the eye. The center stone of the Water Blade is the All-Seeing Eye of the Present. I don't know what I just witnessed but I know that you once were enemies, but the last glint of the memory is gone from my sight because it is now in your past and no longer either of your truths in the present." Christoph fell to his knees as tears of emotion flowed from him. "I saw it. I saw the whole thing for what it was at that moment. I felt you. I felt you both, and I am aware of how much both of you mean to each other." Christoph tried to catch his breath but there was no use. He was in some sort of vision state now and the information was flowing into his body, his mind, and his soul. "I can't see the fight. I can't see how you were enemies because it's in the past, but I can see that today you are brothers, and either of you would stand before the Chaos Dragon herself and tell her where she could stick it if it meant standing with each other. In all my life I have only seen a bond as strong as the one you two have made, maybe a handful of times, and how you made it may be the most beautiful thing I have ever seen."

Dalen helped Christoph up. "It seems that the wielder of the Water Blade is imbued with certain... gifts."

Master Peace was on Christoph's other side helping him to his feet as well. "If you wish to wield the Water Blade you will first have to wield its power." Master Peace drew his Dragon Claw. He did not extend the chain but just held it like a rod. "Many of the Brotherhood of Light consider this weapon to be a sign of great power, and that anyone who wields one is near unbeatable. This has been known to confuse many who do not comprehend how the weapon truly works. I am not empowered by my weapon; my weapon is empowered by me." A ball of light ignited from the Dragon Claw. "It is empowered by my faith." As he spoke the ball of light grew from the size of a fist to slightly larger than a watermelon and turned a bright deep orange resembling a small sun on the end of his weapon. "With this, I can cause great pain and suffering." The ball turned pure white. "Or heal almost any wound." The light changed to blue. "And cure illness." The light flickered out and Master Peace put his tool away. "There are many things I can use this tool for, but in each case, I had to learn how to wield it, so that the power wasn't wielding me like the Water Blade is wielding you now. We know you can wield a blade, of that, there is no question. The question will be can you wield the power of the Water Blade, and will you see it as a weapon or a tool."

"You are right Master Peace." Christoph had regained his senses and the visions had stopped. "If that happened during battle it could mean the death of me. I will have to learn to control it as a tool, not a weapon." Christoph thought about it for a moment. "Well, also a weapon. I saw Blizzard practice with it once or twice and he could make the blade change shape to be any weapon he wanted. I believe you, Master Peace." He drew the Water Blade and looked at it closely. I am going to have to learn much more than I thought." The eye in the sword gave off a small indigo glow for a moment, and Christoph smirked at it. "And all the things that I will have to master, I will need as skills to be King."

272

Christoph just stared at the Water Blade for a moment and then blinked a couple of times. "Anyway." Christoph sheathed the sword and continued from one awkward conversation to another. "So, what I saw made me think that you two might need some time to talk privately."

Dalen stopped him there. "Not a bit of it." Dalen gave a small push off the ground and began to hover about knee-high. "What you witnessed was personal, but at the same time not private."

"You are respected by both of us." Master Peace added. "What you saw was not uncommon in the Brotherhood of Light. Often this is done from student to teacher, but also happens between the brothers from time to time. It's a sign of understanding and respect."

Christoph took a step back and pondered for a moment. "That's how you say thank you?"

"Only when you really mean it." Master Peace said and then he and Dalen gave each other five down low, and then as they gave each other five on the side they stopped with their palms touching and then slid into a galaxy and then pointed at each other.

Christoph gave them a moment and then asked, "Alright then what's next?"

Dalen flashed a smirk at Master Peace who nodded in agreement, although neither of them had specifically thought it. "Now we train."

"Train?" Christoph protested. "I am so tired. Grelf and I

tend to... talk all night, and I have gotten no rest."

"Good," Dalen said, and as he said it, it reminded him of Master Ki. "You will only train for two hours and then rest. While you sleep, I will slow time down to a crawl and you with it. During this time Master Peace and I will train as we planned. We will talk then. While we are training, your mind will do what it normally does while sleeping, and process everything it just went through including the two hours of training, imprinting it in your memory. Then after what you consider to be hours of sleep, Master Truth and I will wake you up for two more hours of training and then breakfast. I will do the best I can to have all of that happen within the next couple of minutes."

Christoph agreed to the plan but asked, "Why bend time? Why not do all of that in the normal time that it takes?"

"Two reasons honestly. The first has to do with the big giant death clock that hangs over all our heads." Dalen explained. "The second has to do with timing the jump. We want to be rested and feel refreshed as we arrive at our next location, which in a few minutes will reach mid-day."

Both of the reasons were solid, and Christoph nodded but then Master Peace added, "The third reason is that we are traveling with a time jinn, and he likes to do his time jinn thing."

Dalen looked to Christoph but pointed to Master Peace. "He's not wrong."

They joked for a moment and then went to work. It was clear that the All-Seeing Eye, as they began to call it, was affecting all of them as if its very presence allowed them to see and understand each other's perceptions. For Christoph, it was much stronger and more powerful. Dalen had experienced moments of sight as Christoph had, but Christoph now had sight as a constant companion. An untrained sight that now needed to be honed, or he would not just be a danger to himself but to anyone around him. For now, Christoph would have to do his best to wield such power on the fly as he learned. Dalen Pax and Master Peace would have to do the best they could to teach him to focus and prepare him for the mantle he would have to bear.

Christoph did as Dalen suggested and trained for a few hours working on trying to get the Water Blade to hold the shape that he wanted it to. Attempt after attempt he tried to make it take the form of a longsword, but the Water blade would not obey. He squeezed the handle extra hard and even screamed at it to change.

"What am I doing wrong?" Christoph asked after hours of fighting with the Water Blade.

"You want my opinion?" asked Dalen, "Or do you want the guy with all the good lines?"

Master Peace stood up and brushed his shoulder off with a swagger. "I think I could lend a helping hand."

Christoph looked into the eye and remembered that the more of the truth you can see the more of it you can understand. "I want to hear from both of you. Dalen Pax. Jinn of Time, what truth can you offer me?"

Dalen smiled. "You want to make a deal with a jinn?"

"Indeed, I do." Christoph stepped forward without fear. "I know your heart Master Pax, and I believe you wouldn't harm me or this quest."

Dalen raised an eyebrow. "That is a lot of faith. Are you sure I am worthy of such praise?"

"I trust you to the end of time Master Pax." Christoph watched as the stones in Dalen's body began to glow.

"All magic has a price. Just speak the words and we will pay it together." Dalen floated higher.

"Together?" asked Christoph as he prepared his thoughts to be clear about his intent.

Dalen nodded. "Yes. If I am right, I will be fine, but if not, it might go really bad for me, but don't worry, I have done this before and I survived, and that time I didn't even know it was coming."

Master Peace looked up at Dalen with surprise, "You are going to drink from the fountain again, aren't you?"

"Yes." Dalen admitted, "I know that I end up drinking from it often. That last time...last time doesn't count, I wasn't ready, and I was using it for myself, I think it will be different if I am answering his wish."

"Why?" Master Peace crossed his arms and waited for an answer.

"I don't know. I think it has to do with the point that I am a jinn and granting wishes." Dalen pulled his cup from his small pocket dimension that he kept his things in and activated it and it filled with a clear viscous fluid. "And this may sound corny..." He looked at his brother and laughed, "I have faith that I can do it."

"Alright, Brother Truth." Master Peace prepared himself to heal Dalen as he had done before. "If you have faith, you can do it, I have faith in you."

"What happened last time?" Christoph got between them with concern. "What's the price?"

"When activated this cup stays full of whatever it was last filled with. The last thing I filled it with was the Fountain of Truth. The last time I tried drinking from it, I almost died." Dalen looked at the cup closely. "One of the reasons I do not call myself Master Truth is because I have not mastered the ability to perceive it. Once I can master drinking from this, I will accept the title of Master."

"How did it almost kill you?" Christoph put his hand over the cup. "I do not like the idea of you risking your life to answer my request."

"As King you will often request people to put their lives on the line. You better get used to that now." Master Peace had no reservations about being blunt.

"Sure. When it's needed." Christoph turned and faced Master Peace. "As King, I will have to order people to their death. I understand that it will be a part of the weight I must bear but this is not required."

"Agreed," added Master Peace, "but there are two things to consider. The first is that you did not order him to do it, and I even warned against it. This is something he feels he needs to do. The second is, as soon as you turned to face me, he drank."

Christoph turned back to Dalen and saw that Master Peace was right. Dalen was already beginning to drop to his knees. "What have you done?"

"I have chosen to grant your wish. I am about to know what you must do to wield the Water Blade." Dalen's eyes began to flutter, and his breathing was forced.

"Stay with me, Dalen." Christoph shook Dalen a little. "This was a bad idea."

Master Peace was at Dalen's other side and ready to do what was needed, but he directed his attention to Christoph and said, "He doesn't need you to tell him why this won't work, he needs you to back him as he faces the hardest thing there is to do."

Christoph looked up at him questioningly. "What is that?"

"The impossible." Master Peace held one of Dalen's hands and began to build his ki and both he and Christoph held Dalen as he relented to the power of the Fountain of Truth.

17

A TASK IMPOSSIBLE

TO FAIL

"Water. Not just the substance, but the concept of it as an element, and the way one can be of it. Body. Mind. Soul. Where all elements can be seen as forms of change such as fire... the bringer of new things, and earth, with its ever-changing patterns, water is the element that changes form and aspect by being both the thing it was and, the thing it changed into. Like a hand that becomes a fist, although it changed form and is now a fist, it is still a hand."

The voice came from everywhere and filled Dalen's mind with memories. "Water can change its form too. Put it into a cylindrical cup and it will be cylindrical. Pour it into a hollow cube and it becomes a cube. It takes the form of its environment. When its environment gets too hot it changes form and becomes a gas; if it gets too cold it becomes a solid, yet both are still water, whether ice or steam. These are just different forms of one element, two sides of the form, both of which are true. Like your coin, which has two completely different sides, each equally as true as the other."

Dalen looked around and recognized that he was in the courtyard of one of the temples of the Brotherhood of Light, it had been carved out of the rock behind the Falls of Birth. As part of his training, he was brought here every day to learn the basics, such as the rules that the brotherhood had and the philosophies they adhered to. Master Ki's voice echoed off the rock making it sound as if they were in a large cathedral.

"That is the nature of it. The concept of water within itself is a myriad of concepts that ebb and flow to the environment, but now the environment is the point of view of the individual and what is being perceived. It can be seen as the substance that changes, or as a concept of how oneself changes. Both are true but different. This is just a reflection of its ability to change. Without it, people would die quickly, and though it has been called the liquid of life, drink too much of it and it can kill you. Submerge yourself in it and it becomes death." Master Ki's voice became quiet, forcing Dalen to listen closely. "Again, two completely different aspects of an element that are each true. That example is just another aspect of water reflecting the same idea that I have been talking about with each different example I've given."

Dalen remembered this day clearly. It was one of the first times he began to learn the Path of Truth. He had made an offhand comment to his teacher, Brother Faith, about stepping in the same water twice. It was a cool, wise-sounding thing, he had heard once in a movie, but his teacher decided that his comment was a wonderful place to start, so Dalen had been tasked with understanding the true nature of the question. Could one step on the same water twice? Brother Faith suggested that both yes and no were a correct answer. Dalen was then tasked with understanding how that was possible. "The mind, the persona of the self, it moves like water. One person could be a father, son, brother, friend, and foe all at once. That persona is shaped by those who perceive them. To their children they are fathers, and to their fathers they are sons. Controlled by the environment. By the container that holds it. The observation of others." Master Ki's voice continued to echo in the temple and then faded. The next time he spoke, his voice seemed directly in front of Dalen. "Again, another aspect of the element. You can move like water on all three spheres, which in itself reflects itself. Like every aspect of itself I have mentioned."

Dalen was in a large pool with the water level about waist high. His teacher, Master Ki, had taken his water form and was hiding somewhere in the pool. In this state, he was made of water, and his stones of power were not visible, so as he submerged in the water, there was no way to discern him from the pool.

He was tasked to tag Master Ki once. Master Ki would pop up a distance from Dalen, scoop up a ball of water, and hit him with it. As Dalen tried to push through the water Master Ki would dunk himself in the water and move to a new location, blending perfectly with the pool, remaining undetected. Then he would rise out of the water and hit Dalen with another water ball. It had been going on for some time now and Dalen was worried that it could still be quite some time before he would be able to tag Master Ki.

"Once you go into the water I can't see you. How is this fair?" Dalen swung around and looked for where he thought Master Ki would emerge.

"You're right." Master Ki's voice came from behind him. Dalen turned quickly and leaped forward to get Master Ki, who wasn't there. Just then a ball of water came from the direction he had just been looking. "It's not fair." Dalen got back on his feet and was ready to jump again. A liquid form of Master Ki was emerging from the water, playfully tossing a water ball up and down. "I gave you a task you couldn't possibly fail." Dalen leaped for him again and Master Ki dropped back into the pool, but not before throwing the ball of water in Dalen's face as he advanced.

Dalen screamed. After a few breaths, he looked around, with frustration soaking him more than the pool. Quickly he turned again and asked "What are you talking about? What is this? Some sadistic full-contact word problem?"

"All of life can be seen as a full contact word problem." Master Ki laughed and hurled another ball of water at Dalen from across the pool, hitting him square in the face and splashing up his nose, sending him spurting and coughing. "But it's not sadistic. I mean. Sure, I am having a lot of fun with this, but not because I want to see you suffer."

"Dalen did his best to run toward Master Ki but running in water was difficult at best. "Oh yeah? Then why?"

"Two reasons." Master Ki hurled another water ball at Dalen from across the pool. This time Dalen put up his hands and covered his face in time to block the water ball, but when he brought them down again Master Ki was right in front of him. Dalen was surprised and gasped at the sight of him. As he did Master Ki placed a water ball in Dalen's mouth, and he began to choke. "I love teaching really." Master Ki dropped down just in time to dodge Dalen's wild swing at him while he coughed. Master Ki popped back up about ten feet away.

"Secondly... How is this...," Master Ki reached out with his arm, and it extended like a tentacle until it stopped an inch from Dalen's nose. "...not fun?" Like an index finger, the tentacle extended the last of the distance and touched Dalen's nose. "Boop." The moment that it touched Dalen it turned back into water and fell with a splash leaving Master Ki with a normal-sized arm again.

Dalen let out another frustrated scream. His anger was flaring, and his frustration was palpable. "You move too fast, and I am hindered by the water. It's not fair and there is no way I can catch you."

"Wow." Master Ki rose from the water again, but this time he took a more physical shape. And the power stones in his body, hands, and feet began to glow. Waves of light projected on the walls and ceiling as the light from his stones sent ripples from his ever-moving body. "You went from shifting the blame away from yourself to saying it was rigged, to saying it was impossible, all in one breath." He cocked his head to one side quizzically. "How's that working for you?"

Master Ki hadn't directly scolded him, but Dalen realized Master Ki was right. He took a breath and tried to calm down. "I'm frustrated and I'm mad and I'm completely miserable."

"Then stop doing that. It's not working for you." Master Ki scooped up a water ball and began to casually roll it up and down his arm.

"Stop what?" Dalen asked because he still did not understand.

"Stop trying to work so hard to not do the work. Stop trying to force your perspective." Master Ki had only been working with Dalen for a couple of weeks and was still trying to be gentle with him.

Dalen had been practicing the idea of being able to see more than one side of truth. He had recently learned his first real lesson, which had to do with understanding that the truth was much like a coin. Each side was different, but they were the same coin. He pulled the Initiates Coin from his belt. It was silver and bore the symbols of magic that he was learning. Flipped over and it was the Master's Coin, gold with the head of a dragon.

"There is something here that I am missing." Master Ki nodded. "Whatever it is I am missing, it's obscuring my view of the truth?" Dalen asked.

Master Ki nodded again. "The reverse could be said as well. Your view of the truth is obscuring you from seeing the thing you are missing."

Dalen didn't feel like a master at that moment and turned his coin back over. "How am I supposed to know what I am not seeing, if I can't see it?"

Master Ki held out a ball of water. "By paying attention to what is going on around you and not just assuming you know what it means. Stop looking at it from such a narrow point of view." Master Ki's lights began to get brighter. "Be like water. Allow yourself to see more than just one drop in the ocean."

"What am I supposed to see?" asked Dalen. He had gotten himself refocused and did his best to pay attention.

Master Ki tilted his hand and let the water ball slip from his fingers and drop back into the water. Dalen watched it fall and stared when it submerged and waited for something to happen. After a few moments, he looked to Master Ki for help.

Master Ki shrugged and asked, "Where did it go?"

Dalen looked back at the water and then back to Master Ki. "What do you mean?"

"Dalen." Master Ki reached into the shape of his tunic and pulled out a cup made of water and took a sip from it. "Would you agree that this all started when you asked if it was possible to step in the same water twice, and then that question led you to how you gained your coin?"

Dalen had been there for two weeks, but he had already learned to be weary of agreeing with Master Ki, yet in this case, he was correct. "Yes."

"Good. If we agree on that, would we also agree that once you learned that lesson, I tasked you with this one?" Again, Dalen timidly agreed. "Good. Then if we agree, I will expect you to use that lesson here. If I ask you a specific question it is because the answer will hopefully lead you to the understanding that allows you to change your point of view from, this being a sadistic torture that you cannot win, to a lesson that ends with the acceptance that in the task I have set before you, there is no possible way to fail?" Master Ki chuckled to himself as he took another sip from his cup. "As you and I both have said, this test is unfair."

This is why Dalen didn't like to agree with Master Ki. It always ended with everything being up to Dalen and all the responsibility for his actions and thoughts left in his hands. He nodded. Master Ki put away his cup and allowed himself to take the form of water again. He scooped up another ball from the pool and held it out. He dropped it, but by the time it hit the surface of the water, and he had turned his empty hand back over, a new ball had formed, the same way the tentacle had formed from his arm. He dropped the second ball too, which promptly reproduced in the palm of his hand.

Dalen understood that Master Ki was just moving and shaping water. He was pulling up water from the pool and because

Master Ki was made of it, he was just shaping it how he chose. Dalen explained his thought process and Master Ki agreed. He explained that he didn't have to scoop up a ball, he could just form one anywhere he wanted because the water was all one form. Master Ki turned his hand again and let another ball of water fall into the pool.

Master Ki showed that both of his hands were empty, and then asked, "Now. Where is the ball?"

Dalen had to think about it. He knew that Master Ki could create one at will but where was it while it wasn't a ball? It was like asking where someone's fist went when they opened their hand. It was physically there, yet it had changed its shape. "It has become one with the pool."

Master Ki folded his arms. "So, what does that mean?"

Dalen thought about the original question and the truth about water. "It means that it is all of the pool because it has become one with it."

Master Ki nodded. "If that is true, then how can that knowledge be applied to this task?"

Dalen was doing his best to keep his mind clear of his thoughts, but he had not yet learned how to focus beyond his frustration and stress and all he could see was his point of view. "It means that in your water form, you are one with the water and so it is impossible to catch you because you can choose to be anywhere you want to be within the pool."

"Good!" Master Ki practically shouted it, but then he got quiet and the water that made up his body ceased its motion. "Flip the coin. What is also true?"

Dalen flipped it over and stared at the Master Coin. He asked himself clearly, "What is the opposite of that truth... Yet is still true?" Time slowed down in Dalen's mind and for a second he became distracted by a drop of water that was about to fall from his hand. In that moment it was the only thing he could see. He watched as it let go of his hand and fell. It was beautiful. Refusing to let go of that moment Dalen stretched time to almost a standstill as he watched it fall. In his mind, he saw it glow as if it were made of light and as it touched the surface of the water and was enveloped, he watched the light become a part of the entire pool and the whole thing began to glow, including the water that formed Master Ki. Dalen laughed as time began to move normally. "All I must do is tag you? Right?"

Master Ki scooped up another water ball and taunted him. "If you can."

Dalen reached one hand out and pointed down. He dropped his finger into the pool and said, "Tag."

Master Ki laughed. "This is why you will be a master one day. Because you already are. It is only when you accept this can you claim it as your own."

Then there was a great flash, and Dalen was no longer in his memory. He had just been under the control of the Fountain of Truth, his body was in pain, and he couldn't move more than a little. He looked up and saw that both Master Peace and Christoph had their eyes closed. He had activated the Eye of the Beholder before he had drunk from his cup and in this moment, they were probably seeing through his eyes.

A voice called out to Dalen, he looked toward it and saw Master Truth beckoning to him. His mind obeyed and at his summons, Dalen left his body to join his master. The pain stopped and time stood still.

"That was an ill-planned and risky move." He still looked the way that Dalen had always seen him. When they first met, he thought he was a ghost because he was completely made of smoke, but the smoke took the form of an old man with a beard wearing robes with a hood. Every morning, they would have tea and watch the sunrise, but this wasn't a memory, this was happening now.

"Yes, but it was the right one." Master Truth in all respects was Dalen himself, or at least a future version of himself, but Dalen understood that it was the aspect of his own higher consciousness that he was talking to.

Master Truth smiled. "Yes, it was."

"Master, I know that this is an illusion. I know that what I see before me is what I choose to see because I am not ready to see myself as a master. But I also know that I will not find my truth by waiting for it."

Master Truth took a sip from his cup. "Agreed."

"What must I do?" Dalen asked. "I want to take this step, but I don't know what I am truly aiming at."

Master Truth took another sip from his cup. "You will not be able to call yourself Master until you have come to the truth of who you are."

Dalen nodded. He has had much more training now than he did that day with Master Ki. He focused his mind and allowed what was said to be true. "What are the steps I will require to achieve this goal?"

"Every time you use the Fountain of Truth, you will be given one more piece of the puzzle, but be warned, it comes at a great price. Not only on your body but your mind and soul as well. Learning who you truly are is not for the meek." Master Truth took another sip from his cup. "Each time will get you closer and closer to the final revelation. It will be there, that you will find out the truth of who you are, and only then will you be able to call yourself Master Truth."

"I have two questions." Dalen had no idea if Master Truth would answer them, but this was the opportunity that he had. "Why is the question of how to save David, the most important question I will ask?"

"I am not going to give you the answer you want. I am sorry about that. The answer you seek must be learned by experiencing the moment and not by me telling you. It just won't mean the same. So, I will give you the answer I can." Master Truth took another sip from his cup and Dalen watched as answers washed over him. "As I said, you will have to train yourself to be able to withstand the power of the Fountain of Truth, the same way that Christoph will now have to train in using the eye. Each time you do you will get closer to the truth. It will be on the question of how to save David that you will reach your goal. I am sure that you understand that moment will only come after the Time Mage has been dealt with. DeSalvo put..." Master Truth smirked. "In his place."

Dalen put his hand over his heart and gave a small bow. "Thank you for that."

"You will know when it is time." Master Truth began to fade away.

"No wait...My second question. What do I do about that?" and pointed to his dying body.

Master Truth smiled and raised his cup to Dalen suggesting something deeper than Dalen could perceive in that moment. He took a sip, and said, "If only you had a way to focus your vision." He gave a small bow and with a phantom gust of wind, he was gone.

The moment Master Truth blew away Dalen was back in his body. Time was moving at full speed and his pain was unbearable. The pain snapped both Master Peace and Christoph out of their trance and they both started to try and revive Dalen.

Dalen couldn't reach his Vengerian Pin, but he hoped he could concentrate hard enough to send a message telepathically.

Eye

Christoph looked at Dalen with surprise. "I heard you." He drew the Water Blade. "What am I supposed to do?"

Dalen was exhausted and was running out of time. Twice, he tried to send, but the pain was torturous, and it took everything that Dalen had to stay conscious. On his third attempt, he focused with everything he had left and activated the stone in his third eye. Christoph put it together and touched the Eye in the Water Blade to Dalen's third eye stone. Dalen harmonized with the moment he was in, and the vision he was having in that moment. The All-Seeing eye spoke to him directly through his third eye, directly into his mind. Dalen could see himself and everything around him the way that Dorn had shown him, and when he looked at himself, he could see the strands of reality that made up not only him but the water from the Fountain of Truth. True sight on a level that Dalen did not know was possible and the eye was teaching him reflexively as it showed him the truth of that moment. He saw how and even more importantly than how, he saw why, the fountain was affecting him on a level where magic becomes intent, and intent becomes reality.

From this state, Dalen could see what needed to be done. The All-Seeing eye guided him toward the understanding he needed in the present, and how he could heal himself from within. The pain subsided as his system acclimated and adapted. Dalen smiled as he looked up at his friends. "What a ride."

18

MADDICUS OF THE BODITES

It had been four days since we had used the Quantum Compass and traveled to the closest location to the Verris Desert. We had been fortunate, and the Fire Blade had been where Blaze suggested, but it was still unknown if where we were going was the correct choice, and if it wasn't, we were running out of time.

We stopped off where we could find civilization to resupply and rest, the last place had been more than a day and a half ago. Now, we were moving toward the last beacon of civilization before entering the Verris Desert, a desolate wasteland of sand. The sharp wind created sandstorms, and the temperature could swing from sweltering heat during the day to freezing temperatures during the night. Only a sparse amount of life that had evolved to live in such a climate survived out there for long, except for nomadic people who seemed to find a way to not only survive but make the Verris Desert their home.

Our goal was a small village called Mopet, on the outskirts of the desert. We had talked to locals along the way, and they told us that Mopet was one of the only places on this side of the desert that the nomadic tribe would trade with, because it was the outpost that was furthest into the desert.

They were known as sand-folk generally, but the name of their tribe was the Bodites or Bodarians. They had their own dialect of common that seemed to be more about concept than structure. A single word could be used for many concepts, and how it was used would give it meaning. It was also explained to us that they had perfected a form of flying carpet that allowed them to travel great distances, and it was the reason they were able to live deep within the desert.

When we arrived in Mopet we discovered it was not much more than a general store that doubled as a tavern and a few other structures that were for minor requirements of travel. There was a metal worker who had a few weapons in his shop. Mainly simple blades and knives. Most of his wares were mining tools and supplies. There was an individual who was selling water. It was warm from being out in the heat, but it was clean. He said that he and his family collected the water from a spring that was on his property. The only other vendor was a woman who was selling large pieces of cloth. She demonstrated how the locals used them as wrappings to protect themselves from the elements.

We bought something from each vendor and casually began to ask questions about the area. Each of them seemed happy to talk if we were buying. We asked if there had been any Bodites here recently because we were looking to hire a guide. Each of them said that they believed that there was a young woman from the tribe in Mopet and directed us toward the tavern.

To get to the tavern and store you had to first enter a single space room that was made of sandstone and wasn't much bigger than the vendor's small rooms. The room itself was empty except for a stairway that went down. The building's main purpose was to be a structure to keep out the light and heat of the desert. As we traversed the stairs that went down three flights it was like going into a cave. The further we got away from the surface the cooler the air became and as we reached the tavern it was cool enough that the team decided to change their attire for cooler weather. I didn't care about the temperature, and I liked what I was wearing so I stayed in what I always wore.

As we walked through the door only a few people looked up. Travis counted in his head as he scanned the room. ‹I count six. Eight if you count the two behind the bar and tending shop. Out of those six, four of them are men and look more like locals than someone visiting from a nomadic tribe. One of them is wearing desert wraps over their face, but the frame doesn't suggest someone that the vendors described as a young woman. My guess is on your forward left. Young woman, with blue hair.⟩

Sir Adam followed with his eyes to where his brother suggested. ⟨Got her, and it looks like she is not alone.⟩ Two of the larger men that Travis had mentioned were sitting at a table with her.

⟨I'll see if I can't get close enough to hear them.⟩ Oubliette whispered.

Travis looked to his left where he thought Becky had been but found nothing. ⟨You just straight-up ghosted me.⟩ He scanned for her but to no avail and while he did, he switched his communication to just Becky. ⟨Okay. That was kind of hot.⟩ and then reconnected to the group.

Somewhere in the darkness, Oubliette smiled. The room was lit by large stones about the size of a man's fist that gave off light as bright as a torch. They were placed strategically around the room to create enough light to see but the atmosphere gave off a feeling of shadow. She walked right up to the table, and no one noticed a thing. With one leap and a swing, she positioned herself in the rafters directly overhead. She activated her pin so that everyone could listen in.

At first, she couldn't understand anything that was being said so Oubliette tapped her pin again and accessed its magical ability to translate what they were saying. It worked well for languages like Elven that were structured. In some cases, terms were used differently but what you would hear is an understanding of what was meant. But this girl was speaking in a way where the Vengerian Pin allowed for translation, but the words offered little meaning.

I was fascinated because she was doing something I would have never expected. She was speaking in a diminished form of Grey Speak. *Oh Brother.* I asked myself. *What have you been doing?*

I will show you when you get here. Hip-Gnosis's voice was clear, and I recognized who he was instantly. *I can't wait for you to meet them.*

I asked again but no answer came. I knew my brother well enough not to be afraid. There is no one in this world I trust more than Hip-Gnosis. In a strange twist of fate, he is one of the only people I must trust because he is one of the only people whose actions I cannot see as the narrator of this world. Whatever we were going to find in the sands of the Verris Desert, I only knew one thing for sure. It was going to be a surprise.

I focused my attention back on the moment at hand. The young woman was speaking to the two men, and from what I could tell they were trying to make a deal with her. She was sitting at the head of the table; we entered the room from her right. She was tilted back in her chair and had one leg on the table. She was wearing leather shorts with knee pads and was barefoot. She wore a matching top that kept her decent but showed her midsection and arms. Over that was a leather long coat that she had draped off her shoulders and held by her elbows, revealing a strange pack on her back. She was still wearing the sleeves, but the fabric was bunched between the elbows and wrists, allowing for the fingerless gloves she wore to still be seen. Her hair was cut slightly shorter than her shoulders and she had it swept back and out of her face by a pair of goggles she was wearing along her hairline. Her hair was faded blue, and gray, and looked more wind-swept than unkempt. Multiple strange blue lights were twinkling about a foot above her head. They would appear, then drop toward her, but fade before they reached her head, making it look like it was snowing blue light around her. Oubliette noted that from her position she could see that she also wore a necklace that was glowing the same color of blue, and the area directly around her seemed colder.

"Look, lady. I'm not trying to be difficult. I want to buy them. Three of them in fact." The first of the two men sitting with her sounded frustrated but still trying to be nice.

"We have the money." said the second. "We can pay you right now."

She looked over to the first guy and said, "Bro." Then she looked over to the other. "Bro... I'm vibing with all the things you're saying, but if you want it, you're going to have to say it. Straight up." Then she shrugged as if to say, 'Nothing can be done.'

The first man pointed to the lights and said, "Those." Then he pointed to the chain that hung around her neck and disappeared into her top. "Those."

The woman covered herself with her arms playfully. "What do you mean?"

"Come on!" The second guy pleaded. "Don't make us say that stupid name."

"Disrespect!" She reached over her head and behind her and grabbed the back of her seat, as she did, she arched her back and pushed off the table with the leg that was on it. She was as nimble as a circus performer and folded herself backward over the chair, flipping her legs over, leaving her standing behind it. She pointed at the lights and said with contempt, "These are Twinkle Freezy Lights, and you will speak their name, or you will be thirsty with no canteen."

The two men looked at each other and both held their heads down in defeat and shame. In unison, they spoke as if the words tasted bad in their mouths. "Can we have the Twinkle Freezy Lights please?"

"Bros!" Her entire mood had changed. She was no longer mad and seemed truly happy to do business with them. "That was soaring with the clouds. Y'all be glidin'." She produced three necklaces from her coat pocket, and they slid over to her a sack the size of a watermelon filled with gold. She gave a fist pump and said, "Bro. So, gliding." She handed them all three necklaces and added, "Swag."

Both men seemed relieved to have them, and they each put one on. Small blue specs of light began to appear above their heads. "Thank you Maddicus. You saved our lives and our brothers too."

"I didn't save you, bro. This sick move you swayed. You sought me out. You made a good trade and even spoke the Word of Bodi about the Twinkle Freezy Lights and then bought my stuff. You saved yourselves." They nodded, and just as they were making it past our group she called out, "You be cool!" As we approached her, she waved at the person behind the bar, when she had their attention, she held up the sack of money, pointed at herself, and then held up three fingers and pointed at the table. Once she knew the barkeep had her order she turned her attention to us. "Bet. Hours before they get the cool joke." She saw the confused looks on most of our faces and rolled her eyes, "Those charms keep you cool, even in the sun."

‹Ten crowns say she's the Bodite. Any takers?› Grelf didn't expect a response, but she loved her team more because they did.

‹Pass› Sir Adam's thought happened as easily as conversation or as if he had been ready for her to ask.

‹Hard pass› Travis was quick to pick up on signals, so he waved to the barkeep and when he had his attention, he pointed a finger and spun it in a circle in the general direction of the team. He then held up two fingers, pointed to the table, sat down with his notebook open, and continued to write.

Maddicus stared at Travis for a moment. He looked up from his notebook and gestured to her seat. She looked up at the bartender who was waiting for a signal to see if she was going to allow them to drink at her table. She did some trading here from time to time and when folk knew she was coming business was better, but when it came to people walking in from the desert, they were sometimes customers and sometimes problems. She gave him a nod and he began getting the drinks together.

‹I want a Twinkle Freezy Light.› Oubliette whispered from

her shadowy perch above the table.

‹How much is a crown?› Travis had turned to a different page in his notebook and looked over to Grelf for an answer.

While Grelf tried to explain the monetary exchange for the coins of the realm I took the seat to the right of Maddicus and started talking so hopefully we didn't look like a bunch of mutes staring at each other. "Hi. I need you to say something to me directly for this to work, so if you don't mind, hello. I am Will of Grey. Who are you?"

She flopped down into the chair and tossed her head back just a little as a gesture of hello. "Sup Bro? Maddicus. You looking to trade?"

Telling and learning stories had always been my thing. When someone spoke to me, even once, I took on the knowledge of the stories they knew. And I could speak them back to them in their native tongue. Six generations of legends and lore of the Bodite people were imparted to me. I knew every story and myth that she had ever been told around a campfire by her grandfather, and I knew of Bodi, Keeper of The Way, and the Maker of Dreams.

I didn't think about anything. I opened my mind and allowed myself to speak from my soul. "Flow. Trade's sweet." I scooted my chair in and got down to business. "Sis. We're trippin'."

Maddicus physically relaxed. "Why the sand?"

I could hear the confusion from the Vengerians and in that moment I was glad that I was not listening to them. I was only focused on Maddicus. I understood now that it was a spattering of slang and Grey Speak. It didn't have the potency of Grey Speak in the sense it would knock people over, but it was a language where slang could be understood and learned at near telepathic levels. So, it didn't matter if they knew the language, as long as it was slang, euphemism, or even colloquialism, it could be understood and the more they understood, the faster the rest of the language was telepathically picked up until they could speak to anyone within a matter of a single conversation. I decided to start with terms she knew and slowly added our own so that she would be able to understand everyone else as well. "Trying not to crash on the dunes."

She gave me a respectful nod. "Heard." The drinks came. Three shots for her and two for each of us. I tossed one back, not knowing what to expect. I winced and guessed it to be two parts cactus juice and one part lamp oil.

"We need someone who... knows the dunes and never bails. Hear you're the bibitz." I drank my other shot and regretted it as much as the first.

"The bibitz? That's gliding." Maddicus took her two shots one after the other. "You speak the Word of Bodi. I never bail. I ride those dunes like we are family. I know their heart."

"Righteous." I looked back at the rest with a smile and a nod. They caught on and followed suit.

"Where you flyin'?" Maddicus scanned each of them to see who was going to answer.

It was Grelf that obliged her. "The Immovable Stone."

Maddicus snorted. She got up from her seat and drank her last shot. "Don't waste my water."

I had picked up a lot of slang from each of them as they spoke. Not just Maddicus and Grelf but the other Vengerians as well. They had come from another world, and I did my best to keep them in the loop by using phrases they would understand. I stood as well but then took a step back. "Slow your roll."

"Slow my...?" She thought about it for a moment. "You're right. You're trippin'. I can't."

I folded my arms and with as much sass as I could put on it asked, "Can't or won't?"

Maddicus gave me a nod acknowledging my point. "Respect. Still, one creates the other, follow? And both are true either way you look."

"Word." I couldn't help but agree. She had a good point. "How come?"

"Two-day ride. Bro, if I'm babysitting, five... and I get paid by the hour." Maddicus stopped in her tracks and took a deep breath. She looked at Grelf and the others. "Sorry." She grimaced. "Disrespectful."

This was one of those moments where knowing the lore of a people was helpful. Understanding people by their dreams and stories is how we of the Grey Continuum fulfill their needs, but when my brother is given enough time, he can build lore so that it leaves a message or opens a door. I knew of one of their oldest myths. A myth with a prophecy of a fire princess, who would be the person who would finally move the Immovable Stone, and more importantly, I knew that once she did, she would claim the sword that was inside it.

"Your Highness. This woman will protect that stone at all costs. It is a part of her belief and a part of the myths and legends of her people. You just asked to see one of their sacred places. She would never willingly lead an outsider there." I gave Maddicus a respectful bow. "But all of this is unimportant. In just a moment Maddicus here will completely change her mind and take you to her people and then to the stone."

"You're not just trippin', you're straight trippin'." Maddicus folded her arms and shook her head. "Suspect."

"I swear." She still looked at me with doubt. I gave her a wink and said, "Your Highness, leave nothing out. Tell this guardian who is a guardian of her people's sacred places, who you are and why we are here." I watched Maddicus's face as Grelf retold what had happened since the moment Dalen and his friends arrived and explained in detail what she had gone through so far and why she was trying to get to the Immovable Stone. There is almost nothing in this world as amazing and joyous to watch as looking into the eyes of someone as they believe. All the details were too close to the myth, and Maddicus started to believe that Grelf was the Fire Princess from the old stories, finally here to claim the Earth Blade that had been there since the dawn of her people. To her knowledge, the Immovable Stone had always had a sword inside it like a mystical geode, and she and her people had been the guardians of the stone further back than her grandmother could remember.

"Gliding. I'll take you to the Wise. They will know what to do, but I can only take one of you." Maddicus shrugged. "I only have so much room on the board."

"That's not a problem. Take one of my Vengerian Guards and when you get there, we will use the skills and abilities of Master Grey here. I guess that he can get us there." Grelf tipped back one of her shots and then looked at the glass like it insulted her.

"That sinks like a stone." Maddicus pointed to Grelf. "Two days ride." She looked at Travis and Sir Adam... "Respect. No man rides my board I don't know, and ugh... Stranger Danger."

"I'll go." Whispered Oubliette as she dropped from her position and landed quietly next to Travis.

Maddicus was noticeably shaken, and she even made a yelp as Oubliette came down. She slowly turned toward me and asked, "Do y'all see that ghost or am I trippin'?"

"That's Oubliette. She does that." Grelf shrugged. "She is also a Vengerian Guardian and a trusted friend."

"And my girlfriend." Travis didn't have to say that, but he wanted to. Partly because he was head over heels for the girl and tactically speaking, when introducing your girlfriend to another attractive person, it never hurts to declare it right away. It makes them feel safe and lets anyone else know where you stand.

Maddicus noticed it. "Respect." She sat back down in her seat and leaned in. "Trust is a river that flows both ways. You want to go to a guarded sacred place and want me to trust you, but in trade, you have to trust me to take the Fire Princess to my people."

"We can't let you take Grelf without us." Sir Adam argued.

"Disrespectful." She got up and turned her chair to face Sir Adam and then sat back down. "Protector. Guardian. Gliding, but Bro, I need time to ponder. I have questions and only she has answers. Two days ride and I will know if she is the one."

"Dude." Adam took a breath and refocused. "I understand what you are saying but I have taken a vow to keep her safe, we all have. We can't just let her leave with a stranger."

Maddicus was getting frustrated. "Grey guy can port you to her?" Sir Adam looked to me to see if I could confirm that. I gave him a nod and he then refocused on Maddicus. "Fly. If anything happens, port to where we are, and you can totally waste me."

She stood up and put her hand out to shake. Sir Adam realized at that moment she was serious. She was offering her life as collateral for Grelf's.

Sir Adam looked to Grelf, and she replied, "In the end, you can't take this journey for me. Christoph and I just talked about this. None of you can take this path for me. You can come with me, but it is my journey. I am going to have to insist."

"Very well." Sir Adam looked deep into Maddicus's eyes and said, "Rule number nine: Trust is not given it's earned, but how can it be earned if never given the chance."

She shook Sir Adam's hand, "Gliding."

Maddicus tried to let go but Sir Adam held on. Plainly and without threats he simply said, "Take care of her. Please."

Adam's words touched Maddicus's heart, and she smiled and hugged him. "You're a good dude." She looked up in the rafters and asked, "Are there any more ghost girlfriends?"

Sir Adam laughed. "No. My brother is the lucky one."

Maddicus lingered on her hug for a moment. "Maybe I am." She squeezed him tightly once more and before she let go, she pecked Sir Adam on the cheek. Maddicus pulled up her coat back over her shoulder and gave Sir Adam a devilish wink. Then tugged on Grelf's sleeve. "Girl talk. Besides, we should go before we go. Two-day's ride is longer than you think."

Both of them disappeared into a door at the far end of the tavern and as they went in Becky removed her hood and said, "Hey Adam. You know how you always say that you can't tell when a girl is flirting with you?"

Sir Adam turned towards Becky and carefully responded with, "Yeah."

Becky pointed in the direction of where Maddicus and Grelf went. "That was it." Becky headed toward the door, and when asked where she was going, she didn't even turn around, just called out, "Girl talk."

19

A DEAL WITH THE TEACHER

In the northern part of the Koa Vod province, a man came to the edge of a farm, unpacked a brazier, and prepped it. He looked up at the sky and said a prayer to all who might be listening as he lit the brazier, and a thick white smoke began to plume from it. He was sure that would get someone's attention, so he kneeled and waited until someone from the farm found him. He dared not disrespect the owner of this land by trespassing.

He was found quicker than he expected, and it filled him with excitement and something akin to fear. He remained kneeling and didn't raise his eyes higher than their feet. They asked why he was there, and he answered that he wished to speak to the master of the house and then begged forgiveness for his unannounced arrival, swearing that there had been no other way within his means to contact him. He explained the smoke and then put his forehead to the ground and waited for them to decide what was to be done with him.

They decided that his actions were honorable enough to allow his head to remain where it was for a time. They allowed him to extinguish the brazier and collect his things and then they explained to him that though he lived he was not trusted. A bag was placed over his head, and it was not taken off again until he was standing before the master of the house.

"You worked very hard to get to me alive. I am curious why you would risk so much?" The lines in Master Bo's face showed he had laughed more than he cried but both had left their toll. He kept his hair short for many reasons but mostly just because it was easier to keep clean and practical. Everything about him could be described as such. Everything he wore was clean and kept, and everything was practical. From the Midnight Blacks that he wore to conceal himself in shadows and the shadow blade on his back, to the face mask covering the lower half of his face, so that his identity would remain concealed. All were nonreflective black and most of him looked like a walking shadow. The sword and mask were practical for the safety of them both. For as long as this man had not seen his face, he might have the chance to do business and leave with his heart still beating... or perhaps not."

"I am here to make a deal with you, Master Bo." As the man said it, he dropped to his knees and touched his forehead to the floor.

"That part is obvious." Master Bo had a disdain for people who wasted his time and wanted the man to get to his point. "Impress me with the next thing out of your mouth."

"I want to offer you access to your own personal magic portal that will allow you access to locations all over this world." The man just stayed there without motion.

"Why would you want to offer me this?" The true meat of the question. Why was he here, before Master Bo? Many people would be interested in something like that, so out of all the people who he chose to speak with, why was he here?

"After the question I am asking now, which I apologize for doing, I humbly request to ask a single question first that will allow me the ability to navigate your questions more easily?" The man lay motionless on the ground.

This man was going out of his way to not get killed. Master Bo liked that. "I forgive your question without permission, and I allow you your one question."

The man paused for a moment as if he were deciding if this was the right course of action, and then asked, "May I have permission from you directly, to speak and move freely?"

"Just because I grant you freedom does not give you license to be disrespectful." Master Bo leaned in. "Keep that in mind, but you may rise and speak."

The man got up and stretched the crick in his back. "Thank you." He turned all the way around and tried to take in the ambiance of the place. He was standing in a great hall. The ceiling was four stories high and held by six onyx pillars which had dragons made of jade that wrapped themselves the length of the pillar. Each of the dragons reached the top of their pillars and were carved to look like they were holding up the ceiling. Their eyes glowed with a purple hue, and it looked as if black smoke was exuding from them. "That is one of the most terrifyingly beautiful things I have ever seen."

"Thank you." Master Bo waited for the man to answer the question he had been originally asked, and he was in the habit of never asking twice.

"I would guess that you are the type of person who wants me to be direct and to the point. So, I will make this simple." The man took a deep breath and began. "I believe you have the ability to care for the portal and protect it. Other people will want to share it with the world for all to use. A greater light for all people, and I would rather know that there is at least one in this world that is protected by someone who understands its worth and wants to keep it a secret."

"What does it do?" Master Bo signaled one of the servants and they began to prepare tea.

The man took that as a sign that Master Bo might be interested in his deal. "I am going to create a portal with many places to step into and step out of. Your portal would allow you access to every single one of them."

"How many?" asked Master Bo.

"Three hundred and sixty known locations, across this world." The man replied. "I will also grant you a magical compass that is tied to the portals and will allow you to access them as desired."

"What is the catch?" Master Bo accepted his tea and then offered some to the man.

The man accepted his tea and bowed not only to Master Bo but also to the servant who brought him his tea. "The offer will be made to more than just you."

Master Bo took a sip of his tea and swallowed it slowly. "And if they tried to use their portal to access mine?"

"They would be met at the gate by your finest Shadow Warriors and be slain on the spot for daring to trespass onto your lands without your permission." The man took a sip from his cup. It was made with Kalerium, a very potent truth drug. Made from a root that grew naturally in those parts. "Kalerium? You didn't need to drug me, I have no reason to lie but, if it makes you happy." The man tilted the glass back and swallowed his tea with one gulp. He felt its effects take control immediately. "Okay. Ask away."

"Price." Master Bo asked simply as he considered his choices.

"A few things. I want free access to your portal. I can think of a hundred different reasons why it could be useful to be able to step into the Temple of Shadow and not have to worry about whatever was on the other side following me. The Temple of Shadow is a good place to hide. I want access to all my portals, and I don't want to have to throw myself on the floor and beg every time my need requires it. As well, I request the knowledge that allows you to create Gnosis Stones."

The creation of Gnosis Stones had been a secret that only a few in the world knew. Master Bo and his Shadow Warriors had spent their lives protecting their knowledge of crafting Gnosis Stones from the outside world. "Why would you require such knowledge?"

"I have studied the use of Gnosis Stones for some time. Mainly through your divine temples. But it is the nature of those temples to only share such knowledge with those who choose to join their order. I wasn't about to give up 30 years of my life and my work so I could get the piece of information that I required. Please understand that I am fascinated with the entire concept of how they work. Instead of putting a specific enchantment on a weapon with magic, the weapon is merely imbued with the ability to harmonize with multiple enchantments. The addition of a Gnosis Stone grants the weapon enchantment from whichever type of stone is used. Because of this, the same blade could harmonize with the enchantment of fire or electricity, the temperament of the blade would alter depending on the stone." The man gave a bow of respect. "Truly fascinating. I discovered a specific enchantment that I believe would be beneficial to both of us. The means to create a Gnosis Stone is an ability, that for as many years as I have been walking this world, has eluded me. Eastern magic differs from Western magic, and where I have knowledge about spells and cast work unknown to the world, I do not know how to imbue it into a Gnosis Stone. If you are willing to share the knowledge of how to create a Gnosis Stone, I will share with you knowledge that is unknown to the rest of this world, and we will both be able to create something that will benefit us. A Hidden Stone. Its enchantment allows the user to be unnoticed. Not just unseen, or invisible, but truly not perceived by the mind." The man gave Master Bo another deep bow. "Which is why I am here and am willing to grant you access to one of my portals." As the man stood back up, he smiled and added, "Yes. Anyone who can access any of the portals would be able to access yours, but if you place the portal in a location that you have absolute control over, it won't really matter. Anyone who dares use it to enter your stronghold would undoubtedly be met with certain death within two steps of making it through. But what you will have is three hundred and fifty-nine locations that you can get to and retreat from. You will be able to contract your work over the entire world and all it will cost you is giving me a free pass to use it if needed, and the knowledge of how to craft a Gnosis Stone."

"You have not answered my question." Master Bo reminded the man.

"Indeed. I require a Hidden Stone for the same purpose that you would want one. I don't want people to know what I am doing."

"What is it you are doing?" Master Bo finished his tea and handed the cup to the servant with a small bow.

"Things that I am willing to go through this much trouble to hide. With your line of work, I am sure that you understand there is a reason I don't ask about the contracts you hold. I am sure you can respect the point that I would be without honor if I were to divulge the nature of mine."

"What is it that you have not yet told me?" Master Bo was ready to agree but had to be sure of what he was getting involved with.

"Wow. The Kalerium is powerful." The man staggered for a moment as he felt the need to answer the question. "The part I have not mentioned is this. All the portals are tied together. You would be required by a magical pact to never destroy it once you agree to open it. It will grant you the ability to slip into almost impossible places, but you will never be able to close it, which means you would have to dedicate yourself to its protection."

"Those are the only terms? It's protection, your free access, and the knowledge of how to create a Gnosis Stone?" Master Bo thought about it carefully. While he waited to see how the man would answer.

"Yes. By my word, that is the price, and of course, no doubt from time to time you will have to dispatch someone foolish enough to enter your domain, but beyond that, I am being completely honest with you. Of course, there is always the possibility of an unforeseen disaster or some such event that is beyond my control, but that is a risk we all take every moment of our lives."

"I will agree to your terms. How do we proceed?" Master Bo took the man's hand, they made eye contact and bowed together.

The man reached into a small pouch and provided Master Bo with a seed. "Plant this seed and take care of it well. The tree that grows from it will be your portal. It is enchanted with a powerful spell and connects that seed to all of these." The man showed him a handful of seeds from his pouch.

"How does it work?" asked Master Bo.

"Quantumly. All of them are the same seed." The man tried to read Master Bo's eyes to see if he understood. "There is only one seed, that I had magically forced into over three hundred and fifty locations. Although it is in multiple positions, there is only one seed. When it grows there will only be one tree. The thing is, that one tree will be in three-hundred and sixty known locations. Which is why you must take care of it. Kill one tree and they all die, because..."

"There is only one tree." Master Bo looked at the seed in his hand. "Very well. I am in. What should I call you?"

"You can refer to me as The Teacher." The Teacher gave another bow out of respect. "Now, let's get all of this in writing." He pulled out a scroll and unrolled it. It was a magical contract. Impossible to break. "Please read it and make sure we are in agreement, and while you have me in the grips of your truth drug, I know that you have searched for the knowledge to move past death and become..." The Teacher allowed the grin to stretch across his face. "Something more."

Master Bo's demeanor changed, and he became very interested in what the Teacher had to say. "What do you know of my quest?"

The Teacher instinctively pivoted his weight to his back leg, knowing that he may have tipped his hand too far. "Two things, Master Bo. The first is that you wish to protect all that you have built by becoming an ancestor spirit of your clan and be able to watch over your house forever." The Teacher changed his stance and shifted his weight forward while intentionally looking Master Bo in the eyes. "The second thing is that I know how to achieve it. Not only would you be a guardian spirit of your clan, but I can make you a god of this temple."

While all of this was happening, Dalen Pax was watching the scene take place from an incorporeal state. Due to the knowledge gained from drinking from the Fountain of Truth and then combined with being touched by the All-Seeing Eye and the words that Crystal had told him, Dalen had awoken from the vision with the ability to see through time. Dalen had just begun to understand the power and was still weakened by the Fountain of Truth but while in his incorporeal state, he was strong enough to slip in through the tree and take a few moments to scan this place somewhere in time. Controlling it was a skill, and he was still unpracticed, so he had no strong control over it. Initially, he meant to only go back a day or two so he could see the patterns of when the tree was being guarded. He had moved back much farther than intended and was watching a moment that had long since passed, but he was not sure exactly when it was. He did know that when they used this tree they would be met with great hostility.

This Tree of Travel was one of the places that no one went

to, and if someone did, no one came back and now Dalen knew why. He was somehow watching the moment that these Shadow Warriors got their tree and although that man who was making the deal somehow seemed familiar, Dalen was more fascinated with what he was peddling. Dalen had never thought about where the trees had come from and never thought about the idea of some guy calling himself The Teacher, making deals with magic Shadow Warriors to get them all in place. He wondered what other deals that man would have had to make to get them all in position. In this case, it was a position of danger and treachery. Aside from this location, the nearest tree to their goal put them on the edge of not being able to make the distance in time. So, they believed that this tree would be their only option.

Master Bo called to the spirits of the temple to be with him, and Dalen could hear growling and hissing from the jade dragons. Dalen was relieved at first knowing that he was watching an event from long ago when out of nowhere, he felt the spirit's eyes upon him. He tried to ignore it, but the sensation was too strong. He looked up and into the eyes of the dragons and as he did, their eyes glowed brighter. Master Bo noticed Dalen and looked right at him.

"Who is your friend?" Master Bo asked, but The Teacher gave his word that he came alone. "In that case, we have an intruder." Master Bo pointed directly at Dalen. "You move in the spirit realm, but the Shadow Dragons give me sight."

Dalen did not hesitate to let go of that moment and return to the present. When he did, he still felt as if the dragon statues were looking at him. Master Bo's voice began to come from everywhere. "I knew one day you would return." Master Bo appeared in front of Dalen and looked directly at him. "After our last encounter, I have been here, in the spirit world to watch over my clan. What are you doing here Master Truth?"

"I require use of the tree. Me and two others." Dalen was surprised that this ghost knew him and more importantly knew him as Master Truth. "There is a great danger coming and we require the help of the Gold Dragon of the East. This is the closest tree to its location. If our situation were not dire, we would never have trespassed, but we had no choice."

Bo began to hover to meet Dalen in the air. "You always have a choice. The next closest location is eight days from here. Go around."

"Not a choice. We have little time and if we do not use this passage, the world could be in jeopardy." Dalen gave a respectful bow.

"I am the founder of the Brotherhood of Shadow, and I have been the ancestral spirit guardian for a thousand years, and in all that time, no outsider has ever used our tree." Black smoke began to envelop Master Bo. "The Brotherhood of Light should know better than to come here. The Brotherhood of Shadow will not allow you passage."

Master Bo extended his hand and the black smoke that had enveloped him shot out toward Dalen. When it touched him, it felt cold and there was a sensation as if his life were starting to be pulled from his being.

Dalen cast a spell turning his body into pure sunlight. Master Bo let go of Dalen and screamed in pain and anger. Dalen didn't waste time using the tree while Master Bo was distracted. Instead, Dalen prepared himself to teleport directly back to Christoph.

"So, you have some fight after all. I honestly didn't think you had it in you," said Master Bo. "I will respect the treaty that was set forth by you and me together when we created our sects. You will be granted access if you can prove yourself to be worthy. If you come here, be prepared to fight. We will grant you passage if you survive our trial, but be warned... Master Truth, we will show you no mercy!" The jade dragons roared, and the room began to fill with Shadow Warriors as they poured in from other locations to protect the tree.

Dalen moved his quantum location to directly in front of his friends. Dalen refocused his energy and became corporeal again, surprising them both. "I have good news and bad news."

Christoph shrugged and said, "Sounds about right. What's the good news."

"The good news is I know where this tree will take us." Dalen Pax moved his line of sight from Christoph to Master Peace. "The bad news is that it is protected by the Brotherhood of Shadow, and they will be expecting us."

Master Peace knew what that meant. "I would like to avoid a fight if we can help it, but I believe that any other location will not get us close enough in time."

"I also can't let you do this for me. I must take each step. Is there a third option?" asked Christoph.

"I can drink from the Fountain of Truth again, but I am not yet at full strength, and it took me an entire day to recover this much. A day, that if we had moved would have given us enough time to use another route." Dalen took a deep breath. "I know that we do not wish to fight, but there is a real possibility that it may be required. The spirit I talked to used to be a Master of the Brotherhood of Shadow, and no matter how we differ, I know he will hold true to his word. If we go, there will be a trial, and we will have to fight. Fight for our very lives."

"Understood. Council." Christoph looked at the two monks. "Is there another way?"

"After drinking from the Fountain of Truth, I am still too weak to alter time for anyone but myself. If I were at full strength, I could just slow down time and we could travel the longer distance, but in my weakened state I do not have the strength to take you with me." Dalen hung his head. I am sorry. Trying to reach my own goals, I may have put the larger mission in trouble."

Christoph remembered what Gavin had told him, and this was not the time for Dalen to begin to doubt himself. "I don't think so. There is danger yes, and because of your weakened state, we can't just cheat. I guess we will have to do it legitimately." He smiled. "You did the right thing. And I am going to have to ask you to start believing in yourself and that we are still on the right path."

Dalen took a breath and nodded. "When push comes to shove, I am going to need you to not second guess yourself."

"Easier said than done," added Dalen.

"Not true. There is something you can do to help keep from second-guessing yourself." Christoph slapped Dalen on the shoulder. "Make sure that the choice is right before you make it."

Dalen nodded, "Heard."

Then Christoph looked to the bigger picture. "Is there a chance of success?"

Master Peace closed his eyes and nodded. "At a great price. They will be trying to kill us, and there is a real chance that we will have to kill some of them along the way."

"Have either of you killed a man before?" Christoph's eyes jumped back and forth between the two of them.

"I have never had to kill someone," said Master Peace. "Got close once and have avoided it since, but if it means the salvation of this entire world, I will."

"Same." Dalen gave a small nod to Master Peace. We have trained to do what is needed, we have just been fortunate to not have the need arise, we will both avoid killing if either of us can help it, but I believe I can speak for both Master Peace and myself when I say that we are ready to do what must be done to save this world." Master Peace nodded. "How about you? Have you had to?"

Christoph nodded. "More than once, and it stays with you always." Then he thought for a moment. "If this is too much for you, what if we wait a few days and let you get your strength back and once you can move others through time again, we take the long way?"

"That is a possible answer." Dalen considered it for a moment. "The question is, how long will it take me to recover? What if it takes me nine more days to recover? Then all is lost."

"Yeah, but what if you recover in an hour? Then there would be no need to go this way." Christoph argued.

"You are absolutely right." Master Peace gave Christoph a small bow. "There are two paths in front of you. One path offers a chance of failure and has great peril. The other provides little peril, if any, but the price for that safety is the blind chance that it will work."

"But what if the first way is too dangerous?" Christoph took a moment to look them both in the eye. "What if we don't succeed?"

Together Master Peace and Dalen spoke. "Even if it means my final breath, you will not fail."

Dalen smiled at his brother and they both exchanged nods, then Dalen added, "I guess your only course of action is simple."

Christoph smiled and asked, "Of yeah? What's that?"

Dalen slapped Christoph's shoulder as Christoph had done a moment before. "Make sure that the choice is right before you make it."

Christoph knew he should have heard his own words coming. He laughed and said, "Heard."

20

THE BALLAD OF

MOON CROW

When it was time to leave, Maddicus took Grelf outside. The wind had calmed down, but the heat was intense. Grelf gave us instructions to stay at our current location. She wanted us to try and find out as much as we could about the Bodites from the locals and when she got to her new location, they would join her.

Maddicus removed something from her pack that was painted with designs that were both tribal and aerodynamic. The markings looked to be written in a language none of them spoke. It was a small board that was about the length of her forearm. It seemed like nothing more than a plank with rounded edges on the front and back and along the sides. She leapt into the air and placed the board under her feet. As she did it grew in length and width and just as she got her feet planted, it began to hum quietly and hover about a foot or so off the ground.

"The stories mentioned that you use flying carpets." Travis was making notes. "Looks more like a surfboard."

"Surf...board? Dude I'm bailing. Wha'?" Maddicus' face scrunched up like she was trying to do math in her head.

"You know? Water?" Sir Adam mimicked the waves with his arms, but Maddicus just looked at him puzzled.

"Their people have a partial magic ability to understand any language, but the part she understands is the slang. The more slang you add to your words, the more she will understand you." I gave Maddicus a thumbs up. And winked. "It's a variant of Grey Speak and because I have been here to translate, it has been easier, I was helping a lot in the tavern. But...good news, now is your chance to see if you can do it without my help."

All four of them slowly turned and looked at Maddicus with confusion and disbelief. She had seen this look before with outsiders. The moment that it dawned on them what was really going on. She just smiled and raised an eyebrow.

Now it was Travis who was solving some sort of a riddle in his head. He blinked a couple of times and nodded and then addressed Maddicus directly. "Yo, What up? Girl, this board is fresh." It was coming out awkward as if he were speaking in his third language.

Maddicus smiled and bobbed in agreement. "Fresh. That's gliding." She thought about it for a moment and then said, "Yo, I'm Maddicus."

Sir Adam cocked his head back as a hello and said, "Sup?" She returned the motion with a subsequent "Sup." "Madam I'm Adam." It was something he liked to use from time to time because not only was it an introduction, but it was a palindrome. He used it enough that it became one of his sayings and translated.

Maddicus looked over to Becky and gave her a nod of recognition. "Spooky."

Becky didn't skip a beat. She nodded back and whispered "Word." Although her mask was down those who knew her, knew that this was the first time they had ever seen Oubliette's face. She shifted gears quickly and Becky walked over to Maddicus and smiled. "Like totally whoa. Like you and me aren't besties and I'm like, no way. Like totally gag me. I was all like, 'What?'. Like my grandpa is like totally Japanese and when I was a kid, I heard stories about how like really old ancestors and whatever, were like ninjas, I was like sweet. I always wanted to be a ninja, but now it's like whoa. I can be like, one with the darkness, and I'm like, whoa. That's chill."

"Chill?" Inquired Maddicus.

Becky put her hands up. "So, chill. Straight up peace. I mean yeah, I was all like peek-a-boo on your butt. My bad, but girl..." Becky pointed to Travis. "...That's my boo. I kinda had to be all, sup?"

Maddicus crouched down so she was the same height as Becky. "That's bustin. Respect." She looked at Travis and laughed. "You're just marking your dune." Maddicus put out her hand for five. "Besties?"

Becky gave her a five. "Like, totally."

Travis cleared his throat. And when the girls looked over, he began to read from his notebook. "Yo Maddicus. You be all like..." He put his fingers up to make quotation marks. "Surfboard?" Maddicus nodded. "Surf and Turf."

Maddicus comprehended but the idea of that much water in one place sounded either magical or absurd. She looked to Sir Adam for confirmation, and he did the same motion with his arms and said, "Ride the waves, dude."

Maddicus blinked a couple of times and then gave up on trying to imagine what that would look like and said, "Not a surfboard. Dune Board. Respect the Bodi board. It will set you free." She pulled up a sleeve and showed them that she wore a manacle on her right wrist." She saw that they were not quite understanding. "Surf the dunes. They are my sisters, they call to me, yo."

All of them knew that they needed more information about these sand surfers if they were going to get through this. Maddicus said her fair wells and helped Grelf climb aboard. Grelf stood right behind Maddicus and held on to her waist. Maddicus leaned forward slowly, and the Bodi board began to move with her. They picked up speed smoothly, but quickly, and within a short period of time, they were out of sight.

For two days the Vengerian Guardians and I waited for Grelf to make it to the encampment of the Bodites. She checked in three times a day. Once when she woke, once in the middle of the night, and once before she went to sleep. They often slept during the day and traveled by night.

After two and a half days they were beginning to get nervous because they were running out of time, but the call came in and they were summoned to wherever Grelf had been taken. I waited until they were all ready to go and then I asked each of them to close their eyes. "Alright." I began. "I want you all to picture the three of you standing together in the desert. I'm not there. Just the sound of my voice. Can you picture it?" Each of them kept their eyes closed but one by one they all nodded. "Alright picture everything you can about where you are. Everything from the little shops nearby to where the sun is in the sky. You got it?" Again, they nodded. "Okay now listen to what I am going to tell you."

They listened. At first, they couldn't hear anything other than small gusts of wind that were slowly erasing their footprints, and the ghostly hint of a song that each of them felt they knew but could not place. It was only when they heard the music that they began to hear me speak as well. They were still imagining their environment and the main thing they noticed was the sun with its heat and although their eyes were closed, they could tell that it was bright. But as they focused on the music and my voice they began to cool as the environment changed around them. In their minds, they pictured a large tent wrapping itself around them and protecting them from the heat and light of the sun. Then they noticed that there were many people in the tent with them. One of them was Grelf and they felt a pull toward her as she drew close and stood right next to them. It almost startled them when the images in their heads began to talk amongst themselves, and they could not just hear it in their minds, but it was a tangible sound that was coming from an outside source, and they collectively chose to open their eyes. They found themselves in a large tent. In a semi-circle in front of them, there were seven elders and two younger folks.

They had bamphed directly to Grelf's position, so she was standing between the twins, and Becky was standing behind her. Sir Adam leaned into Grelf and asked, "Sup?"

"We are standing in front of the 'Wise' to explain our case. This is the first of two meetings." Grelf looked around. "Where is Will of Grey? We could really use his assistance here."

I do love walking into a room on cue and that time was no different. "Hello. I am here." I walked past the guards with a nonchalant gait and even waved at someone behind them. In truth, there was no one behind them, but it made them look away to see who I was waving at. The moment they took their eyes off of me they forgot all about me, which granted me the opportunity to join my friends.

"Good. I am glad you're here. You said it was easier to translate when you were here. This may be an opportune time to demonstrate this ability." She huddled everyone together so she could talk to them as a team. "Alright. The reason for the two meetings was explained to me but I only 'think' I understand. The first meeting will be simple yet by the time we are done both sides will want to take a break."

"Alright, I'll bite. Why?" asked Travis.

Grelf patted Travis on the shoulder. "I'll bite... that's great. The meeting is so we can give them every single slang word or phrase and colloquialism we can think of."

"That doesn't sound too hard." Becky was trying to look at the bright side, but the light of hope was clouded by Grelf's next sentence.

"Yeah. For the first hour." Grelf was trying to compile as much as she could. "They said the meeting will last three hours to give us a chance to think of more after the first two waves of memory and inspiration... Whatever that means." Grelf took another slow breath. "It means that we are going to be here for a while. After they take it all in, we can then make our case. I could push the issue, but in this case, I think that we should wait. No doubt we could wipe them out and take what we came for, but that is not the first thing I want to do as the Bloodline of Venger, so for now we are going to give them what they're asking for. Agreed?"

Each of them agreed and so, they did. They spent the next three hours thinking of every slang word and saying they could think of. At first it was fun. Becky gave her best 'valley girl' and Sir Adam gave his best 'surfer boy'. Travis tried to give them all the urban words that he could remember and Grelf, of course, gave them bibitz. Toward the end, once they had spoken everything they could think of, new words and phrases would only come in waves of memory. Remembering one word or idiom would spark an entire set of new words that created a chain reaction with others until that train of thought ran out. Their minds were tired, so I saw it as an opportunity to give them a break and show them that I had learned much about them through their stories and wanted to give Grelf and her team the opportunity to get to know them as well.

I pushed my Grey Speak enough that all could understand me but decided it was not a wise choice to hit them with the full effect all at once. I eased everyone involved into something that looked like a harmony of thought. "If you don't mind. In honor of your hospitality on this glorious day, I wish to honor you by telling the story of The Creator of Dreams and Moon Crow." I bowed and awaited their response.

"He speaks like The Way." said one of the elders. They looked at each other back and forth and for the first time, the team got to see what a telepathic conversation looked like from the outside.

‹We don't look like that when we talk do we?› asked Becky.

‹Probably worse.› Answered Grelf. ‹They have gotten used to it. See how smooth they are. My guess is that we look like a group of six-year-olds when somebody asks who smeared jam on the rug.›

The elders gave permission, so I pushed my Grey Speak to full function and the night crept into the tent like smoke. "It started on a dark night, many years ago." As I spoke the world vanished from them, as their minds opened completely to the words of a Grey Bard, and they watched as the scenes of my tale played out as if they were there, silently watching.

...

It started on a dark night, many years ago. Two peasants were starving and had lost their homes after soldiers had come through and burned them out. Unspeakable acts had taken place that night and although they survived, neither of them was well. They had lost everything and although they did their best to mend their lives, they could not salvage it. The events that they had witnessed and the things they had to endure had broken them. They knew that they had to save their son and find him a new home because staying with them meant starving and undoubtedly death. They sold their son to a toy maker as an apprentice and were never heard from again. The toy maker watched as they took the money and disappeared into the night, knowing that in the end, this was going to be better for the boy.

The toymaker named him Moon Crow and cared for the boy for two years before the woman he loved swindled him and he was left with nothing. When bill collectors came to collect, the toymaker eventually had to give up Moon Crow. Over the next few months, Moon Crow was moved from owner to owner and ended up with a cruel man who was a magic items broker known as Dakas. He swore to Moon Crow that he would never be sold again, but this truth brought Moon Crow no peace. Dakas was known for two things: his cruelty and his greed. Both traits created a need for him to keep any slave he owned, and he marveled at the idea of keeping a slave until they died.

Dakas wanted to make sure that none of his slaves could ever escape so, Moon Crow was fitted with a Manacle of Property. A very magical tool, built for enslavement. Within its enchantment, there was a location spell and Dakas could use it to know the location of anyone who belonged to him, and as long as Moon Crow was property, it would never come off. For as long as he was a slave it would remain magically locked to his wrist. It was the only means that Dakas used to keep track of his many slaves. Moon Crow tested his resolve a couple of times and tried to run, but Dakas always knew his location and would send out his two bounty hunters who would always find him. The beatings that followed over the next couple of days persuaded Moon Crow to stop any attempt at escape. It was torturous. No chains or bars but imprisoned just the same.

When Moon Crow was twelve, he had been in the service of Dakas for five years and had learned his place and all but accepted his fate, except there was still a spark of life left in him. For years Moon Crow had waited for the toymaker to save him or someone to come, but after five years of abuse and slavery, Moon Crow had given up on anyone other than himself to come to his rescue.

Moon Crow was often told to clean Dakas's shop and clean all new items coming in. After five years, Moon Crow's long wait finally paid off. Dakas had acquired a flying carpet in trade and Moon Crow was ordered to clean it.

"I can fly this away from here." Moon Crow looked at the

manacle on his wrist. "As long as I am his slave this will not come off, but I would rather be a slave on the run than just sit back and agree to be a slave." Moon Crow understood that Dakas would know the moment he tried to run, but with this carpet, there was a chance. A chance that Moon Crow could outrun him and his bounty hunters. Yet, Moon Crow knew he could only run for so long. He would either have to find a way to lose the manacle and obtain his freedom or he would have to fly to a place where Dakas and his bounty hunters would not follow.

Moon Crow waited until the shop was quiet for the evening and when he thought that it was safe he stole the carpet and climbed to the roof. Dakas unfortunately was there. Waiting for him.

"Hello, Moon Crow. After all this time I thought that you would have learned this lesson." Dakas backhanded Moon Crow and the blow picked him up off the ground. His face stung and the pain set in as he landed with a hard thud. "I thought you learned this years ago, but I guess some slaves never learn."

Moon Crow pulled himself to his knees, looked up into the stars, and prayed that someone would hear his soul beg for release. "Are you going to kill me?" asked Moon Crow.

"Kill you? Why would I do that?" Dakas laughed. "Even after the beating I am going to give you, you will still be able to do your job and thus have value, and I will never give that up willingly." Dakas struck Moon Crow across the face and blood began to pour from his nose. "If you had stayed with your family, you would be dead by now, or worse, you would be nothing, or worse than that you could be a burden on everyone and everything around you and be worth less than nothing." Dakas struck Moon Crow again, "You should thank me." Dakas' eyes flashed with violent intent. "At least with me, you have value." Dakas picked Moon Crow up just so he could backhand him again to the floor. Anger was beginning to build up in him, but Dakas wasn't explosive with his anger. He was quiet and terrifying as an all too familiar look began to take shape across his face, and he began to feel the thrill of the pain he was about to inflict on such a small being. His eyes glinted in the moonlight as he smiled with vicious intent "Now... thank me for giving value to your life or I will give you another."

Dakas picked up Moon Crow by his neck and dangled him over the roof. The shop was nestled on the edge of the Verris Mountains which were located at the southern end of the desert. The fall was easily far enough to kill him if Dakas dropped him.

"Drop me." Moon Crow looked into Dakas' eyes and didn't flinch. "Drop me. You abusive piece of lizard dung."

"What did you say to me?" Dakas put a pinky from his free hand in his ear and pretended to clean it out. With his other, he began to grip tighter. Not enough to cut off Moon Crow's air completely, but enough to instill panic. "There is no possible way you just said what you said to me so, could you repeat that?"

"Drop me, you coward." Moon Crow spit in his face. "Are you so afraid to lose a profit that you are going to let me talk to you like that? You blind albino flea in the armpit of my life. Drop me." Moon Crow was past frightened and far beyond anything that looked like self-preservation. His only hope. His only preservation was death. "I dare you."

"Now why would you say something like that when you know you will have to pay for it." Dakas pulled him back from the edge. "I won't kill you." He leaned in close and looked Moon Crow right in the eyes. "I am going to break you, boy. If I killed you, how would you learn your place." Dakas struck Moon Crow again, this time open-handed across the cheek. "Oh, you won't be dying today, there is no escape for you. Dakas kicked the rolled-up rug off the roof and threw Moon Crow down near the edge. "You will regret ever crossing me boy."

Moon Crow pulled himself to his feet. "That's where you are wrong." Moon Crow looked back at the fall that called to him. "Your threats of pain and suffering are at an end, for I would rather die right here and now than live a single moment longer a slave." Moon Crow leaped from the roof before Dakas could stop him. For a moment Moon Crow felt the sensation of freedom and for a moment he could have sworn that the manacle loosened and almost came off, but Moon Crow became distracted as he hit the lower ledge of the shop which stuck out further than the building roof.

As he hit, he realized that the rug had been stopped too. Moon Crow grabbed it as he slid off the lower roof and began to plummet down the mountain. Moon Crow franticly tried to untie the rope that was binding the rug. When he got it undone it unrolled, and Moon Crow grabbed two of its corners. He was moments from hitting the ground, but he pulled back hard on the rug, and it responded just in time. The rug was now flying along the ground, and Moon Crow knew that Dakas would be after him, so he headed north into the Verris Desert in hopes that the desert would slow Dakas down, or at least give him some time to formulate a plan.

From the rooftops of his shop along the top of the mountain Dakas watched as Moon Crow began his escape. "Run all you like. I will always be able to find you because you will always belong to me, and as long as you are mine you will never be free."

Twice during the first day, Moon Crow tried to stop and think, but within moments of him stopping, Dakas's hunters showed up to bring him back, so he had to take flight once more. After nearly being caught twice Moon Crow decided not to stop again. He flew into the desert for three days and nights, bearing the freezing temperatures at night and the unrelenting heat of the day until he was dehydrated and exhausted. He was still flying as he faded in and out of consciousness, lying there on his back staring at the stars. He was aware that his body was giving out and he had no idea if he was going to wake again, but alive or dead, in that moment he was free.

Sleep took him and Moon Crow dreamt of flying in the stars. As he floated amongst the universe, he allowed his mind to wander. He watched as galaxies bloomed into existence and he watched them expand as time slipped away. They appeared and disappeared like explosions in the void of space. They collapsed inward on themselves in fractal patterns and twinkled out of existence.

Moon Crow came across another who was gliding through the stars. He was humanoid in form but had no distinguishing features except for masculine. His body oscillated with every color imaginable and a few that weren't. He was lying on something alongside Moon Crow, but instead of a carpet it was a board, his legs dangled from the knee, and he was resting the back of his head in his hands.

Few make it here who can still claim to be alive. His voice was like music and Moon Crow wept at the beauty of it.

Moon Crow hoped with all his heart that he had died. He prayed that the desert had taken him, and he could finally be free. He looked at his right hand and wept to see the manacle was still attached. "Don't make me go back."

The being sat up on his board and swung his feet back and forth. *I would never force you to do anything that you don't want to, but if you die now, you will stay a slave forever, if you go back, I can help you find the way to free yourself.*

Moon Crow sat up as well. "There is a way?"

Not just a way. Said the being on the board. *The Way, and if you can find it, you can free yourself from your bondage.*

"You know a way to get this manacle off?" Moon Crow asked.

The being got up from his seated position and stood up on his board. *That cuff has no power over you. It is merely a symbol of your bondage and slavery. I am saying that if you go back, you will have the chance to truly be free.*

Moon Crow stood up as well. He had not stood up on the

carpet before and it took him a couple of tries to find his footing. "I don't understand the difference, but I have nothing left. Teach me The Way."

The being spoke a few words then Moon Crow's carpet folded and changed to take the shape of a Bodi board and changed colors the same way the being did. Together they flew through space. The being shared with Moon Crow the secrets of surfing the stars. Moon Crow called the being The Creator of Dreams because as he spoke visions would appear in Moon Crow's mind. Dreams were outside of actual time and space, and Moon Crow had no idea if they had talked for moments or centuries, but when Moon Crow awoke, he found that his board had stopped while he slept and as fate would have it, the Bodi board had stopped at an oasis. Moon Crow rolled off his board and crawled to the water. He was suffering from exposure and close to death. He drank deep from the watering hole and felt his strength begin to return but he only had moments to rest.

Dakas's bounty hunters were on him in moments. They traveled with stone unicorns. One was made of marble and the other from obsidian, yet they moved as if they were real and wore magic armor that granted them special abilities. They were fast and never got tired. The bounty hunters were both wearing enchanted garments that maintained their temperature even under harsh environments, but he knew who they were. It was Tongo and Pontoon. They were known as the Sand-Spiders and were some of the most notorious men in the Verris Desert. They also wore desert goggles and head wraps to keep the sand out of their faces but although they had their faces covered, there was no question in Moon Crow's mind of who they were.

They told Moon Crow to stay where he was, but he was not about to give in and start thinking like a slave again. He knew if he went back, he would never have this opportunity again. Instead, he jumped onto his board, took a wide stance like the Creator of Dreams had taught him, and leaned forward. The board took off and the bounty hunters quickly took up chase.

Their mounts had enchantments on them that would make them aware of, and be able to locate, anyone wearing a manacle and be able to teleport to their general location. If the slave ran, they had other enchantments to make them fast. With all the enchantments available they were built to run down anything that escaped, but they were slowed by the sandy terrain. This is how Moon Crow was able to always escape them, but this time he had no intention of escaping. Their mounts were fast, but they could not fly.

Moon Crow tried to go high, but the riders were bowmen and after no more than a few moments of getting above the dunes and seeing the terrain before him, Moon Crow was struck by an arrow in his left shoulder. Moon Crow pivoted his Bodi board back toward the ground quickly and began to move sporadically in hopes of dodging any more incoming fire.

The arrow had not gone deep, and he was lucky that it hit where it did. Less than the width of two fingers towards his center the arrow would have gone into his joint. Another finger width deep and it would have pierced an artery.

Moon Crow knew he could outrun them and get out of range if he could just fly in a straight line, but dodging like he was slowed his pace, and the bounty hunters were keeping up. He had gotten higher to get a feel for the terrain and it paid off. Seeing the desert from a greater height had given him the advantage over the bounty hunters who could only see at ground level. There was a cliff that dropped down and it was coming up fast.

Arrows cut the air around him as the bounty hunters were learning to anticipate his movements. The desert was more mountainous here and the unicorns were beginning to gain on him. Moon Crow had nowhere to hide and was only armed with a terrible idea made up by a scared twelve-year-old on the run.

"I am so scared!" He screamed as he dodged two more arrows. "I don't know if I can do this alone. Are you still with me?"

Truly being alone is a task that you will never be able to achieve.

As the Creator of Dreams spoke to Moon Crow all his fear faded from him, and hope became something he could believe in. "What am I supposed to do?"

Do you remember when I taught you to dance amongst the stars?

Memories from his dream flooded his mind of how they flew through the rings of a planet for fun and the time they played tag in an asteroid belt. They were games. They laughed together like brothers as they dodged in and out of danger and tried to do tricks to impress one another. Fear was never part of the equation.

Moon Crow looked over and saw the Creator of Dreams riding beside him. "You came!"

Show me what you got. I'm watching.

Simple. But powerful. This one quote is the foundation of everything that the Bodites adhere to within their belief system. In every aspect of the choices and actions that they take and live by.

Moon Crow's perception of the entire situation had changed, and it had now become a game. He imagined that arrows were burning balls of light that looked like shooting stars and he and the Creator of Dreams began pushing their boards to the limits of speed and performance, as they flew closer and closer to the edge of the asteroid they were shooting across the surface of.

The Creator of Dreams was swaying with Moon Crow, but he wasn't dodging anything. Moon Crow noticed this and asked, "Are you really here?"

For you, I am really here. The Creator of Dreams turned around on his board, looked at the bounty hunters, and sighed. *They are not ready.* He spun on his toes and landed with a nice strong stance on his board. He looked over at Moon Crow and then back at the edge that was rapidly approaching. *Are you?*

"You have known me long enough to know my answer." They had been weaving back and forth, making harder turns, in part to dodge the incoming asteroids, but there was another purpose. They were drawing the bounty hunters in. It was dangerous, because the closer they were the better their aim, but Moon Crow needed them right on top of him as they reached the edge. "Some might say this is either terrifying or crazy." Moon Crow wept as he began to understand. "It is nothing compared to what happens if I give up now."

His timing was good. As Moon Crow cleared the edge, he grabbed his board and removed it from his feet deactivating it, and Moon Crow fell. One of the mounts was able to stop in time but the other, along with its rider went over the edge as well. The mount had tried to stop. The momentum from the abrupt move separated Pontoon from the steed as they both went over the precipice. Pontoon screamed in desperation as he tried to get back to his mount, but he was too late and wasn't touching it when it sensed its mortal danger and teleported back to the top of the ledge. Without its rider, the marble unicorn was forced to shut down. It went to sleep as if its rider had dismounted and was now waiting for them to return.

"Give me your board or I'll kill you!" screamed Pontoon, grasping for an arrow as he fell.

Moon Crow knew that if he helped him, he would just overpower him, take the board, and return him to Dakas. It made Moon Crow sad. It made him sad that there was no way to save him and save himself. It made him sad that he was going to have to choose for someone to die, but most of all, it made him sad that Pontoon would be so stupid as to threaten the life of the only person who could save him. "Too dumb to live, Brother." Moon Crow slid the board under his feet, and it quickly slowed him to a hover. Pontoon took a shot, but it was wild and missed Moon Crow by more than his arm's length.

Another passed much closer but that one had come from above. Tongo screamed "I will kill you for that!" and fired again.

Moon Crow got to the ground as fast as he could and as he reached the bottom Tongo's mount teleported itself and its rider to the bottom of the cliff. In a rage, Tongo continued his pursuit. "This is it!" Tongo screamed as he chased the boy. "You are finally going to be free of Dakas. It will be costly but accidents...do... happen!" They raced along the desert and Tongo pushed his mount to its limits. "I am going to set you free!" He whipped his mount with the reins. "Because I am going to kill you!"

Tongo was so locked on to his target that he didn't notice the sandstorm that they were flying towards, and if he had he wouldn't have cared. They both went into it at full speed. Moon Crow dropped into another canyon as they hit the wall of sand and wind.

Moon Crow wasted no time and pushed forward with Tongo closing in. They flew out of the sand wall and Moon Crow stared in horror as he understood where he was. He had only touched the edge of the storm. The sandstorm was just the outer ring of what was known as a sand spire. It was a magical storm with a giant wind wall larger than most cities that surrounded it. In the center was a maelstrom of magic creating a tornado made of magic and wind. They were almost myths and only formed in places of great power.

"I'm going in." Moon Crow yelled to Tongo. "If you want me, you are going to have to catch me."

Together they raced along the desert floor. All the sand had been pulled away by the sand wall and now the unicorn was able to get a sure footing, slowly Tongo crept in on his prey closer and closer. He pulled an arrow and took aim, ready to fire and end everything, but his instincts forced his attention, and although he wanted to kill the boy, he did not wish to die. He chose to pull away and tried to stop the mount before it hit the tornado but both hands were busy with his bow. It was his moment, and he flinched. A flinch that cost him everything. By the time he could get his hands on the reins to stop his mount, it was already leaping headlong into the maelstrom. It reared as it was hit with the magical storm and Tongo was picked up and smashed by the force of the cyclone.

Moon Crow did not flinch. He powered into the center of it and rode the currents of its power, heading toward the top. He and his board were hit with winds and debris, but Moon Crow held his path and found The Way, and somewhere in the middle of the chaos, in the middle of the storm, Moon Crow let go. As he glided in the power of it all he saw the Creator of Dreams riding with him. He pointed to his wrist and then to Moon Crow's. Moon Crow looked down and to his amazement he watched his manacle unlatch itself and fall off.

You are now free. Free from the bondage of that which has enslaved you.

Dakas, or Moon Crow's former life was never mentioned. Instead, they rode the currents of magic together. When the storm died out Moon Crow saw that there was something at the center of the storm. It was there, that Moon Crow found the Immovable Stone and swore to protect it. At the heart of the storm, and that is why it is still considered a sacred place to the Bodites to this day. Because it was where Moon Crow found The Way.

...

As the image faded and everyone who had heard my story was no longer in the desert with Moon Crow, but sitting in the tent at the Bodite encampment, it took them a moment to realize where they were. Like waking up from a dream that was thought to be real, their minds needed a moment to remind themselves that 'this reality' is what was actually happening.

While they were all still clearing their minds I bowed and stepped away before they could ask me too many questions. I had to speak with my brother, and I was pretty sure I knew where to find him.

21

THE BROTHERHOOD OF SHADOW

Dalen Pax arrived with Master Peace and Christoph into the Temple of Shadow via the Tree of Travel and were met by ten Shadow Warriors and their Shadow Lord, Master Blade. They moved slowly away from the tree and toward the center of the room. As they moved forward the Shadow Warriors closed in behind them and moved with them as a single group.

The Shadow Warriors were wearing the same Midnight Blacks that Oubliette wore, and they were almost indistinguishable from the shadows that filled the room. They were also armed with short swords that had the same effect on the scabbard and handle, but for the time being, they all had their weapons sheathed. The only part of them that didn't seem like shadows were their eyes which caught the dim light like an animal and gave off a low purple glow. From those eyes came black smoke that mingled with the shadows.

"You know that moment right after the Shadow Warriors surround you, and you think to yourself, this might have been a mistake?" Christoph was doing his best to keep his temperament in check. "I think this is it."

"I know what you mean." Master Peace made eye contact with Master Blade. Master Blade looked through Master Peace's soul with a piercing stare that normally sent fear into a man with an icy grip. Master Peace was all too familiar with that look. He used to wear it when he trolled the halls of his high school, looking to intimidate anyone to make himself feel powerful. Master Peace batted his eyes dramatically back at Master Blade.

Dalen glanced around at the Shadow Warriors and remarked, "Did you ever get the feeling that you are being watched?"

Christoph stopped mid-step and turned around to face Dalen. "You feel it too? So, it's not just me?"

"Enough!" Master Blade was now furious. These two monks from the Brotherhood of Light were an example of everything he hated about them. They were disrespectful, loud, and arrogant. "The light has dared to walk the shadows and the shadows reject you!" He was speaking with hatred that dripped from his words like venom. "You come here and show no respect. The same respect that you would demand from us if we were standing in your precious Temple of Light."

"In all honor and respect, thank you for seeing us today, I am sure you are a very important man with more important things to do than answer the petty request of two lowly monks of an order that has nothing but respect for you. Our actions were a sad attempt to keep ourselves from being overpowered by the sheer magnificence of the Brotherhood of Shadow and we would never intentionally mean to cause any dishonor or disrespect." Master Peace gave a very formal bow of the Brotherhood of Light. "That said, if the roles were reversed you would find yourself on the other side of a chasm from the Temple of Light, and the only way to get across is with a leap of faith. If you were standing in my Temple, it means you earned the right to be there, and if I were to greet you there I would do it as an equal brother."

Dalen and Christoph looked at each other and respected the burn, but then returned their gaze to Master Blade. All three of them discreetly and without breaking eye contact reached up, made a quick galaxy, and then readied themselves again for the battle to come.

Master Blade was furious. Again, they had disrespected him, but what could he expect from an ignorant Brother of Light? Master Blade thought of the teachings of the Temple of Shadow and reminded himself that while anger is a useful weapon cast outward, it is an even greater tool reflected inward. He turned his rage inward and let it burn his soul, fueling his power, all the while changing his temperament outwardly and speaking with a calm and almost friendly voice he said, "How true, well then, allow me to offer you the same." Master Blade stomped his foot, and the circle of Shadow Warriors opened a path directly to him. "I have spoken with the shadows, and our Ancestor Guardian, and they have told me much. You are a master? Are you not?"

"I am Master Peace of the Brotherhood of Light." His words were clear and strong.

Master Blade bade him to come forward. "Please Master Peace of the Brotherhood of Light. I am Master Blade of the Brotherhood of Shadow, and I ask you to come forth and stand with me..." Master Blade gave a formal Bow of the Brotherhood of Shadow. "As equals." Then all the Shadow Warriors copied the bow and stayed in that position.

"You got this." There was a sense of assuredness in Dalen's voice. "Remember. Every second that we aren't being murdered by creepy glow-eyed shadow people, the plan is working."

Master Peace gave a nod to Dalen and Christoph. ‹Here we go.› He gave a smile and walked up to meet Master Blade, who was a little more than a third into the room. Together they gave each other the standard bow of their respective school of learning. The healer and the killer.

Black smoke poured from the jade dragon heads along the ceiling and came together as a shadowy mass in the center of the room. Within it, two glowing purple eyes could be seen. "Behold!" Master Blade called out. "The ancestor guardian has come!" All of the Shadow Warriors stood up and gave a different bow that ended with each of them lowering their heads to the floor. Master Blade gave a different bow, and though his head was still up, he was now on his knees.

From within the shadow, a whisper of a voice spoke. "I am the founder of the Temple of Shadow. You are within my domain. I will speak to the holder of truth. Now."

Dalen knew he had to go, but he first turned to Christoph and asked, "Are you going to be okay?"

Christoph looked around and put his hands on his hips. "Can I handle ten guys who have their heads on the ground?" He shrugged. "Sure, and look they aren't even using their weapons. I got this." Dalen began to protest his answer, but Christoph laughed and pushed Dalen towards the smoke. "I got this. Go. I order you as King."

"You are the king that the shadows spoke of." Master Blade looked over to Master Peace and added, "This will be fun."

Dalen Pax inverted his form and turned incorporeal. Viewing through the lens of the spirit world the room they were in now looked different. Darkness hung in the room like black fog. Light was being produced by the jade dragons giving everything a sickly green hue, and Dalen could feel their glowing purple eyes upon him. Glowing lines of green light made out a pattern on the floor and it was all too familiar. He looked back and saw that three concentric circles covered the entire floor. Christoph was standing in the outer ring that was recognized as the body, Master Peace was standing in the middle ring that was recognized as the mind, and in the center where Dalen stood, was the circle for the soul.

Dalen looked over to Master Bo, who could now be seen while Dalen was in this state. "This is it...isn't it? Your Trial?"

"Indeed, it is Master Truth...or should I say, Brother Truth. The shadows have told me much." Master Bo smiled and gave the slightest of bows. "Also, you come to me injured and not at full strength." His lip pouted for a moment and mockingly he said, "How terrible for you."

"What's the trial Master Bo?" Dalen knew the trap had already sprung. They had separated each of them.

"Ah. Master Blade is about to explain." Master Bo's smile was almost demonic as he spoke.

"Here is the price for using our tree." Master Blade pointed to Christoph. "You! The would-be King. It is said that a king should fight like ten men. Here is your opportunity to prove it." Then he turned to Master Peace. "You will only face me healer. One on one... as equals."

"What of Brother Truth?" Master Peace began to charge his ki. Although they were still talking, he knew the fight had already begun.

"Oh, don't worry about him, he faces the shadows themselves. You should worry about yourself. So, you are the master of the Temple of Light?"

"I am a master. I am not The Master." Master Peace took a

breath and let his mind go blank.

"Ah but, you are the master who is here." Master Blade began to crouch down low and circle Master Peace. He drew his blade from his back and the blade itself was shadowed. "Do you like it? It is a Shadow Blade, and this is what it does."

Master Blade had been holding in his rage and hatred. He held it as it burned him and caused him pain, and now he focused his ki and directed all of his pain and anger and hatred of this monk through the Gnosis Stone in his blade. As he did, the Shadow Blade turned completely black and began to exude black smoke.

Master Blade held his Shadow Blade aggressively at Master Peace as he continued to slowly circle him. "Show me how a Master would handle this."

Master Peace responded by activating the Dragon Claw. The three-toed claw opened wide as a ball of light appeared in it. Master Peace readied himself as he began to wield it like a mace. He had been focusing his ki and had a strong charge built up which he channeled into the ball of light. He took a deep breath in and as he let it out the dragon claw opened wider, and the ball grew to about the size of his head.

"The shadows have spoken to me about you." Master Blade began to shift the focus of his ki from his Shadow Blade. He paid enough attention to it so that it would hold the charge he had given it but refocused most of his ki on the mask in his other hand. He used his ki to give it a charge, and as he placed it over his face, he spoke the word required to activate it.

Master Peace watched as Master Blade faded from his mind. As it happened, he understood that his senses were being played with. Master Blade had not turned invisible. Master Peace's mind refused to acknowledge his presence, and so it was just not drawing him in. He knew it but could do nothing about it. Even though his adversary had vanished Master Peace knew that he was there. Peace was ready to strike but could not use any of his physical senses to detect him.

From all around him, Master Blade's voice echoed. "What chance do you think you have? You have claimed the title of master for what? A week? I am the Grand Master of the Brotherhood of Shadow. What possible hope could you possess?"

Master Peace winced in pain as a cut appeared on his left arm. It wasn't the deep slash of a sword strike. It was a cut. Deep enough to hurt but made with precision and accuracy. Master Peace fought against his instincts as they tried to act in fear. His mind was racing, trying to figure out what to do. Had Master Blade just walked right up to him and cut him in the arm, and he couldn't do anything about it, because his mind refused to register that he was there? Master Peace believed that his only chance would be to draw him out. "So, that's the Brotherhood of Shadow's big secret. Hide like a coward."

Master Blade was standing to Master Peace's left, but he was sure he couldn't be noticed, so he passed behind him and took another stance to his right. Master Blade believed that it was more honorable to attack someone on their weapon side, so he was preparing to grant him this honor. He was going to kill this whelp and spill the blood of a Master of the Brotherhood of Light on the floor of the Hall of Shadows. In his mind it was not a matter of whether he was going to win, but a matter of whether he could milk his victory for everything it was worth. He reached out with his blade and with the precision of a surgeon he made a small cut on Master Peace's cheek.

Master Peace reeled back and swung defensively as blood dripped from his cheek. He reached up and touched the wound and then looked at the blood on his hand. "Too scared to face me?" He tried to push past his own mind, but still could not see Master Blade.

Christoph wasn't having the same problems. He knew that each of the Shadow Warriors had activated some form of magic, there was a warble that appeared around them like the distortion of heat, but as it did, he felt the Water Blade awaken. The eye in the hilt began to glow a beautiful indigo. Christoph's mind entangled itself with the eye and its power and vision became his own. The eye allowed him to see the present and within that vision of the present, he could see the Shadow Warriors. It took him a moment to understand what had happened. The warriors believed they were invisible to his sight so each of them relaxed their stance and defenses, believing themselves to be safe.

Another useful gift was granted to him because of the eye. Aside from being able to see the warriors as if they were not cloaked, he could also discern what their move was going to be with the first twitch of a motion. He understood the meaning of their actions with great clarity, and it was unlike anything he had ever experienced. All of this occurred to Christoph as he watched the ten Shadow Warriors begin to sneak up on him in plain sight. He had to stifle his smile and continued to pretend to look past them as if he couldn't see them.

One of them made their first attack. As he lunged forward with a thrust, Christoph reached across his own body and then swung the Water Blade back as the thrust came in, safely pushing the attack far enough to the side so that it would miss him, leaving the Water Blade between Christoph and the Shadow Warrior's Shadow Blade. He pivoted his weapon using the Shadow Blade as a fulcrum, moving it from a vertical position to a horizontal position, and pushed down on the Shadow Warrior's Blade as he quickly took a step forward. The Shadow Warrior was not ready for the block and was surprised by the motion. Christoph reached up and grabbed the back of the Shadow Warrior's head and thrust it forward as he brought up the Water Blade and smacked him with it, making his face hit the flat blade with a satisfying 'thunk'.

Christoph stood his ground and flourished his weapon, and the Water Blade turned back into water. "You are going to have to do a lot better than that." Christoph didn't hesitate. He turned around and swung a horizontal attack. Water sprayed out toward a quarter of the circle that surrounded him freezing in mid-flight and three of the Shadow Warriors were hit with ice stilettos.

Dalen's first thought was to save his friends. They had been separated on purpose and either Christoph or Master Peace could really use his help, but Master Bo forced his attention back to his own trial as black smoke began to emanate from him. It became thicker and as it began to envelop Master Bo, he stepped back into it and blended into the shadows and smoke. The jade dragons began to pour shadow and smoke into the room and soon Dalen was surrounded by darkness and shadow.

Master Bo's voice came like a whisper but echoed from everywhere. "And now Brother Truth, the darkness shall eat your soul." Dalen was surrounded by darkness and in every direction he looked, he could see multiple sets of glowing purple eyes, out in the darkness, watching him.

Christoph had dispatched about half of the Shadow Warriors, and they retreated long enough to review a different approach and strategy. Christoph had a moment, scanned the room, and locked on to Master Peace. He was bleeding from multiple cuts and while he was trying to take a defensive position, Master Blade kept moving around Master Peace, who didn't move as if he could see his opponent. Christoph touched his pin and activated the Eye of the Beholder and although he was still surrounded, he kept his eyes locked onto the two Masters.

Master Peace had already taken five cuts and had not yet been able to overcome the abilities of Master Blade. Fear was doing all that it could to take control of his mind. He knew that if he were going to win, he would have to do it without the mind-numbing effects of fear and pain. He closed his eyes and cleared his mind of all thoughts. In the silence, he found his peace and let his mind go blank, but in that peace, there was something that he had not expected. Another's thoughts. Within that peace, his mind opened to what Christoph was sending. He saw himself and Master

Blade. He used Christoph's vision to know where Master Blade was but made no physical response to tip his hand.

Christoph held steady even as the Shadow Warriors began their second attack. He fought them with his peripherals and continued to keep his eye on Master Peace and Master Blade. Master Blade stepped in to make another cut and that is when Master Peace acted.

Master Blade had moved in slowly to make another cut. Master Peace waited until the last second and with all his speed reached up with his off-hand and grabbed the wrist of Master Blade while at the same time sending his light mace careening into Master Blade's face. The blow found its target and Master Blade's mask took the main hit, knocking it off of his face, making him instantly perceivable to Master Peace.

Dalen was unaware of any of it. Every direction he looked hundreds of eyes stared at him from the darkness and Dalen had no idea which was Master Bo or if any of them were. He was not at full strength and acting within the spirit world was not something he had grown accustomed to yet. With all of that against him, coupled with whatever Master Bo was doing, Dalen could feel what strength he had slowly fading from him as if the darkness itself was draining his life force.

From within the dark, Master Bo's voice taunted Dalen again. "I am going to kill you, and you are defenseless to stop me. How does someone as pathetic as you ever become Master Truth?" At that moment... Dalen didn't have an answer.

As Master Blade got to his feet he tried to locate his mask, but it was now on the other side of Master Peace who was standing at the ready. Master Blade refocused his ki and channeled it all into his Shadow Blade. The blade began to hum and black smoke poured from it.

"Well done, but all you have done is convince me to stop playing with you." He came in at Master Peace with an attack and although Master Peace blocked it, it left them in a lockup with each of them pushing against each other. Slowly Master Blade began to push in on Master Peace. "Now I am going to show you the power of shadow, and then... you will die." Master Blade's sword began to push into the ball of light. "You may call yourself a Master, but your light is weak."

Christoph had taken down another while trying to keep Master Peace in sight, but once he saw that he had knocked off Master Blade's mask and was able to see him again, he was able to refocus on his assailants. The final four had him surrounded and fought together as a team, Christoph was being attacked from all sides. He had lost his momentum helping Master Peace, and taken a few hits, now that they knew that Christoph could see them, the Shadow Warriors were fighting him with all that they had and were on the defensive.

Christoph had been chosen to defend Venger for his abilities with a sword. He was one of the greatest swordsmen of his time, but these were fully trained Shadow Warriors that had trained to fight as a team, and if possible, to attack where their opponent could not see it. He had done well but he was losing.

Master Blade was not only a strong man, but he was channeling all his anger, pain, and frustration through the Shadow Blade, and it gave it the power to push through Master Peace's light. Peace was now injured and doing all that he could to keep his mind focused.

"You, see? You are no master. How could you defeat me? The Brotherhood of Light has no idea what it means to stand in the shadows. You have no idea what power there is within it. This is why you fail. My Shadow Blade is powered by all of my hate. All of my pain!" Master Blade pushed in harder, and Master Peace's Light began to diminish. "What do you have, Healer? Your faith?" He leaned all his weight on Master Peace and sneered. "Hope?"

Master Peace realized he was right, but not in the way that Master Blade had planned. He was a healer and the thing that he did have was not just his faith but the faith and hopes of thousands of people over thousands of years. Power, that was given to him the first day he arrived in Venger.

"Thank you for reminding me." Master Peace smiled and closed his eyes. He took a breath in and as he let it out, he let go. His mind harmonized and he remembered who he was. Master of Peace. The ball of light changed color to a brilliant white and it exploded into a concussive sphere of light and magic that launched Master Blade away from him and saturated Master Peace and the entire room with healing light.

Less than an hour had passed since Dalen and Master Peace connected themselves as brothers, in a ceremony they both had learned while being trained at the Brotherhood of Light. Unlike the

Brotherhood of Shadow which focuses on gaining power and prestige for oneself, they had built a connection that focused on sharing the power to strengthen each other, together, and as Master Peace lit up like he had a choice, it rippled through their connection and the silver stones throughout Dalen's body began to glow.

All of Dalen's life force returned to him and he was at full power. All the weakness that had been brought on by the Fountain of Truth was healed and Dalen Pax felt like his old self. He looked around with the eyes of a jinn. They pierced the darkness as they glowed blue and violet.

Dalen sensed Master Bo everywhere and he realized that all the eyes that stared at him from every direction were all him, he had become one with the darkness. Dalen flipped over the Master Coin in his mind and remembered the lesson he had learned all those years ago with Master Ki in the water.

Dalen reached out with one hand. He focused all of his energy on the center of his Heartstone and then split it. Sending energy going both directions within himself at once, activating his Divine connection at his solar plexus and activating his Arcane power through his throat chakra as he spoke a single word.

Tag. As Dalen spoke a bolt of pure divine light shot from his hand. Since Master Bo had completely melded with the darkness and shadow, hitting him with the bolt of light was a task that was impossible to fail.

Master Bo howled in the darkness. His surprise was palpable. The strike forced him to retake his form as he lost concentration. He looked at Dalen with anger. "I will destroy you!"

"Fascinating." Dalen aimed his hand randomly into the darkness again. *Tag*. The bolt shot into the darkness, but the light still found its mark. It knocked Master Bo to the floor.

"Shadows, protect me." Master Bo barely got to his feet when he was hit with another blast of divine light that sent him sprawling again. "Stop that!"

Dalen aimed both hands at Master Bo and asked, "Do you yield?"

As the light rippled through the room it hit Christoph and as it phased through him, he found that all of his wounds had been healed. Christoph took a deep breath of relief. "Gentlemen, this is your chance to flee."

The Shadow Warrior that was directly behind Christoph thrust his sword toward Christoph's back, but as he moved Christoph innately knew what move the warrior was going to make. He spun in place to his right and brought the Water Blade around so that he was able to block the thrust. He continued his spin and stepped forward, bringing his left fist hard across the Shadow Warrior's face. Christoph swung his right arm out toward the rest of the Shadow Warriors and took aim. He launched a ball of water from the Water Blade roughly the size of an orange, and as it splashed into the Shadow Warrior's face that was farthest from him, it froze in place, blocking not only his vision but his air supply, he dropped his Shadow Blade and began to fight to remove his mask so he could breathe.

The Shadow Warrior that Christoph had punched recovered. His head was still ringing, and his head was still spinning so his attack was off balance, but he came back in toward Christoph. Christoph switched hands, parried the attack easily with his off-hand, and followed up with another punch that lifted the Shadow Warrior off the floor, rendering him unconscious before he could return it.

Christoph's vision allowed him to see that another Shadow Warrior was trying to attack him from behind. He switched hands again and the Water Blade froze solid. Christoph brought the sword over his head and laid it diagonally across his back just as the strike came in and blocked it. Christoph turned his head to look at them directly, and the Shadow Warrior could see that Christoph's eyes were glowing indigo. He gave her a small nod and said, "Ma'am." As he spoke the Water Blade grew colder and it began to freeze her Shadow Blade. She stepped back and Christoph took a half turn and used his momentum to attack her. She blocked his attack with her Shadow Blade, and it shattered into a thousand pieces. She stared in disbelief for a moment then tried for a frontal attack, but as she stepped forward, she stepped directly into Christoph's kick to the side of her head and fell to the ground unconscious.

Christoph turned to face the final Shadow Warrior. "And then there's you." Christoph and the Water Blade were now in harmony and were flowing as one. He would think what he wanted it to do, and if it was within its power it obeyed. "For you, I've got something Blizzard himself used on me in a sparring match, and I am going to be honest with you, I hated it. Are you ready?" The Shadow Warrior took a new stance to suggest he was ready. "Alright. But when you wake up later, don't feel bad. I never figured out how to handle it either."

Christoph tilted the Water Blade back and began to take running steps toward the Shadow Warrior. When he was about a body length away, he leaped into the air and brought the Water Blade down with all his might. The Shadow Warrior brought up his blade horizontally to block it, but just as their weapons made contact, the Water Blade returned to its liquid form. The Shadow Blade cut right through it with no loss of momentum and the Water Blade solidified as it passed through, bringing the final blow crashing down on the warrior's mask at full force, as if the warrior's blade were never there. Christoph had turned the Water Blade, so the strike impacted the Shadow Warrior's head flat-bladed but the concussion was strong enough to leave him knocked out on the floor. Victorious, Christoph looked across the room to check on Master Peace.

Master Peace had now extended the chain on his weapon. He swung the ball of light around himself and then, with a simple action, he released the chain, and the ball flew out fifteen feet and was barely blocked by a retreating Master Blade. Behind him was a dark shadowy cloud, with flashes of light pulsing through it like flashes of sheet lightning.

"I will never yield to you!" screeched the ghost of Master Bo. He moved through the shadows, latched on to Dalen's back, and actively tried to drain his life energy. "I am darkness.

I am shadow."

At first, Dalen tried to maneuver in a way to be able to get a hold of Master Bo. There was no way to reach him effectively. Dalen struggled to break free, but Master Bo's ability to siphon his life energy was strong, and Dalen's vision began to grow dark. "This is your last warning," Dalen said defiantly.

Master Bo reveled as he drained Dalen's energy. "I am Death."

"Those are great names. I have a few myself." In his mind, Dalen opened his magic circle and began to harmonize the Soul Sphere. "You know me as Master and Brother Truth, but I am so much more. I am Dalen Pax, the Reality Bender, and The Jinn of Time." Dalen had stalled long enough to harmonize the Divine Element with its counterpart the Arcane, to ignite the Soul Sphere. "Oh yeah, I am also known as Father Light. The 'day' that I seize." Dalen's stones began to radiate Divine energy. Feeding off Dalen was now like trying to stand under a waterfall to get a drink. He was no longer drinking, he was drowning. "I am a divine being and I have more power than you could possibly hope to drain. I warn you again if you do not stop, it will end you dark spirit."

Master Peace retracted his chain and when the ball of light was once again connected to the rod he reattached it to his belt. "Yield now, or I am going to have to give you a demonstration of the truth about me. You think the Brotherhood of Light is weak because we don't understand the dark?" Master Peace opened himself up for Master Blade's next strike and stood there with open arms waiting for the attack. Master Blade took the bait and came in with a thrust, intending to stab Master Peace in the heart. As the sword came toward him Master Peace stepped forward and to the left. He deflected the Shadow Blade and as it continued its forward motion, he ran his hand along the flat side of the dark weapon until he got passed both blade and handle. Then he reached over and around Master Blade's right arm hooking at the elbows. Master Peace continued his motion, reaching further under Master Blade's arm and grabbing his uniform. As he did, he fiercely pulled Master Blade toward him, locking them in place together. Since Master Blade had built momentum from his thrust, he was pulled off balance and only stopped when both of the masters' right shoulders collided. Master Peace unceremoniously reached down with his left hand and firmly gripped all the material he could, just slightly lower than Master Blade's tailbone, and with all his might lifted the poor fellow off his feet.

Master Blade's toes were barely scuffing the ground, and he dropped his sword. He breathed in deep and clutched at Master Peace's tunic.

"Yeah. Hard to do shadow magic while you have your loincloth pulled up into what I like to call The Divine Atomic Wedgy." Master Peace pulled a little tighter and raised Master Blade off the floor completely. Master Blade let out a high-pitched squeak. "Uh-oh. I know that sound, I caught one of the boys, didn't I?" Master Peace just held him in the air while indescribable pain and dishonor filled Master Blade. Master Peace got right next to Master Blade's ear and whispered. "Most of us at the Brotherhood of Light are not there because we do not know the

dark. We are there because we know the darkness all too well."
Master Peace let Master Blade go, when he did Master Blade's
first action was to reach behind himself with both hands, bend
over, and try to remove his undergarments from their uncomfortable
location. Master Peace had seen this too many times and knew he
could count on that maneuver. He retrieved his Dragon Claw and
activated it. With one hand he grabbed the back of Master Blade's
head and shoved it down further, while the other hand brought up
the Dragon Claw, which had been transformed into a swirling vortex
of light, shoving his face into it. "Light swirly!" He charged his
ki one last time and blasted Master Blade with enough energy to
knock him out.

Christoph walked up clapping. "Well done Master Peace. If I
had to guess, you have done that before."

"A former profession." Master Peace picked up Master
Blade's mask, placed it into his satchel, and took Master Blade's
Shadow Blade as a souvenir.

Christoph had two Shadow Blades slung over his shoulder.
"What changed?"

"Dalen Pax." Master Peace looked over to where the flashes
of light were happening. "I wonder how he is doing."

The flashes stopped for a moment and then one bright
light began to grow in the darkness. It grew brighter and in size.
Christoph backed up a little. "I think we are about to find out."

The light grew in intensity, but the shadows seemed to try
to suppress it. It engulfed the light with all its might, but it was to

no avail. The light erupted in an explosion and cast all the shadows from the room sending Master Bo howling back from whence he came.

Dalen Pax was corporeal again. He was floating in the air and taking a deep breath in. "I warned him." Dalen let out his air slowly and as he did his stones released their light and diminished back to the silver tones. He looked at both Christoph and Master Peace. "You both all right?"

"I feel ten years younger." Christoph looked around. "Thanks for that pick me up in the middle of that fight. Saved my life, Master Peace."

"Agreed." Dalen Pax hugged Master Peace. "That is why you are a master. I was losing until right then. I am pretty sure I can say that if it weren't for whatever you did, I would have died at the hands of that evil spirit.

"I was only able to do what I did because Christoph wouldn't break eye contact so I could see. If it weren't for your sacrifice, I wouldn't have been able to see Master Blade and I would have met my end as well."

"Yeah, well..." It was becoming fun to try to blame victory on the other, "If it weren't for Dalen risking his life to drink from the Fountain of Truth, again, I would have never received the vision that taught me how to use the Water Blade."

"Oh yeah well...wait, what?" Dalen didn't understand. The vision was about a water trial, true, but the vision that he had gave him the information he needed, to be able to defeat Master

Bo because he was hiding in the shadows the same way that Master Ki was hiding in the water. "I am glad that it helped you, but how was my lesson with Master Ki helpful in learning the Water Blade?"

"Lesson with Master Ki?" Christoph scratched his head. I have no idea what you are talking about. When I watched what you were seeing through the Vengerian Pin I had a vision of when Blizzard and I would spar in Venger. I fought him for years. Years and years, all spent learning how to fight him while he used the Water Blade. I remembered every trick and tactic he ever used on me. It was like he had been training me to one day wield it. The Water Blade is very intuitive and knew what move I wanted it to make as I thought it."

"The vision I had was a memory of how I was trained to defeat my trial." Dalen looked to Master Peace, and then back to Christoph puzzled. He took out his coin and studied the symbol etched in silver, and then turned the coin over and looked at the gold dragon. "I am a fool to think the truth seen by two different people would be the same."

"An understanding that brings you one step closer to being a Master." Dalen looked over to Master Peace and smiled. Master Peace nodded and then added, "I too had a different vision than either of you which led me to an understanding that allowed me to be victorious. Being shown why I chose to become a healer and spending a day as my former self reminded me of two things."

"Oh yeah?" asked Christoph. "What's that?"

"The first is the understanding that I did not find my peace and become a master because I destroyed who I was, but because who I was, and who I am, are the same person. I just make better choices, and two... Since my past is a part of me and will always be part of the foundation of who I am..." Master Peace shrugged with a smirk on his face. "Never underestimate the power of a good wedgy."

22

THE FAITH OF ONE

I knew I had a bit of time before the council was ready to talk. Time I was going to use to contact my brother and get to the bottom of all of this. The Bodite people didn't have a church specifically. They believed the true spiritual connection that each of them was searching for, was out there, amongst the dunes. But I knew from my knowledge download that there was a medicine man who would be able to help me.

Often there is truth in myth, but truth is often just an ingredient to a larger reality. The next part of Moon Crow's story is that he found a caravan that had gotten lost in the desert. Among the crafters and weavers of the caravan, one of the proprietors sold and traded in rare incense and herbs that were grown for many religious and spiritual purposes.

The myth goes that Moon Crow found them in the Verris Desert and led them to the very same oasis that he had woken to the day he created his freedom. It was an enchanted spring in the middle of the dunes, with enough good soil around it to grow crops. Once they were there the proprietor began to grow his herbs and make his incense.

I would guess that the myth came about to explain why they were in the desert, and how they found a location to grow things. That is often how myths are created. Someone asks the question, 'How did we get here?' and then whichever wise man or medicine woman or shaman or priest does his best to explain. Often the truth is lost in history, and so new stories are created. That story is believed to be true and once the entire tribe believes it, it becomes real, whether it is fact or fiction. Therefore, a myth is created. Chances are there was no real Moon Crow. He was an icon. An image. A metaphor that could be shared to help explain the path of The Way, but that is all just a guess. What I knew was the myth as it was understood by Maddicus. As the legend went, there was a holy herb that Bodi, the Creator of Dreams, himself chose to bless with divine power, and if it were used together with a mixture of incense and another plant that was often used in meditation, you could create something called Bodi's Own. A truly powerful hallucinogenic with the ability to break the user's mind free of reality and allow them to connect to a higher plane and speak with Bodi himself for a short while.

I sought out the medicine man and after asking only a few people, I was directed to his tent. I asked permission to come in and when it was given, I slipped into the dark tent away from the watchful eyes of the tribe.

Nearly all the tents were built to create shade, but most were rather open. This tent was dark inside. Large pelts hung from the center of the room and created a dark place filled with intoxicating smoke and incense. In the center of the tent, there was a small fire, the smoke pulled upward and away toward a small vent at the top.

"I am here to speak to Bodi," I explained to the old man who was sitting on the ground on the far side of the fire. I wasn't using Grey Speak at its full power but enough to make sure that he understood me. "Please, will you help me?"

The old man didn't say a word, instead, he offered me a seat in front of the fire with a gesture of his hand, and when I knelt in front of it, he got up from where he had been and came close. "You speak like The Way, and you sound like the Creator of Dreams." As he spoke my mind opened to him. Just as I had done with Maddicus, I took in his knowledge of every myth and story that he knew. I found it endearing how much he believed in it. As a medicine man that would be important. He accepted it completely. It wasn't a matter of faith for him. It was a matter of fact.

"I am a follower of The Way, and the Creator of Dreams I

know well. I know that I may be a stranger to you, but I am not a stranger to your ways. I laced my fingers together and pleaded. I know what I am asking, and I am ready for what awaits me. Please Wise One, help me speak to the Creator of Dreams."

He reached into a small pouch on his belt, produced some silvery powder, and sprinkled it over the fire. As the powder burned it turned the fire green, and the room filled with the smell that comes with a lightning strike. The medicine man opened a clay pot and produced a reddish powder and a vile of myrrh. He poured them both into a stone bowl, added lavender and then ground it all together. He then took a plant from the pouch around his neck and held it up for me to see. As he moved it, small traces of where it had been flowed behind it like a ghost image. He took the plant and sprinkled the mixture on it. An abalone shell about the size of his palm was nearby and he placed the plant coated in his mixture into it. He demonstrated for me without words to find the hole that was naturally created within the shell, and to draw from it with a deep breath. I showed him I knew what to do, and when I motioned to do it a second time, he took a small stick from the fire and touched it to the Bodi's Own as I drew air. My breath pulled along the mixture, and it produced a thick white smoke that I took into my lungs. The old man pinched his nose and put his other hand over his mouth. I understood he wanted me to hold it within me for as long as I could. I did as I was told, but I did not have to do it for long.

I was no longer in the tent; it was as if I had been whisked into the story of another grey bard. I was kneeling on a Bodi board, floating through the galaxy. I looked to my left and saw that I was not alone. There was a being that held the basic form of a man yet was not anatomically correct. His entire body was oscillating with variant rings of color that shifted through the color spectrum. It reminded me of my brother Hip-Gnosis's tie-dye shirt.

"Hello, Brother." I had made it. I was in the presence of Bodi, which meant I could finally get some answers.

Hello Brother. It's good to see you. The voice came from everywhere at once, but I knew the familiar sound of my brother's voice and was not afraid.

"What have you been doing? Why have you hidden these people from the continuum? The one person I can't see, and you have been hiding things." I looked at the being floating next to me on their board, which also moved in shifting colors, and asked, "Why?"

I had to be sure. Hip-Gnosis very rarely spoke directly. His power to create and destroy with a single word was much too potent for him to be able to speak normally. A single slip and he could undo creation, so more often than not he spoke with telepathy. Of course, when he took the form of a god, such as the God of Magic, he spoke directly because he was speaking through the god, and not with his true voice, so it concerned me when he still chose to communicate through telepathy.

"Be sure of what? Hip-Gnosis, you know how I don't like surprises. What have you done?" I trusted my brother, but I also knew that he was known to take an irrational idea to its inevitable end, just to prove the theory wouldn't work under any circumstances. In all the many cases where he had done so, he had always communicated with us. There were times when we would suggest that he could have foreseen the answer, and he would argue that until you have actually done it, you could not know if you were right. It was sometimes difficult, but he had never specifically kept things from the continuum.

You told the story of Moon Crow. Come on storyteller, are you going to suggest you can't see it? His words were biting, and I knew he was just trying to get a rise out of me.

"What I know is the myth that Maddicus knows, but I also know that the truth and the myth are often different. What am I not seeing?" I ran over the story in my mind. It was an interesting metaphor for life. The concept that all people are slaves and the boundaries that people put upon themselves are the prison that we all live within. The Way was a path to find not only yourself but also the ability to truly be free within your lifetime and live with ascended enlightenment. Many religions and beliefs follow a similar pattern. Even the Brotherhood of Light was built on the premise that the true boundaries one faces are created in the mind. Their Leap of Faith is based on this concept. "Why is this one so special that you had to hide it until you were sure, and sure of what?"

Bodi swung out and did a complete horizontal circle, followed by a vertical one, both times with me as the center point, and then came back alongside me.

It has to do with how many people were required to create what stands before you. Hip-Gnosis sounded giddy, like he was excited, but was trying not to ruin the surprise.

"I am assuming the entire tribe. Eighty or so?" It is a small number. It took a thousand people praying every day for years to create the Goddess of the Sea. It's a small number but it is not unheard of. Especially in such a closed-off environment.

Not even close. Hip-Gnosis was about to burst. Bodi started to pull up for a moment and shot out to catch what looked like a falling star. He swept alongside it, reached out with a single hand, and plucked it from the sky.

"Wow. Less than eighty. Considering the tribe started as a caravan that got lost, my guess then is twenty. Got lost in the desert? Almost died? Found the oasis and stayed?" I was guessing at this point. All I had to go on was the myths and stories, and Hip-Gnosis wanted me to grasp some secret that I couldn't see.

Bodi flew back to me then I heard my brother's voice from all around me. *Guess again.* Bodi reached out and handed me the glowing ball of light that he had caught. As I held it my ability to know the truth about an object ignited as a reflex and I saw in my hands a single soul. One being made of pure light. I looked up at Bodi and in perfect Grey Speak he said, *there was only one.*

My mind opened up to a new truth. The myth was not some made-up event used to explain away a history that was no longer committed to memory. Moon Crow was real. The legend I had just told was an accurate accounting of the events that happened nine generations ago. It had not had time to become a myth. Moon Crow saved the caravan, and he became their teacher, and slowly they began to learn The Way.

The Way itself was the Way of Grey. Not only were they producing people who were Bodites, but they were also Followers of Grey. It was unprecedented. Unheard of, but as I stared at the soul in my hand, there was also no denying the truth of it.

"There's more. Hip-Gnosis's giggle reverberated throughout the galaxy.

"More?" I asked, almost afraid to receive an answer.

He ascended. Hip-gnosis was many things, but a liar was not one of them.

"I believe you, but what do you mean, he ascended?" I got up from my kneeling position. It was tricky because I had never been on a Bodi board before. I leaned in towards Bodi until I was right next to him. "Moon Crow ascended? You mean like *a* master at the Brotherhood of Light?"

I mean like a Grand Master of the Brotherhood of Light. He, himself, became a God. Hip-Gnosis was now very serious, and I began to understand why he had to make sure.

I looked at Bodi closely. "Moon Crow?"

This time it was not my brother who spoke, but Bodi who answered. He spoke in Grey Speak and said, *He is the Creator of Dreams, and I am the Dreamer.* He spun all the way around on his board and then added, "But I'm not the only one."

My mind saw generations of Bodites live their lives and continue to find The Way. Every man woman and child of the Bodites wears a manacle of property. They are all slaves. Born into it, but their captors are themselves. Each their own property, but a slave, nonetheless. As they pursue The Way they slowly become closer and closer to the truth that the slavery they are bound to has nothing to do with chains. All of them were asleep, and only the masters knew it was a dream. As they learn that truth they are freed of their bondage and ascend.

I stared with wide-eyed fascination. "They all ascend, how many of them?" Hundreds of souls flew overhead like a meteor shower, and I wept at the beauty of them. "Brother... What have you done?"

I'm telling you I did not do this. As Hip-Gnosis's voice filled the vastness of space it echoed in my mind, and I knew he was telling the truth. *All this was made by a scared twelve-year-old boy. I only facilitated the connection.*

I stood there slack-jawed for a moment. What I was being asked to believe was impossible at best. The idea that a single boy could have the power to manifest a god was legendary, but then to ascend to godhood and take over the faith was unheard of. But then, to suggest that his followers also reach ascension, which had never taken place in any of the dynasties was borderline crazy. "What does this mean?"

I almost fell from the board I was riding as Hip-Gnosis spoke amongst the stars. *It means that we are at the start of the Fourth Dynasty.*

Grand Master Truth of the Brotherhood of Light had made many prophecies. Some of them had come true and some of them had not yet come to pass. Three of those prophecies were specifically about the end of the Third Dynasty and the beginning of the Fourth. The first prophecy was about the first Herald of Time. A monstrous genie who would destroy his own world. It said that he would be successful and that when he destroyed the world, he would find himself in this one. The second prophecy foretold the second Herald of Time. A Jinn who would travel here from the Fifth Dynasty would bring all things into balance and usher in the existence of the God of Time. The third spoke in detail of signs that would signal that the Fourth Dynasty was at hand. It suggested many signs, but one of them went as follows; 'Bathed in the light of the sun and the stars a single soul will call forth divinity and help free the world from its self-made cage.'

It fits but prophecies are often that way. Hard to interpret until after the event, and in hindsight people look back and recognize the connection. I wanted to argue the point but, in my heart, I knew it was true. My mind quickly put things together and I stood there floating in space, too shocked at the truth in my mind to be able to notice that the vision was beginning to fade.

"Brother. I have been traveling with the second Herald. At this moment, the Herald of Time is with the other half of our team. We have come to reclaim the Earth Blade because the children of Dorn can no longer carry them." I looked around and could tell I was about to wake from my vision. I pushed with my mind and tried to stay in that state for another moment. "A new bloodline has been forged through fire and we have but two days to return to Venger. At the end of that time, the first of the heralds are going to try to take action to awaken the Chaos Dragon."

I dropped to my knees and as I did, I felt the ground under them. I was back in the tent of the medicine man. I was half in and half out, but as this reality faded into existence, I heard Hip-Gnosis say, *Then, it is time, and you know what must be done.*

23

THE COUNCIL

I returned to the main tent and located Grelf and her
Vengerian Guardians just as the council had called them back.
They had processed the new information and were ready to speak
to these outsiders. I knew that Grelf would not only have to
convince the council to let them go to the Immovable Stone but
then tell them that she intended to break it and remove the
Earth Blade from it. I knew Hip-Gnosis had created the lore for
this moment. No doubt he had spoken with Grand Master Truth,
who was known to be a seer of the future, and asked him what

would come. So that he could cultivate and prepare the myths and stories in a way so that as we stood before the Bodites, we would be the very people that the prophecy was about. This was Hip-Gnosis's wheelhouse. He had spent two dynasties perfecting the skill of making the myth match reality. I relied on that when she gave them her reason, that they would recognize the myth just as Maddicus had.

"When Moon Crow left this world, he tasked his people to protect the Immovable Stone, and they will guard that place with faith that it was an edict from God." The council was gathering, and I knew I had to make it quick. "They would never let an outsider near the place."

Grelf looked concerned. She whispered quietly from the side of her mouth. "What do we do?"

"When Moon Crow found the Immovable Stone, it is said that the Creator of Dreams suggested that now he had found it, it was his responsibility to protect it, until the day that the Fire Princess would come forth and claim the heart of the Immovable Stone. Which is a sword that lies within it."

Grelf smiled. "Thank you, Will, I understand."

I took a step forward, gave a respectful bow, and said, "Good afternoon." They all gave me a response as one would expect and as they each spoke; I used the same ability I had used on Maddicus and the medicine man. I took each of them in and knew them. Each of them in their respects had assimilated all the colloquialisms and slang we had taught them. Yet, each of them only used the ones that they flowed with. Choosing the words that fit their personalities and who they felt they were.

On the far right and left were Skip and Bounce. Two men in their thirties who exuded strength. They were two of the tribe's protectors, known as Sand Dogs. Both were respected within the tribe and expected to be treated as such.

Next to each of them were Sun Sprite and Dawn Star. Both women had reached an age where they were considered elders but still had years left in their spirit. They were recognized as matrons of the tribe, were highly respected for their wisdom, and often directly consulted in matters of the health and life of the tribe.

Next to them moving inward were the youngest of the council. Both were about the same age as Travis, Sir Adam, and Becky. The male was Bail, and the girl was Glide. It was decided many generations ago that it would be wise to have younger members on the council so that an understanding of the entire tribe could be known, and it became tradition.

Finally, there was Sway. He was the oldest and wisest on the council. His hair had lost its color decades ago and his leathery skin spoke of the years he had spent in the sun, but it wasn't just his age that made him the leader of the Bodites and head of the council. It was his wisdom and knowledge that granted him those titles. He was respected throughout the entire tribe and trusted implicitly. If he told them to destroy their homes and burn their boards, they would do it, because of the faith and trust the entire tribe had in him.

It was Sway that began the meeting. "Sup?" He smiled at all of us. "It's groovy you're hear man. When Maddicus brought Grelf I was all like, whoa. Then she was all like, 'It's cool,' and I was all like, cool. So, awesome. It's groovy you're here."

Bounce waited for Sway to give the opening greeting and then as one of the main protectors, he started asking security questions. "Yo, Dog. Word up? You chill?"

Grelf had only just heard this slang herself but had been paying attention to what they had been saying and felt that she understood well enough to answer. "We chill."

Skip pulled their attention to the other side of the council. "Yo, Sup?" Grelf and the rest looked over to him and gave him a nod. "Dog, you trippin'? Go to the stone, and you are gonna get jacked."

Sun Sprite responded to Skip's threat. "Like totally oh my god." Her tone was bright and bouncy. "Skip, you are like totally out of bounds. They didn't go wheezing on the Immovable Stone. Like, as if. They are trying to be gliding, and you are all up in their grill. Like totally gag me."

Dawn Star Spoke slowly and sounded as if she were intoxicated. "Hey." She waved at us. "Skip is chill. He just wants the four-one-one on the sitch. Don't harsh his ride. He do what he do."

Skip hit his chest a couple of times with his closed fist. "I do what I do."

"Whoa, Skip." Dawn Star held up her hand and Skip

stopped and took a breath. "It's all good."

Grelf nodded to the council but looked to Skip and then slowly moved her focus across each of them, ending her thought while looking at Bounce. "I understand that you are the guardians of the Immovable Stone, and I respect that under almost any circumstances, but I need you to hear me out before you make your decision."

"Gliding." Bail slowly moved his hand, palm down, across a horizontal plane. "We'll lend an ear, but this is very suspect."

"Very sus," added Glide. "Maddicus spoke mad words about you being the Fire Princess." She cocked her head to one side and asked, "Pardon? I mean wha'?"

Sway raised his hand, and everyone fell silent. His command of the room was undeniable and absolute. Grelf thought to herself that this is what it looks like to have your people respect you, and she hoped that one day she could learn from such a man.

When all eyes were on him, he gave a small nod to recognize the respect and then began to speak. "Maddicus is awesome. She glides. She knows these dunes like they were family, and she can feel the storm before it comes. You feel me?" The council nodded. "I know she's on it, so if she talks mad hype about Miss Thing here being the Fire Princess, chances are she's bustin'. I want to hear it from the horse's mouth." He gestured to Grelf. "Show me what's up."

Grelf shrugged and stepped forward. "Okay. Here we go." She took a deep breath and addressed the council. "You. What up?" She gave a small bow. "Y'all know Venger?" The elders nodded. "They're in some bibitz. The world is in some bibitz. Word?" She looked around and gave them a moment to murmur to themselves. "Time Mage is gonna wake up the Chaos Dragon." She looked directly at Sway and added, "Cringe." She continued to swing her vision back and forth so that she had the opportunity to look each of them in the eyes. "Venger put yours truly and the posse on a quest to get the Fire Blade and then the Earth Blade. Clocks ticking." She thought about their society. They were a bunch of sand surfers, and so she tried to devise a sentence that they would understand. "If I bail, the whole world bails on the dunes with a broken board and no water." The message was clear, and it showed in their faces.

Bounce scoffed. "Proof's in the pudding."

Grelf took a moment to look at both of the Sand Dogs and cautiously said, "Things are about to get real." She drew the Fire Blade and as she did it ignited. As the flame appeared the fire surged and engulfed Grelf in fire and light. It was only a moment and when it faded, she was once again in the garments and jewelry of the Wielder of the Fire Blade and Princess of Venger, and her hair glowed like molten steel.

They all stood dumbfounded for a moment, but it was Sway who found his words first. "Wow, man. Groovy."

Sun Sprite clapped her hands and twirled all the way around. "Totally bitchin'."

Both Sand Dogs in unison leaned back and gave an

elongated, "Daaaaaaaaaaamn." And then Bounce added, "That's what I'm talkin' 'bout."

Again, Sway raised his hand and the council fell silent. "Okay. Gliding." We will go to the stone, and then we will see what's up." He began to scan the outside of the tent for Maddicus. When he found her, he pointed to her and then pointed directly in front of him. She walked over and stood where he suggested. She showed no sign of being nervous to be called in front of the council and even gave Grelf a thumbs up as she walked by. "You killed it today." Sway put his hands together and gave her a bow and the rest of the council followed suit.

Maddicus almost teared up. "Fly."

Sway walked over and hugged her. "Ride by our side. Share our dunes." He then stepped back as the council stepped up to meet her. Each of them one by one hugged her and gave her their blessing. Both Sand Dogs knelt behind her and placed their hands on each of her calves as a representation that they were there to support her. The matrons stood on either side of her and took her hands in recognition that they were there to guide her. Both council that were her own age stepped forward, one to each side, and placed a hand on one of her shoulders, to recognize that they understood her. Sway once again stood directly in front of her and placed one hand on her head, as a father might do to his daughter. "You are a true child of Bodi, and we will ride with you until the sun sets on your life." They pulled in close and together as a family they held each other.

I knew what this meant. I leaned in close to Grelf and

asked, "Would I be correct to say that you are ready to do what is needed to obtain the Earth Blade?

"You would be correct." Grelf was speaking in hushed tones like I was. She paused for a moment and then asked, "Why?"

"I believe you have just gained a new member of your team." I knew this ceremony. They were saying goodbye. "Part of the myth of the Fire Princess is that a Bodite will leave the tribe and travel with her. It seems that the council has decided that since she was the one to find you and bring you to them, the honor is hers."

Grelf took a deep breath in and looked up at the tent. "If we bring her, we will be taking her into the lion's den. Once we leave here, we are headed home, and once we get there, we have to face the Time Mage and whatever monster she has on her leash. With a real chance that the Chaos Dragon herself might awaken and destroy everything. How could I possibly ask anyone to risk their life?" I could feel Grelf's concern, as did everyone in the room. She was no longer speaking quietly. I could tell she wanted to cry but would never let herself. "The Verris Desert is far from Venger. On the other side of the world. There is a chance that if we fail in what we are doing the blast won't reach them. There is a good chance that I'm dead, you're dead. It's something we accepted when we started all of this. Becky. Travis. Sir Adam. They knew the risk and made the oath, and I know in my heart that even if it means their last breath... I will not fail, but even so, I may fail anyway." Something was stirring within her, but she stopped for a moment and took a deep breath. She was not going to show weakness and cry in front of her Vengerians or this council. "I talked to her for two days while we rode across the desert. She is a good person, and her soul is one of the bright spots in the universe. How could I actively choose to take her into the heart of darkness?"

"Grelf?" Maddicus's voice stopped Grelf in her tracks. She had been staring straight up at the tent the whole time and had not noticed that she had gained the attention of the entire room. "It is in darkness the brightest light is needed." I recognized that what she was saying was part of the teachings of Moon Crow.

Bounce began to bounce up and down like he was hearing music. "Yeah."

"Do not run and hide from the maelstrom of your life. This is the way of the slave. Stand and live in your last few moments." Maddicus's voice was strained. She was terrified of the notion that what was to come next was fear, danger, darkness, and death, but her strength did not fail her. "Even if you die, you die free."

Skip howled and started bouncing in time with the other Sand Dog. It wasn't until that moment that the team noticed the sounds of drums. It was quiet at first but once they could see that the Sand Dogs were bobbing up and down with it, it began to grow louder. Both matrons had begun to dance. Sun Sprite began to Belly Dance while Dawn Star's dance was more of a Flamenco from Travis's point of view. Sway, like Bounce, was living up to his name.

As Maddicus continued Bail and Glide began to bob to the drum but they both were young and lively, and their dance reflected that youth with hand gestures that moved and swung to the beat.

The other Bodites that had come around to listen were dancing. Music could be heard, coming from all around them. The tribe had joined in. Drums and musical instruments were played throughout the encampment. It was infectious and Grelf and her team began to move to the music as well.

This was what my brother had wanted me to see. A single people united in faith. Held by the creation of a single song. They were creating Grey songs together as a tribe. I looked at them with astonishment and joy. "Oh, Brother." Tears rolled down my eyes. This was the beginning of the Fourth Dynasty. Hip-Gnosis was right. I took it in for what it was, and in my arrogance, I thought I understood, but what happened next still caught me off guard.

Maddicus was no longer speaking scripture but now was speaking from the heart. "Yo. I never bail. I be gliding. Your hood sounds jacked. Time Mage? Monster? Sounds cray cray."

Grelf looked Maddicus in the eyes. They stared at each other for a moment as the music grew louder. "It is cray cray. I can't ask you to go."

Maddicus cocked her head to the side. "You didn't ask."

Grelf didn't break eye contact. Something had happened out in the desert. The two of them became friends and she had sincerely grown to like Maddicus. Grelf channeled her fear through the Fire Blade and allowed it to burn away. "There is only a slim chance that any of us will survive."

"I have no chance to ever live if I turn back now." Maddicus's face was streaked with tears. She stood strong and proud. The tribe cheered and howled at her answer. The beat had been picking up speed in increments and the tribe's dance moved with it as the sound grew ever louder.

Grelf knew in her heart that Maddicus should go, but one fear remained. It was the fear that she had been carrying with her and it weighed on her as she saw this amazing young woman who was beautiful and strong. She asked herself if she could have her risk her life for a fight that was not her own. She knew she had to face it, as she did at the Fire Falls, and she knew she would have to face it again when she stood before the Immovable Stone. If she succeeded, she would then have to face the fear again with the Chaos Dragon, and then every moment of her life for the rest of her days as Queen of Venger. "What if I fail?"

Maddicus reached into the bottom of her soul and stood before The Fire Princess as her true self. "Even if it means my final breath. You will not fail."

The music and drums went quiet, and everyone stopped dancing. The manacle from around Maddicus's wrist made a clicking noise as it unlatched the locking mechanism and fell to the ground.

24

THE WIND CAVES

Dalen Pax had been traveling East with Master Peace and Christoph for five days. Christoph refused magical help from Dalen as they traveled. He was determined to take every step himself. They had traveled the greatest distance from the Temple of Shadow within the first two days due to a rather easy terrain that was hilly and lush as they moved through the thick forests of the region of Kar. But the ground became mountainous and for the last two days, they had been climbing.

The Gold Dragon of the East made its home in the Wind

Caves of Kar, atop the Mountain of Divine Understanding. Dalen had suggested that he use his magic to fly them to the top and while the offer was tempting, Christoph believed that he needed to climb the mountain himself. Master Peace respected his choice and chose to climb with him for safety reasons and Dalen flew ahead to scout out paths that had strong handholds. Even with Dalen looking ahead and finding the best ways to traverse the mountain, it had still taken two days for Christoph and Master Peace to get to their current position. They were nearing the top and the winds had become dangerous.

⟨I found a cave entrance.⟩ Dalen was only thirty feet ahead of Christoph and Master Peace, but the winds were too strong, they could hear each other's voices but weren't able to make out what was being said. ⟨It's just ahead.⟩

Christoph looked up toward Dalen, who was hovering and then looked down to check Master Peace. The switch in depth caused him to have a moment of vertigo and he had to look straight forward at the rock face and breath a couple of times to clear his head. ⟨How is this not the Earth Challenge?⟩ All three of them had a much-needed laugh.

They still had a day but none of them wanted to push that timeline. The wind hit them again and almost pulled Master Peace off the rock face. He gripped the ledge that he had reached and hoped his strength would hold. ⟨I am pretty sure this is an Air Challenge.⟩

Christoph made it to the ledge where Dalen was at the mouth of the cave. He was just getting his footing when another gust of wind hit them. It was so strong that it ripped Master Peace off the edge. Dalen used his magic to sever the rope that tied them together and let Master Peace fall. He knew that in four feet the rope would have gone taut, and the weight of Master Peace falling would have yanked Christoph off as well.

"You cold-hearted bastard! You are going to just let him die?" Christoph looked over the edge as Peace began to fall. He couldn't watch so he turned his attention to Dalen. He reached over and with both hands grabbed Dalen by his tunic, pulled him in close, and screamed in his face. "He was your friend! Your Brother! Why?"

Dalen didn't back down. Instead, his eyes began to glow. "Two reasons." Dalen also grabbed Christoph's tunic and floated them both about three feet in the air. "First. There was no way I was going to let him pull you off this ledge and have to go play, 'Oh no! Which one do I save,' as I tried to save you both. Second, Master Peace was ready to sacrifice himself to get you through this, even if it meant his final breath." Then Dalen floated him back down and stood him right next to Master Peace. "What makes you think I was going to let him fall?"

Christoph reached down and touched the eye on the Water Blade he was wearing on the side of his hip. He turned his head and looked at Master Peace with a mixture of joyous surprise and shock. Master Peace smiled and waved. "Hello."

Christoph hugged Master Peace with the temperament of a charging elephant. He picked Master Peace up off his feet and swung him around. He sat him down and then while laughing like he just got the joke, he said, "Right." He remembered Dalen could move people through the quantum field. "Right." He turned to Dalen and offered his hand. "My apologies. The shock of what I saw blurred the truth."

Dalen's eyes had stopped glowing, and he was laughing. Dalen took Christoph's forearm tightly. "It's all good brother."

With his other hand, Christoph hugged Dalen. "I need to have faith in you."

Dalen hugged him back but was surprised when he saw the look in Christoph's eyes. There was concern and fear in them and Dalen began to feel the stress off Christoph as if there was something wrong. "Christoph, what you did was show faith in me, by being in complete shock when you saw what you thought you saw."

"Thank you. But listen." Christoph placed his left hand on the hilt of the Water Blade. The crook of his thumb rested on the handle of it, but his fingers draped over the hilt and naturally rested on the eye. It granted him the ability to see Master Peace and Dalen for who they were. He could see their strengths and faults and knew them as the individuals they were at that moment. "While I spoke with Gavin, I was shown an image of what was to come. I was shown two possible futures. In either of them, the Chaos Dragon is released."

Both Dalen and Master Peace looked at each other, and then back to Christoph as Dalen spoke. "We know that much. There was a part of us that hoped that we could find a way that the Dragon wasn't released, but the memory of the past that we have is that in the end, it is you who defeats the Chaos Dragon."

Christoph didn't know if this was the right choice. He knew that he was meant to help Dalen, and he hoped this was the path that he was meant to take. "I understand why that would be your target, but the two ways this all goes down has to do with a choice that happens after the Chaos Dragon is freed."

"Yes. I can imagine." Dalen got close to Christoph and patted him on the shoulder. "To be able to defeat such a thing you would have to have a life-altering moment. A moment where there is a choice that dictates whether or not you make that leap of faith."

Christoph stopped Dalen there and said, "I need you to shut up and listen for a moment."

Christoph's eyes were giving off a slight indigo glow, and Dalen looked down to see Christoph's hand on the eye. "You got it." Dalen opened himself up to what Christoph was saying and allowed his mind to accept whatever Christoph was about to say as truth.

"We are moving toward a moment where the world that you know will hang in the balance. The future I saw. Gavin. Hope. Venger. It all comes down to a single choice, and it is not me who makes it Dalen Pax." Christoph's eyes grew brighter, and his hair and clothes moved as if he were underwater. "It is you."

Dalen could feel the truth in it. That wasn't in question, yet he didn't understand. "What do you mean? How is it my decision? I know from history that it is you who defeats the Chaos Dragon."

"We believe you." Master Peace stepped next to them and formed a small circle. "Now help us understand." Master Peace put out his hand to form a galaxy and the other two joined in. As they connected, Master Peace added some of his ki and light to it. As he did, Christoph channeled the energy from the eye into the galaxy. In turn, Dalen opened all three parts of the Reality Sphere and created a connection to have them be as one, both physically and mentally, and then allowed the power of the universe to flow through him and empower this moment.

The three of them were in sync with one another. They were able to see the truth of the moment, but Dalen could control what moment was seen. Because of Peace, what would be seen was bathed in a healing light so that understanding did not come with pain or suffering. It was almost like drinking from the Fountain of Truth but without it killing them.

Each of them could feel and hear the other as if they were just different parts of a single being. They could recognize themselves as themselves, but they could also feel each other as if they were them as well, much like the relationship between the right hand and the left. In that perfect connection, they had become one.

Dalen was used to this feeling. He had felt it many times while perceiving different aspects of himself, like Father Light or Brother Truth. He could now feel that this new part of himself that was Master Peace, was simply marveling at this new connection, and another part of himself, that was Christoph, was confused and apprehensive about what was happening.

He felt the part of him that was Master Peace began to center and calm the part of him that was Christoph and in the same moment he could feel the part that was himself calm. They reveled in it together for a moment and allowed it to flow. There was no holding back from it. Trying to hide something from each other at that moment would be as difficult as hiding something from themselves.

Christoph looked at himself from the point of view of Dalen and then from Master Peace and together they laughed at the amusement of it all. Master Peace and Dalen did the same. They remembered each other's childhood memories and remembered every joke that each of them ever knew. Christoph marveled at the brotherhood that Dalen and Master Peace had. Dalen now knew that as far as Master Peace was concerned, Dalen was already a master as well, but it was for Dalen to decide when it was true. Both Dalen and Master Peace felt the weight that was on Christoph, and the events that they were rushing toward, trying so hard to achieve. Then both Dalen and Christoph noticed a radiance that seemed to come from Master Peace as if he were standing in front of a light and it was shining from behind him. No matter the angle they looked they couldn't see the source, but it shone past him with brilliant white beams of energy that surrounded Master Peace.

Master Peace had been carrying this light with him since the day he arrived in Venger. Like the rest of those he traveled with, he had come upon a garden that had statues of each of them in the center grounds. The statue of him held the weapon he now carried.

For thousands of years, people had come to give prayers and give thanks to him, because he was one of the champions who saved Venger. They prayed, and they gave thanks, and they gave their strength. Each gift was collected and stored in his Dragon Claw, and once he claimed it from the statue, it was imbued to him. He hadn't learned how to tap into it, but the power was there. Waiting to be discovered. Master Peace had all but forgotten about it until the Temple of Shadow. He had touched it, even if it was for only a moment, and now it was beginning to awaken in him. In their shared thought, Christoph came to know that this power would have to be given to him at one point because he would need it if he were ever going to defeat the Chaos Dragon.

It took a few moments to be able to focus on anything other than the novelty of what was happening. It wasn't what they had meant to do. It was amazing, exciting, and terrifying. Dalen reminded himself that this was much like being under the effects of the Fountain of Truth. He knew there was something to that thought, but had to focus on the moment at hand and decided he would try to take apart that puzzle when they were not so attached.

Master Peace argued if Dalen were going to solve the problem of the Fountain of Truth, it would be wiser to look at it from the perspective they were already in.

Christoph agreed and so they took a moment to look at it. What was different now? They concluded that Christoph's connection to the eye was creating a similar but different effect from the Fountain of Truth. One where Dalen was being protected while seeing the truth rather than being poisoned by it. Together they noticed that while Dalen had the Reality Sphere activated and was at full strength his form changed. Dalen could see the same vision of himself that Christoph and Master Peace could see, which was that Dalen's Stones of Power were all activated and surging with energy. As they got brighter his physical body faded as if he were only an illusion or made of smoke. It reminded Dalen of Master Truth.

Together they rolled back through Christoph's memories to the moment where he watched Venger fall to the sea as the Chaos Dragon ripped itself from the ground directly underneath the city. They watched as Christoph relived the moment the image of the Chaos Dragon reveling in its victory was shown to him. The image freezes and Christoph is told that the choice that happens right here is not made by him but made by Dalen. The information burned itself into their memories. The Chaos Dragon was big. Bigger than they had thought and each of them felt themselves pull their hands away to break the connection. As they did, each also felt as if they had become smaller, just being themselves gave them a sense that they had lost something.

"Why?" Dalen blinked a couple of times as his body became fully corporeal again and his stones dimmed and returned to normal. "Why is it me and the decision of the entire world is in my hands?"

"Because you can control time." Christoph's hand was still on the eye. He knew in his heart that time and time again, Dalen was given almost no information and then told by everyone that he had to figure it out for himself. Sure, he knew the understanding behind the logic, but they were coming close to the end and Christoph had always disagreed with the philosophy of having to let people just wander around in the dark until they stumbled on to the right answer by accident. Christoph knew for a fact that was the wrong answer this time. "I am going to do something that no one ever does. I am just going to tell you what you need to know. Most of the time people around you keep information from you, they keep the truth and let you find it on your own, well let me tell you something. I can see this moment for what it is, and I am telling you that you just need to know what's going on because how the hell are you supposed to become the person you are supposed to be if no one tells you what you are supposed to do?"

"Oh my god, Thank you!" It was all that Dalen had wanted since he started all of this.

"There is this prophecy told by Grand Master Truth about the beginning of the Fourth Dynasty. In the beginning, there was supposed to be a God of Time, but he didn't show up. Through any of the dynasties. But when he finally does appear he is going to be preceded by two heralds. Both will have the ability to control and change time itself, and Gavin believes that you are supposed to be one of those heralds. The other he thinks is some demented genie who decimated his own world named DeSalvo." The look on both Master Peace's and Dalen's faces let him know that they knew who he was talking about. "This DeSalvo is trying to destroy this world and is behind the Time Mage and the release of the Chaos Dragon."

"So far, I am with you. We knew that he was behind the Time Mage and the dragon." The part that Dalen didn't know, was what happened next.

"I don't know what the actual choice you make is, but I know why it's you." Christoph took a drink from his water skin and tried to figure out how to explain what made Dalen different. "If you are one of these heralds, it would make sense that you are a time jinn. Time is something that is not easy to mess with. Look, I am going to do my best and I will make choices based on the information at hand and my own free will, and at that moment it will be my choice, but what I choose is known. It is in your past. We know what I do. I defeat the dragon, and as long as everything goes to plan, that is exactly what I will do. I have met my older self, the version who did it, and I am not worried about me. I'm locked in time and no matter what, defeating the dragon is what I am going to do; it is the thing that I inevitably would choose. Have chosen. Will choose again... for the first time... but not you. You and DeSalvo have the ability to change time at will. I saw the future. Your present. I met Gavin and Hope and saw Venger, a port city at water level, so no matter what I inevitably choose, my actions are going to create that reality. But with a single choice, you can change everything and have it go terribly bad. With one wrong choice by you or DeSalvo, all of it can be destroyed and none of it will have ever existed."

"Because I am a time jinn and possible herald of this supposed Time God?" Dalen was getting frustrated and the idea that he may still destroy everything that he had come to cherish weighed on him. "How am I supposed to be a herald to some Time God I have never met?"

"I don't know," admitted Christoph.

"Okay, forget that part. It's prophecy and hearsay. No better than a rumor." Master Peace took a moment and focused his ki on sending them both some peace. "Just go on a fact we do know. You are a time jinn who can bend the reality of time and have the potential to actively alter it."

"It's one of the reasons I made sure you came with me. I was hoping that if you were to alter reality you would do it with me. History says Grelf gets back with her two swords. She makes it, but I didn't know if that would remain true if you went with her. The only way I could protect her and make sure she succeeded was to make sure you didn't go with her." Christoph was almost ashamed to admit it, but it was the truth, nonetheless. "This way if you alter time, it happens here, and I hoped and prayed that I would be able to fix it if something went wrong. It seems though, that the moment it is going to matter, is after the Chaos Dragon is released and before I am able to kill it."

Dalen took a breath and allowed Master Peace's energy to saturate him. "Okay, but how do I find out what that choice is and why I make it?"

"May I make a suggestion?" Christoph was wearing his old smile again. "I know this is my challenge, but I know for a fact that each of us has a gold coin that allows us the opportunity to speak with the wisest corporeal being in the world. Maybe we should ask him?"

Dalen and Master Peace blinked a couple of times and

stared at Christoph. Both began to understand how much power the eye really had, and both agreed with his perception.

Master Peace nodded. "You're right. We should really focus on the task at hand." Christoph's wisdom couldn't be argued with, so they tried to focus on the challenge.

Christoph still had his fingers on the eye. He looked directly at Dalen and peered into his heart and soul. "I'll tell you this. If the whole world comes down to a life-or-death choice, and that choice rests in your hands, I have no worries. I have faith in you Dalen Pax."

Dalen was still trying to accept the weight of this new truth that had been laid upon him. It was a lot to take in. He needed a moment and asked Master Peace to lead the way. Master Peace looked around the small alcove that they had climbed into and found a passageway leading into a cavernous room with large airshafts that filled the chamber they had moved into.

Dalen slowed down time and sat in his thoughts for hours, just meditating on all that had transpired and once he felt that he was ready to move on, he let go of his hold on the frame of time and allowed it to flow naturally. He was now refocused. He knew that if he kept his mind on the possibility of problems in the future, he would lose sight of the present. He took in the immense size of the chamber that was open on the far end to the open sky. As they got closer to where the rock ended, they could see that there was a drop-off straight down, and massive gusts of wind slammed against the rock face creating gusts that blew upward into the cave. "Gentlemen. Welcome to the Wind Caves of Kar."

"It is said that the blasts of air or so strong that they can lift a man off his feet and carry him to one of the chambers above." All three of them looked up and saw that the cave's ceiling had multiple holes in it.

"I see two questions." Master Peace leaned over the edge and tried to gauge the air bursts. "Is the updraft of the wind strong enough to launch a man into one of those shafts, and if so, which shaft do we take?"

Dalen turned to face Christoph and spoke. As he did his voice held a certainty to it that was strong and hard to argue with. "I know you want to take every step, and you will, but for a moment, allow me to check the passages and figure out which is which. Then you can defy death and dismemberment and attempt to reach it. Fair?"

Christoph walked out to the edge and looked down towards the drop-off. He got hit with a large gust of wind that made him step back. "Fair."

"I'm going too." Master Peace stepped to the edge. "This was everyday life at the Brotherhood of Light. You would not believe how many times I have jumped off a sheer cliff. And that was before I learned how to do it."

"Do what?" Christoph asked.

Master Peace turned to face him and smiled. "This." He closed his eyes and intentionally tipped off the edge backward. He howled as he dropped, and his voice was lost for a moment. They began to hear it again and it grew louder and louder until they saw him pop up past them as if he were flying and shot upwards into one of the shafts above. Then over the Vengerian Pin, they heard him say, ⟨You have got to try this.⟩

Dalen whooped and hollered as he launched himself off the ledge and was shot upward into another shaft. Christoph watched as these two crazy monks played tag through the shafts, laughing the entire time with no concern of falling. The entire time singing an odd song they both knew about Dalen having silver balls.

It wasn't long before he decided to no longer sit back and just watch the fun. He tightened the straps on the pack he was wearing on his back and made sure his weapons were secured before he touched his pin and changed to a pair of pants and a shirt with boots. "Hey Christoph," he said under his breath. "How'd you die?" He laughed nervously to himself in half disbelief. "A couple of crazy monks convinced me to jump off a cliff." Christoph scratched an itch along his hairline. "Fascinating." Now just talking to himself, he shrugged and said, "Right?" He took two quick strides toward the edge and leaped out, not knowing what to expect.

Fear was the first thing he discovered as he began to fall. He fell more than far enough for him to question his actions, but now he was in the wind and there was no turning back.

A gust of air caught him and changed his direction so fast that he felt his stomach drop to his feet. Christoph was running on pure instinct, howling as the wind launched him past where he had jumped from and sent him hurling toward the ceiling of the rock formation. He made it into one of the shafts. He almost missed but he used what he had learned from his water trial to help direct his body to alter its course. The shaft led him to a dead end and when the wind ran out of power Christoph began to fall. He fell through the shaft and as he popped out of it, he was facing the business end of an eight-thousand-foot drop.

‹I bet you're thinking 'Oh Bibitz' now, aren't you?› Dalen was falling right next to him. The wind was too strong to talk verbally so Dalen had chosen to use the Vengerian Pin. ‹There ain't nothing like the first time you willingly step off the edge.› They fell together past the cliff edge where Christoph had started and just long enough to give Christoph concern, but the wind was strong as it dashed itself against the mountainside and channeled all its force upward, pushing against gravity on both of them.

Dalen used that opportunity, as they slowed and changed direction, to perform some aerial acrobatics. Master Peace had found the exact spot where if he held his body a certain way, the wind was just strong enough to hold him in place, neither moving up nor down. ‹Both of you seem so at home.› Cristoph mentioned as he tried not to soil himself.

Dalen slowed time and brought both Peace and Christoph with him. ‹I spent a thousand days jumping off a cliff every day, trying to create a leap of faith›

‹Two years for me.› Master Peace had timed his ascent to match theirs and was level with Dalen and Christoph.

The idea that they would choose to jump off a cliff every day befuddled Christoph. ‹Why?›

‹Because.› Master Peace looked straight down at the ground

and the thousands of feet of open air between. ‹Like many things, sometimes first you must learn to fall.›

Christoph saw the layers of Master Peace's answer. ‹Teach me.›

Peace gave a nod to Dalen who let go of time and for the next hour straight, Peace and Christoph used the wind to keep them in a continual fall, while Dalen explored the shafts looking for the one that would lead them to the dragon.

Christoph and Master Peace had been practicing maneuvers, using their bodies to catch more wind or less, allowing them to dip or rise as they desired. Falling continuously for an hour was something neither of them had ever experienced and the two of them had created a bond with one another in their comradery. Dalen found them hovering in place just talking about life. Conversing as if their situation was commonplace. ‹I have been exploring the shafts. This is just one level of this. Aim for this shaft on your next push.› Dalen pointed upward to the ceiling and when Christoph looked, one of the shafts in the rock began to glow.

Christoph pivoted his body so that his feet pointed down and brought his legs together with his arms tight along his side. It made him drop but after a hundred feet or so he opened himself up and caught as much wind as he could. It shot him upward and he maneuvered himself to pass through the suggested opening. The gust pushed him about one story higher than where the passage let out, into the open air, and deposited him by the edge of the shaft on a small plateau near where the mountain began its ascent. Christoph looked around but couldn't see the nesting place of the Gold Dragon. ‹It must be a shaft that leads to an internal chamber.› He took a deep breath and enjoyed the view.

‹I think I found it.› Dalen's voice sounded excited with a hint of fear. ‹Second shaft to the right and then directly forward.›

‹Excellent. I am on my way.› Christoph took one more look at the beauty of the view and then leaped back through the shaft he had come through.

He dropped back into the open air. Falling from a tube into open air was a lot for anyone to process and his heart missed a beat while his stomach tried to escape his body through his throat. He said a small prayer as he, for a second time, dropped past the ledge he had initially leaped from, and hoped that another gust would send him flying back upward. Because he was falling faster on this round it took more time and space to change his direction. He had fallen farther than before so when the wind launched him upward again, he barely caught the top of the ledge he had just passed and had to pull himself up.

Christoph turned back around and stared out from the cliff edge while he caught his breath. ‹At least one thing is going to come out of all this.› Christoph thought as he stared out and let the vertigo spin him.

‹What is that?› asked Master Peace.

Christoph had to catch his balance, and he let the ripples of adrenaline wash over him. ‹By the time I get through this, I will have conquered my severe fear of heights.› Christoph looked up to the ceiling and allowed the world to stop spinning. He found the shaft Dalen had suggested and maneuvered to where it was.

‹You have a fear of heights?› Dalen's voice suggested surprise, considering Christoph chose to climb the mountain for two days.

Christoph put his hands on his hips and momentarily laughed at himself. ‹Not for long.› He held his arms out like a competitive swimmer and dove headfirst off the cliff.

His first thought was how much of a bad idea that was, but it was forced out of his mind by the part of him who whooped and hollered. He guessed where the wind would hit and folded himself up into a ball. As he got to where he believed the wind was going to catch him, he unfolded himself so that his head was upright. He timed it perfectly and as it launched him upward, he let out his most impressive yell as he flew toward the second shaft. He hit with speed but unlike the shaft before, the gust only got him high enough to reach the end of the passage. His momentum quit just as he was level with Dalen and Master Peace, who reached out as he became parallel with them and pulled him to solid ground.

Christoph stumbled onto the ground and while catching his breath began to look around at his new location. They were in another chamber that was more like an alcove. Looking outward, they saw nothing but sky. Christoph looked up and saw another shaft high above them. There was no rushing wind around them like below, so they were able to speak freely. "How are we supposed to get to that?"

"Not sure yet." Dalen began to fly up near it. "I am pretty

sure that is where we are supposed to go. I can fly you up if you wish."

"No. There is something we are missing." Christoph began to search the area. "There must be another answer. How does anyone else who doesn't have a jinn with them get there?"

"I don't know." Dalen floated back down to him. "The air gusts are noticeable here, but nothing strong enough to lift a person."

Master Peace sat down and dangled his feet off the edge. "Sometimes when you run out of options it's a good idea to go back to basics with fresh eyes."

Dalen and Christoph agreed so all three of them stopped what they were doing and considered looking at this from a new direction. "What do we actually know? I think it is reasonable to assume that other people have made it through the Wind Caves and have seen the Gold Dragon." Christoph stayed standing and kept one hand on a rock formation nearby to steady himself. "I mean, has anyone actually met him?"

"When I was at the Brotherhood of Light I was given this coin." Dalen pulled out his coin and held it out so that Christoph could see the golden dragon on it. "I was told that if you had one it granted an audience with the Gold Dragon, so I believe that you can."

Christoph pulled out the one that Crystal had given him. When he held the coin, it was silver side up and he looked at the etching of the eye that was on it. "What am I supposed to see?" He turned it over and looked at the golden side that had an embossed representation of the Gold Dragon on it. As he did, he felt with the scruff on his cheek that the wind began to pick up. "Are you sure that the rule is you have to have a coin to have a meeting with the dragon?"

Dalen was looking past his coin at Christoph. He could see that he was on to something. "Yes. Why do you ask?"

"I think I got it." Christoph held his coin tightly and stared at the Gold Dragon, the wisest being in the corporeal world, and he hoped that the dragon's wisdom was with him at that moment.

Dalen looked at his own coin. He flipped it over so he could see the dragon and as he did, he felt the wind. "It's a promissory note to have an audience with the dragon." The wind was getting stronger quickly. "Master Peace get your coin out."

Master Peace saw how the wind was affecting them both but could not feel it himself. He laughed. "Magic coin. You really do need it to get to the Gold Dragon." He pulled out his coin and stared at the dragon and began to feel the wind as well. This time they didn't have to leap. The wind grew so strong it lifted them off the rock ledge where they were and carried them upward toward the opening in the rockface above. It carried them through the shaft, gaining speed as they flew higher and higher through the rock. A void in the stone opened and they were deposited into a shadowy chamber. The lair of the Gold Dragon of the East.

25

THE GOLD DRAGON OF THE EAST

Dalen still looked to be a young man, but after spending eighteen years on earth he left and began his training. He spent the better part of three years training with the Brotherhood of Light. That's when he received his Initiate's Coin, the first lesson at the Brotherhood of Light. The coin demonstrated how one truth could be completely different depending on how one looked at it. Dalen flipped it over and stared at its other side. The Master Coin. It had been told to him that he needed the coin to have an audience with the Gold Dragon, but he had no idea that it was a magical coin or what it would do. Dalen believed that he had still not learned everything there was to know about the coin and thought to himself how interesting it would be if the coin still had something to teach him, and how strange it would be if that lesson was the thing that helped him reach becoming a master. He flipped it back over and stared at the image of the Gold Dragon for a moment thinking about how funny time was. After spending his time at the Temple of Light, he spent twenty years learning magic at the Temple of All Faith. Late at night after the candles had been blown out, and the only light came from the moonlight that saturated Dalen's bed from the window next to it, he spent hours looking at that Dragon, wondering what it would be like to stand in its presence. Now that he was here and seeing the Gold Dragon of the East in person, he knew that even in his best guess, his imagination paled in comparison to the real thing.

They stood on the edge of a large circular room that was carved from the rock and illuminated by a single shaft of light that was coming from an opening in the center of it. The opening was large enough to allow the Gold Dragon entrance and egress yet was still less than a sixth of the size of the entire ceiling. The shaft of light stood in the center of the room and gave illumination to everything around it. The light faded and dwindled as it moved further back into the room, where Dalen and his companions stood. They had been brought to the edge of this circular room and where they stood, they were in near complete darkness. Something moved in the shadows on the far end of the room. It was hard to make out details at first but based on size alone, the three of them knew that it must be the Gold Dragon.

As it emerged from the shadows the light began to dance upon its scales. They twinkled at first as the beast moved from the shadows and then they grew brighter. It was like watching a constellation appear first in the dusk sky and then come to life, stepping out from the heavens in the darker night sky. First to emerge from the shadows and directly move into the light was its head. It looked much like a lion's head, but its snout was longer, and it was covered in scales and not fur. It had two large horns that grew from either side of its head that flowed with the shape of its mane and had tendrils at the end of its muzzle and chin that gave it the look of a long mustache and goatee. It was so huge that if it opened its mouth completely it could swallow a person whole.

All three of the Gold Dragon's guests instinctually stepped back. Dalen was hovering, so it didn't affect him, but Master Peace and Christoph stepped backward into the open shaft. They both scrambled for their balance which gave Dalen enough time to use his telekinesis to push them back onto solid ground.

The Gold Dragon chuckled to himself. "That never gets old." He brought his head low and laid down so it could see them at their level. The dragon had found it made him seem smaller, and less frightening. "I give you my word that I mean you no harm. You have come to see me. I am here." His voice was deep and rich, and it echoed through the chamber and reverberated in the hearts of Dalen and his companions.

"Our apologies. You caught us off guard. We meant no disrespect." Master Peace gave a bow from the Brotherhood of

Light that was usually saved for masters or high-end people of power such as a queen or king.

"Ah... pleasantries. Your apology has been heard, noted, and accepted." His head moved in closer, and it breathed them in deeply. "While that is all true, it is also true that there was no requirement. I found it quite amusing."

Dalen finally found his wits and gave the same bow as Master Peace. "I am Brother Truth, and this is Master Peace. We are from the Brotherhood of Light, and this is Christoph of Venger. We seek an audience. Your Excellency."

"I know exactly who you are Dalen Pax. I see you are calling yourself Brother Truth at this point. You remind me of another member of your sect, a...Master Truth." The Gold Dragon moved closer and stared at Dalen with his glowing eyes. "I swear you look just like him."

Dalen smiled and gave him a much more informal bow. "I know that I eventually become Master Truth."

The Gold Dragon leaned in even closer and smiled. "I abhor wasting a good joke on someone when I have to explain it to them."

"So, you know Master Truth?" asked Master Peace.

"How else would I know that Dalen looks like him?" The Gold Dragon turned his gaze to Master Peace. "But to answer the question you did not ask; I know who each of you are and why you are here." He pulled back a little and chortled deep in his throat.

"Then you know that I have come seeking the Air Blade,

your imperial majesty... what should we call you?" As Christoph bowed, he winced and told himself to get it together.

"Thank you for your acts of honor. I have gone by many names." The Gold Dragon thought for a moment. "His Holiness. His Majestic Brilliance. I like Imperial Majesty, but none of them are who I am. Do you follow?" He scanned each of their eyes. "I have many names and all of them I am, yet the opposite can also be spoken, for none of them are who I am."

Christoph wasn't sure if it was because he had been spending too much time with the monks but what the Dragon said made sense. "Then please tell me. Who are you?"

"I'll make you a bargain, Christoph, son of Modok, First Duke of Delthor. You wish to know who I am. I will tell you, but once I have, you must answer the same question." The Gold Dragon began to float and as he raised himself off the ground he moved into the light. He was more beautiful than any of them could have imagined. He was wingless and long like a serpent. He had two pairs of legs and three pairs of arms. As he floated there, suspended in the sun, his scales caught the light and reflected it in many directions. Flashes of light hit their eyes as multiple scales caught the sunlight perfectly and sent beams directly at their faces. "I am Han Bo Fang. Last of the ancient Dragons, and keeper of the lost wisdom of my people. That is who I am. Every other name and title are granted to me by another." Han Bo Fang turned his attention for a moment to Dalen. "It is only in this name that I hold my truth, for it is the only one that is real." Then Han Bo Fang looked at Master Peace, "No matter how much they wish the other names were so." The Gold Dragon drifted back to the ground, moved away from the pillar of light, and brought his head down low.

Christoph bowed and said, "It is an honor, and a pleasure to meet you, Han Bo Fang." Then he began to introduce himself, but he was stopped by the dragon.

"Not like that." The Gold Dragon's tail swished around Christoph and guided him to stand in the light. "You now stand within the light of truth. Do not dishonor this sacred place by speaking a falsehood."

Dalen felt a ripple of magic as Christoph stepped into the light. Dalen knew this was somehow all too familiar, but he wasn't able to explain why. "Is this his trial?"

"Perhaps." The Gold Dragon said with great amusement. He swung his attention to Dalen. "If it is, I would say it is way too late for you to do anything about it, and as you well know, once it starts you are not to help him. So, I expect you both to hold to the honor of the Brotherhood of Light and keep even your thoughts to yourselves." As he said it, they were all too aware that somehow Han Bo Fang knew that they could be in telepathic communication with Christoph. Both Dalen and Master Peace reached up and deactivated their Vengerian Pins. When they did, he bowed his head to the monks and said, "I will be with you in a moment. Hopefully, our conversation will inspire Christoph." Then Han Bo Fang dedicated all of his attention to Christoph. "Son of Modok. This is your one chance to save the world and all you have to do is answer this question correctly. Not by the terms that others see you..." The Gold Dragon looked up into the light and declared, "From the only perception that matters in all of this, who are you, and why are you the chosen one?"

Christoph felt the weight of each moment as it passed by him. He looked up into the light and asked, "How can I possibly know this answer?" His mind froze and stagnated. Many people have dedicated their lives to the pursuit of being able to answer the question of who they truly are, and only a handful have been able to answer it.

It seemed like such a simple question. Who are you? When he asked Han Bo Fang, he had meant it as a simple question. Christoph laughed at himself for a moment and thought that he should have stuck with the question, 'What should I call you?' instead he had paraphrased and asked a completely different question. Who are you?

He was Christoph, son of Modok, but that wasn't who he was. That was his name and lineage. There were other people called Christoph, and his brother Kal had the same lineage, so those weren't the things that made him who he was. Christoph touched the All-Seeing Eye and believed he knew what the dragon wanted. He had to know his truth and be able to stand in the light as his true self.

It was during that moment that Christoph decided that if they survived the days to come, he would implement a decree that said anyone of the royal line needed to spend some time with the Brotherhood of Light and be trained for such things.

The dragon backed into the shadows and when he did, he let

smoke bellow from his nostrils and mouth. The smoke was white and thicker than the deep fog that blankets the coast in winter. From the smoke stepped an old man with long white hair and facial hair that resembled the Gold Dragon. He was dressed in an outfit that closely resembled the Brotherhood of Light, but where theirs were black and white, all of the black had been replaced with golden silk. The dragon was still in the shadows billowing smoke, but now this image continued to talk for him. He spoke with the same voice that filled the room. "The first part is simple. All you need do, is get rid of everything that does not come from the source."

Christoph looked at the old man and understood he was still talking to Han Bo Fang. "What of the second?"

"Why are you the chosen?" Han Bo Fang laughed. "That part is even easier once you understand the first, yet it is also the key to the first."

"I don't understand."

"You are the chosen one?"

"This is what I am told."

"When you understand who chose you, you will know the perspective required to answer the first part, with that you will know why you were chosen." Christoph stared at him confused with eyes that pleaded for help. "I will not hold your hand any further than this. If you are to be King of Venger, you must know who you are and you will have to do it on your own. Meditate on it, while I speak with the other travelers who have come so far from where they started to arrive in this moment with you. You have until I return." Han Bo Fang bowed to Christoph in the same manner that Christoph had bowed to him and then walked over to Dalen and Master Peace while Christoph drew the Water Blade and placed its eye on the center of his forehead.

Dalen first looked at the old man with the fu-man-chu and robes of a grandmaster, then set his gaze past him to the Gold Dragon in the shadows. The old man stopped in his tracks and turned to look back at the Gold Dragon. The dragon waved and the old man waved in return, then turned to face Dalen and Master Peace again. Dalen considered his options carefully and bowed to the actual dragon in the room then turned his attention to the old man. From Dalen's point of view, the old man looked Asian in appearance and skin tone. His hair was white and there were wrinkles around his eyes that gave him the appearance of being old, but he moved like a man in his prime. During Dalen's training, he had come across many teachers. Most of which never appeared to him in their true form, but instead under the guise of something that his mind would understand, this was no different. Instead of trying to talk to an enormous dragon, he was granted the opportunity to talk to someone his mind could easily grasp, using images that he could subconsciously interpret. Old. Older than you would think, but still powerful and vibrant, he wore the robes of a grandmaster, suggesting his levels of power and wisdom.

Dalen gave a very sincere bow that was normally reserved for masters. "Han Bo Fang, I have waited many years to be in this moment. It is an honor to speak with you."

Han Bo Fang smiled, and to Dalen's surprise, returned

the same bow to him. "Master Truth and I have talked about you before. I have waited far longer for this conversation than you might guess." Then he turned his attention to Master Peace. "Benjamin Watts, son of Richard, it is an honor to speak with you as well. There is a prophecy that one day, you will heal the Tree of Sorrow. It is a blight in this world and all the Dragons of the West are born under its influence. Most of them are born dark and mean because they were saturated by its sadness until it broke their hearts even before they hatched. One day, it will be you who heals the tree and gives my kind a chance to let go of their hatred and finally find peace."

Master Peace's eyes widened as he stared at Han Bo Fang. He lost his balance and dropped to his knees. "In my time, I have already healed the tree, but I had no idea of the consequences."

Han Bo Fang walked up to Master Peace and helped him back to his feet. He closed his eyes, took a deep breath in, and as he let it out, breathed smoke directly into Master Peace's face. Master Peace breathed it in a couple of times and began to cough aggressively. Han Bo Fang waved Dalen off as he tried to help his friend. "It is fine Dalen Pax. Master Peace of the Brotherhood of Light will be alright. His body must accept what is happening to him."

Dalen watched as Han Bo Fang caught Master Peace and laid him on the floor. His body was now convulsing, and he held onto his throat as if he were choking. Dalen had learned a long time ago to heed the words of those who knew more than himself and stood back, but asked, "What is happening to him?"

Han Bo Fang held Master Peace in his lap and slowly rocked him while Master Peace coughed and fought for breath. "The dragons of your time will recognize him as a savior of their kind. They will build a monument to him, in his very footprints at the exact location where he healed the Tree of Sorrow. And the name of Benjamin will be carried in the lineage of dragons that are born years after he leaves the corporeal plane, for they will be born of peace. They will hatch with peace in their hearts and that generation of dragons will bring forth a new perspective that will bring the Dragons of the West back from the brink of their own destruction from hate and sorrow." Master Peace began to relax, and his coughing began to subside. "What I have given him is known as the Blessing of the Dragon. From now on, he will be able to understand and speak our language. His throat had to change so that he could make the sounds needed." Han Bo Fang helped Master Peace to his feet. "With this blessing, you will now be able to learn our magic. Consider it a thank you for what you have done for all my kind. When you return to your own time, please come back here and visit me again."

Dalen checked on Master Peace. "I'm fine. A little sore in the throat. I am going to need a few minutes." His voice was now deeper and had a rasp to it. "I don't know how to take in everything that was just said and I, like Christoph, need to meditate on what is before me."

Han Bo Fang then turned his attention back to Dalen. "Two in meditation and one still left with questions. Are you ready for what you are about to learn?"

It was an interesting question and a highly appealing offer. Dalen prepared himself the best that he could, and only when his mind was calm and free of doubt, did he continue. "I am."

Han Bo Fang cast a spell and a cup of tea appeared in his hand. Dalen watched him in slow motion as he stretched out time. He activated the Spheres of Reality and watched as the dragon conjured the cup into existence, complete with the beverage he desired. Dragon Magic was vastly different than the magic he knew as a jinn, but in the end, the components were the same, just brought about from a different point of view.

Dalen allowed his sight to return to normal as his body became corporeal again. With it, time began to move normally. Han Bo Fang smirked and asked, "Did you get all of that?"

Dalen was surprised for a moment that Han Bo Fang knew what he had just done, then he thought twice about it and remembered who he was talking to. "Yes, I did. Thank you. Dragon Magic is fascinating. You truly do live up to the title of Wisest Being in the Corporeal World."

"Thank you." Han Bo Fang gave a small bow. "Then I am sure you will trust my wisdom when I suggest that we toast to your question. I will drink from my cup, and you will drink from yours."

Dalen retrieved his cup and activated it. "I know you abhor having to explain the joke, so I am going to skip asking if you know what I carry."

"Thank you." Han Bo Fang smiled. "A far better question would be whether you knew what you carry."

"I know there is much I do not know. It is not a matter of what I do know that drives my question, but the vast amount of knowledge that I do not." It was almost unbearable to admit it, but Dalen had been trained to do the impossible. He had swallowed his pride and let go of his ego, and in a moment of truth, he admitted his ignorance.

"And yet you refuse the title of master, Brother Truth." There was a look of query on Han Bo Fang's face.

"I am trying to reach it. That's why I am here. I have even found my challenge. I have been putting myself through hell to try and become what I am supposed to be." Dalen could feel tears of frustration began to swell in his eyes. "I am here to try to understand if what I am doing is correct, and if it is not, then to understand what I am doing wrong. I am willing to do the work, and I am willing to take leaps of faith. I am ready. I am willing, but I beg you please, I need guidance."

"Very well." Han Bo Fang took three slow deep breaths before he continued. "First we will drink, but you will drink from my cup, and I will drink from yours." He reached over and switched cups with Dalen. He tipped the cup toward Dalen's face and Dalen had the choice of drinking or letting it spill down his chin. He chose the former and was surprised when he realized he was drinking his favorite drink in all the world. It was a special mint tea that grew at the Temple of Light. "Master Truth and I are old friends. I know the location of every coin I have ever made. I knew it was you when you arrived at the mountain because you carry the personal coin of Master Truth."

Dalen's mind wandered for a moment as he tried to imagine when the coin was originally made, and how long Grand Master Truth had it before he gave it to Dalen. He watched as a stitch in time created a paradox in his mind. He would carry it with him from here for thousands of years and eventually give it to his younger self who would carry it for thousands of years. Was it possible that his coin was older than the universe? Questions began to fill his mind, he thought; if he carries it until he gives it to himself, in a loop, when was the coin originally made?

"Focus." Han Bo Fang's voice brought Dalen out of his thoughts, and he snapped his focus back to the present. "There was more than just mint in that tea, and you drank from my cup. With it, you drink in my wisdom. Pay attention, because I will only do this once." Han Bo Fang turned and pointed to the Gold Dragon who looked up at them and winked. "What I hold in this cup would have the same effect on him as it does on you. His body would reject it, and it would begin to kill him while holding him in a state of massive visions, leaving him helpless while his body died. Then where would you be? Live the rest of your life as the guy who killed Han Bo Fang. You would be…unliked." Han Bo Fang turned back toward Dalen and added, "Yet, although it would kill the dragon…" Before Dalen could stop him, Han Bo Fang drank deeply from Dalen's cup. Dalen tried to stop him, but he was far too late. Han Bo Fang's eyes rolled into the back of his head for a second or two. He closed them and Dalen could see that his eyes were moving as if he were dreaming, then he opened them again and sighed as if the experience was refreshing and handed Dalen back his cup. "I was right. I seem no worse for the wear."

Dalen just stared at him with shock for a moment and finally whispered, "How did you do that?"

"Like I said, Brother Truth. It would have killed the dragon. The Fountain of Truth would have poisoned his body." Han Bo Fang handed Dalen back his cup. "But you and I know I don't have a body now do I?"

Dalen's mind expanded like a fractal, each facet an understanding of the events that had just taken place and Dalen could see them all. He slowed down time so that he could take in each one, but as his mind expanded, one became two, and two became four. Tens became hundreds and then thousands as the infinite possibility of perception unfolded in Dalen's mind.

The understanding of it inverted in Dalen's mind and folded in on itself until there was a clear singular image of comprehension. "It poisons the body and kills it, but you drank it from an incorporeal state." Dalen activated his Spheres of Reality. He felt his body change as he took his true form. He was now halfway in and out of reality, both there and not. Dalen then inverted the field of his own reality, rendering him truly incorporeal, and marveled at what he could now see. He could see the very fabric of reality much like he had learned in Dorn's, but now he could not only read the magic, he could understand it on a new level. A level that could only be categorized as lucid dreaming while not dreaming. Looking at reality itself with the same level of control and understanding that a lucid dream state offers. He looked at his cup, the liquid from the Fountain of Truth had changed and was now putting off a glowing light.

Now drink. Han Bo Fang's voice echoed in Dalen's mind. *Trust in me. Drink.* Dalen didn't question him and took a drink from the Fountain of Truth.

The vision began but there was no pain. The water from the Fountain of Truth had transmuted with him and had become something that was no longer a threat.

There were no longer shadows in this room, and he could see the Gold Dragon in all his splendor. He sparkled and glittered in the light that Christoph still kneeled in. Dalen now knew where he had seen that light before. In the Temple of All Faith, there was a light that continuously shined through the stained-glass window that formed a large circle in the middle of the ceiling. It shined down on a casting circle, and as the light passed through it would create markings on the casting circle for whatever was required of the caster. Those memories flashed through his mind as he looked at Christoph kneeling in the light, and he understood why the mountain, the home of the Gold Dragon, was called Divine Understanding.

Han Bo Fang had moved into the spirit world with Dalen and congratulated him on his bravery and faith.

"I said I was willing to do the work and risk it all. I meant it with all my heart." Dalen watched as waves of energy poured from the light in the center of the room and formed ripples of magic that passed through each other and created reality. Dalen began to study the line that seemed to tether the man to the dragon. It reminded him of the lines that had connected him to the Fire Jinn who had taught him magic so many years ago. He began to follow

430

it back to its source and as he thought of her, she began to float near him in all her glory.

"It's umbilical by its nature." She floated alongside him and hugged him.

Dalen squeezed her and then let her go. "It's good to see you."

Her flames burned brightly, and she said with a wink, "It's good to be seen."

"As thrilled as I am to see you," Dalen had noticed that there was a line connected between them that was directly attached to his Heartstone. "I have learned that I only see you when I am about to go through a fast change."

"Fire does tend to do that. Burn away everything so something new can grow." She pointed to the cord that connected them. "But I am not here for that. This you already understand. The same way that you and I are the same being, and because of that, you and I are connected always, the dragon and the man are one, and talking to either of them is talking to both, but that is also not why I am here."

Dalen finished memorizing the lines of magic that made up the connection and began to float back to the position he was in the moment he drank from his cup. "It's because of what is about to happen." The Fire Jinn nodded. "What am I about to do?"

The Fire Jinn laughed, and her fire flared, filling the room with light. "I believe you are about to ask the wisest corporeal being a question about your path to truth. I believe that you are going to get an answer that you weren't quite ready for, and when it comes it will change your point of view and begin you down the last leg of your journey. A journey that will take you to the heart of truth, and your mastery."

Dalen nodded as he got back to where he was. "Then I am glad you are with me"

The Fire Jinn touched her Heartstone, and the cord began to glow. The light traveled down the cord and touched Dalen's heart and within that light, Dalen could feel warmth and love. "I am always with you."

"I know. You are my soul. Ageless, with no race or gender, because you are incorporeal. I remember the day we met you showed me who you were, but I couldn't understand then. I do now." Dalen paused for a moment. "I have always tried to do what you have asked, but now I have a request."

The Fire Jinn felt Dalen's heart through their connection and said, "If it is within my power to grant you a wish I shall."

"You, Master Ki, and Master Truth. The three of you are aspects of my body, mind, and soul. With the other two, there is a harmony of balance. I feel I know them better because I can call them by name. It gives me a sense of knowing them. I only know you as the Fire Jinn, and although I connect to you deeper in some ways than either of them, I feel disconnected from you.

"The very point that you call them by a name and see them as anything other than yourself is what keeps you separate from them." The Fire Jinn turned to move toward the light in the center of the room, but Dalen grabbed her hand and turned her back.

"That may be true, but I am taking steps toward that understanding. Please. I wish to call you something other than the Fire Jinn, which in my mind, separates me from you anyway. I can't call you Dalen either, because that doesn't seem right. From my understanding, Dalen is the person you are being... me. Not the name you truly are, and I just wish to know you better."

"I know my friend; I just wanted you to be aware of what you were asking." She caressed his cheek. "I will tell you. The day we met I told you that I would tell you my name when you were ready to hear it." Her fire became stronger, and she moved forward so that Dalen and she shared the same location in the universe. Her light joined his as she spoke in his mind. *You can know me as Moment.*

Dalen thought it was a beautiful name. "Do you mean moment, as a measurement of time, or do you mean it like having a moment?"

It depends on what side of the coin you are looking at. With those words, she faded from his mind, as the vision from the Fountain of Truth subsided and Dalen returned to the corporeal world.

"Well Done!" cried Han Bo Fang as he applauded. Together they gave each other a bow of respect and then Han Bo Fang smiled and slapped Dalen on the shoulder. "Now let's see if this king of yours is as wise as we all hope. Let Master Peace know that it is time."

Dalen went to check on Master Peace who had recentered himself and had come to grips with what had happened, and what he had been told. He looked up at Dalen and rose to his feet. "Truth." His voice was still deep with a hint of a rasp. "It has one hell of a kick."

"Indeed." Dalen tried to put his arm around Master Peace but found that he was still in his jinn state. Dalen paused for a moment and looked at the man who had just slapped his shoulder, shook his head, and chuckled to himself. Then Dalen looked at his own hands. He found it odd that he was still in his full jinn form. "Hmm. After something like that, I normally would have reverted to my normal state."

Master Peace smiled with pride at his brother. "Maybe you have finally gotten close enough to your truth that this is, your natural state."

"I am not sure what to do." Both of them started to make their way over to Christoph. "Up until now, this state has been something I had to do on purpose. Like making a fist. Something I had to continuously think about because once you stop concentrating, the muscle relaxes and returns to its natural state. I have no idea 'how' to make myself corporeal, except allowing myself to revert to it. I should be solid."

Master Peace just stared at the beauty of Dalen's jinn form. "I will think about it, but right now we need to be there for Christoph." Dalen agreed although it concerned him, and he tried a few more times to force himself back into a more physical state to no avail.

"Are you ready to tell me who you are?" asked Han Bo Fang.

"I believe so, and you have given me more than a fair chance to think about it." Christoph got up and sheathed the Water Blade. "I heard a lot of what was said, and I believe that Dalen and I have the same question."

"Fascinating." Han Bo Fang crossed his arms in front of him. "Then you are ready?"

Christoph stood proud and strong. "I am."

"Then if you would please, hand me your coin." Christoph did as Han Bo Fang asked, and once he had handed over the coin, the man stepped back into the cloud of smoke and faded from existence. The Gold Dragon began to move again and brought his head forward so that he was eye to eye with Christoph. "Who are you and why are you the chosen one?"

Christoph stood in the Light of Truth and spoke from his heart. "I thought long and hard about what you said. I used the eye so I could see myself as clearly as possible, but all that it would show me was that it was up to me. At first, I didn't understand, but the words that you said stayed with me. I had to let go of what everyone else thought and listen to the one opinion that mattered. I had to decide what that meant, and you hinted that the opinion of the only one who mattered would also be the perception of the person who chose me. So, I had to start there. I knew I had to understand who chose this. Why is it that I am the one to be King? Why is it that I am the chosen one? To know that I would need to know who chose me. It is something I have been struggling with since we started all of this. I believe in the First Law of Free Will. Always have, but I have never understood how fate played a role in all of this. Destiny is the outcome of your choices, but how does fate fall into all of this? Who chooses my fate, and if there is someone who is choosing my fate, how can free will ever exist? If there is fate, that means before I was born someone decided my path. I thought to myself that it must be a god or goddess, but then it brought me back to free will. So, I was left with only one conclusion. Before I was born, I chose my path."

Christoph looked to the Gold Dragon for confirmation. Han Bo Fang just smiled and said, "Don't let me stop you."

"That means I chose my fate, which means I am the chosen one, because I chose it, and now to fulfill my destiny, I must choose it again, and so I do. This time on my terms."

Han Bo Fang held out his claw and opened it. He reached out to Christoph and gently slid something into Christoph's hand. "Who are you?"

Christoph looked at the coin in his hand. It was silver and had the Royal Seal of Venger on it. He flipped it over in his hand to reveal the golden side that had the embossing of Han Bo Fang on it. "I am Christoph. King of Venger."

"Yes. You finally are." As the Golden Dragon spoke a small spark of condensed light passed through the opening and slowly fell toward Christoph.

Dalen watched with eyes of a jinn as a small piece of

divinity fell from the heavens and touched the coin in Christoph's hand. The coin lit up and began to alter its form. Now in Christoph's hand was a physical handle and hilt of a sword made of condensed light with the gold coin as the center stone in the hilt. The blade was made of open air, and the only reason Dalen knew it was there because of the aura of magic that outlined the blade. "You have done it!" Dalen cheered. "You have the Air Blade!"

Han Bo Fang bowed his head and said, "Long live the King."

26

THE GUARDIANS OF THE IMMOVABLE STONE

Grelf and her companions were given a ride in a cart that was used to transport large goods and supplies, like the large pelts for tents and long poles used to hold them together. They were going to be traveling to the Immovable Stone, taking with them most of the tribe, who were hoping to witness this momentous occasion they had been hearing stories about their whole lives.

Most of the tribe traveled by Bodi board, but a few were controlling much larger versions. They had the same features as their small counterparts but instead of being created for speed and maneuverability, they were built for power so they could be used to tow other things. The oasis was their home, and although they would return, they had packed enough to create a small mobile pavilion of tents and were ready to move quickly.

They traveled south, the Immovable Stone was on the other side of the dunes where the ground became rocky. Instead of dunes, there were canyons and cliffs, with stretches of ground that were nothing but cracker rock, baked under the heat of the sun. They traveled a distance that would have taken a day or two if they had traveled by foot, but instead, they glided along the desert with great speed and reached the cliffs within a couple of hours, stopping at the edge of them. Most of the tribe continued to the east, following a route that took them down sloping paths to allow for the tribe to easily get to the bottom, they moved ahead to set up camp at the Immovable Stone, but there was something that Maddicus wanted to show us and had asked our driver to stop. She hopped off her board in mid-flight and grabbed it with her hand. As she did the board shrank down again and she attached it to her pack just as her feet hit the ground.

As she looked at them, they could see that there was a new spark of life in her eyes that had not been there before. "Check it out." She waved them to follow her and began to walk east along the cliff edge.

Each of us had been given a Twinkle Freezy light and it was helping in the blistering heat of the sun. As Grelf traveled with Maddicus she had learned that the days could get so hot the Bodites would have to spend time in the shade, out of the direct sunlight because it had killed people exposed to it for long periods of time. But the heat had not bothered her one time since she came to the desert, and she was sure that the Fire Blade was keeping her safe from the damage of the heat and the sun. The rest of us were not immune and were very thankful for the gifts they had given us. What was more of a concern were the nights. In the Verris Desert, there is no moisture except at that oasis, so there was no moisture in the air, and with no cloud cover, the heat escaped, meaning that there were two ways to die in the Verris Desert. During the day you could roast alive and at night you could freeze to death.

We moved along the ridge to something that was standing on the edge of the cliff. It was a beautiful marble statue of a unicorn whose shoulder stood as tall as Travis. The saddle and armor were intricately forged in steel and inlaid with gold. The carving of the unicorn itself was still in perfect detail and showed no sign of being an object that had spent decades in the elements.

"What's the buzz, cuz?" Travis had already pulled out his notebook and was sketching the unicorn looking over the ridge.

"Look around you," I said, checking the terrain. "Doesn't this place look familiar?"

Slowly the team looked around. Travis flipped to another page that had a rudimentary map. He followed it with his finger and then looked up at the unicorn. "It's the mount of Kontoon, isn't it?"

Maddicus gave him a hand gesture that looked like she was

flipping him off except her thumb and pinky were also extended outward. "Bussin'."

Sir Adam took a moment to inspect it while his brother finished the sketch. "It's been here the whole time?"

Maddicus walked over to the front of the unicorn. Its head was down low and Maddicus bent over a little to be eye to eye with it. She placed her forehead against it directly underneath its horn, as if she were saying hello to an old friend. "Waitin' for a worthy rider."

Grelf stared at the mount while she allowed her mind to replay the story. Both Kontoon and the unicorn went over the edge and Kontoon was thrown from his saddle. The mount had teleported to the edge before Kontoon could get back to it during the fall. Without a rider, it went into a shutdown state until its rider returned. "Waiting forever for a rider that will never return. Why wasn't it ever retrieved?"

Maddicus was standing dangerously close to the edge of the ridge. She leaned out and looked over the edge. "Kontoon and Tongo bailed on the dunes. Moon Crow was free. Nothing to track and no one to track it. Dakas bailed hard in the dunes looking for them." She reached out and stroked the unicorn's nose. "Now he's free too. Like I said, he waits for a worthy rider." Maddicus patted its nose once more and then leaned out, over the edge again, and pointed further south. "The Tribe thinks this place is haunted for real. They say Kontoon still calls out to his mount, but it refuses to respond. Nobody ever comes here except me. We have been friends since I could glide. I say he did it on purpose because he

didn't want to be Kontoon's mount. Now he guards the stone, bro."
A few miles out, there was a large ring in the desert. Its edge was
a mountain of sand. A giant dune that went around the entire area
creating a perfect circle. Within the circle, the Verris Desert was
void of sand.

"Maddicus. You need to be careful." Sir Adam was moving
toward her cautiously. She didn't notice but the ground under her
feet was crumbling.

Maddicus turned back toward Sir Adam as she asked,
"Suspect?" The weight change deteriorated the ground further, and
pieces of the ridge around her began to fall.

Sir Adam tried to step closer but as he did more of the
ground began to give way. Maddicus only had a moment to look Sir
Adam in the eyes and reach out for him as the ground gave way and
she began to fall.

Sir Adam never had time to think about what happened
next. There was no time. His first conscious thought was the
acknowledgment that he had already leaped off the edge after
her. He never broke eye contact as they began to fall together.
They were very close together and were falling at the same rate
of speed, but neither one could reach the other as they both
reached out.

Maddicus had tipped over backward as the ground had given
out and she was falling with her back towards the ground. She
looked over her shoulder to see how close they were to the ground
and then locked eyes with Sir Adam who was falling headfirst,

vertically, toward her. She opened her body to catch as much air as she could. Adam was gaining on her, but the question was whether he would get to her in time. She just held his gaze as she hit the speed that was as fast as she was going to fall. It felt like flying. She howled with excitement and reached out her hand to Sir Adam. "Come on Sir Adam," she coaxed. Daring him to catch her. "Save my life!"

They hit the point of ground rush as their hands made contact and Sir Adam pulled Maddicus close and swung an arm under her knees and another behind her shoulders. "Hold on to me tight!"

Maddicus bit her lip and then smiled. "If you insist." She intertwined one arm over his left shoulder and one under his right arm and grasped both of her wrists behind him while wrapping her legs around his waist.

They were falling inches from the rock face and if he had extended his arms far enough Sir Adam could touch the cliff as he flew by it. As he drew his sword the world fell dark as if there was an eclipse, and his blade glowed with the light of his faith. He secured Maddicus the best that he could with his left arm, switched his grip so that the blade was near the bottom of his hand, and held it up in a stabbing position. The ground was getting closer, and he had no time to decide if it would work. He just believed with all his heart that it could be done, and in one swift motion, he plunged the blade into the rock and held on with one hand and all his might. From deep within Sir Adam, something began to awaken. A power that had been granted to him by the wishes and dreams of the thousands of people who went to his statue for thousands of years. It empowered his body, and his strength held as he tried to stop their fall.

The sandstone rockface was nothing against the power of his sword and it cut through it like a hot knife through mashed potatoes. It was so sharp that it wasn't slowing their momentum, so Sir Adam began to twist the blade which pulled them hard to the left but now there was something besides the impossibly sharp edge pushing down upon the stone and their speed began to diminish the more he turned it.

Maddicus held on tight as Sir Adam brought them to a complete stop. They were still a couple of hundred feet in the air, but for the moment they were safe. She pulled herself up to be able to look eye to eye with him and then clung to him closely as she spoke. "You saved me."

Sir Adam had done it. He had stopped there decent. There was no fear or thought of failure when he leaped, but staring into Maddicus's eyes as they dangled there, her agile form pressing against him while she held on for dear life, Adam found himself at a loss for words.

Maddicus readjusted herself when she could tell that Adam wasn't going to answer. "You know. I don't know if I am going to get another chance like this."

Adam could tell by the way she moved that her intent to press close to him had changed. "Chance for what?"

Maddicus's smile was mischievous and seductive. "To say

thank you." Maddicus kissed him deeply as she held him close. They hung there for a moment, neither of them remembering the peril they were still in.

Sir Adam's strength was beginning to wane, and it demanded his attention. "As much as I would like to stay here forever, I know my grip alone will never hold us both that long."

"Word." She kissed him again. "But if we hold on together..." Maddicus Removed her board from her back and put it under her feet and at once the weight Sir Adam was carrying was relieved. "The sky's the limit."

Sir Adam's feet contacted her board, and he felt almost foolish. "Of course, you had your board." He looked at her with puzzlement. "Why didn't you pull it earlier?"

"And steal your sick move? It's not every day a man jumps off a cliff for you." Maddicus kissed him sweetly. "So, what? I had my board, but I had faith in you, and you did not disappoint."

Sir Adam pulled his blade from the cliff face and returned it to its sheath. He could see that she was watching him closely to see how he responded to all of it. He took her by the hands and got his balance so he could give her his best as he spoke. "I have made vows to protect queens with my life, and although both of them trusted me to uphold that vow, you are the woman who has truly left the fate of her life in my hands. I am honored beyond words."

Maddicus was expecting an ego fueled by embarrassment or something close to anger. Instead, he met her with respect and honor and Maddicus began to see something noble in him. She still hadn't let him go. "Now that you saved me, let me save you."

Sir Adam allowed her to turn around so that they were facing the same way and then held her close around her waist. "I'm all yours."

"Damn right." She leaned forward and began to fly, she and Sir Adam flew back up to the top of the cliff where she sat him down right next to his brother.

Travis applauded and asked them how things went. Sir Adam hugged his brother with excitement and relayed the entire death-defying event to us.

Becky was concerned and asked them both,
"Are you alright?"

"I am now." Maddicus snuggled into his chest.

Travis waited for Sir Adam to finish his entire tale before he high-fived him and asked, "Bro! How did you know that was going to work?"

"I didn't." Sir Adam admitted. "I was hoping it did, but I didn't know."

"Wait." Maddicus looked truly impressed. "You didn't know it would work when you jumped?" and then gave him a playful wink.

"Adam! One of these days your sense of adventure is going to get you killed!" As Becky scolded him, she hugged him with relief that they were okay. "What were you thinking?"

"I didn't think. If I had thought about it, I wouldn't have had enough time to catch her." The power that Sir Adam had tapped into surged in him again. "I didn't think about the point she had a Bodi board." Something had awoken in him, and it was getting bigger.

"Then why did you leap?" asked Grelf, continuing to be truly impressed by Sir Adam.

"I just... knew." Sir Adam swore that he saw the unicorn's head move. He stepped away from everyone even though they were still talking to him and walked up to Kontoon's mount. In his mind, he could hear it calling to him, and the urge to touch its horn was beginning to become overwhelming.

"Tell me..." asked Maddicus as she walked up behind Sir Adam and put her hand lightly on his shoulder. Everyone could feel a surge of energy building in Sir Adam as he looked at the marble unicorn with its beautiful steel and gold armor. "What did you know?"

Adam couldn't take his eyes off the unicorn. "I don't have words. It was less like a thought and more like..."

"A feeling?" As always, Becky was able to finish Sir Adam's sentence even before he understood it completely.

"Yeah." Adam touched the mount's horn and as he did, what had woken inside him surged as the power of thousands channeled through him. The power bestowed on him by all who had come to the statue of Sir Adam the Pure Heart, patron saint of all who face the darkness with light.

The power that rippled out broke the magical restraints that had been put on the unicorn when it was trapped and enslaved all those years ago, and it awoke from its slumber. Its body turned to flesh once more, and with a shake of its head, the barding that was placed around its horn enslaving it disintegrated and revealed the face of a living breathing creature. After all the years of waiting, it had found someone whose soul was worthy.

Grelf leaned over to me and under her breath asked me, "Did you know about this?"

I responded in kind with, "I only know the myths that they know. Kontoon's mount being a real unicorn is news to me."

The unicorn made a high-pitched sound that resonated like a silver horn. Sir Adam nodded and said, "Yes. I can understand you." Travis tried to ask a question but was hushed quickly by Sir Adam. The unicorn looked at everyone and made the sound again. "No. These are my friends. I trust them with my life."

The unicorn stomped his right leg a couple of times and then let out a sigh. It looked over to the place where the Immovable Stone was and then let out a sorrowful call that almost broke the hearts of everyone there.

Sir Adam hugged the unicorn and wept with it for a moment. "We will do everything that we can." The unicorn let out another sorrowful cry.

"Sir Adam." Grelf approached slowly. "What's it saying?"

The unicorn sensed her approaching and began to back up making grunting noises as it retreated.

"She is Grelf, the Fire Princess of Venger and she is here to open the Immovable Stone and retrieve the Earth Blade." The unicorn reared up and made a series of high-pitched sounds. It took Sir Adam a moment to calm the unicorn and once he had he tried to explain. "None of you can hear him?"

"We hear animal sounds, but I can tell that he is upset." Grelf had already begun to back up and give the unicorn some space.

"This is Kargen. He says that he has been under a curse. He and his mate Pipim had been captured and bound by magic, and then used by two vial men. He and Pipim had been trapped here for longer than he can remember." Sir Adam stroked Kargen's mane gently. "He was trapped here and just at the edge of his sight Pipim has been trapped as well." Kargen gave off a high-pitched sound that rang out like an angel's voice. "She was transformed by the maelstrom of the desert spire."

Becky held Travis's hand and leaned her head against his shoulder. Becky was naturally empathic to the needs of others and listening to Sir Adam explain that Kargen had been able to see his love for decades but not go to her, touched the center of her heart.

Grelf was moved as well. She took a couple of steps closer to Sir Adam and the unicorn slowly. "How was she transformed? If it is within my abilities, I will free Pipim."

Kargen responded to her. It was obvious that he could understand her. He blew out some air and made a couple of quiet sounds. Sir Adam smiled and gave Grelf a nod. "He says thank you." The unicorn reared up for a moment and then dropped back down with another angelic tone. "Kargen wants to go. He says he has grown tired of this view and wishes to look upon it no longer." Kargen nudged Sir Adam's head with his nose and made another sound. "Yes, alright. Let's go." He climbed up into the saddle and held onto the reigns.

Maddicus watched as he got on, and her heart skipped a beat. She reached behind her back and pulled out her board. She got on and readied herself. "Sir Adam?" She waited for him to look over. "This time, I'm gliding."

Grelf had spent two days on Maddicus's board and trusted her to get her down alive, "Yo, Sis. Can I hitch a ride?"

Maddicus waved her over and pulled her on board. "Hold tight. We're goin' for a ride."

Becky pulled up her hood and retrieved her weapons. She kept the blades retracted and readied herself to leap off the cliff.

"Hey, umm Adam?" Sir Adam looked over to his brother. "You're riding a unicorn."

Sir Adam grinned. "I know! Right?"

I could tell that they were all about to go off this edge and I knew that it would be a moment I would want to remember. "This ought to be good. I am going to watch it from up here."

Travis pulled out an odd device from his pack. He tapped it a few times and then handed it to me. "This is called a phone.

For all intents and purposes, this is a magical device that will remember what it looks at so it can be seen again later. Just keep the action where you can see it through here."

This world is not the only one I have seen, and I was familiar with the concept of the device, once Travis showed me what to do, I felt I could provide what he asked for. "Okay, are you ready?"

Travis pulled out his bow. "Ready." He reached back, pulled an arrow, and strung it. "Brother. I need to hear it one more time."

I put Sir Adam directly in the center of the shot as the unicorn reared up and Sir Adam threw one hand into the air. "These are the moments we live for!"

Together they leaped from the edge of the cliff. Kargen and Sir Adam turned into stardust that twinkled in the sun and then dissipated. Sir Adam was in the middle of a whoop, and his voice faded out like a ghost. Unicorn magic is often described as majestic or mystical and for a moment everyone forgot about the cliff they had leapt off and watched as they disappeared. New sparkles of stardust appeared at the bottom of the cliff and Sir Adam and Kargen appeared from it, with Sir Adam still whooping.

When Oubliette leaped from the cliff, she dove forward headfirst. She activated the hilts of her weapons and as they locked into place in mid-air, she allowed her momentum to send her into a forward swing. As the swing caught the apex, she clicked off the hilts and allowed her momentum to carry her outward with a slight ascent. She arched her back and allowed herself to go into a back flip, so she was now facing headfirst. She reactivated her hilts and used them as a fulcrum for her next swing.

Maddicus and Grelf cheered her on as they descended at the same speed as Oubliette and circled so they could watch the show.

Travis leaped off the cliff and screamed all the way down. He flew past the girls like a shrieking comet. He waited until he was almost at ground level then fired his arrow ahead of him. As the arrow hit, Travis teleported directly to it, but didn't take any of the momentum with him, so he found himself smoothly landing at the bottom of the cliff with his twin brother and a unicorn. I liked their view, so I decided to continue recording the girls from their location. I handed the phone back to Travis still recording.

Oubliette finished with a triple summersault when she reached the bottom. Grelf, Maddicus, and Becky were still squealing about how fun their trip down had been when the cart finally made it to us after taking the longer way, which didn't involve a sheer cliff face. While everyone was getting back in the cart to continue their adventure forward to the stone, Maddicus began talking to Kargen and Sir Adam translated for him. Kargen had been awake the entire length of his imprisonment. He knew his resting site was a place that she had been hundreds of times. She had talked to him about her life and what she was feeling. He told her that she had pulled him back from the edge of his madness. His solitude had been unbearable for decades, but her talking to him for years became the only joy he ever felt since the days before Moon Crow. He promised that he would never share a word of what she said. It was precious to him. It was sacred. She hugged him like she had for years, and then he placed his head against hers so that her forehead rested just below his horn, then told her how proud of her he was now that she no longer wore a manacle. She told him she was proud that he no longer wore one either.

During their two days in the desert Maddicus had been teaching Grelf how to ride a Bodi board. It was the final leg of Grelf's journey and Maddicus thought it was only right that Grelf flew it. So, Maddicus and Grelf switched places, putting Grelf in the drivers position. Grelf gained her balance and pushed forward, and the Bodi board began to move.

Travis and Becky got in the cart. Sir Adam and Kargen rode together, and alongside them, Grelf and Maddicus flew across the desert. They raced along the floor of the Verris Desert until they came to the edge of the massive dune. The sand slowed Kargen down, but once they got past the dune the ground was void of sand and he began to move with greater speed.

At the center of the large circle, that sat like a wound in the Verris Desert, the tribe of Bodites had already begun to set up tents. The tents encircled about thirty yards from the center point. In the heart of the circle stood a statue of a unicorn up on its hind legs, about the same size as Kargen. The statue itself, like the ground it stood on, was made of obsidian. The rich black rock reached out with hundreds of tendrils along the ground that resembled the pattern lightning makes when it strikes the ground. It appeared as if the statue and the area around it were carved from a single piece of obsidian.

The Bodites had come out to officially welcome the Fire Princess, but they were unprepared for what they saw. The Fire

Princess arrived flying a Bodi board, and alongside her one of her men had not only awoken but was now riding the unicorn guardian of the stone. The entire tribe stopped what they were doing, and stared slack-jawed at their arrival. Many of them dropped whatever they happened to have in their hands at the time and knelt in honor at the site of them riding in together. They prayed. They sang. This was the moment they had heard about their entire lives. A legend from their fathers, fathers, fathers. The prophecy was coming to pass.

Kargen made a quiet grunt and Adam dismounted him. The unicorn walked slowly up to the statue timidly. His heart cried out in mournful sorrow and his voice echoed against the dunes that surrounded the location.

Sway of the Bodites joined Grelf and Sir Adam as they stood next to Kargen. The entire front of the second unicorn's torso was transparent. Looking into Pipim they could see that she was a geode lined with hundreds of crystals and in the center of it, was an obsidian sword.

Sir Adam translated for Kargen, as he spoke directly into Sir Adam's consciousness. "She is still alive."

Sway reached out gently and allowed his hand to stroke Kargen's mane. "Far out." Then, even slower and as gentle as he could, touched the clear torso of the statue. "This is the Immovable Stone. The crystals in the geode reflect kinetic energy two-fold sis. The harder you hit it the more energy reflects."

"It's the sword that keeps her in this form. It somehow

is imprisoning her. He says that it has been here since the time of Moon Crow." Sir Adam seemed puzzled. "Kargen. How is that possible? The Earth Blade of Venger has only been out of play for a couple of weeks. How can it have been here for generations?" Kargen's angelic voice echoed across the sand. "It was the tempest. The sword was caught in the vortex of time and space, rendering the time of its actual disappearance irrelevant. A lot of things have no meaning in the eye of a tempest, not even time." The unicorn pawed at the ground with his hoof and lowered his head. "He says that if you can remove the obsidian blade, they will be eternally grateful."

"Then you will be glad to know that retrieving that sword is why I am here." She looked directly at Kargen, "I have no intention of hurting her, but I will need to break the stone to remove the sword."

Kargen snorted. "He understands that you must do what is needed." Sir Adam gave Grelf a nod. "We talked. I let him know what's happening. He said that he will trust you until you prove it unwise to do so."

"That's really all I can ask of anyone. Thank you." Grelf meant every word, but she didn't look away from the stone. "Sway?"

"Word?" the old man said.

"How hard would I have to hit it to get past that barrier?" Grelf tried to touch the Immovable Stone, but she moved way too fast, and her hand bounced back as a small force wave returned her kinetic energy two-fold with a small whooshing sound.

Sway chuckled. "No such thing."

Grelf stared at him wide-eyed. "What do you mean, no such thing?"

Sway brought up his left arm palm facing his right. Then with his right hand, he slowly touched a finger to his left palm and said, "Bing", then acted like his hand got pushed back. Next, he doubled up his fist and punched his left palm as hard as he could. And said, "Hawang!", his hand flailed in slow motion as he pretended it was a man screaming, illustrating him flying through the air until his hand couldn't reach any further.

Grelf swallowed hard. She looked up into the heavens and asked with exasperation, "Why can't it ever be just hit it really hard?" Kargen popped his front legs up and vocalized his disapproval. Before Sir Adam could say anything Grelf held up a hand. "You don't have to translate, I understood that one just fine." Grelf looked apologetically to Kargen with a real sense of contrition. "I'm sorry. Just frustrated. I don't want to smash your mate." Grelf took a deep breath and looked at the sun. It's going to be dark soon, and when it gets dark it goes below freezing. I have tonight to come up with a plan because tomorrow morning I must do this." Grelf stared into the eyes of Pipim. "Tomorrow is the last day. We have run out of time."

27

DALEN'S

VENGERIAN GIFT

Dalen had moved the three of them quantumly. His desired location was the Vengerian throne room but in mid-transit, something happened, and their Vengerian Pins became ineffective. The pins were required to get them past the magical security the City of Venger had in place. Without them, any teleportation attempt into the city just sent them to the closest location allowed before breaching their defenses, which landed them at the White Tree of Travel across the fields of wildflowers from Venger.

The first time Dalen had ever stood here was the first

moment he had ever seen this world. He was only seventeen at the time and had only just met Moment. When Dalen arrived, the tree was on the edge of a bowl-shaped valley resembling a large outdoor amphitheater, with the City of Venger center stage right along the coast. Now he looked out upon a prairie of grass and wildflowers and Venger was settled on the edge of a cliff that stood thousands of feet above the water's edge.

He had had a vision of the Chaos Dragon erupting from the ground. The vision that Christoph had shared with him confirmed what he had seen. There was only a day or so left before the Chaos Dragon would be freed, and when it manifested it would need mass to create itself. Dalen guessed that it was going to use the earth and stone to generate itself, and when it did, it was going to be so large that the void left would form the valley that he had seen the day he first arrived.

"I wonder why our Vengerian Pins didn't allow us into the city?" Dalen looked around for an answer. The one that he found was the last he would have wanted.

"Your precious Vengerian Pins will no longer work for you here." A black smoke that had small red lights of castoff energy giving him the look of the inside of a structure fire, appeared without warning, and DeSalvo walked out of it. The smoke dissipated after his arrival as fast as it had formed. "The Time Mage has asked me to protect us from the threat of people teleporting in and surprising us while we do our..." He chuckled insidiously. "...work."

His appearance was that of a very old man. Much like Dalen,

he had black stones over his third eye and throat chakras. Matching them his eyes were black and sunken into their sockets with dark circles around them. He was pale and due to his age, his face looked more like a skull than a person. He was dressed all in black except for a cloth that he wore over his left shoulder. It was a long cloth that draped down to his knees in the front and back. Going up the cloth was an image of fire. The cloth had to have been enchanted because the fire moved and danced as if it were real.

"You must be DeSalvo, right?" DeSalvo made direct eye contact with Christoph and as he did Christoph could feel fear beginning to build in him. "Why are you doing this?"

"If what you are asking me is if I have some sort of reason to want to destroy Venger and all that entails, I don't." DeSalvo reached out with his magic and continued to actively try to induce fear into Christoph. "If you think it has something to do with power and greed, you would be wrong again."

Christoph rested his hand on the eye in the hilt of the Water Blade. As he did, he could see what DeSalvo was doing at that moment, and he was able to break free of his grasp. "Enough of that." Christoph blinked a couple of times to refocus. "One. You aren't nearly as scary as you think you are and two, you didn't answer my question."

DeSalvo put his hand out and shrugged. "Well, 'Almost King' what can I say? You have a mental acuity stronger than that of a nine-year-old, look at you paying attention to what I am saying." His eyes narrowed and his tone became threatening. "I am a servant of the Chaos Dragon, you naive dolt. I want her to wake up and shower this world with her gift of destruction." DeSalvo took a few steps forward and smiled as Christoph stepped back. "But to answer your question even further since I know that you will not accept such a simple answer, I am doing this because of him." DeSalvo pointed to Dalen.

"Why?" Christoph found his courage and took a step toward DeSalvo in defiance. "What has Dalen done, that this is your response?"

DeSalvo turned his attention away from Christoph and turned his attention to Dalen. "You want to know why I am doing this, Almost King? Because Mr. Pax over here took something very valuable from me. Something I asked for nicely for him to return, and instead in an act of defiance and misguided importance, he intentionally let it fall from his fingers and let it get lost in time itself." DeSalvo turned back on Christoph. "Ask him if it's true. Ask your friend, if this is all his fault. Ask him if he took what was mine and intentionally lost it in the frames of time." Then he uncontrollably screamed with rage. "Ask him!"

It made everyone flinch. Christoph blinked a couple of times and wiggled his finger in his ear up and down suggesting DeSalvo's scream was too loud. "Do either of you have any idea what he is talking about?"

Dalen nodded. "The thing he is talking about is called the Beads of Fire. I intentionally lost them in the frames of time. He did ask for them and then tried to take them and left me with no choice."

DeSalvo was furious. "You had the choice of giving them to me."

Dalen was also getting angry. "Why should I give them to you?"

"They belong to me." DeSalvo was snarling, almost growling at Dalen.

"No, they don't!"

"Yes, they do!"

Dalen was now snarling at DeSalvo as well. "NO! They don't! If they were yours then why are they tied to my soul?"

All of DeSalvo's rage and anger drained from him and was replaced by amusement. "You still don't understand." DeSalvo cast a spell, and as he did Dalen slowed down time and watched the magic play out. Dalen knew this spell. It was a spell that forced the target to speak only the truth. DeSalvo, being a genie, gave him the ability to overcome the spell, but there was another piece of magic to this spell, and Dalen watched with the eyes of a jinn. He saw that this extra piece was built into it making it impossible for DeSalvo to break it. Once Dalen knew what it was, he allowed time to flow normally. "You know this spell Mr. Pax?" Dalen nodded. "Good. Then you know that until I dispel it, I am unable to lie to you."

Dalen calmed his heart and mind. "I'm listening."

"The same way when you activated them, they connected you to your soul, they would have connected me to mine. I was there when they were created and without any question, they belong to me." Once DeSalvo finished speaking he folded his arms and waited for Dalen to accept the truth.

Dalen had no choice but to accept what he said as truth, but there were more questions to answer. "Then why did Moment tell me to keep them from you?"

"Moment? Cute." DeSalvo rubbed his hand over his mouth and chin while he thought. "I would guess that it believed that I would have taken them and tried to heal my world. Unfortunately, in the process, your world may have come to an end." DeSalvo shrugged again. "Omelets. They are funny that way."

"From what I understand you already destroyed your world, and then you wanted to destroy mine?" Master Peace scoffed. "I wouldn't want you to have it either."

DeSalvo turned on Master Peace with a rush of new anger. "This is between me and Dalen, Ben! I need him alive for a short while longer, but I would have no problem destroying you without a second thought."

Master Peace pulled his Dragon Claw of Light and activated it. "How about, no." As he activated it, he tapped back into the power laid dormant within him. As if in this moment it knew that it was needed, the power awoke within him, and it ignited the Dragon Claw and became a white ball of pure energy that throbbed and hummed with raw power.

DeSalvo put up his hands as if the light were hot or too bright. He was noticeably bothered by it but put his arms down and tried to ignore it. "Did you really think I would allow myself to physically be here and have all of this come down to whether Ben Watts could give me a magic swirly? You are dumber than I ever guessed. How about I put you back in that little hell I put you in before? You know? The one that broke you?"

Master Peace's surprise was obvious. "It wasn't an accident? You did that to me on purpose?"

DeSalvo was now getting cocky. "Yeah. You tried to kill Dalen." He swung around and looked at Christoph. "I bet you didn't know that did you?" DeSalvo glared at Master Peace. The day all of this started young Ben here, got three of his friends and tried to kill Dalen, and this was before he knew magic. If it wasn't for me, he would be dead now, because of this noble Brother of Light."

"It was Mathias who healed me," Dalen said defiantly. "I have already learned that Mathias was me from another time. I saved myself. You had nothing to do with it."

"If you remember correctly my dear boy, Mathias was a student of mine and working for me to retrieve the Beads of Fire." DeSalvo leaned in and spoke in hushed tones like he was giving away a secret. "Who do you think put him on that corner that night? I was watching you even before that. Earlier in that same day when Ben planned on attacking you at school, I was there, watching. You even saw me for a moment in your principal's office."

Dalen had seen DeSalvo that day. He had not thought about it in years but as DeSalvo spoke he remembered not only that, but DeSalvo still had the truth spell on him. "Then why did you try to kill everyone?"

DeSalvo feigned insult and pain. "It was Mathias. You, by your own admittance, tried to kill your friends. It was you who slit the throat of your David. I showed up afterward and asked for the Beads of Fire."

"But it was you who made the knife." Dalen knew he was telling the truth, but Dalen was ready to bet everything that he wasn't being honest. "A knife you gave to him to use on us."

"Look, Mr. Pax. I know you want to blame me for all your problems, but you are going to have to take responsibility for your own actions one day." DeSalvo got right up in Dalen's face. "By now you know that the only person that can free your friend is the being who made Soul Freezer. Nothing's changed, except I will also free your friend from his curse. All you have to do is give me what I want."

Christoph had stayed out of things until now, but he couldn't hold his tongue any longer. "What is it that you want?"

DeSalvo was looking into Dalen's eyes with hate. "Almost King wants to know what I want. Maybe he will make a deal with me? What do you think?" DeSalvo just stared into Dalen's eyes for a moment and then stepped away from him and addressed Christoph. "I want the Beads of Fire. If Dalen truly lost them and can't get them back, I will take his heart stone as compensation. If he does, I will end the trouble with the Time Mage and Chaos Dragon immediately. I only did it to get your attention and to make it absolutely clear how far I am willing to go to retrieve my property. I am under a truth spell, and Mr. Pax can tell you if I say it, it is true, and because I don't want any bad feelings, I will also wake up his friend."

"Truth spell, okay. Then answer a question." Master Peace sounded skeptical. "Besides the being who created the knife releasing the victim, who else can break the curse."

"You know, there are moments where the truth is far more damaging than any lie that I could ever conceive." DeSalvo gave a dramatic bow. "Dear Ben, I regret to inform you that there is no other way to save David, and I will do it willingly and with a smile on my face." DeSalvo's smile dropped and turned into a look that would haunt a normal man. "You know my price."

"I won't let you destroy this world!" Dalen said with defiance.

DeSalvo chuckled. "That is now completely in your hands. I'll give you one day to produce the Beads of Fire or hand over your Heart Stone in compensation. One day, and then after that, it will be too late." DeSalvo turned around as if he were about to walk away, but then turned back and looked out over the field. "And just to make sure you don't try something extremely heroic and equally stupid; I will leave you with this." DeSalvo waved his arm and countless shadow creatures appeared between them and Venger. They howled and snarled as they took up ranks to block anyone who would try to get to the city. They were created from nightmares. They were the things that hid under the bed in children's minds. They were dark monsters of people's worst fears, brought forth through dark magic to keep them from being able to physically enter

Venger. "One day. Make your choice."

Black smoke with red embers began to appear around him until he was fully enveloped, then just as quickly, it faded away and he was gone. The smoke smelled of sulfur and Christoph fanned his nose to get rid of the smell. They were far enough away that the shadow creatures were not bothered by them. "Let's fall back. Don't bother Grelf but get ahold of one of the other Vengerians and inform them of what's happening. "

They moved to a nearby farmhouse that had been recently abandoned. It was further from Venger but kept the Tree of Transport in sight. While Dalen used his magic to reach out to Lady Venger, Master Peace reached out to Travis and let them know that they were back and what had happened, then gave him directions to find them when they returned.

This was going to take planning. They were so close and now they had to contend with an army of nightmarish creatures made of pure darkness and fueled by hatred and fear. Dalen cast a spell that provided food and drink for the other two. He no longer felt hungry since he had no longer been able to slip back into full corporeal form.

Christoph sat down and began to eat and took a drink from a mug that Dalen created with his spell. "Report. What do we got?"

Master Peace put up a finger and then Dalen followed suit with two. "Grelf is at the Earth Blade now. Travis is hopeful that they should be back soon. They are aware of the time restraints.

His response was, 'Now we know why we only had ten days.' He also said something about Sir Adam finding a unicorn and maybe falling in love with a sand surfer. They know where we are and will meet us here."

Christoph nodded and then turned his attention to Dalen. "Lady Venger says that they are fine. Their protective magic has kept the Time Mage and DeSalvo in the middle ring for now. They are attempting to get to the Heart of Venger and are slowly pushing their way through. They believe that the timeline he gave us is based on how long it will take them to get to the center of the city where the Heart of Venger is. The actual crystal is both the heart of the City of Venger and also Lady Venger herself. We only have until then. She says that if we can get through the Great Seal of Venger our Vengerian Pins will work again, and we can teleport directly to the throne room. Since the day that we left, they have been evacuating people from Venger. Both her and Dorn wish us luck."

Christoph listened carefully, the entire time one of his hands rested on the hilt of the Air Blade, and he was keeping his fingers touching the gold dragon coin in its hilt. While his other hand was draped across the eye of the Water Blade, still on his hip. Dalen suspected where the Eye of the Water Blade was all-seeing and granted him the vision of Crystal, the Coin of the Air Blade was all-knowing and granted the wielder the wisdom of Han Bo Fang. "Gentlemen I would like to give you my thoughts on the situation. Master Peace. Something happened to you back there. I have never seen your ball of light do what it did today, and I could feel the power coming off it. What happened?"

Master Peace pulled out his Dragon Claw. And looked at it introspectively. "When I got the Dragon Claw of Light. It had the power of thousands who had given part of themselves to it. That power is eventually for you, and I don't know if I could truly call it mine, but I am now able to tap into it and use the power that was given me."

Christoph slowly nodded, "We are going to need that power to fuse the two Elemental Blades back together to create the Eye of the Dragon you mentioned. Perhaps all four. Dorn said it would take a considerable amount of power to wield it." Christoph pondered again for a moment. "Master Peace. So, what you are saying is that your Dragon Claw holds within it, the power given to it for years by thousands of people? DeSalvo didn't seem to like it at all. Were you the only one who got that?"

Master Peace looked up from his weapon and glanced over to Dalen and then back to Christoph. "No. Each of us received something like this."

That's what Christoph was hoping to hear. "Dalen. What was the object your statue had?"

Dalen reached over and opened his dimensional pocket in midair. Using his magic, because he could not hold the physical object, he pulled out the backpack that he packed the day he left his home to begin this adventure. He opened one of the small side pockets and used his magic to pull out his white stone. "This is what my statue had."

Christoph inspected it as it floated near him. "Why don't you use it?"

"When I first got it, I still thought I was human. When I first took it, it changed me into a jinn. It was an amazing amount of power, but it was hindering me. I had not obtained my true Heart Stone, and I had begun to rely on this false one to sustain me. It made me weaker in the end. I set it aside so that I could earn my true Heart Stone."

"It also made him too solid. Like he was a living statue and not a real person." Dalen looked at Master Peace with a little indignance. Master Peace shrugged and said, "Well it did."

"Perhaps that's what you need now." Christoph laughed at the ideas that were running through his mind. "Master Peace. Before the day you got the Dragon Claw of Light, had you ever trained in that kind of weapon?"

"It was my favorite weapon. I had trained in it for three years before I got it." Master Peace smiled. "I see where you are going with this. Travis was familiar with archery and Becky had been trained in gymnastics. Adam had no choice but to be the pure knight that he was. He even befriended a unicorn."

"Then why would they give you an object that was never meant to be used?" Christoph pondered.

It was a good question that Dalen didn't have a direct answer for. "I don't know. Now that you mention it, it doesn't make sense that they would give me an item that I wouldn't use, but I never needed it."

"Until now." Christoph was sure he was right. "You had to earn your heart stone first. I'll grant you that, but now. Now when the end is so close. Now you need something that will make you more solid. Something that will diminish you just enough to make you real."

"You know what. I think you are right." I don't believe that they meant to harm me, and the stone does the exact thing I need right now. Dalen reached out and put his hand around the stone. All of Dalen's stones lit up and began to glow. The stone was transforming him, but this time it was different. The stone flowed with all the Stones of Power that Dalen already had and harmonized with him.

He could feel the power that had been lying in wait. He could sense all the people who had given of themselves at his statue. He could hear their prayers and feel their wishes and desires. He could flow to any moment in time when someone had knelt at his statue. There were thousands of them, but all of them began to harmonize until he focused on the first person who had ever given anything of themselves.

It was Christoph. Dalen saw him as a King of Venger. He walked up to the statue and knelt. He looked up at the eyes of the statue and said, 'When you see this, you will be at the abandoned farmhouse three years ago. This is the moment when you first touch the power you have been keeping secret. Later you will tell me about this moment and how it created something that you call a stitch in time. It's funny how time works." He smiled as he bent down to touch the circle to give his gift. It was his respect and thanks. "Standing on this side of it I know what takes place, and there is something you should know. Do not give in to DeSalvo's demands. He doesn't know nearly as much as he thinks. The best thing you can do is be the best that you are. No one can ask more from you than that."

After that Dalen's eye refocused where he was. He was still floating but he was corporeal again. Now that he was, he was starving. Dalen reached into his backpack, retrieved a mirror, and looked at himself. His stones had turned white once more, but his complexion was still good, and he didn't seem to have any ill effects from the stone. In truth, he felt more powerful than he ever had.

Christoph hugged Dalen. "Solid enough and it looks good on you Dalen. How do you feel?"

Dalen thought deeply about it and realized Christoph had been right. The stone was meant for him now. When he was corporeal it affected him by making him more dense and real, to the point he was losing himself, but now that he was a fully formed jinn to the point his true form was less real than not, this stone harmonized him and allowed him to channel all of the power that the stone held.

"Good call. I have tapped into the power same as Master Peace, and I am pretty sure that I can now help the others find theirs."

"Now we're talking." Christoph took another long pull on his mug, walked outside, and looked out past the tree towards the horde of monsters waiting for them. "Do you think if all of you can tap into the power and Grelf and I have full use of all four Elemental Blades we can get through that army of shadows?"

Master Peace gave Christoph a nod. "Yes. I believe that is a reality that we can create."

Christoph stood next to Master Peace and looked toward the nightmare creatures that stood between them and Venger. "First, we wait for Grelf and the others to return. Hopefully, they will be here soon."

Dalen floated behind them in his new form. "And second?"

Christoph turned and looked at Dalen with a devilish grin. "We take back Venger."

28

THE STRENGTH

TO RELENT

Grelf had spent the night in one of the tents that had been erected for her and her people. She had been told the temperature drop was extreme and advised to be inside before the sunset. Each tent had been enchanted to keep the cold from creeping in on them. No fire was allowed because they would need to vent the tent to let out the smoke and along with the smoke the heat would escape, so instead they were given a Fire Stone. This stone was enchanted to produce light and sufficient heat to keep everyone warm and safe. Only Kargen remained outside. He refused to leave Pipim now that he was free and assured Sir Adam that the cold posed no threat to him. He had spent many nights in this desert and was ready for what would come, but even if he weren't, Pipim would never be without him again.

Grelf had been asked to stay in her tent unless she had a need. Just before the sun went down the Bodites showed Grelf and her team which tents were designated as lavatories. There were a couple of them, but one was set up and designated for Grelf and the Vengerians. Inside the lavatory were three sections. The first was directly in the center and connected to the flap that acted as a door. In the middle was another Fire Stone that kept the tent from freezing. On each side, large pelts had been erected to give a private room on either side. In both rooms, was a large pot with a wide smooth rim that could be sat on. Like the Fire Stone, the pot was enchanted and continually created the magical effect of 'clean'. With the spell in effect, anything put into the pot would be magically cleared away and disappear. They were warned that once night descended if they needed to use the lavatory, dress as warmly as possible and move quickly from one location to the next.

We stayed up for hours trying to form a plan. In his notebook, Travis detailed all the ideas the team agreed were worth attempting. The next morning when we woke, he would bring his notebook as a map to our plan of action. The plan was for Grelf to try each one until something worked.

The morning had still been cold, and they were still wearing clothes designed for winter when they stepped out of the tent. I was fortunate to be able to ignore the temperature at that level and so I was dressed in my usual attire. We talked to Pipim as we ate breakfast around her. Through Sir Adam, Kargen said that he had spoken to her all night to no avail. Sir Adam suggested that he try to awaken her by the same method that he had awoken Kargen. But although Sir Adam could now tap into that power, it did not have the same effect on Pipim. Kargen believed that Sir Adam's act of selflessness as he leaped off the edge to save Maddicus was the precursor to Kargen becoming free. That, mixed with Sir Adam's awakening, is what brought forth the connection between Kargen and Sir Adam. Sir Adam was Kargen's rider now, and because of that, it could not be him who woke her. It also made sense that it had to be Grelf who achieved this. It was her challenge and Sir Adam could not achieve it for her.

In the afternoon Grelf went through a myriad of attempts. Everything from talking to her and explaining the situation, to demonstrating her prowess with a blade. She tried to impress Pipim and prove that she was a worthy candidate. She was even willing to try and sing to her. She rubbed her belly which showed patience, to be able to touch her without creating enough kinetic force to get her hand kicked away. Although she was opposed to it at first, she even danced for Pipim.

When she made it to the part of the list where it was time to try physically hitting the stone with all her might, the Bodites began to make marks behind her and bet on how far she would get launched backward. For two hours she tried hitting it with all her might, getting launched backward with every strike. The tribe would bang their drums, building the rhythm to a near drum roll waiting for her to strike the stone and then they would cheer as she flew back. Where she landed was now the new mark to beat and then they would wager again. Maddicus explained that over the years many had tried to break the Immovable Stone in this manner, so often, that the tribe had created this game.

In the afternoon when the sun was at its hottest and many of the Bodites retired to their tents, she continued the list. Her Vengerians never left her side and Kargen never left Pipim. She had waited for that part of the day to try her Flame Blade. When the sun was at its hottest, she pointed the Fire Blade at the stone and hit it with a fountain of fire that erupted from the end of it.

Time was running out, and without knowing the exact time of pending destruction, every minute could be the last. "Melt, damn you!" Grelf screamed as she dropped to her knees and allowed the fire to stop.

We wanted it just as much as she did but her strength, like our hopes, was beginning to dwindle. We had tried everything on our list, and she was no closer to beating the Immovable Stone than the moment we had first arrived.

"It's not fair." Grelf was on the edge of breaking down. She hated to lose control, especially around other people. She saw it as a sign of weakness, and so she made it a point to not cry when others could see her, but she was at the end of her rope and out of faith. She walked up to the Immovable Stone, slowly and as gently as she could she slid her hands onto Pipim's belly. "I don't know how to save you, which means I don't know how to save anybody else." Slowly she rested her head on Pipim. "I'm out of ideas and

I'm still at step one. This is my biggest fear." Tears began to well up in Grelf's eyes. "That it would all come down to me, and I would not be able to be strong enough. I'm not strong enough to save the world." She had all but given up but still, she kept herself from crying.

"Hang on." Travis grabbed his notebook and began to feverishly flip through his notes until he found what he was looking for. He stood alongside Grelf, and she turned her head so he could not see her eyes. "Grelf. I am going to need you to do something, and it's important."

Grelf scoffed. "More important than this?"

"Actually, yes." Travis's tone was very matter-of-fact, and it caused enough confusion in her thinking, that she pursued his line of thought. "Fine. What do you want me to do?"

"Travis put his hand on Grelf's shoulder and spoke with compassion. "I am going to need you to accept that everything you have done hasn't worked. So far, you have failed."

"What are you doing?" Becky scolded him. "Can't you see she already feels bad enough?"

Travis bent sideways and closed one eye so that he could get a different view of Grelf. "Umm. I would have to disagree with you, My Love." Becky just stared at him slack-jawed. She had never seen him be so callous. "Grelf, there is a difference between being too weak to finish the job and being too weak to admit that you have not succeeded. I know you think you are being strong by keeping it all in, but you are not. It is a sign of weakness to be unable to admit the truth about yourself, agreed?"

Grelf was now on the verge of tears, but she took a deep breath and tried to refocus. "Agreed."

Travis was now getting louder as if he were frustrated. "Stop hiding from it!" He knelt next to her so there was nowhere to hide her face. "That also means facing the truth about what you feel. Every time you try to bury it, you are burying a piece of your heart and soul, and you are lying about the truth of who you are."

"What are you saying?" Grelf was fighting her emotions, she wanted to scream and cry, but a part of her kept fighting to be strong.

Travis reached out and hugged her. "Stop trying to be the Orc Slayer. Just be Grelf."

I felt my sister approaching so I moved alongside Grelf opposite Travis, but it was my sister who was there to speak. "Your friend is right. You are still trying to be the Orc Slayer. Only the Queen of Venger can free the unicorn."

Grelf knew it was Reflection of Grey who was with her. She kept her forehead against the Immovable Stone and spoke from her hopelessness. "It's impossible. There is a reason it's called an Immovable Stone. I can't affect it. I am not strong enough." It killed Grelf inside to admit it out loud, but she had reached a place where it was the only thing she could see.

"Nothing is impossible. End of thought." Reflection stroked Grelf's hair. "I am an immovable object, and I have been defeated many times."

"How?" Grelf whispered. "How do you move an immovable object?"

"From within." Reflection, without question, is one of the strongest of the Grey Continuum. Anyone who has ever faced her was met with equal force reflected at them. She has only been matched by Angel, but he is a literal unstoppable force. The Gods of the First Dynasty would concur. "I have faced many opponents in my time, both in this world and others, and the only enemy I ever faced that was able to defeat me, was my own mind and heart. Just as yours are defeating you now. Right now, you are battling on too many fronts, and you will not be able to defeat this trial until you can defeat the person who is keeping you from your goal. Yourself."

Grelf flexed her fingers and pushed her head against the stone, and it pushed back against her kinetic force. "How? How do I defeat myself?"

"Stop fighting. You are putting all your will and strength into not feeling what you are feeling. Every part of you focused on not letting anything in, but the truth is that the thing you are now fighting is already in. What you are fighting is yourself, trying to get out." Reflection leaned in close and whispered. "Stop. Stop trying to defeat yourself. One of the most profound ways of defeating an enemy is to have them become an ally."

Reflection had said what she needed to and fulfilled her promise, so now it was me who was stroking her hair. "It's okay Grelf. Stop fighting."

Grelf's emotional damn broke and she let go. She sobbed

into the chest of Pipim. "I am so sorry I couldn't save you... or anyone." Tears rolled down her cheeks and although there was force against them, they finally settled on to the statue of Pipim.

Out of respect for her, we let her cry it out in peace. No one tried to stop her or told her to be brave. What we did was give her space and stand in quiet reverence. Bodites who were still watching quietly went from tent to tent until the entire tribe came out and bore witness. They chanted and sang in quiet low tones. And I could feel the presence of the Creator of Dreams.

Hip-Gnosis spoke to my soul from the Continuum. *The trials are not arbitrary. Each one prepares them. Reflection, as always, shows great wisdom. The unicorn was never the Immovable Stone she had to defeat.*

We stood with her in her moment of strength and weakness. As the sun went down and the desert began to get cold, the Bodites left in groups, but only long enough to wrap themselves in the warmest clothes they had, and mothers brought out their Fire Stones to keep their children warm. They were still the length of a ship away, but we could hear them as they began to sing and play their instruments.

Night fell completely and the Verris Desert's temperature dropped quickly. The Vengerians tapped their Vengerian Pins and were now wearing clothes that would keep them alive for a short while. They did not want to disturb Grelf, but they were beginning to get concerned about her freezing to death. They knew Grelf was immune to heat, but there was a question of the possibility, that the Fire Princess would not be able to function without heat of some form.

"Please Grelf." Maddicus's voice was riddled with concern, for she knew what being in this Verris Desert at night could do to a person. "Please, let's take a break and get you toasty."

Grelf stood back up, and with eyes swollen from tears, she looked Maddicus in the eyes and said, "No. There is no time. The world could end at any moment." She smiled and hugged her new sister. "I refuse to move from this spot until I have the Earth Blade, or the Dragon destroys us all." Maddicus hugged her back but tried to take her hands and coax her away from the statue. "You aren't hearing me, and at this moment, I need you to respect my wishes."

Maddicus let go of Grelf's hands. "Okay, Grelf. But if you aren't moving then neither am I." With purpose, she stood beside Grelf, and the tribe began to play louder.

The temperature was still dropping but Becky and Travis stepped forward together. Kargen and Sir Adam stood on the other side of Maddicus.

"Even if it means our final breath." Sir Adam said with passion. "It's not just something we said because it's the thing to say. We are with you till the end."

"Sir Adam." Grelf empathized with the heart of this knight who was ready to stand with her until hell froze over. "You are a true hero, and I know, for a fact, that you will stand here and freeze to death to hold yourself to your word, but there is no need for you to die."

Sir Adam smiled and puffed out his chest with determination. "Are you kidding? These are the moments we live for." And he began to sway with the music. "Besides, what are you going to do? Turn us all away?"

Grelf turned and looked. Everyone was standing with her. Everyone. The entire tribe stood no more than the length of a carriage with horses from where Grelf stood. They were singing and playing their song. Closer still, was me, the Vengerians including Maddicus, and even Kargen standing with her. As she turned and saw them the tribe exploded with song and music.

Maddicus held Grelf's hand. "Being alone is the only task that you cannot achieve."

From behind Grelf came a sound like ice crackling as they're dropped into a drink. She turned and stared at the Immovable Stone. For hours while she wept, her tears had been absorbed into the surface. The temperature had dropped significantly, and they froze into the stone. As they froze, they expanded, but inside the stone, there was nowhere for them to expand, creating a kinetic force within it. That kinetic force was then reflected two-fold. That energy also had nowhere to go except back into the stone, which then reflected two-fold again. It had caused a chain reaction and there was a charge building up within the Immovable Stone. Its strength had now been turned inward, building exponentially, and it was moving toward becoming an unstoppable force.

Inside the geode, all the points of the crystals began to glow, and current began to arc between them. Grelf ignited and the fire engulfed her. It swirled around her and lit up the night, then as it burned out, Grelf was wearing the dress she had worn when she emerged from the lava, and now standing directly in front of the Immovable Stone, was the Fire Princess and future Queen of Venger. As she stepped forward the tribe began to vocalize, holding a single tone, like monks in a meditation. Together, the voices grew louder and stronger.

Grelf's hair ignited as she drew the Fire Blade and held it with her left hand. Slowly she moved her other hand and touched the solar plexus of Pipim. The charge had built up so strongly that it was only moments from exploding, but the energy that was being produced also created heat. Enough heat to melt stone. The immense heat would have caused anyone to combust, but she was the Fire Princess of Venger and immune to it. Her hand turned to pure light, and she pushed it through the stone in its viscous state.

The tribe built their sound into a crescendo until their voices filled the air and harmonized with their echoes. It built and built and together as a single sound it stopped, leaving only silence.

There was a flash of light that rippled outward and faded exactly at the edge of the dune. Grelf was made of obsidian, but her hair was still pure fire. She pulled back her hand to her chest and she was holding the Earth Blade. She had her eyes closed at first but when she opened them, they gleamed like two stars in the night against her obsidian skin. She looked into the eyes of Pipim, who knelt her front legs so that she could bow to the new Queen of Venger.

Sir Adam was the first to his knees followed by the rest of

the Vengerians. Kargen moved to be near Pipim and bowed as well. Grelf turned around just in time to watch the entire tribe bow down and even the children understood what they had witnessed. None moved, we merely just knelt there in a perfect moment of silence and listened to the planet turn.

It lasted for as long as it could but finally, Sir Adam threw up his hands and called out to the sky. "These are the moments we live for!" It fully translated to the Bodites and together the entire tribe echoed it back.

People quickly remembered that everyone was freezing to death and although they wanted Grelf to stay, they understood that there was no time to waste. They had to leave. Maddicus went to tell people goodbye and by the time she was back, Grelf looked like a flesh and blood person again.

Pipim was now free, and she and Kargen were reunited. Sir Adam heard from the Bodites that they were going to continue to protect her because she and Kargen were the last of their kind, so Adam decided that he needed to speak with Kargen before they left.

"As much as I enjoy our connection, I believe that your place is here with Pipim." Sir Adam stroked the nose of Kargen. "You have been waiting longer than I have been alive to be with her again, and where we are going is beyond dangerous. So, it might be wise for you to stay here and be with the one that you love." Kargen's voice was beautiful and filled with love and joy. Sir Adam nodded and stroked Kargen's nose. "Of course, but I had to offer." Kargen touched Sir Adam's forehead with his own and then reared up and sang more of its beautiful song.

"What did he say?" asked Travis.

"He appreciates what I was trying to do for him, but he would consider it a disgrace if he were to leave me now when I needed him the most." Sir Adam looked out to the dunes and for a moment seemed lost in thought. "I am glad he is coming, to be honest. Now that we are connected, it would have been near unbearable to say goodbye."

Travis looked out over the dunes as well and took in the moments before the battle that was to come. "What about Pipim?"

"They will arrive together. After we get to this farmhouse that Master Peace told us about, Kargen will come to me when I call, and Pipim will teleport to Kargen." Sir Adam turned his gaze to Travis. "I am not in denial about any of it."

Travis met his brother's gaze and asked, "What do you mean?"

"I remember what you said when we were with the oracles. Becky... We both know she doesn't handle loss well, and we both know that she uses logic to hide from the truth." Sir Adam's voice wavered as his emotions got the better of him. "I don't know for sure what is going to happen next, but I know this..." Sir Adam let down his guard and Adam hugged his brother. "Whatever happens next, I believe in you, and I know that no matter what it is, you will do what you have to, to save this whole world." Travis tried to speak but Adam stopped him. "Don't say anything, just hear me. Travis, I am so proud of you, and the man you have become. Before everything happens, I had to tell you."

Travis hugged his brother, and both of them held on to the moment. "Adam. You are my living breathing hero, and even though I give you a hard time with your sense of adventure getting the better of you, I pray that you will never change. I love you." Travis could feel his brother sob. And he held him tighter. "You are my inspiration, my strength. Within minutes we are going to face an army of nightmares and shadows. There is no one in this world I would rather stand at the gates of hell with, than you."

Adam looked up and saw that Becky was approaching, so Sir Adam whispered her name to his brother, wiped his face, and started laughing.

Becky saw Sir Adam wiping his face and said, "Damn Travis, you broke him, what did you say?"

"I tried to let Kargen stay to keep both of them safe, but he refused to leave my side and when I told your boyfriend here, he decided to remind me that unicorns are drawn to virgins." Sir Adam slapped Travis in the arm.

Becky covered her mouth in shock. "Oh no he didn't?"

Travis had had enough time to get himself back together. He gave his brother a nod and said, "I only said what I did, because it's true. He turned around to face Becky rubbing his eyes. "Oh... That was a good one."

Becky put her hands on her hip disapprovingly. "Just because you aren't..."

Sir Adam stopped her right there. "Hang on what?" Sir Adam looked at his brother. "When did this happen?"

Travis just shrugged. "You should appreciate that an honorable man doesn't kiss and tell."

Becky liked that answer and gave him a sweet kiss. "We are leaving in five." Becky grinned at the look of surprise that still wore an entire Sir Adam suit and said, "It happened on the island after the fire trial."

Sir Adam looked at the both of them and asked, "You made love after a phoenix burn ceremony of fertility presided by the Goddess of Rebirth? Good luck with that."

Becky and Travis had not thought of that until that moment, and both looked at each other with concern. She couldn't think about that right then, so she laughed nervously and tried to change the subject. It took her a moment, but she remembered what she had come for. She asked Travis what he had looked up and Travis started flipping back through pages. "Do you remember our first day in Venger?"

Becky nodded. "How could I forget?"

Travis found the page but gave his attention to Becky. "I asked Dorn if there was something he could tell us before we left."

"Yeah. It was a bunch of random things, but you were sure that he was helping." A lot had happened since that day, and Becky couldn't remember what was said.

Travis smiled. "This is one of the reasons I write stuff down.

I remembered the first one during the fire challenge. Dorn said, 'Sometimes you have to walk through fire.' Which is exactly what Grelf had to do for the Fire Blade. One of the other things he said was this. He turned around his notebook so Becky could see it.

Becky looked right where Travis had pointed out and read it aloud. "An immovable object can only be affected by an unstoppable force, so relent and let the tears of your defeat be the thing that helps you find victory." She read it twice, just to make sure that it really said what it did. "Travis. This is why I love you." She kissed him and he kissed her back.

"Get a room, you two," Adam said jokingly.

"I got a room," added Maddicus as she batted her eyes at Sir Adam flirtatiously.

"You can all have rooms at the castle, but first let's go save the world." Grelf waved goodbye but she knew it would not be forever. She had bonded with these people, and she knew she would be back to see them once all of this was done. "We are out of time. Will of Grey. Tell me you can get us home quickly."

"Sure." I huddled them together and had them close their eyes. "Let me tell you a story about how you are already there."

29

THE EYE OF THE DRAGON AND THE HORN OF THE UNICORN

Time. So abundant that it fills up forever both toward the future and the past, yet so scarce that every being has witnessed it running out when it was needed the most. Time was running out for Christoph. For Venger. For the world. Christoph could do nothing but wait until Grelf arrived. Until then, his mind chose to play the possible outcomes of what would happen if she didn't make it back in time. To try to ease the stress he had resorted to pacing. He crossed back and forth looking out different windows hoping to see their arrival. It came as a shock to him when on one of his passes Grelf and her Vengerians were just standing in the kitchen with their eyes closed.

I finished describing the scene to them and gave Christoph a wink. "Go ahead. Open your eyes."

It had only been ten days, but it had seemed like a lifetime apart and when they opened their eyes, the Vengerians joined the two monks from the Brotherhood of Light with hugs and high-fives, while Christoph and Grelf enjoyed a much-needed embrace. Sir Adam stood close to Maddicus, and introductions were made. Much to the monk's delight at the concept, it was explained that the more slang they used as they spoke to her, the better she would understand them.

"Dalen Pax." Dalen gave her a bow. "Jinn of Time. Sup?"

Maddicus gave Dalen a head-to-toe scan. "Gliding. Sup?"

Dalen gave the slightest of grins from one corner of his mouth. "Chillin', 'Bout to go do this thing."

Maddicus gave a hand gesture that resembled a peace sign but the only finger she held down was her ring finger. "That's what's up."

"Master Peace." He offered Maddicus his hand to shake. "Word."

She slapped it five and then came back and tapped the back of her hand against his and made a fist. "Word." They tapped their fists together and she smiled as he pretended that his hand exploded in slow motion, complete with sound effects. She mimicked the move and added. "That's cap."

Grelf laid out the Earth Blade and the Fire Blade on the kitchen table. "I got mine. Did you get yours?"

Christoph picked up Grelf and spun her around in celebration. He kissed her and then sat her down. "I never doubted you for a minute." Christoph laid the Water Blade and the Air Blade next to the others with a gloating playful grin. "Of course I got mine."

"That's odd. Travis was staring at the Earth Blade with his head nearly sideways. "Something might be wrong."

"What is it?" asked Becky.

"Everything was happening before, and I didn't have time to notice, and this is my first real chance to take a look at the Earth Blade." Travis flipped his notebook open and scanned a couple of pages. "We were with Queen Hope when she obtained the Earth Blade and saw it appear." He then pointed out something from his notes. "Here it is. The Earth Blade was Damascus made of obsidian and celestium. This is a different sword."

Christoph's eyes shot to the swords. The Fire Blade's hilt and handle were made of gold and adorned with rubies with an inlay of a black metal that he had never seen before. The blade itself looked like it had just been taken out of the kiln and he could feel the heat of it. The Earth Blade was a single piece of obsidian as if it were a carving of a longsword. The hilt and blade were one piece, and both had intricate etchings to accent its beauty. The handles of the two blades were unique and if he had to guess Christoph would have said they were fashioned from the horns of unicorns. "He's right. I have seen all four blades up close. On Water and Air, the only physical part of the weapons are the eyes. They can create and control their elements, so the blades themselves change to fit the needs of the wielder. Size, shape, length, style of blade... all of it can be altered because the blade itself is the element that it controls, but Earth and Fire are material. Real, tangible, forged blades and this is not what they look like."

"Oh, my Goddess," Grelf exclaimed. "I got the wrong sword!"

"If I may?" I was treading on delicate terrain. Not getting directly involved is often our policy, but I knew that I could stop the panic that they just didn't have time for if she began to think in these final moments, that she had gone through all of this in vain, that she had collected the wrong swords. "I would like to ask a question."

It was already beginning to build in all of them and I could feel the story begin to change, but Grelf stared into my eyes with hope. "Is there still a chance?"

"I don't know until I ask my question." I sent with my words a sense of ease to relax her enough to find out what the story was trying to tell me.

"Yes, Master Grey." Grelf was now just trying to be brave. "Ask your question. I'm ready."

I smiled sheepishly as I approached. "It's not a question

directed at you." I rested my hand on the hilt of the Earth Blade and quietly whispered, *What's your story?*

The story of this blade flashed through my mind as I watched thousands of years of history. It was the Earth Blade, but like its brothers, it controlled the element directly. She was merely the handle and created the rest of the blade through her power. Her heart was tied to Grelf, and this is what she looked like being bound to her. If the wielder changed whether it be a personal change or a new wielder, it would create itself in the image of the bond it shared with the queen who held her.

Then it began to send flashes of its time with Blaze, and I could feel that it was not just a part of something, but a whole. The connection to the blade known as Dorn's Promise was on the edge of my ability to withstand. It had a power too big to be wielded alone. The kind that leaves scars just by holding it, and powerful enough to destroy a god or even one of the Grey Continuum. As the thought crossed my mind another flash of its story going back to its origin came before me, to a time before time. A time before this world existed, when I stood at the borders of Heaven and defended the gates as my other half plunged her sword into my heart and cursed her blade to become the Sword of God's Wrath.

I let go and stumbled back. Someone tried to help me, but I yelled, "Don't touch me!" They let me be while I regained my composure. Finally, I was able to get out, "It's the right blade." My voice was quiet for my power had dwindled. "It changes for each wielder."

"Are you alright?" Master Peace, always being a healer, was ready to respond.

"Yes, Peace. I'm good." I had then caught my breath, and the color had come back to my face. "Just got a reminder."

"Don't ask questions if you're not ready for the answer?" asked Dalen.

I nodded. "It's a lesson we all get reminded of from time to time. Wouldn't you agree?"

I hadn't aimed the question at anyone but all of them in unison said. "Agreed."

I let out a strong high-pitched, "Woo." My strength was coming back. "That will wake you up." I offered up my hand to Master Peace who shook it. "Top me off brother?" Master Peace used his ki and healed and reenergized me. "Thank you. So... Yes. Indeed, the right swords. Both of you. You did amazing."

Christoph ran his hand over the Fire and Earth Blades now knowing that how they looked was somehow connected to who Grelf was as a princess and queen. "They're beautiful."

"Yours are as well, but not as nearly as beautiful as you princess." Grelf raised an eyebrow and before Christoph could argue she kissed him. "Damn good to see you Christoph, but now is not the time for me to demonstrate how much I have missed you, but I tell you what. After this is all over and we are in bed tonight, and all of this is all over..." She leaned up and whispered something into his ear and Christoph's eyes widened.

"Then, in that case, we better win." Christoph started to speak but stopped and looked back over at Grelf who just smiled and batted her eyes at him. He stared at her for a moment and then smiled, but then took his attention back to the group. "Everyone ready?" The Vengerian Guardians all nodded or made a woot. "It's bibitz out there. We have no time. They are going to break through at any moment and we must move now." He grabbed his two Elemental Blades. "Follow me and I will show you what we are facing."

Grelf took her Elemental Blades and followed him out. Becky, Travis, Sir Adam, and Maddicus were already packed and ready to travel so they were next out the door, followed by Master Peace and Dalen.

They walked in silence. Each of them had faced a threat in one form or another but what was in their path, ahead of them, gave them a need for inner reflection. It wasn't long before Christoph signaled them to be quiet. Immediately they knew they were on duty and the feeling of the group changed. They crouched down low and began to move as stealthily as they could. Becky pulled up her hood and turned into shadow, and Sir Adam began flexing his hands to warm them up for the fight he knew was inevitably ahead of him.

Once they made it to the White Tree they stopped. Starting at about half the distance to the castle was an army of shadow monsters five thousand strong.

"How are we supposed to beat that many?" asked Travis.

"We won't need to. This is merely a distraction, built to keep us out." Master Peace gave a respectful nod to Christoph and Grelf. "The only thing that matters is getting Grelf and Christoph across the Great Seal."

Adam made a face in agreement. "That makes it a lot easier." He called out Kargen's name and he and Pipim appeared in a dazzling stream of stardust.

Kargen nuzzled Sir Adam and Pipim walked over to Grelf and made a high-pitched sound with a voice that was even more beautiful than Kargen's. Grelf smiled and said, "It would be an honor to ride with you."

Master Peace watched as both riders mounted their unicorns. Although he had seen many amazing things he had never seen something as beautiful as Kargen and Pipim. He gave them both a bow of respect and then addressed the whole group. "That means that this is just an obstacle." He took his Dragon's Claw from his belt. "My time in the Brotherhood of Light taught me that obstacles, by their very design, are built to be overcome."

Travis looked out toward Venger and scanned the army that lay before them. "May I pose a question?"

Grelf was staring at the nightmare army and almost didn't hear him. She broke her attention from the sight of them and focused on Travis. "If you have questions. Now is the time."

Travis stepped forward and turned his back on the nightmare hoard as if they weren't there. "Here are my questions... Grelf, did you complete both challenges and become both the Fire Princess of

Venger and its Earth Queen too?"

Grelf closed her eyes and thought about all that she had been through since she had last stood in that very spot and started her journey. "Indeed." She readjusted her grip on both of her Elemental Blades. Her hair ignited with fire and light as her skin turned into obsidian.

Travis then looked at Christoph and asked, "Have you succeeded in your trials?"

Christoph's chest swelled and with assured strength, he drew both Elemental Blades into ready position. His left eye turned blue, and his right eye turned gold. "I am the keeper of both the sight of the All-Seeing Dragon and the wisdom of the All-Knowing Dragon. I know who I am. I am Christoph... King of Venger."

Travis gave them a bow. "Your Majesties." It hit Grelf and Christoph hard. It was the first time someone had called them that since they had earned the right. Then Travis pointed at Maddicus. "Bodite." He grinned from one side of his mouth. "Are you free?"

Maddicus pulled out her board and leaped aboard. "You know it."

"Oubliette. This army is made of nightmares and monsters. All of them come from the darkest parts of the mind and this world. My question to you is simple." Travis looked over his shoulder and scoffed at the army. "Are you ready to go play in the shadows?"

Oubliette answered by drawing her blades and extending them.

"I thought you might." Then Travis turned to the monks. "Master Peace. I understand that you have tapped into the power that we have been holding and you can channel it through your Dragon Claw. Once you did, you were able to defeat the Master of the Brotherhood of Shadow." Master Peace nodded, "Is there anything else you could possibly do to get ready for this moment?"

"Actually, there is." Master Peace opened his satchel and retrieved the Shadow Mask. "Picked up a souvenir, thought that Oubliette might like it." He tossed it over to her and told her the word to activate it. Oubliette caught it and added it underneath her hood. She whispered the activation word and disappeared from sight completely. "Besides that, I have never been more ready for anything in my life."

"Dalen Pax. Jinn and Master of Time... Up until now, you have been very conservative with your magic, but you are an all-powerful jinn. Wouldn't you agree that now would be a great time to stop holding back?"

Dalen raised himself off the ground. It got the attention of the shadow army, but he didn't care. One by one he activated the Spheres of Reality and Magic. He intentionally took his full jinn form, his body began to phase out of the corporeal world and all of the stones in his body began to glow.

Travis turned and looked me in the eyes. "Will of Grey. Same question."

I grinned at Travis slyly and said, "You don't want me at my full potential."

Travis gave me a double take, lingered on a look of concern for a moment, and then nodded. "Do what you can." Travis shook his head. "Sir Adam." Travis looked at his brother and smirked. "You're ready, I don't even have to ask."

Sir Adam Drew his sword, and the blade shined brighter than the sun. The light from it engulfed both of the unicorns and they began to glow like Sir Adam's blade. That got more of the Shadow Army's attention, and they howled and snarled as they started to advance.

Travis removed his bow and pulled an arrow. "We have the King and Queen of Venger, a shadow being who can't be seen and moves through shadow as a fish moves through the water, an ascended free master of the Bodites, and a Master from the Brotherhood of Light. A Knight of the Light so pure that he can call forth unicorns. A bard that seems to be directly related to every god and goddess that we have come across and we have a reality bender who is also the jinn of time."

"What about you Travis," Christoph asked as he looked through the Eyes of the Dragons and saw that Travis had already tapped into the power that he had been holding. Somehow Christoph knew that he had tapped into it almost as soon as he received it and had been holding the truth of his power like a secret.

Travis notched his arrow and faced the army that was slowly approaching. As he drew his bow the string began to glow as did the arrowhead. He let go and sent the arrow towards the heart of the Shadow Army and while it was in flight he turned back toward his King. "Me?" The arrow hit its mark and an explosion of light that was shaped like a sphere with a thirty-foot radius went off at the impact sight, obliterating anything that was within that area. "I am Lord Travis of Venger, and I am ready to walk through this army like it is not even there."

"Then I have a question." Grelf raised her Earth Blade into the air as Pipim reared up. "What are we waiting for?" Pipim dropped back down and Grelf stood up in the saddle. "Sir Adam! Make me believe it!"

Together the nine of us cried out, "These are the moments we live for!" and charged full long into the army of shadow.

I reached out with my telepathy and connected to Dalen. We had spent a lot of time in a dream state together at the beginning of Dalen's journey and I knew how to connect to him again. *This is the first of three moments when you must make a choice. Will you choose to connect to the power that has been entrusted to you, or will you play it safe?*

Time slowed down past the point where the frames of reality began to flicker and the space between the frames became longer and longer. It finally ceased altogether, and Dalen found himself floating in a place that was no longer connected to reality. Dalen had mastered the Spheres of Magic, and he could see his training circle in his mind's eye. As he did, he could see himself in each of the six elements on the outside ring, but now he had to take a new step forward, inward, and toward the truth of who he really was.

He was standing on the glyph of the observer. In the center

of the training circle stood a version of himself that he had not seen since he first drank from the Fountain of Truth.

"You are aware that you are a version of myself?" he asked. Dalen's silence answered his question. "You have mastered the seven Elements of Reality, and it is time to step forward into your next stage."

Dalen took a deep breath. "I am ready, but if I have mastered the seven Elements of Reality where do I stop?"

The version of himself in the center acknowledged his question but then added, "This circle doesn't have just seven elements, does it?"

Dalen looked at the space between where he and the other version stood. Dalen had spent hours in this circle and had never paid attention to the fact that there was an inner ring of empty circles that sat between each element and the center of the circle. Now that he saw it, it was so obvious to him that he felt dumb.

"I know." said the version of himself in the center. "Becky would be disappointed."

Dalen laughed and nodded. "You really are me."

"No. You really are me." He pointed at the inner set of six circles. These are the Elements of Existence, and as the Jinn of Time, this is where you belong." One of the elements began to glow, and a new glyph appeared. "This is the Element of Time." He beckoned to Dalen. "Step forward and claim your power."

As Dalen stepped into the Element of Time, he saw visions

of the past, present, and future. He watched as time unfolded itself in all its complexity. He relived his vision of the Chaos Dragon erupting from the ground, and he watched as Venger fell. The vision froze in his mind, and he watched as it moved backward in time until the moment before the Chaos Dragon was released.

"This is the moment that you will have to make your next decision, and it is almost upon you." The other version of himself in the center of the circle reached out and took his hand. "It will be one of the hardest choices you will ever have to make."

Dalen was still coursing with the power he was now connected to from the stone that he had received. No longer was it a poison and it only strengthened him. He stopped resisting and relented to its power. "What is the choice that I must make?"

"Save the world... or save your friend. Either way, it will be in your hands." Then the vision moved forward until the moment just before the Chaos Dragon was going to destroy everything.

"And this one?" asked Dalen.

"Save the world... or save yourself."

Dalen understood. This was the real question and the real choice in the end. Would he lay down his life to save the world? It is a question many have wondered, but only those who have stood in those moments can know the answer for sure.

Dalen looked himself in the eyes and without flinching he said, "Oh, I thought it was going to be hard."

The other smiled and hugged him. "I did too." He stood

Dalen up straight and tall and wiped away the tear that had fallen from his eye. "The good news is that if everything goes right, you end up here."

"Alright. I'm ready." Dalen closed his eyes and when he opened them again everything was void. Then a flash of reality happened as a single frame came into existence, and then another and another. They began to speed up faster and faster until he was moving at the speed of time that everyone else was moving and he knew he was in control again.

Dalen was connected to his power, and it flowed through him, with him, and from him. He was tapped directly into the unending source of all magic. He reached out with his mind and connected to the beings that had stood witness with them during the trials. The residual of our connection was still with him, and he harmonized with my power. As he did, he spoke like a god. *Come forth and stand with us now.*

The sky opened up and the first to appear was the Phoenix, it screeched as it tore through the sky with trails of fire. It dove down into the Shadow Army and pulled up about ten feet off the ground. As she flew over the army everything in her wake caught fire.

Christoph was attacking the shadows head-on. As he swung with one hand, a handful of the shadow monsters would freeze into place, and with a swing of his other, he would knock back ten of them into the air. Master Peace was watching his back. He was using his Dragon Claw as a blade whip. He would wrap the chain that connected the claw to the hilt around his arm while keeping it swinging, and as something drew near, he would let go of it, shooting it out toward his target. As the radiance hit the shadow monster it would be engulfed in the light and be obliterated.

Dalen's voice entered their thoughts through the Mind Sphere. *Look up.*

Christoph and Master Peace instinctually looked up and they watched as the Western Dragon of Sight and the Eastern Dragon of Wisdom appeared overhead and began to lay down suppressive cover fire with breath weapons made of pure energy.

Time slowed down for Becky until everything around her was no longer detectably moving. Dalen was standing next to her sipping from his cup. She glanced over to where she thought he was and was surprised to see that he was still there, frozen like everyone else.

"Dalen, what is happening?" whispered Oubliette.

I am using the Mind Sphere to manifest in your thoughts. He pointed at the other Dalen floating over the battlefield. *That's still me too.*

This new version she saw in her mind was transparent like a ghost, but his Stones of Power were casting so much light that Oubliette had to block her eyes because it stung. "Your light is so bright."

I am not really here. This is an image of me that your mind is creating, trying to understand what it is experiencing. Dalen smiled as he finally understood why he saw Masters Truth and Ki along with Moment the way that he did. *The light that you see is coming from you. Do not turn from it.*

Oubliette shrugged, "I am a creature of shadow."

There are two sides to every coin. It creates a balance, but the balance is only true when both sides of the coin are real.

Oubliette tried to understand. "Two sides of every coin?" Then from the heart of Oubliette, Becky spoke. "Becky and Oubliette."

Dalen nodded and touched them both with his magic. Becky and Oubliette stood in front of each other. It had taken Becky a while in the beginning to accept Oubliette. At first, she saw her as another person. But with time, she learned that the power bestowed on her had only amplified her strength and dexterity. It gave her abilities, but it never once changed who she was. Oubliette was a part of her, always had been. She had come to grips with being most comfortable in the shadows, and after a while, she saw herself as one of those shadows. There were moments when Becky still saw Oubliette as another part of her, but there were moments when Oubliette saw Becky the same way.

"I have been looking at this wrong, haven't I?" Dalen raised an eyebrow and shrugged like he didn't know Becky's question and waited for her to come to her own conclusions. He had absolute faith in her. Since he had known her, she was the one who could answer the riddles and solve the puzzles in the games they used to play. "I have always seen Oubliette as who I would be if I had power, and the power that was bestowed upon me created her, but it's not true. It awakened her. Awakened me."

Dalen took another sip from his cup and said, "Keep going."

"I am not someone who is either light or darkness." Becky's eyes widened as Oubliette took off her mask and hood and stared into her soul.

"I am not the darkness that shrouds the light," Oubliette whispered as she stared at Becky in amazement. It felt as if she was looking into her own soul. They reached for each other and held each other close.

Who are you? Dalen's voice slipped into both of their minds and as he asked the question, they both knew the answer in their hearts.

Both Becky and Oubliette spoke as one. "I am the light that shines in the darkness."

Dalen smiled and made a gesture toward the army of shadow. They were moving at normal speed again and when she looked back, she was alone, but she could still hear Dalen's voice in her mind. *Show me.*

Oubliette was now directly tied to her power and Becky knew exactly what to do with it. She ran at full speed toward the army and as she moved her blades began to glow. As she got to her first target, she dove into it and exited through another that was twenty feet away. As she landed both shadow creatures dissolved into smoke and dissipated. She landed with a forward roll and leaped into another. She exited through another further away and they too turned into smoke. Oubliette continued with this method heading toward the front gate.

Master Peace kept his Dragon Claw spinning above his head and would extend the chain and then retract it as needed as he drove a path through the heart of the Shadow Army. He retracted the chain, swung the Dragon Claw like a mace, and sent a shockwave of energy out obliterating twenty shadow creatures to his right. He held it directly overhead and focused his ki. The ball pulsed out and every shadow creature and demon were instantly destroyed within a hundred-foot radius of Master Peace.

Travis stayed where he was, but he used his position to start launching arrows in front of his team to help create a path for them. Huge orbs of light erupted on the front lines of the Shadow Army wiping out twenty or so of them at a time.

Sir Adam rode next to Grelf and both Kargen and Pipim lowered their heads and pointed their horns as they charged at the villainous hoard. Waves of light and energy began to exude from their horns and created a shield shaped like a plow made of light. They didn't even slow down as their shields repelled the shadow creatures and knocked them away.

Maddicus flew above them and called out where she could see weak spots forming in the Shadow Army's defense due to the arrows that Travis fired overhead.

They cut their way through and made it to the front gate. Both Grelf and Sir Adam leaped from their unicorns and when they landed, they began to fight off the shadow monsters to hold their ground. Grelf and Sir Adam were standing on the Great Seal and so were in direct contact with Lady Venger. She explained that the Shadow Army had been trying to push past the Great Seal, and with DeSalvo trying to push past the barriers to the Heart of Venger, the city was fighting off too many things at once and needed their help. They said they understood and continued to clear out any shadows in the area to fortify their position, making sure the others had an open shot to the gate.

An arrow flew toward them and landed a foot in front of Grelf. The arrow disappeared and, in its place, Travis was now standing, picking off monsters and boogiemen one by one. He grabbed another arrow from his quiver and created another blast that knocked back the army. "Why aren't we moving?"

"Keeping them at bay is allowing Venger to focus all her attention on DeSalvo. If we move the whole thing might fall." Grelf reached out with her left hand to blast a shadow monster with the Fire Blade and as she did another leaped at her from the side and bit her arm. It yelped as its teeth broke against her arm. She looked at it with puppy dog eyes and frowned. "I'm made of obsidian sweety."

Adam saw it and obliterated it with his weapon before it could respond. "We have to find a way to strengthen the protective barrier."

Another shadow beast leaped at Travis. As it flew through the air it burst into smoke as Oubliette leaped out of its body and landed next to him. "Hello, my love." It was Oubliette that spoke, but she said it in Becky's voice.

Christoph was dropped off by Crystal who had flown him over much of the battle. Han Bo Fang arrived, and both shrunk themselves down to something that greatly resembled their human images but was still distinctly draconic and stood on the seal with Kargen and Pipim.

"I know what you are about to do," Crystal called out. "This is where the four of you transfer your powers to Grelf and Christoph."

"What about Dalen?" asked Travis.

Dalen shifted his existence to the corporeal plane and was standing next to them. "I am going to give you the time you need." He focused all of his energy and created a barrier of light and power with all of his will and strength. His power was pulling a lot of force, and he had to yell to be heard over it. "It's like flexing a muscle!" He called out over the sound as he continued to push against the onslaught of the remaining strength of the Shadow Army. "It is strong enough, but I can't hold it forever." On the other side of his wall, the power of shadow and darkness was building and trying to push through.

Crystal advised Grelf and Christoph to stand on either side of the Great Seal, which was three concentric circles. Travis looked in his notebook and found the page he was looking for. In our time there are characters of The Dragon and The Unicorn. This isn't complete."

"This is how it has always been for us," Grelf said as she looked for symbols that were not there on the Great Seal. Travis pointed to two locations. Grelf took one of the positions and Christoph took the other location Travis had pointed to.

"Okay, Grelf, you are standing directly where the Unicorn should be, and Christoph is standing where the Dragon should be." Travis was sure of it. "It is the recognition of the royal family. Great power ascended to their greatest potential."

Becky pulled back her hood and cried out, "I know what needs to be done!" She grabbed Travis and had him stand on the other side of Grelf from her. She had Sir Adam and Master Peace do the same for Christoph. "Unicorns... Dragons... We are going to need your blessings.

"And do it quickly. I am not going to be able to hold it much longer!" Dalen called out.

Grelf and Adam both heard the unicorns as they spoke from their minds. "We, as the last of the unicorns grant you, our blessings. Now and for all time."

Han Bo Fang and Crystal both spoke in Draconic, but it was clear what they were saying and as they finished, they both bowed in reverence.

"I am glad I got to connect with the power before I had to let it go." Master Peace said, and Sir Adam agreed.

"I just finally came to peace with all of it. I know I shall miss it," added Becky.

"Travis smiled at her and blew her a kiss. "It's better to have loved and lost than to never have loved at all."

Becky smiled at him and blew a kiss back. "You're right. We went into this knowing that we were on borrowed time."

Travis could not help but let the tears flow. "Okay, we are ready. What do we do?"

Crystal looked a few moments into the future and said, "Each of you pull out your instruments. We are about to make some music." All of them, including Grelf and Christoph held out their weapons and activated them.

It was time so I moved my perception from the edge of the battlefield to the center of the circle between them. "You are each going to choose whether to relinquish your power."

"I accept that as truth," said Master Peace. "What do we need to do?"

I didn't want any confusion, so I spoke to them in Grey Speak. *You know the words.* I could see it in their eyes that they understood. I turned my attention to Dalen who was beginning to get exhausted. The power he was wielding was endless, but he still had limits. "Dalen!" I called out. "Drop the Barrier!"

"I can't!" Dalen cried. "If I do, they will break through. I can barely hold it now!"

The moment was on us and there was no time to argue. I touched his heart and mind and soul with my power and said, *Brother. Let go.*

Dalen heard me and took a leap of faith. He let go of the barrier and it began to fall. He watched as Phoenix flew through the open passage, as I reached up and allowed my fingers to physically brush her as she flew over, the power moved through me like a channel and went into the Great Seal. It lit up with magic and power and the four Vengerian Guardians spoke as one. "Even if it means our final breath. You will not fail."

Light filled the front gate as they relinquished their power. It felt like their life was being drained out of them and it dropped them to their knees. It reminded Becky of the moment when Queen Hope had to give of herself to the Mother Tree for her challenge. "Don't just let it take you," Becky called out. It was hard for her to catch her breath. "Mother Tree." The others understood and they slowly took a breath in and as they breathed out, they pushed with the current.

Grelf and Christoph's minds began to fill with the memories of thousands of people coming to pray at the statues. Their bodies tingled like the sensation of being electrocuted. It was overwhelming and the worst part was that there was more. Each of them had carried more power than they could know what to do with, and now both Grelf and Christoph had to hold twice as much.

Christoph relaxed and flowed with the current as he had learned in the maze, and he held his thoughts on what he was doing and why he was there. He felt his body become stronger and his mind become sharper. Grelf allowed the energy to change her and as it built, she did not fight it or try to be stronger than what she was feeling. Instead, she allowed herself to release the strain, and she let her head fall back and screamed.

Their Vengerian Guardians gave everything they had. They felt the power that they had been holding leave them. In the beginning, when they had first received it, they had barely noticed it, but one by one they had found that power and had learned how to tap into it. Now that it was gone, they felt diminished, and they could sense what they had given up.

Grelf and Christoph both felt like they were going to die. There was so much power, and their bodies were physically altering so that they could survive the ordeal. Their bodies were humming, and it felt like every nerve ending was alive. Their bodies were trying to adapt as if they were in a constant state of pain, although there was no damage to speak of. There was just more energy than they could process. Like eating a raw lemon, it won't cause pain, but the body will respond as if it did.

"I don't know what to do!" screamed Christoph. "I'm losing my mind!"

Dalen tried to help ground them, but this was larger than he imagined. He called to them as the nightmare hoard poured into the front gates. "You have to bring them together!"

Christoph and Grelf fought for any control that they had left in their beings as the power surged through their systems. Both of them cried out with all their fury, from the center of their being, as they brought their hands together and with them the Elemental Blades of Venger. The Fire Blade and the Earth Blade merged and as the fire ignited, the obsidian began to glow and turn into a sword made of pure light. A sword that had not been seen in thousands of years known as the Horn of the Unicorn. The Water Blade and Air Blade vanished as the Eye of Sight and the Gold Eye of Wisdom became like two sides of the same coin and formed one blade made of mist known as the legendary Eye of the Dragon.

An image of the Dragon and Unicorn appeared underneath Grelf and Christoph's feet as a blast of energy from the creation of the two relics transfused itself into the barriers that were protecting the City of Venger, amplified a hundred-fold. The shock wave blasted outward from the seal and passed through the Vengerians without harm, but once it reached the edge of the wall the wave rippled out in a single ring and devastated everything that was left of the Shadow Army. Leaving nothing, not even the dust of the adversary.

30

MASTER OF TRUTH

Dalen used the healing magic Master Peace had taught him to help his friends. Each of them had built a charge within them as they passed the power to Grelf and Christoph and they were not completely spent, but they were exhausted. They felt as if they had not slept in days and like part of their souls had been ripped from them. The healing revitalized them enough that they could function, but they felt weak, and it was hard for them to concentrate on anything other than the loss they felt in their hearts and souls.

Dalen knew what came next and that they would have to be

able to act. He touched the stone centered at his root chakra and then moved up one and activated that one as well. In doing so he activated the Natural and Kinetic Elements. This connected him to each of his friends as if they were one being, and then he shared his energy and ki through that connection with each of them. While still touching the Kinetic Element he reached up and touched the top of his head, then moved down one stone to the one connected to his third eye. That opened the Mind Sphere and allowed their minds to be connected while still being tapped into his ki. Their minds began to refocus, and they became more alert and aware of their surroundings.

The hand that was on the Kinetic moved to his solar plexus and the hand touching his third eye moved one place down to his throat chakra. Dalen connected to the Divine field and its unlimited power, he channeled it through his words as a single concept and spoke through his soul. *You are going to be alright.*

Each of the Vengerian Guardians began to recharge and come out of the fog that they were in. They looked around and took a couple of cleansing breaths. Travis and Becky held each other and checked on one another and Sir Adam and Master Peace helped each other keep their balance as they got to their feet. Maddicus was with Sir Adam and Peace and offered a handhold on her board if they needed to regain their footing.

Dalen brought both of his hands together over his Heartstone and made a wish and as he did, their pains and aches dissolved, and they felt enough like themselves that they were ready to travel.

While Dalen was helping them, I focused my attention on Grelf and Christoph. They were all right, but they were still trying to deal with the amount of power surging through them. I knew that they must be fighting to keep calm, so I focused my power and spoke to them in Grey Speak. *Prepare yourselves. You face the Chaos Dragon here. Together you hold the only weapon that can defeat her. No matter what happens here today I promise you that your story will never be forgotten.* I shook Christoph's hand and hugged Grelf. *Maddicus and I are going to head for the castle. We will be Venger and Dorn's last line of defense. If you fail, we will do all we can to protect them and get them to safety.*

They thanked me and through my abilities, I could hear not just their words, but I could feel the sincerity in their hearts. They were exhausted and overwhelmed, but it brought them a small amount of peace to know that Dorn and Venger would not be alone.

Maddicus shoved Grelf in the shoulder and scoffed at them. "Why you trippin'? You're the bibitz."

"Damn right." Grelf playfully pushed her back.

Maddicus gave a nod to Christoph. "King Dude." She took his forearm as tightly as she could muster. "Keep your head on a swivel. Don't bail."

Christoph smiled. "Good advice. I'll do my best."

Maddicus let go of his forearm and gave him five. "Gliding."

She and I checked on the other Vengerian Guardians. Dalen had just about gotten them to the best that they could hope for under the circumstances. The nine came together and formed a galaxy. We took a long look at one another as Dalen allowed all of us to connect to the Natural Element and for a moment, we were all one. None of us spoke. None of us had to. We felt the bond and knew at that moment we were family. We had gone through so much to reach this point, but this is where everything came to an apex. We understood what was on the line and we knew that this may be the last time that any of us ever saw one another. The future was counting on all of us, and these next few minutes were going to decide the fate of this world.

Unless all of time changed, the Chaos Dragon was going to be released and Christoph and Grelf were the ones who were supposed to stop it. They had become the Dragon and the Unicorn, defenders, and protectors of this world, so they began to prepare themselves for the battle against a foe from another form of existence, that was more powerful than the gods.

Maddicus gave me a hand on to her Bodi board and we flew off to the castle as Venger's last line of defense. I knew Venger City well and navigated for her while we flew through the empty streets and made our way to the center of the city.

Dalen and the other Vengerian Guardians knew where they had to go as well. When they were in Venger for the first time it was known as the Saviors Garden, and they were told it was where they stopped the Time Mage. There had been statues of them depicting who they were at that moment, it was also where they received their weapons and powers.

When they arrived, they found only a small courtyard and a well. It seemed like an ordinary water well, but it was out of the way for anyone to collect water and somehow, because they had been there before, it felt like coming to a sacred place, or a long-forgotten memory from their childhood. Built into the inside of the well there was a ladder going down and one by one they began to climb into the shadowy depths.

Travis was stalling and made sure that he and Dalen were the last two to go down. He pulled out his notebook and wrote down some new notes. Then he went to the back and ripped out a strip of paper from the final page and used it like a bookmark. "Dalen, can I ask you for a favor?"

Dalen drew close and tried to see what was written on the page that Travis marked but Travis closed it up before he had a chance to read anything on it. "Yeah man, anything."

"You know that pocket in time and space where you keep your backpack and other things? I would like to use it real quick. I may need to find certain notes quickly down there and I may not have the time to pull everything out of my pack on the run. Can I have you hold on to it for me in your cool little time space pocket thing?" Dalen agreed and opened his pocket dimension and put Travis's notebook in it. Then Travis pulled out his cup and tapped his Vengerian Pin to have his backpack saved in it. He activated the cup, took a sip, and then offered a sip to Dalen. It was still filled with crangrape juice, which was what he had asked for when he first got his cup. "Here's to everything going to plan."

Dalen knew that Travis believed he was going to have to sacrifice himself that day. He believed that he was somehow responsible for the destruction of the Time Stone, which imprisoned the Chaos Dragon. And in doing so he would be ripped from time, and like the Beads of Fire, would be lost in the fabric of time and forgotten.

"You know that things can go differently, right?" Dalen was doing his best to give Travis hope. He could see it in his eyes and feel it in his heart, Travis had already accepted his pending fate as a truth.

Travis looked at Dalen like he was surprised that Dalen could be so dense. He deactivated his cup and tossed it into Dalen's pocket dimension. "When this all started you made me a promise, do you remember it?"

Dalen nodded. "I promised that if it went down the way that you thought it might go, and you were lost in time, I would find a way to bring you back."

Travis looked him in the eyes and did his best to fight off the tears. "I wish for you to stop trying to save me, Dalen. Go save Venger. Save the world, and for the love of all that matters, go save David, but stop wasting your time trying to save me. My fate is my own."

Dalen had no intention of hiding his emotions. As he closed his eyes a tear fell from each of them. He took a deep breath in and sighed. "As you wish."

Dalen closed his magical pocket and he and Travis made their way down the well. When they got to the bottom Sir Adam asked what had taken them so long. Travis said he was sorry, but he had to take some final notes before everything got crazy.

At the bottom of the well, there was a passage that led towards the center of the city and as they moved through it, they could hear voices. Someone was talking to somebody else.

"This barrier isn't going to come down anytime soon." It was unmistakably DeSalvo. He sounded irritated, but he was masking it with syrupy sweetness. "I think that we are going to need my friend to get through this."

A sweet and innocent voice asked, "Do you mean the magic dragon?" She sounded excited and oblivious to the destructive nature of the Chaos Dragon.

"Yes. She is super strong and could get through this magic barrier, no problem." The Vengerian Guardians came around the bend and found DeSalvo kneeling in front of a small nine-year-old girl with sandy blond hair that hung about her shoulders. "So do you wish for me to release her?"

"Don't answer that," Dalen spoke with easy tones, trying not to scare the little girl. The corridor that they were in had opened into a natural cave and there was enough room for all of them to confront both DeSalvo and the Time Mage at once.

"Oh no, Xoxy!" DeSalvo was smiling with a look on his face that made none of them feel safe. "It's Dalen, and he has brought his friend to take me from you."

The little girl looked at Dalen with abject fear, took a step back, and began to cry. Dalen tried to calm her but when he took a step forward, she screamed in terror and held up the clear stone in her right hand. A wave of energy pulsed from it and washed over all of them.

‹What the hell was that?› asked Sir Adam, using his Vengerian Pin.

‹I believe we just got hit with the same wave that blasted Jed, Jax, Blizzard, and Blaze.› Travis looked back at his brother. ‹We are still disjointed from time because we used the pillar to get here. If it wasn't for that, that little girl might have just killed all of us.›

All at once they understood the threat they faced. DeSalvo had convinced some poor little girl to take the Time Stone. Whatever DeSalvo had done to her, she believed that he was her friend and that they were villains. She was terrified as if they were monsters, and that terrified little girl was wielding the Time Stone to protect her friend from monsters.

DeSalvo was glaring at them with contempt through black eyes made of onyx. His withered yellow teeth made his smile terrifying. *Go ahead. Stop her, if you can.* DeSalvo's thoughts seeped into their minds like black tar.

Sir Adam stepped forward and took a knee. "We don't want to hurt you. We want to help you. DeSalvo has been lying to you."

Xoxann shook her head and screamed, "Liar!" She pointed the Time Stone at Sir Adam, and a portal opened up directly where he knelt, and in a blink, Sir Adam fell through time. Dalen let go of his corporeal body, left it standing there as a time anchor, and leaped in after him.

From the point of view of everyone else Sir Adam fell

through, and the portal closed, leaving him trapped in time. DeSalvo laughed and said, "Good job. Now get rid of the rest of them."

. . .

Sir Adam was standing in a forest on fire. All around him, he could hear men screaming in terror. A Dragon flew over, and with a single breath, lit five acres of earth on fire near where he stood. Through the fire and the screams, he also noticed a man huddled down, praying near some ruins as the trees around him burned.

He was a Vengerian soldier. His platoon had marched from Venger to help protect the Elven kingdom south of the city. They were told that if they wished to stay and protect their homes, they would be allowed to, but if they stood with the Elves, together, there was a chance for the war to be over. So, he had volunteered because he knew the devastation that the dragons had already created, and if there was a chance to defeat them, he had to try.

The initial surprise attack had gone well and four of the ten went down before they could understand what had happened. But they were vengeful creatures and began to target the most sacred places of the Elven Woods as punishment for the loss of the four. The soldier had been sent to this location to protect it. When the dragon first attacked, they had been hiding in an old stone ruin. They had found one with an intact room made of stone. It only had one entrance to defend and there was enough room for them all to fit in. He had run out to face the dragon just as it flew over. It clipped a tree and broke off the top of it which came crashing down at him on fire. He had leaped clear, but the log was blocking the only exit to the ruin, and the fire was going to slowly cook his men alive. He reached out, grabbed the nonburning end of the tree, and tried to lift the weight, but it was far too heavy to lift. His team was pinned down and he was alone. He dropped to his knees and in hopes that this place was truly sacred, he began to pray to anyone who could hear him and begged for help.

"We can do it together." The man looked up and saw the face of Sir Adam the Pure Heart. One of the Saviors of Venger.

The soldier couldn't believe his eyes. He rubbed them and looked again but Sir Adam was still there. "Help! I can't lift it on my own. Please! Help me save them." He positioned himself to pick up his end of the log.

Sir Adam nodded he grabbed on as well. There was no place safe to hold on to the tree and although he was wearing full armor, it was still made of metal, and it was going to get hot fast. Sir Adam ignored the heat and grabbed on. "What's your name?"

The soldier stared in awe as he watched Sir Adam step into the fire. He looked like his whole back was wreathed in fire like some kind of guardian angel with burning wings. When Adam asked his name, his training kicked in and he replied with, "Ferris, Sir."

Sir Adam's back was getting hot, and he knew he only had moments before it began to burn. "Ferris." Sir Adam positioned himself to lift the heavy load. "These are the moments we live for."

They both lifted with all their might and together they moved the burning tree. Ferris took one more look at Sir Adam and then turned his attention to getting his platoon out. It was right then that Sir Adams's back felt almost ice cold and Dalen's voice entered his thoughts as if they were his own.

You did well. You saved their lives, but we must go. There are many more lives to save. A portal opened and Sir Adam stepped through it with a smile and a nod.

Ferris swore to his men later that Sir Adam was there, but only Ferris saw him that day. Sir Adam could still remember him coming up to the statue later and thanking him.

. . .

"Good job. Now get rid of the rest." DeSalvo pointed at the rest of them. Go ahead, sweetheart. Make a wish and save us from Dalen."

Another time portal opened, and Sir Adam stepped through. "Miss me?" Sir Adam was hit with multiple telepathic messages of relief.

Dalen retook his corporeal form and added through a smirk, "I can do time magic too."

Xoxann panicked. She didn't know what to do. "Dalen, I wish that as a baby you get pulled from this world to a place with no magic."

DeSalvo rubbed his forehead with resolution. "We can't run from fate, can we Mister Pax?" The Time Stone sent out another pulse and DeSalvo reluctantly cast his magic at Dalen.

All the Vengerians just stood there as the energy hit Dalen and rippled backward through time. Dalen looked down at her and with the sweetest voice he could he said, "I spent the first seventeen years of my life in a world with no magic."

Xoxann began to cry because nothing she tried seemed to work. Her anger and her sadness were getting the better of her, she dropped to her knees and sobbed.

Dalen was still trying to keep her calm. "Why are you afraid of me?"

Xoxann looked up at him and screamed, "You hurt Kim! It's your fault she's dead."

Out of all the things that the little girl could have said at that moment, that was one of the few things that would completely confuse Dalen and his friends. Dalen was keeping an eye on DeSalvo, but he was so confused that he allowed his eyes to look at the scared little girl. "Who?"

"Kim, my friend. You took her to the ball and then left her there all alone after you hurt DeSalvo." She was getting angry, and her temper began to flare.

Dalen slowed down time and brought his friends with him so they could think.

‹Is that possible?› Dalen asked in disbelief.

‹There is a real possibility.› Becky had already put it together. ‹We never took DeSalvo's proverbial lamp.›

‹Lamp?› Sir Adam's mind was building the puzzle quickly. ‹You mean like a genie's lamp? The thing that whoever owns it, is the genie's master?›

‹I have seen it.› Dalen remembered seeing it when he fought DeSalvo the first time. It's a small black piece of twisted metal.›

‹If I may?› Everyone held their thoughts so Travis could speak. ‹I believe that pure evil doesn't lie. It just doesn't tell you all the truth. That's the problem. I would guess that Becky is right.› Travis's voice was sullen. ‹We didn't get the object that connected him to the physical world after he was defeated. At the time we didn't think about it. Kim Collard must have found it, and when she picked it up, there was old 'dark and spooky' over there waiting to tell her that he knew you and that he could help find you. All true, but who knows what half-truths he told this poor girl.›

Xoxann pointed the stone at Dalen threateningly and forced everyone back into real-time. It was jarring and made them slightly nauseous. "DeSalvo brought her here so that they could find you, but they were on a raft, and she was going to starve. All because of you!" She started sobbing uncontrollably.

"Oh, I think I have had enough of this." Dalen turned to DeSalvo. "What is she talking about?"

DeSalvo laughed in Dalen's face. "You heard her. It's the truth."

"The truth?" Dalen was getting sick of this demented madman. "You want truth?" Dalen activated the Spheres of Reality within him. "I'll give you truth."

Each of Dalen's eyes had always been different colors. One of them was blue and the other violet. The blue one began to glow, and Dalen saw the truth of the moment at hand. In his hand, he held his coin. He didn't look at it but turned it over in his hand and as he did his violet eye also lit up. Through the Quantum element, Dalen could see the possibilities this moment could bring. As he looked at this moment through both eyes, he reminded himself the coin was only whole when both sides were understood.

In that moment he remembered that very first lesson, and for a moment he was there at the monastery as an initiate once more. Brother Truth took a deep breath and closed his eyes, and he heard the words of the Master within him.

It's easy to be happy on a sunny day.

The first lesson he learned the day he became an initiate was the lesson of the coin. Truth has more than one side, and he would have to see both sides to know the truth. This was taught by hearing someone speak their opinion, which to them was truth, and then watching them accept the opposite as truth as well. Not instead of, but as well. The words that Brother Truth heard had been the wisdom that had been taught to him that day.

Master Love and Master Truth were debating in the courtyard, and Brother Truth had been allowed to watch. The debate was about where on someone's path they are the strongest. Master Love had argued from the perspective of a healer and argued that, once someone had been healed of their pain and their suffering, they were stronger for it. She cited that once people let go of their pain and their trauma, they become stronger individuals. They find peace and oneness.

"It's easy to be happy on a sunny day." It was the only rebuttal that Master Truth gave. Master Love remembered her own path and found that it was at her lowest when she took impossible steps that her pain and her trauma would not let her believe were real. She remembered how hard she had to fight in her own darkest moments. She remembered the day she became a master and redeemed the soul of the man who had tried to sell her innocence on the street at twelve. She remembered it was the hardest day of her life, and she remembered it was raining on that day too.

He remembered when Brother Faith told him how he honored the weakest parts of himself, for they were the ones who were strong enough to make the Leap of Faith in the first place. The first time he leaped he was wounded and broken and had a brother on his back dying.

Brother Truth saw himself facing DeSalvo, trapped in the earth slowly crushing him, and realized that was his moment. Then his mind moved forward to the moment he was in, and looking from an outside point of view, he found himself facing off against DeSalvo once more. He examined it from both sides with eyes that could see through time and understood how this moment was a linchpin in many truths. He looked at himself and DeSalvo and could see them as two pieces of something still yet to come. Something that was both. This was Dalen's mirror. Throughout time, they had both been needed to keep a true balance in all things, but that time was coming to an end and soon there would be a choice... and it belonged to neither of them. It lay in the hands of a frightened young girl and in that moment the only other person in the room besides the two heralds, who could change the reality of everything.

He stared at it like it wasn't real. He stopped it, turned the world in his mind, and looked at it from every angle. His consciousness opened to impossible truths and Brother Truth understood that DeSalvo was the other side of his coin. But he could not see the coin as a whole. Brother Truth thought that perhaps their connection, whatever that was, would be the answer to how he was going to save his brother David from the curse he was under. They were told that only the being who created the knife could free him, but perhaps there was a way that he could save him because he was connected to DeSalvo directly, and two parts to a common whole. It was the question he had been waiting to ask and now the time was here. He took out his cup, activated it, and watched as it filled with the Fountain of Truth. Brother Truth believed that by learning the answer to how to save David, he would understand how he and DeSalvo were connected. He closed his eyes and spoke. "DeSalvo is the only being who can remove the curse from the knife he created. If there is a greater truth out there, how do I save David?" Then drank from the Fountain of Truth once more.

The vision was dark, and Dalen spent a thousand years there while he watched another reality play out. It was of pain and death. Darkness and betrayal. Betrayal of everyone and most of all himself, but after the dark and twisted years in a world of suffering...the timeline that led him to become Mathias pushed passed that moment and ended with him becoming DeSalvo.

DeSalvo had found a way to create an intentional loop in time and in a moment of desperation he got his hands on the Beads of Fire. Armed with an ill-conceived wish from his master, and someone he only knew as The Teacher, to destroy the world... he did just that. He ended his world by wishing it out of existence. Dalen was once told that he had destroyed his own timeline in an alternate version of time but had never been told that he was DeSalvo when he did it.

DeSalvo's world was destroyed, and this one took its place, but for some reason, he was still here. DeSalvo's wish was meant to reset his timeline and for himself to be Dalen but instead he found someone else living the life that he had wished for himself. Now he wanted the Beads of Fire back or Dalen's Heartstone so that he could free himself of his misery. He was willing to kill everyone here because he intended to remake his timeline and still save everyone he cared about. This world meant nothing to him and there was no length he wouldn't go to save his original timeline, but everything hinged on getting Xoxann to wish what he wanted her to. Dalen's mind was reeling as DeSalvo's memories awoke in his own mind. Dalen followed DeSalvo's memory backward and learned of the Breath of Time and that it needed to be sealed before it created a hole in this world that would destroy it whether the Chaos Dragon did or not. He watched as DeSalvo manipulated Xoxann and got her to take the Time Stone. He saw how they met, and he watched as the ghost of Kim told her exactly what DeSalvo told her to say. Once she did, he freed her soul from the curse of a Soul Freezer. Brother Truth went back and watched it again, and again until he could memorize the magic that DeSalvo used. He knew how to save David. This moment was it. Dorn had been right. This was the only way he would have asked the right question with the right intent. It was at this moment, and not until now was he ready to accept the truth he was being shown. This was the question that changed everything and now his world had changed.

In this, the hardest moment that Brother Truth had ever experienced in his life, as the pain and suffering of a thousand years of torment and pain by the hands of his master and The Teacher washed over him, and the things he was forced to do while in their service came unapologetically crashing into his mind, Brother Truth looked past the darkness and stared into the mirror of his most brutal and broken moment and understood...everything.

As was the nature of the Fountain of Truth, it had told him more than he could have ever guessed and in hindsight, more than he wanted to know, but there were no longer questions in Dalen's mind. He knew what was happening and why DeSalvo wanted the Beads of Fire so badly. He had told the truth. The Beads of Fire had belonged to him, always had belonged to him and now Dalen understood why the object was connected to both of their souls, for the Beads of Fire were the broken piece of DeSalvo's. The broken piece made the difference between a free-willed jinn and an enslaved genie who had been tortured for a thousand years.

Dalen spiraled at the truth, knowing that this fiend. This villain. This mad genie who was willing to destroy everything was himself. This wasn't some whimsical thought where if asked if he was in the same place, and had to deal with the same events, would he have turned out the same? Oh no. It was far greater than that. DeSalvo was the outcome of who he would be in that timeline under those circumstances. Everything DeSalvo was and had ever been, was also Dalen. There was no question Dalen was shown the darkest places in his heart and soul. The truth of it poured into his mind like molten steel. There was nowhere to hide from it and as he stared into the heart of his enemy by looking inward Dalen found his worst moment.

Brother Truth moved to the position of his corporeal self, the entire time staring at DeSalvo. He was ready to return to the moment at hand, he closed both of his eyes and took in his last breath with faith and joy. Master Truth opened all three of his eyes like a triangle. One blue, one violet, and his third eye was white.

• • •

Hey DeSalvo? You know that spell you cast on yourself so that it would work on a genie and make him speak only the truth? It was a rhetorical question and Master Truth continued without giving him time to answer. *Thanks for showing me the piece of magic needed to have spells like that work on you.* He smiled at DeSalvo as he raised an eyebrow. *By the way, I fixed it.* Master Truth pulled a fast draw on DeSalvo and got his spell off before DeSalvo could stop him. *This version not only makes you tell the truth, but it makes you tell all of it.* A magical choker made of celestium with a beautiful blue sapphire sitting directly over DeSalvo's throat chakra appeared on his neck.

Master Truth looked at the scared girl with the Sight of Truth and as he did, he saw DeSalvo's hold over her emotions and thoughts. *Master Peace, look at her through my eyes.* Master Truth activated the Eye of the Beholder on his pin.

Master Peace closed his eyes and was now looking through Master Truth's, he saw the blackness in her mind. He activated his Dragon Claw and filled the room with healing light. All her pain and fear drained from her, and she no longer felt hatred toward any of them.

DeSalvo fought against the collar, but he was helpless to remove it without a wish from Xoxann. He tried to maintain his hold on her, but he was fighting the battle against Master Truth's power over him and didn't have the focus to battle both fronts. Master Peace dismissed him from her mind. His light was now protecting her, and DeSalvo could no longer enter her thoughts.

DeSalvo began to reach for her, but Sir Adam's blade was thrust between them. Whatever dark and vile thing that made up the core of this wretched beast was afraid of what that blade was and what it could do to him. "Xoxann, don't listen to them. They are trying to take me away from you."

"Damn right," said Sir Adam as he stared DeSalvo down.

"You see, they admit it." DeSalvo was desperate and began pointing at Sir Adam. "They are going to try and take me away from you. Haven't I always been there for you and protected you?"

"Let go of him now Dalen!" She pointed the Time Stone at him, and Dalen could feel its power. Used the wrong way there was a real threat.

"The only thing I did, was make him tell the truth." Dalen gestured to DeSalvo. "You ask him. No Tricks. You ask him what happened."

The certainty in Master Truth's voice made Xoxann doubt so she turned to her friend and asked, "DeSalvo? What are they talking about?"

They had blocked him from her. Master Truth had blocked with magic, and Master Peace had kept DeSalvo from her mind. Sir Adam had blocked him physically and DeSalvo was sure that the thing that Sir Adam was wielding could cause serious harm to him. "They are trying to get me to say things so that they can convince you of something else. They want you to see me as the bad guy."

Xoxann looked at her friend and huge tears began to well up in her eyes. "Are you?"

"I am trying to be a savior," DeSalvo said. He clasped his hands around his mouth, but then removed them to say, "And there is no price too big to save everyone I cared for."

Tell her DeSalvo. Tell her how you tried to kill everyone. Master Truth looked over to Xoxann and told her, *you have all the power. You can make him answer you.* She was holding the item that bound him to her in her left hand and she squeezed it tightly. *Tell her how if she frees the Chaos Dragon, it will first destroy Venger City and try to destroy this entire world.*

Xoxann didn't know what to believe. She gripped his small rod of black twisted metal tightly and demanded, "Is it true DeSalvo? Do you want to kill everyone?"

"No. I don't want to kill everyone. I wish to save an entire world that was destroyed." DeSalvo struggled against the spell, but Dalen's choker held strong, and DeSalvo was not able to break free of it. "Waking the Chaos Dragon and killing everyone was just a great way to get Dalen's attention." DeSalvo shrieked with frustration and used both hands to try and blast Dalen and his friends with magic.

Nothing happened and DeSalvo slowly turned to look at Xoxann. "What are you doing sweety?"

Xoxann had control of DeSalvo and didn't let him use his magic. Travis and Becky stood on either side of her, and they faced the truth together. She held up her hand with his object and said, "Why did you kill Kim?"

"She had her own plans, and it was the only way to control the situation. Once I trapped her soul, she would have done anything to be set free."

"You said that you saved her because she was going to starve to death." She clenched her fist on DeSalvo's 'lamp'. "I wish for you to tell me the truth."

DeSalvo struggled and screamed but he was under her control. "I could have appeared in this world in one of three hundred and sixty locations. But regardless of that, I could have used the tree that was on the island to move to any of the other locations."

"Then why did you take the boat?"

DeSalvo glared at everyone with hatred. "Because getting her on the water was the only way to convince her that she was going to die slowly, so she would wish me to use the Soul Freezer on her.

"Why did you have her tell me what she told me?"

"Because you wouldn't have helped me if I didn't trick you into it."

"How could you?"

"Easily. You are a stupid little girl."

"No, I'm not!"

"I got you to let me erase a kid from existence because he was picking on you. Yeah. You are."

Master Truth entered the other Vengerian's minds. *I know that your instincts are to stop him from hurting her but stay your hand. The world needs her to hear this.* It was hard. Each of them wanted to protect Xoxann from the cruelty of the evil genie's words.

"You really think I'm stupid?" Xoxann cried as she looked at DeSalvo and lost all belief in him being her friend or that he cared at all.

"Without question."

Her sadness and pain turned to anger, and she glared back into his cold black eyes and said, "Then explain this." Xoxann reached out with her left hand and handed DeSalvo's object to Becky.

Becky looked at the piece of black twisted metal and thought about all the horrific things she could have DeSalvo do to himself. Her mind began to race and all of it was of dark vile things. "I can't hold this. It's doing something to me." Master Truth floated over to her and put out his hand. She tried to hand it to Master Truth but there was a part of her that started to think about all the power she could wield. Sir Adam reached out and slapped DeSalvo in the face, breaking his concentration on Becky and she opened her hand and let go.

Sir Adam wagged his finger at DeSalvo and said, "Bad genie. No!"

Master Truth turned to DeSalvo while holding his object. *Before I dismiss you from this world, I want you to know.* Master Truth moved through Sir Adam and Master Peace like a ghost and moved directly in front of DeSalvo. *I know.* He looked past the darkness and the pain, gazed into the eyes of himself, and said, *I know everything.* Master Truth held up the twisted piece of metal and said, *I wish for you to be dismissed from this world until which time I call you.*

DeSalvo was enveloped in a black cloud that had small sparks of red moving through it and as it dissipated DeSalvo simply added, "This is not over."

No, it's not, said, Master Truth. *But don't worry. I'll save you.*

Travis knelt next to Xoxann. "Hi. I'm Travis. That was an amazingly smart thing to do, and I think DeSalvo was wrong."

Tears rolled down Xoxann's face. "I thought he was my friend."

"Yeah. I bet that hurts." Xoxann answered Travis's question with a nod and a lower lip that began to quiver. "Me and my friends came here partly to save the world from mean ol' DeSalvo, and you know what?"

Xoxann looked up at him with the sad eyes of a broken heart. "What?"

"If you like, I bet my friends here would love to be your friend, and I mean real friends. Would you like that?"

Xoxann slowly nodded as she closed her eyes and began to cry. Travis held her and just let her cry for a moment and then he looked her in the eyes and said, "Okay, friends don't lie to each other like DeSalvo did, so I want to tell you something okay?" Xoxann nodded. "We also came here because that stone in your hand is really dangerous and DeSalvo tricked you into using it, and we are going to tell the King and Queen it wasn't your fault because you didn't know, but now that you do know, you don't want to use it anymore. Right?"

"Right." Xoxann wiped tears away with her free hand and handed Travis the Time Stone.

Everyone else had been quietly staying calm and waiting for this moment. Whether or not Xoxann knew it, she was holding a true piece of evil and with the wrong action could have shattered the Time Stone, and in doing so could have been lost in time. Not to mention releasing the Chaos Dragon. Once she let it go, they all breathed a sigh of relief and Becky picked her up and hugged her.

"Let's get her out of here," Travis suggested and pointed

the way out.

They made their way out of the tunnels. They had Master Peace go first, followed by Xoxann so that he could help her out of the well. When he reached the top, he looked back down the well and told her how great she was doing with every rung until he could reach her and help her out of the well.

Sir Adam was next, but he stopped long enough to look back at Becky and Travis. "I watched you with Xoxann. You guys make a good team." He gave Becky a hug and said, "Way to go, being able to tell that thing was hurting you. Sometimes you have to let things go." He looked over to Travis. "Right, Bro?" Travis agreed, then hugged him and pushed him up the ladder.

Travis stopped Becky at the bottom of the ladder and kissed her. She kissed him back and then asked, "What was that for?"

"You know, end of the world events and all." Travis held her close.

She leaned into him and then playfully pulled away. "Later."

Travis had his fingers laced together and she couldn't break his hold on her. "Later doesn't always come."

"My Love. We won. Dalen has control over DeSalvo, and we got the Time Stone back. Venger is safe and we don't even need to face the Chaos Dragon." Becky pushed back and this time Travis let her. "Later is definitely happening," she smiled and climbed up the ladder.

Travis waited until she was up the ladder and then asked

Master Truth, "You know. Don't you?"

I know enough.

"Are you going to try and stop me?"

That is something I had to think about for a long time when I first saw this happen in time. But I have come to understand.

"At any other time, we aren't going to be as ready as we are right now." Travis looked at the Time Stone in his hand. "We are all on rails brother. You can't see it because you are built to see the world differently, and you can choose to make another choice. But this is the choice I always make. Always made. Always will." Travis looked Master Truth in the eyes and said, "There is no way to keep it safe forever. DeSalvo proved that. Next time it will be taken to the other side of the world for all we know and broken there. We won't even know it happened until everybody dies in a wave of death that covers the planet, because that is what it will do if it has the chance to. But today! Today is different. Today, we have Christoph and Grelf here! This is the only moment that we would ever stand the chance to stop it, and I am the only one who sees it."

We can think of another answer. You don't have to lay on the grenade and sacrifice yourself for the world. Master Truth knew that if he tried, he could force this to go differently. He could see it in the Quantum field of possibility, but then he looked beyond that choice. Travis was right. No matter what happened from here, if they didn't destroy it and just tried to protect it, the stone would eventually be taken. When they hid it, it was eventually found, as if were tied to some type of will, and it was leading dark men to do dark things. Master Truth followed the will like he was taught to in the Elven woods. On the day they met the Elven queen, he was taught how to track someone through their use of telepathy. When he found the source, he realized it was the Chaos Dragon herself, and as long as the Time Stone existed it would call out to be found. *Save the world or save your friend. I knew this was coming.*

"So, you understand why I must do this? It's because I always would have, always did. Lady Venger told me that I would sacrifice everything to save Venger and this is it. You remember when I got my bow, you and I knew then."

Master Truth nodded. *I will miss you.*

"No, you won't." Travis began to cry. "None of you will remember me." Travis walked up to Master Truth and pressed his finger against Master Truth's Heartstone. "But that doesn't mean I am not expecting you to keep your promise that you made me that day and find a way to save me."

As you wish. Master Peace hugged Travis and then began to float upward toward the top of the well.

Travis looked up at his friend and with a heart that was filling with anxiety and fear he asked, "Can I ask for one more?"

Master Truth came back down. *For one of my best friends? Anything.*

Travis took a deep breath in and let it out. "I wish for the strength to do this. I am so scared, and I am not ready to let this world go. I'm not ready to say goodbye and I don't know if I can do this."

This was it. Master Truth knew it in his heart. He refocused his spheres and allowed Master Truth to just be a part of who he was, and Dalen forced himself back into a corporeal form.

"As you wish." Dalen reached up and touched his Heartstone and then touched the one that was a part of his throat chakra and with his other hand touched the center of Travis's forehead. "Relax and be at peace." And with that, he knew he had made his choice. "And you are also a fool if you think I will let you do this alone."

"Everything alright down there?" Becky called down the well.

"Everything is going to be okay," Travis called out as he pulled his bow. He tossed the Time Stone into the air and before it reached the apex of its arc Travis pulled an arrow and fired it.

Dalen watched in slow motion as the arrow flew through the air. He brought time to a crawl and looked back at his friend and brother and tried with all his might to remember his face.

The arrow found its mark and the Time Stone shattered into a thousand pieces as Travis was shattered in time.

...

Dalen stared at the empty room. His memories of someone who had just been there faded like a dream, but the harder he tried to hold on to anything, the faster they evaporated from his mind. Dalen opened his third eye and tried to look through time.

Everyplace that there should be another person, there was a blind spot in his vision as if he had looked directly into the sun. He had to look away and flinch from the pain while his mind made tracers of the ghostly afterimages. Tears ran down his other two eyes as he tried to force himself to look into the entirety of time. It made his mind scream, and every part of his being tried to force him to look away, yet still he persisted. He looked at it for as long as he could and cried out. "I will find you!"

31

THE CHAOS DRAGON

Dalen emerged from the well and as he did the Vengerians let out a sigh of relief. "We thought that you broke the Time Stone, but since you're here, everything must be alright." Master Peace could see the pain on Dalen's face and knew that something had happened. "You called out that you would find someone." Master Peace was sure he knew what happened but had to ask to make sure. "Who are you looking for?"

Dalen's heart sank. "I don't know." The ground began to shake as a low rumble grew louder and louder. "I would guess, that is the Chaos Dragon forming itself from the rock in the earth directly below Venger. I still have the power from my stone within me, so I will try and help Christoph and Grelf." Dalen looked at his friends and counted them. It was the same four that he always knew had been there. Sir Adam, Becky, Master Peace, and himself. He forcibly tried to remind himself that there was another, but this was like the spell he had used when he first took the Beads of Fire at the museum. His mind just refused to look at it. "Now that we are in the city, our abilities to teleport within the city using our pins should be active. If you guys were smart you saved a couple of locations along the way. I suggest you get to Dorn and Lady Venger. Maddicus and Will of Grey are with them. Use your Vengerian Pins and hide. Save them and save yourselves."

Sir Adam made a sound like a loud buzzer. "Wrong but thank you for playing. The correct answer is...." He held up his hand like he was reading the answer from a card. "We save Dorn and Lady Venger by not running, and instead by working together and fighting side by side until the bitter end and these are the moments we live for." Adam turned to look at his friends and added, "Which number is, 'never split the party'?" He trailed off and lost track of what he was saying.

Master Peace gave Dalen the bow that is reserved for masters. "I have been waiting for you Master Truth and I have no intentions of missing your debut."

Becky had her finger up and waited until the others were listening. "Question. How is the Chaos Dragon free?"

Dalen lowered himself toward the ground and stepped down

onto it. "One of us shattered the Time Stone."

"But we are all here." Becky clasped her hand over her mouth as she realized what it meant. "Who's missing?" Each of them looked around at each other with blank faces. Becky started to panic and screamed, "Who's missing!"

"I don't know." Dalen hugged her. "I don't know. Every time I try to look, it's like staring into the sun. No matter how hard I try I can't see them."

"We can figure this out." Sir Adam started counting on his fingers. "The Grey Bard, Becky, and I went with Grelf. How many people went with Christoph?"

Master Peace shrugged and said, "Just the two of us. Remember, he specifically said he wanted to take both the monks from the Brotherhood of Light."

Dalen had calmed Becky down enough that she gave a nod indicating she was okay, then walked over to a specific spot in the courtyard. "Right here. My statue was right here." She pointed to another spot. "Adam, yours was there."

Adam moved to his spot and looked around, trying to picture the scene. He pointed to another spot and said, "Dalen, you stood there."

Dalen and Master Peace took their spots and each of them tried to remember the scene. "We are all in the right places, right?" Becky looked around. "Two on the left and two on the right. Right?" They all agreed. "Then who's missing?"

Another rumble and this time the ground shook hard enough to knock them off their feet.

Sir Adam got back up quickly and kept his eyes open for falling debris. "Becky. I hear you and I agree. We all understand that we have lost one of our own and we are not blind to it, but Becky, the literal ground is shaking, and these are going to be the last few minutes of this world unless we do something right now. I have no doubt this person matters, and that we all loved them, but they awoke the Chaos Dragon, and we are going to have to work on this later if, there is one."

"There will definitely be a later." Becky stopped herself as a flash of nearly remembering something streaked across her mind for a fleeting moment.

"Not if we don't first save the world." Dalen changed and took his full jinn form. His stones lit up as he phased into something that wasn't quite there and opened his third eye. His other two began to glow and he floated off the ground. *I am going to help Grelf and Christoph.* He pointed to Xoxann. *She has been through enough. Please get her someplace safe.*

Sir Adam scooped Xoxann up in his arms and said with a goofy grin and a voice to match, "This place is getting crazy. Let's get you someplace safe. Okay?" She nodded. "Okay. Close your eyes and count to three." On two Sir Adam reached up and touched his pin and they both vanished.

"I'm not okay with this." Becky was angry yet tears fell from her eyes. "We all just lost somebody, and you are all acting like you don't care."

It's not that I don't care about who we lost. Dalen put his hand over his Heartstone. *It's that I can't bear to lose anyone else.* He looked to Master Peace. *Do your best to help her find some peace. We are still going to need Oubliette before this is over.*

Dalen moved quantumly and was quickly standing by Christoph's side. Christoph was holding a ghost blade that looked to be as phased from existence as Dalen was. In the center of its hilt was a single coin that seemed to be the only tangible part of his weapon. It was made of both the All-Seeing Eye of the Present and the All-Knowing Gold Coin of Master Wisdom. Within the coin, Dalen could see and feel the power of both dragons. They were surging through Christoph. He had become the Avatar of the Dragon.

Grelf was holding the Horn of the Unicorn which was a beautiful blade made of celestium, with its handle created from a real unicorn horn. She too was surging with raw energy, and her hair gave off as much light as a campfire. Dalen recognized that Kargen and Pipim were still with her. She had become the Avatar of the Unicorn.

They were standing on the grassy field about a mile from the outer walls of Venger City. They were hoping that if the fight happened, they could make a stand here and keep the fight away from Venger itself. They both noticed Dalen as he appeared, and they gave him a nod. "At least we have time on our side." mused Christoph.

"It seems that you were right Master Pax." Grelf gave Dalen a nod. "Waking the Dragon was inevitable." The ground rumbled again, and each of them braced themselves to take the shaking with their legs and knees and remained standing while the world tried to tear itself apart. "At least we didn't get all dressed up for nothing."

The world stopped shaking for a moment and the air crackled as Sir Adam, Becky, Master Peace, Maddicus and I appeared. Sir Adam took a knee. "Dorn and Lady Venger have taken refuge in the Heart of Venger. They are protecting the girl. There is nothing for us to do there. They are safe until the moment the Chaos Dragon destroys everything all at once, and there is nothing there that we could do about it, except stand there and wait to die." He stood up and looked at Grelf and Christoph with resolve. "And before you try to tell us this is not our fight let me say this. Yes, it is. This is the fight of everything that still breaths, because the Chaos Dragon threatens it all, and if we are going to die this day, we would rather face our destroyer headlong instead of hiding in the shadows and waiting to die."

"Wouldn't want it any other way." Christoph smiled at them. "I am glad that each of you is by our side."

"Not all of us." Becky took a deep breath and waved off Peace. "I said I was alright. I'll be fine." But then she hugged Grelf.

"What happened?" Grelf gave Becky her undivided attention. For a moment, there was no Chaos Dragon, there was no end of the world; there was only a girl that needed to be heard.

"One of us broke the Time Stone, and now none of us can remember them. Dalen can't even see them when he looks for them in time. They are just gone, and nobody seems to care." Becky plunged her head into Grelf's chest and sobbed. "Master Peace is connected to his emotions, and Adam's heart is the strongest part of his whole being. Dalen cares about each of us, and he tried to see them, but nobody is broken up about this. I do not understand how all of you could just not care that somebody we knew has been taken from us. Stolen from our minds and hearts!"

The ground rumbled again. Clouds quickly began to form overhead and become dark. Grelf ignored it as if it didn't exist. She looked at Becky and said, "I think that is precisely why. They have been stolen from our hearts and minds. It is hard to mourn someone you cannot remember." The ground sent another rumble, and the shaking began to increase. "Especially when the world is about to end. I am sure once this is over, we will all feel the loss, but in battle, sometimes you have to set aside the pain long enough to survive."

Becky nodded and stepped back to get her balance with the next round of shaking. "So why can't I let this go?"

Grelf took a long look at Christoph and smiled. "Maybe, because they meant something important to you."

"They were important to all of us!" Becky looked around at each of them. "Are you going to say that you are not deeply connected to everyone here? Are any of us strangers? Whoever they were they mattered to all of us."

"Then let us recognize them now. As King, I request it. Take this moment for our fallen comrade." Christoph put his hand over his heart and asked Becky to speak hers. Everyone put their hands over their hearts as well and gave her their attention.

"We have lost someone today, and they didn't just die, they were taken from our hearts and memories. We may never know their name, but I can tell you who they were. They were a friend. A sister or brother to all of us. They were loved and trusted... they were one of us." The ground began to rumble but she just talked louder. "They were someone who knew in their hearts that this moment had to happen. They were willing to risk everything so that we could end this once and for all. So, let us go forth and win this battle in their name. So that their sacrifice will not be in vain!"

The ground began to rise as if a new hill were being formed but then, it ruptured, and the dragon began to emerge from underneath. Dalen had flashbacks of his vision of this moment, and it touched him through time as it came to pass, and he understood that all this time, his vision was him seeing a memory that had not yet happened.

Christoph balled himself up and then stretched out wide, and as he did giant dragon wings spread out from his back, and scales formed over most of his visible skin. He leaped into the air and with a flap of his wings he was airborne and beginning to climb.

Grelf turned into stardust and twinkled out of existence and then reappeared the same way on the top of the Chaos Dragon's head. She held on to one of its horns as it pulled itself out of the rock face and began to stand up.

As the Chaos Dragon rose it created a void in the rock and soil of the prairie that it used to create itself. The ground gave way quickly and began to fall. Becky put one of the handles from her blades under her butt and clicked it into position, and then used the other to stabilize herself as the ground fell away from them. Master Peace leaped out as the last piece of ground fell from under him. It was a true leap of faith, and he flew for yards through the air before landing by Grelf's side.

The ground dropped directly under Sir Adam. He dropped straight down into the cavernous void. As he looked up and watched the hole he fell through grow more distant, he saw Maddicus dive into it after him. For a moment Sir Adam forgot about the Chaos Dragon and the pending end of the world. All he could think about was the smile on Maddicus's face as she reached out for him and they fell through the darkness together, and in that moment, he was falling for her as well.

When she caught him, they pulled each other close. "If we glide, we'll still have the cliff crumbling around us." She was right, they were falling at the same speed as the rocks and earth, and the moment she activated her board they would be under attack. The debris continued to fall at a steady rate. "Venger may be in range to bamph." Maddicus guessed, as she reached up and touched her brand-new Vengerian Pin.

"Where would be the fun in that?" asked Sir Adam as he flipped around behind her, so she activated her board and stopped their fall. They both looked up at the falling rocks and together whooped and cheered as they made their flight out, dodging rocks and debris as they climbed.

Dalen looked at the top tower of the castle. He stared at it for a moment and blinked. When his eyes opened, he was where he had been looking. From his position he could see that the Chaos Dragon had moved out to the shallows of the shore and had stood up on her hind legs, dwarfing the Star Folk boat that was moored in the middle of the Vengerian Bay. She was enormous... taller than the cliffs and she roared at the city of Venger situated at her eye level.

Dalen charged his connection to the Divine Field and prayed. Dalen's form changed to his connection to the Soul Sphere and became Father Light. "At this moment I only ask for the strength to do what is in front of me."

The ground gave way, and the City of Venger began to fall. Father Light reached out with telekinesis and tried to catch Venger as it fell. He channeled all the power that he could, but a dropping city seemed impossible to catch. Instead of holding up the city, he watched in vain as the weight of it just dragged him down.

Father Light noticed that time began to slow. He was focused on trying to hold up Venger, so he knew it wasn't him. He felt her presence before she glided into sight, and he was happy to see The Fire Jinn floating next to him. She smiled and waved like an old friend who was happy to see him.

What seems to be the problem, my friend? Father Light was still holding his spell and was trying to keep Venger from falling. She looked around. *Oh. You are here.* She turned back around and maneuvered to be face-to-face with him. *My goodness look how you have grown. I am so proud of you, and you are so close.* She kissed him on the forehead.

Father Light closed his eyes and relented to her kiss. "It is good to see you, Moment. I could really use your help. I may have grown, but it is not enough. I'm not strong enough to keep Venger from falling."

Moment just folded her arms and shook her head. *Why not?*

Father Light looked at her with defeat in his eyes. "It's too big."

Moment couldn't help but chuckle. *Not enough... I'm not strong enough... It is too big. If Diem were here, he would be sorely disappointed in that kind of thinking.*

Father Light barely noticed as time stopped completely onto a single frame as his mind locked on to what the Fire Jinn had just said. "I am Diem."

Moment leaned back in surprise. *You are? Because Diem would not say the things you have. He understands the hard part is moving something with your magic. Things like size are irrelevant. Either you can do it, or you can't. Wouldn't you agree?* Father Light nodded. *If Diem were here, what would he tell you?*

Father Light relented and let go of his hold on the City of Venger so that he could hug her properly. Time had stopped so the city just hung in the air. "Thank you. There has never been a moment that you have ever let me down." He let her go and refocused and as he did, she lit up with white fire and told him that she would see him soon. She grew brighter until she was pure light as Father Light looked up and said, "Diem would say that the size is a distraction and limitation that I put on myself. The only truth that comes from it is how much I choose to limit myself. He would remind me of the First Law of Magic. That I am only as powerful as I allow myself to be. He would say that I should let go of the garbage that I have filled my head with about the things that are too hard, and thoughts of what I can't do. He would say I am strong enough. I am powerful enough...."

Time kicked back in and Venger began to fall. Father Light was no longer Dalen's truth and as Diem, he looked down at the city as it began to drop and reached out with his very soul and proclaimed, "For I am the day that I seize!" And caught Venger in midair. All the rocks and soil that still clung to the city gave way and Diem began to slowly float Venger down to the ground.

•••

The Chaos Dragon had black iridescent scales over most of her body except for the larger plate scales that were dark purple and covered her chest and belly. There were matching horns and spikes along her bone ridges. Her wings were covered in the same scales along the hard structure of the appendage and the sails that made up the wings were black. Christoph was trying to get close enough to attack her while dodging her arms and wings as she swatted at him like an annoying insect. She was three times the size of a standard dragon and was twice as tall as the highest tower of Venger Castle. Riding on top of her head, Master Peace and Grelf held on to her horns and tried their best to attack her while not being thrown.

Master Peace used his Dragon Claw and sent it out on its chain. On his second attempt, his aim was true, and the Dragon Claw hit and latched to a smaller horn, merely the size of a person, located in the center of the dragon's head. Once the dragon claw latched on, he leaned back on it and made it taut. Grelf waited for a moment until she felt that she could move then let go of one of the Chaos Dragon's main horns she was holding onto. She made a quick movement toward the chain and caught it. She was now using the chain like a rope to move hand over hand toward the center of the Chaos Dragon's head.

Christoph dodged under the Chaos Dragon's arm as she tried to attack him. He rolled over so he was on his back and thrust his sword upwards into the underside of her arm. The Eye of the Dragon penetrated the flesh, and the Chaos Dragon let out a roar, but her scales and flesh healed instantly. Christoph landed on the monstrosity and began to cleave into the Chaos Dragon's body.

The Chaos Dragon roared in pain and looked to see what had harmed her. She saw Christoph and although he tried to evade her grasp and fly away, she caught him in midair. Christoph could see that all the damage he had just done was for nothing as she healed instantly. The Chaos Dragon brought Christoph up to look at him face to face.

She tore into his mind violently and he began to bleed from his nose and ears while she rooted around through his memories and thoughts. *Where is Dorn?*

In that moment Christoph would have told her anything. This abomination had ripped apart the first law of this world which was Free Will. She bypassed it completely and Christoph was now at her mercy, of which she had none, but before he could answer her Grelf plunged the Horn of the Unicorn into the Chaos Dragon's skull.

The Chaos Dragon dropped her hold over Christoph's mind and opened her claw as she roared in pain and Christoph fell out of her grip. He tried to fly but his right wing had been broken when the Chaos Dragon grabbed him. He did his best to open it to glide but the pain was intense.

Sir Adam and Maddicus came flying out of the ground that was still falling below them and saw that he was in trouble. Maddicus flew them to a place where she could intercept him as he fell, and Sir Adam reached out to catch him. Maddicus deactivated her board and as they fell together, Adam and Christoph struggled to get a good hold of one another, but finally, Christoph grabbed his hand and Sir Adam helped him aboard.

"The board's not built for three. Chill or we're gonna bail!" Maddicus reactivated the board, slowly pulled up, and started moving out of arm's length of the Chaos Dragon.

The Chaos Dragon paid no attention to them, for in that moment there was something else on her mind. She reached up with her claw and struck her head. Master Peace had been leaning out from the horn trying to give Grelf stability, with the swipe of her claw he was rendered unconscious. He had wrapped his arm in the chain of his Dragon Claw, and it saved him from simply falling off the Chaos Dragon's head, but it left him dangling from it unconscious and being battered as he hung there.

Grelf had ducked low, but the Chaos Dragon's attack had pinned and broken her left arm which had been holding the chain. With her right, she clung to the Horn of the Unicorn. The Chaos Dragon knew she had caught something and picked up Grelf who gripped the Horn of the Unicorn with all her might and was able to take it with her as the Chaos Dragon brought her around to see what she had caught. Without hesitation, she hit the dragon's claw with her sword again.

The Dragon roared with anger and pain. *You will pay for your insolence!* She screamed in Grelf's head and then unceremoniously threw her to the ground. The Chaos Dragon threw her too quickly for anyone to respond and she hit the ground with a dull thump. Her back had been broken. Shards of bone impaled all her organs, and her body began to fill up with blood. The Chaos Dragon raised her hind leg with every intention of stepping on her and brought it down to smash her once and for all.

As the shadow of the Chaos Dragon's foot began to engulf Grelf, Oubliette stepped out from the shadow. She raised both of her blades, pointed at the Chaos Dragon's foot in two places slightly wider than shoulder length, and locked them into place as the Chaos Dragon's foot came crashing down.

Becky had created enough space that when the dragon's foot came down, there was a small void created by her magically immovable weapons keeping them safe. Her blades did not pierce the Chaos Dragon's flesh, but she immediately stepped back as if she were in pain.

‹I need you to go.› Grelf was too injured to speak physically.

"I am not going to leave you like this," Oubliette whispered.

Tears fell from Grelf's eyes as the pain began to go numb and her vision began to blur. She knew she was dying and wouldn't survive, but as she looked over Oubliette's shoulder, she could see that the Chaos Dragon was about to use its breath weapon at them. It wasn't taking a giant breath like she saw in the vision, but even a small blast would undoubtedly kill anything in its path.

‹I can't move. We are close enough to the city to use the teleporter with your pin. You are going to have to get to a safe place so I can teleport to your location. Now move. I order you as your Queen.› She watched as Oubliette told her that she would be okay and bamphed out of her view. She had lied twice to Becky, and she prayed that she would forgive her. She knew she wasn't close enough for the teleport ability in the Vengerian Pin to work. It wouldn't take her to someplace safe in the city. It would bounce her to the nearest location that was allowed which would be the Tree of Travel. She heard Becky's voice as she told her that something had gone wrong, but she was safe at the tree. The second lie was that she knew that her back and left arm were broken so horrifically that she was never going to be able to reach her own Vengerian Pin. She smiled knowing that at least she was able to save one as she put up her right arm to shield herself from the blast. She was vaporized instantly.

"No!" Christoph, Maddicus, and Sir Adam crash-landed in the small crater where Grelf had just been moments before. Christoph dropped to his knees in the ash and sobbed. "No."

Diem finished setting the City of Venger down and turned to see what was happening. He moved through space to the location of Christoph and saw what had happened.

Master Peace's voice broke the silence. ‹I am still in position. Maybe we can still kill this thing.›

Diem felt sick. Time was warping and he couldn't tell why. A wave of time moved through him and forced Dalen into a physical corporeal form, and he dropped from his floating position and landed on the ground. Something had gone wrong with time, and this was all going to go bad.

Christoph stood up with revenge in his heart and reached down and took the Horn of the Unicorn. He intended to attack the Chaos Dragon with both. The power that he had within him was only enough to wield the Eye of the Dragon and The Horn of the Unicorn was meant to be wielded by the Queen, so when he picked up the Horn of the Unicorn the power was too much. There was a surge of energy and before it could be stopped the power of both swords combined shredded Christoph into nothing.

Your champions have failed Dorn! The Chaos Dragon called out in triumph. She raised her head back, reveled in the moment, and then took a deep breath in.

Dalen didn't know what to do. He knew that he was out of time and yet they had failed. He thought back to the moment when he was first told of this day. He played it back in his mind with perfect clarity. He remembered the pool that was the Fountain of Truth. He remembered the four Elemental Swords and then in the center was a single blade. He had said what it was that day. The Eye of the Dragon... in the Horn of the Unicorn.

Dalen understood where it went wrong. Christoph was never meant to wield them separately, the two blades needed to be forged into one, with the power that both Christoph and Grelf held. All of that was gone the moment that Grelf had been killed. From that moment on they were on a different path.

The Chaos Dragon brought her head forward and with all of her might sent her blast toward Venger.

Time came to a screeching halt with the blast of energy just penetrating the outer protective shield. The shield had failed, and the blast had just begun to push through. Dalen stood there staring at this moment in time and he knew what it meant. He could never let time start again, because if he did, it was over.

32

A SECOND CHANCE

"You can't do it," I called out. I was standing next to him as he stared at the end of the world. "You can't change what's happened."

Dalen stared at everything he had cared about frozen in time. If he lets go of time the blast will engulf half the planet. "Since the beginning of all this, I have been told again and again that I am dangerous because I can change time. So, yeah, I think I can."

I walked in front of him to force him to look at me. "You can make different choices and change what one timeline remembers as the past, as it happens, but once you have experienced the moment, that moment is set in your history. You are moving forward in time so you cannot use the present to affect the past, only the future."

Dalen allowed himself to be Master Truth and opened his third eye. He looked backward in time and began to look for a moment to perceive.

I stepped into his vision of time. "Master Ki went over this with you. He had you relive the moment when you created your rings. He explained to you that you can see it, and look at it, but once you have actually experienced a moment, it becomes locked in time, and you can't change it."

Master Truth looked through time again and again, and no matter how many times he tried to affect it, he was only looking at a memory. He spun it a thousand times but couldn't find an answer until frustration took over and he returned to being Dalen and brought his attention to the present.

"I told you." I looked out over the moment frozen in time. "You can't change it because you are moving forward in time. You can only alter things in the direction you are going."

"Then that is what I will do." He turned and looked up to the Tree of Travel and moved himself to that location through the Quantum Field. Becky was standing there, staring at the carnage. She had her hand over her mouth and tears in her eyes.

I had moved with him because I was not done with our

conversation. "Then what will you do?"

Dalen looked at me and smiled, "This area isn't affected by the cave-in when the dragon rips itself out of the ground. It's safe to stand here when I go back in time."

"You can't..." I began to argue.

"Affect the past if I am moving forward. Okay. So, I am going to move backward in time, or more to the point I am going to make time move backward while I move normally in it."

"That is not possible."

"Why? Because you say so?" Dalen shook his head. "Again and again, I keep being told that I am only limited by what I believe can be done." He opened his arms and looked around. "Here I am! Not moving forward in time."

"That's because you are holding a single frame. Time is still going forward. If you let go, you would still get the next frame."

"Then I will just do what I do to make it stop and do that even harder." He closed his eyes and forced time to a complete standstill. The single frame of time vanished, and Dalen found himself in the void. He tried as hard as he could and held it for a long time before his will gave out and the next frame of reality appeared.

"You see." I wanted him to succeed, but I knew that he would not be able to do it alone. *You do not have the power needed to move it backward beyond this point.*

Dalen flipped the coin in his head and knew he had the

answer. "You're right. Truth is truth, I can't do it alone." For a moment I thought that he had chosen reason as an ally, but then he snapped his attention to me and looked me in the eyes, and I saw him choose a different truth. "But I'm not alone, am I?"

Dalen pulled out DeSalvo's item and called him forth. His black smoke with sparks of red appeared and he stepped through it into the world. DeSalvo looked around at the frame frozen in time and then gave his attention to Dalen. "Why have you brought me here?"

"This is your answer?" I asked. "This genie destroyed his whole world and set things in motion to destroy this one. Why would you ever believe that he is going to help you?"

"Because he is the other half of the coin and the only other being in this world that can change time." Dalen held out DeSalvo's piece of black twisted metal. "I want to show you this moment. I mean really show it to you, and then I want to show you a truth. Once I have, and you have honestly looked at it, I am going to grant you a single wish and give this to you and you will be free. Do we have an accord?"

I needed to make sure that Dalen understood what he was doing. "Dalen, if you give him a wish, what makes you think he will do anything but destroy this world."

"Then we are no worse off than we already are." Dalen didn't break DeSalvo's gaze. "You and I have got some things we need to work out. Do we have an accord?"

"If you are wrong about DeSalvo he will turn on you and

everything you have worked for. You will fail."

Dalen broke eye contact and stared me down. "Then I will fail!" It was the kind of resolve that this moment needed, and I lowered my eyes and gave him a bow. He turned back to DeSalvo and with a newfound calm asked for the third time. "Do we have an accord?"

Dalen had not directly wished for it, and he was giving DeSalvo a choice. DeSalvo wasn't expecting this move, and the rewards were worth the risk. "We have an accord."

"All of this went wrong the day we lost Becky in time."

"Be careful of speaking about things you know nothing about." DeSalvo snarled at Dalen.

"I know a lot more than you think." Dalen stared DeSalvo down. "I know about everything Dalen."

DeSalvo squinted with anger. "You do know, don't you?" Dalen nodded, "Then you know why I must do what I have to do."

"You never learned that whole incorporeal thing, did you?" Dalen put his hand on DeSalvo's shoulder, but DeSalvo pulled away. "Your entire timeline was destroyed. Even if you go back in time, you will go back on this timeline."

DeSalvo laughed at Dalen. "Then you are just as well off as I am." He pointed to the Chaos Dragon who was in the midst of trying to destroy everything Dalen had come to love. "Both of our timelines have been destroyed."

Dalen didn't flinch or skip a beat. "This one hasn't happened yet and with your help, I intend to save both of them."

"How?" DeSalvo was skeptical but he had to look at whatever he was told to. If he did, Dalen would give him his item back, and as his master, would then free DeSalvo to make a single wish, so he bid his time and continued to listen.

"You got your hands on the Beads of Fire and made a wish at the Pillar of Time. Normally whoever makes the wish would be destroyed along with all of their knowledge from the original timeline, the moment that timeline itself is destroyed. Back to the point in time that the wish is made for...the place where time changes. But you are one of the two Heralds of Time and could not be destroyed, so you persisted."

"That's why I still exist? Is that why I still remember?" DeSalvo began to listen intently.

"Yes, but although you survived the destruction of your timeline, your wish still came true. Instead of repeating what had happened before... you were moved six hours ahead, to when you first found the Beads of Fire. You wished that you never lost Becky. Turn around."

DeSalvo turned around and was practically eye-to-eye with Becky. It stopped DeSalvo in his tracks. "This isn't my Becky."

"No." Dalen put his arm around DeSalvo and put him directly in front of her. "That Becky vanishes. This is the Becky that doesn't disappear. This is the Becky that you wished for."

DeSalvo reached up and wiped one of the tears from Becky's face. "The Becky I wished for?"

Dalen shifted their location from where they were, to standing by Adam. "This is Sir Adam the Pure Heart. He is alive and has become everything he has ever dreamed of. He is such a perfect soul that he can call forth a unicorn."

DeSalvo looked at Dalen in disbelief and then looked over to Sir Adam. Dalen shared with DeSalvo the image of Sir Adam on the back of Kargen just as he reared up before their charge.

"Next to him is Maddicus. She loves him for the man he has become." Then Dalen moved to Master Peace. You remember him as Ben Watts, but I know him as Master Peace of the Brotherhood of Light and have come to respect him greatly. He earned his mastery by healing the Tree of Sorrow, which you created as a wound in time, and I have come to know him not only as a friend but as a brother.

DeSalvo wiped a tear from his eye. "What about Travis?"

"Who is Travis?" asked Dalen.

"Travis? Adam's twin brother." DeSalvo's eyes widened as he understood. "Travis is the one who shattered the Time Stone and freed that evil bitch."

Dalen nodded and shifted them back to stand next to Becky. "There is a hole in time where someone used to be, they sacrificed themselves to try and stop the Chaos Dragon once and for all, but something went wrong, and everything didn't go the way it was supposed to."

"Yeah..." DeSalvo turned and looked at the Chaos Dragon. "She has the ability to warp reality through chaos, including time."

He bent over and braced himself just above his knees. "Oh, how I hate her so much."

"The last time, she was in control of you, and then The Teacher..." Dalen started to say.

"You know about The Teacher?" DeSalvo asked with surprise.

"If I think back to before I became Mathias, I remember Travis, but he is only something that happened in your world. He is no longer in mine. Except for that, I know everything you know as if I were you." Dalen paused. "Because I am." Dalen looked at the giant dragon and said, "I have as much reason to hate her as you do. Tell you what...this time neither The Teacher nor the dragon has control over you. How would you like to wreck her plans, and in doing so, The Teacher's plans as well? Send that guy back to square one, and end her forever?"

DeSalvo scoffed. "You wouldn't even have to wish for it."

Dalen threw DeSalvo his piece of black twisted metal. "Here's your chance to prove it."

DeSalvo looked at his item. It had become as black and twisted as his heart, but now it was his. No one controlled him but himself and he was granted a single wish for himself. "What do you think we can possibly do? It's already too late."

"Not if we reverse the flow of time," Dalen said with a dead calm.

DeSalvo laughed. "Impossible. I can impose my will on the

direction and move through time, but I am only a genie and do not have the power to alter time."

"Well. I am the Jinn of Time and can alter it but cannot move backward through it physically." Dalen put out his hand, "Do you see where I am going with this?"

"You want you and me to combine our abilities into one action?" DeSalvo was starting to see a little of himself in this Dalen Pax. His plans went against everything that either of them had ever learned or believed in.

Dalen nodded. "I want you to invert the direction of time so that I can alter the past by acting from the present." Dalen put out his hand. "Let's finish this like we started. As one."

"Both of you need to be aware of what you are doing." I said, "If you break the timeline one of you will have to take the hit and you may very well be destroyed."

"Heard." They said in unison, locked on to each other as they openly chose rebellion.

They stood a short distance apart and each began to focus their power. DeSalvo called forth the power of the Black Flame and commanded it to his will. Black smoke began to permeate the ground. From the center of the wisping smoke arose the six Elemental Stones. Black flames burned along the ground creating the pattern of his casting circle. Dalen focused and harmonized with the Spheres of Reality. Each of the Elemental Reality Stones arose from the ground surrounded by celestium that stretched out between them creating Dalen's casting circle as he began to prepare to bend reality.

Neither of them intended it, but a connection had been made between the two, and something within them both began to emerge.

Dalen observed his circle and saw himself in each Sphere of Reality. He looked to Master Truth who was beautiful and powerful standing on the Element of Imagination and the Observer. His third eye sees through time itself. In the Arcane Element stood Diem. It was the part of him that connected him to the truth of his being. He was a Jinn and by his very nature a divine being made of something more powerful than magic itself. Standing in the Kinetic Element he saw himself in his corporeal form. An older wiser Dalen Pax. He no longer looked like he was seventeen, but more of a man in his forties, he had held that image so that his friends would know him, but the time for such illusions was over. He looked at his face. He had seen it in so many forms. It was the face of Dalen's corporeal age, and not only was it worn by Dalen, but it was the face of Mathias.

Master Ki appeared in Dalen's thoughts. *His is the face you refuse to see. Even Master Truth wears his face if you look closely.* Dalen looked over at the being made of smoke and light and for the first time noticed that Master Truth's features did resemble Diem and Mathias. *They wear it as a truth. A truth you are ready to face. Allow your form to be the truth of all of them.*

Dalen closed his eyes and brought each of his perspectives together. Dalen Pax was finally whole. No more pieces of himself were cast aside and he stood in his power. A physical jinn who could move in and out of his corporeal state. His form had the face of Diem, and his stones looked like celestium mixed with silver. The green element in the center lit up and the symbol of the yin yang wreathed in silver fire began to glow from within it.

...

DeSalvo could feel the presence of the Chaos Dragon. She was the true Master of the Black Flame and his creator. Even in this frozen state, she was aware of him. She had been frozen in a single moment in time for years beyond counting, and in her imprisonment, she taught herself how to connect to corporeal beings through something of their own creation. Those dark souls who wished to see destruction befall this world had begun to pray to the Chaos Dragon as a goddess. Over enough time they began to believe that although she was frozen in a single moment in time, she could hear them and accept their offerings of blood and sacrifice. They believed it so much that they created a path for her to communicate with them as if she were a deity, and now that goddess was incarnate and present, even if still frozen in time. Only a single frame, but to her this was home, and she was still aware of what was happening, and she could still talk to her favorite slave. *What are you doing DeSalvo?*

DeSalvo still wore the mithril collar that forced him to speak the truth. "My opponent is growing too powerful. Dalen has just connected the three spheres for controlling magic. If I do not match him, there is no chance of success."

She was furious with him that he came to her for favors and offered only excuses for how he was not good enough. He had failed her too many times. Perhaps it was because she broke him too far when she turned him into a genie, by forcing him to go back in time and trick himself into becoming her slave, as he had already done, and then tearing him from his connection to his soul or the memories of who he was. So, there was a chance that the reason he continued to fail was because he was too weak to handle losing all she had taken from him. After all of this was finished, she would make him pay for his weakness, but she grew tired of his continued failure and granted what she had previously taken. *I release to you, your connections to your heart and your past. Now finish this, I command you!*

On the Element of Body Manipulation, he saw himself, old and withered from a thousand years of abuse and neglect. DeSalvo sneered at it and the image sneered back. As it did, he understood he was looking at a reflection of how he saw himself.

The Element of Mind Control lit up and Mathias stood before DeSalvo, and with him came a flooding of emotion and memory. It broke DeSalvo's heart as he remembered what it was like to be him. As he did, he remembered that this was not his goal. He had been forced into becoming an instrument of carnage and death, but before they broke him, he was on a different mission. As DeSalvo, he knew what it was... logically. He had seen it in time and knew what happened, but as he stood and stared into the eyes of Mathias, he remembered what it felt like, and what it felt like to want it.

"Becky." DeSalvo looked out across the field. Standing next to the tree, looking out at the Chaos Dragon with tears in her eyes as she watched the world be destroyed, stood Becky. She was here and she was alive. "The one I wished for."

The Element of Heart Conditioning lit up and Dalen at seventeen was bathed in a blue light. "The one you wished for," he said and DeSalvo began to weep.

DeSalvo turned in circles trying to see them all. "What do you want from me?"

The other DeSalvo that stood on the Element of Body Manipulation smiled. "Nothing really." He smiled and even DeSalvo had to admit it was haunting. "You see, we are you, and just like you asked for..."

"You dreamed of...." added Mathias.

"You wished for..." added young Dalen.

"We want to be whole." Hissed the vision of DeSalvo. He held up his hand and displayed the black twisted piece of metal. "We want to be you."

"The real you." Mathias held up his hand and in it was a gunmetal grey figure in his hand.

"The true you." The young Dalen echoed as he held up his silver figure. "You just have to accept us."

"All of us," DeSalvo interjected.

"All of us," Mathias said and offered his piece to DeSalvo. "The good. The bad. It's how we got here." Mathias walked up to DeSalvo and put his figure in DeSalvo's hand. He faded away and

DeSalvo took with him the connection to his memories and the man he chose to become while trying to save his friends.

The other DeSalvo walked up and before he placed his twisted piece of metal into his hands he said, "You have a thousand years of knowledge and training, and now that you get to make your own choices, use your dark times as a lesson. Remember what you are fighting every day not to become. Make better choices and now that you are your own master, never let anyone, especially that dragon bitch, take that away from you again." He put his item in DeSalvo's hand and began to fade away, as he did his skills and knowledge about time and how to bend it to his will became alive along with the knowledge of the suffering that comes with twisting such things. He remembered the pain and the sorrow he reaped across a world he finally destroyed as an act of mercy and knew he would never use the name DeSalvo again. It was his slave name, and a slave was something he would never be again.

"Promise me one thing." Young Dalen walked over and placed his silver figure in his hand but didn't let go. Never forget what you have done, and never forget why you did it, but remember that you are an evolving being who is allowed to change, and that... is who you truly are." He let go of it and faded away. As he did this new version of Dalen laughed. The Chaos Dragon had no idea that he had his figure back. She would never have given him his power back if she thought that he wasn't under control.

He was ready. He decided to meet himself in the middle and take the name and the face of Mathias and as he made his choice the Element of Self Mastery ignited, and the symbol of a yin yang wreathed in swirling black fire lit up underneath his feet.

. . .

Both of their fields worked together like two sides of a
battery and a charge began to form. Together they used their magic
and began to focus their fields towards a common thought. An
idea that until that moment could be nothing more than thought,
but they were in harmony, and they were going to rewrite the laws
of time.

The Chaos Dragon screamed into Mathias's head, "DeSalvo!
You fool! You are creating a time anomaly." She roared in his mind.
"Stop this at once!"

Mathias had spent years being screamed at telepathically
by her and The Teacher. They amused themselves by seeing how
far they could push his mind before it broke. After countless years
he had built up quite the immunity to it and besides, he thought
to himself, "Nobody calls me DeSalvo." He reached down as far
as he could and pushed with all his might. On the other side, he
saw Dalen, but he was wearing black and white robes, his left side
was armored, and his right arm was bare. On his right arm, there
was a light tattoo of three concentric circles. He had a beard but
no mustache and although he was matching Mathias's power there
seemed to be a calm about him.

Dalen stared at the dark mirror of himself. He had found
his balance and no longer looked like a gnarled old man. Instead,
he looked like the Mathias that Dalen met in the alleyway. He
was wearing ceremonial robes that were all in black save for a

cloth that hung over his left shoulder that had an enchanted flame running the length of it that moved and danced like real fire. He had a goatee and short-kept hair. The stones throughout his body looked like silver obsidian.

The Chaos Dragon roared with all of her might into their minds, if they would not listen, she would destroy them.

Together they pushed and Dalen brought time to a complete standstill. The frame of reality that they were in ceased to exist and together they stood in the void. Mathis had been waiting for it, he focused all his strength and power and inverted his field.

And time began to move backward.

At first, it was a single frame, and the Chaos Dragon was still roaring. She could sense them both but then Dalen let go of his grip of time and slipped into the frame before that one. She was no longer roaring in their minds and was unaware of their treachery. With every frame, she began to understand, then another frame would take its place, and for a moment she was unaware of what they were doing. Then another moment of recognition, then a new frame where she still had not become aware of what was happening... nor the one before that, until there were no more moments of recognition.

Time began to move quicker, and Dalen watched as the blast from the Chaos Dragon moved its way upward, "It's working!" Dalen looked over to Mathias and saw that he was still struggling. Dalen had to release his power to let time move but Mathias had to hold his to keep it going in reverse. "How do I help?"

"I will hold the field." Mathias struggled for a moment but regained his control. "I don't know how long I can hold it. Whatever you are going to do, you better do it fast."

"You can't hold this alone," Dalen said as he tried to refocus his power. The force of the charge was something they had built but when Mathias inverted his field it began to push against itself like stirring something one way and then intentionally trying to stir it the other, but the thing they were stirring was time. "We can barely hold it together."

A blast of light came and it nearly broke both of their concentration as the Chaos Dragon took back the blast it fired to kill Grelf.

"I can't hold it alone but look at me. Look at me!" Mathias sent a pulse from his hands, and it made Dalen look up. "I won't be able to hold it for long, but I will hold it as long as I can."

Dalen shook his head. "It will shred you through time like it did our friend if I leave you."

The ground began to rebuild itself as time continued to move backward. Mathias held his will and power against the force that he knew would build until it destroyed him. "His name was Travis. Don't look for him in your memories, look for him in mine. I remember him." He knew there would only be moments and screamed at Dalen, "Now go!"

Dalen heard from deep inside, his own voice echoed the truth he had not understood until this moment. "I can save the world...or save myself," he whispered and broke his contact. He knew in his heart that there was no time. Because they were acting in the same moment, Dalen's memories of this event came into existence, but he remembered them as Mathias had experienced them.

Mathias held it as long as he could, determined to give everything he had. For every second he could hold the time stream was another second Dalen had to save not only his world but theirs. I stood there watching him as he tore the universe apart and for the second time was going to destroy an entire timeline of existence. "You know that the timeline you started in is gone right?" Mathias looked up at me but just focused on holding the current of time. "You just destroyed an entire timeline where the Chaos Dragon destroys everything."

The pressure was building, and Mathias could barely hold on. "Good."

"Good? That means you killed all those people instead of the dragon."

"They were all dead anyway."

I got in Mathias's face as he struggled to hold back time. "So, that gives you the right?"

Mathias began to feel himself being torn in time. The pain was beyond words that any language has devised, but he refused to let go. "I have to save this world."

"Why?"

"Because it's the one I wished for." Mathias looked over to

Becky. "This is my chance." Parts of him began to fracture but he held himself together in the sands of time out of sheer will. "I can save her."

"At the cost of everything?" I looked him square in the eyes "When time starts, you won't be here, and you won't be you."

Mathias looked at the item in his hand and began to move it toward the anomaly that he and Dalen had made. It untwisted as he moved his hand and began to look like Mathias's figure instead of the twisted black piece of metal that DeSalvo had carried for years. "I don't even care if I get to see it or not. I destroyed a whole world trying to do the right thing, and now I have a chance to save one instead."

I scoffed at him. "Do you think saving this world makes up for all you have done?"

"No."

Mathias had held on for as long as he could, and true to his will and his word he was now going to die so that Becky could live. The anomaly became too strong as the will of the universe demanded that time returned to its proper flow and Mathias began to disintegrate, and although he felt every moment of it, he held time for as long as he could. I watched him as he refused to let go. "Do you think that you will be forgiven?"

"No."

Tears rolled down my face as I watched him sacrifice himself, with no hope of reward. I wept as he gave everything to set right the world. "Oh, brother...you have so much to learn."

His deeds had not gone unnoticed, and it was known that most of the terrible things that he brought to his world were the actions of those who controlled his free will. They perverted him and enslaved him, but in the end, when he was free, he chose to save the world and the people he cared for, with the belief that there would be no redemption for the Mad Genie DeSalvo. But that was not what was meant to come to pass. In the last moment of his existence, his figure had turned silver. He would be given a chance to find that redemption. His memories were blocked, and they were set so that once he reached certain levels of understanding and mastery, his memories would return to him. His body was reverted to a younger state along with his mind, and Dalen was going to be given another chance.

. . .

Dalen felt odd, almost queasy and his mind began to fog until there was nothing. It seemed to only last a second, and then everything refocused as fast as it came on.

After snapping back to the reality going on around him, the first thought that Dalen could remember was to ask himself how long he had been staring at the beads. He blinked a couple of times and looked around with a sense of confusion. 'What had grabbed his attention?' he asked himself. 'Had there been a sound?'

Entering the room were multiple individuals. Most of them were clad in navy blue jumpsuits with the museum's logo on their backs in white. There were two armed individuals in security uniforms different than the standard security of the museum. The two women who came in with them wore clothes that suggested they worked here in a more executive manner.

As a second surprise, only after his brain had identified the possible danger, did he look around the room to realize that it was dawn. Dalen could see out the window on the eastern side of the room, past the courtyard, the sun had crept over the trees and was pouring light into the room. Dalen stood there stunned for a moment. He didn't know how to process the time loss. Several hours had gone by. As one of the women began talking his mind was driven back from the depths of his thought and brought back to what was going on.

33

SAVING THE WORLD

"Then let us recognize them now. As King, I request it. Take this moment for our fallen comrade." Christoph put his hand over his heart and asked Becky to speak hers. Everyone put their hands over their hearts as well.

Dalen put his hand over his heart as his memories became complete and he remembered the last moments of his past life. As he lowered his head, he noticed that besides the robes and armor of the Brotherhood of Light, he now wore Diem's prayer cloth over his right shoulder and Mathias's fire cloth over his left. He was whole.

Two lifetimes that were aggressively different, both ending in him having to destroy his timeline to create one that he wished would be better. All of DeSalvo's memories and powers were now his to command as well as his own. He had sacrificed everything to make sure he could be standing right here. Right now.

"We have lost someone today. They didn't just die they were taken from our hearts and memories. We may never know their name, but I can tell you who they were. They were a friend, a sister, or brother to all of us. They were loved and trusted... they were one of us." The ground began to rumble but she just talked louder. "They were someone who knew in their hearts that this moment had to happen. They were someone willing to risk everything so that we could end this once and for all. Let us go forth and win this battle in their name. So that their sacrifice will not be in vain!"

Dalen stopped time just as Becky finished. He knew that everything was about to go sideways, and this was his moment. He reached out with his hand and as he touched Grelf's arm she began to move like him. She let her gaze slowly move to her left as she noticed that everything was frozen and stopped when she saw Dalen smiling at her. "Dalen? Is that you?"

"Yeah. It's me." Dalen looked down at himself and turned around. "It seems that we have all been going through some changes. Being a jinn, my form reflects those changes." Dalen smiled. "My form is no longer corporeal." Dalen smiled again and waved off the statement. "I mean, it's an option, but when I do become corporeal, my form takes the image of the truth of who I am."

Grelf took in his appearance. The first thing she noticed was his age. He had aged thirty years, but she could still see the Dalen she had always known. Then her eyes moved downward and took in all that he was wearing and tried to understand that everything she could see, was a truth about him in some way, made real by his understanding of it. "It's absolutely beautiful, but I don't think that is why you have frozen time. What's on your mind, Pax?"

"I was just thinking." Dalen rubbed his beard. In the earth challenge you obtained the blessing of the unicorns, right?"

"Yes. They are with me now." Grelf took a deep breath in and felt their power within her.

"What of your fire trial?" Dalen asked. "Was there anything special there?"

"Yes. It was witnessed by a phoenix goddess."

"The same phoenix that was there the moment the power was sent to you and helped you transform into the dragon and the unicorn, right?"

"Yes, I believe so."

"Did she give you any other blessings?"

Grelf reached out with one hand and with the other tapped her Vengerian Pin. A luminescent feather appeared in her hand. "She gave me this and said it was for when all else is lost."

Dalen believed this was what needed to be changed. He

mused at the idea that such a small thing as whether or not you have a feather with you would change the outcome of the world. But then again, he reminded himself, look how much change came from just moving a boy six hours ahead in the future.

Dalen felt his old skills from his darker days were at the ready, but instead of using them to manipulate for control, he would use them to guide Grelf to an answer. "In my opinion, the phoenix goddess gave you that feather with a planned purpose, she even gave you a hint as to when to use it, right?"

"Right."

"I have seen a version of this where all is lost, and it came down to the point that this cannot be done without you. End of story. So, it could be said that if you die all is lost. Can you see this as a possibility?"

"Are you saying that something is going to happen to me?" Grelf sounded concerned.

"That is not specifically what I was talking about. If we lost Christoph, we would be lost as well. I am saying that the phoenix gave her feather to you, and I think that means something."

"Do you want to hold it just in case something happens to either of us?"

"I'm not saying anything is going to happen to you, but since she gave it to you, you might want to keep it handy. Perhaps put it in your right arm guard. Who knows, maybe it will help you swing a killing blow on her."

"Her?"

"The dragon? Oh yes and scorned." Dalen shook his head. "So much fury. So yeah... What do you think? It couldn't hurt."

Grelf agreed and tucked the phoenix feather into her right arm guard.

"Okay." Dalen looked back at everybody else still frozen. Officially, it was Grelf that he was talking to, but he sent out a small prayer to all of them. "Focus on what you are doing. We got this. Ready?" Grelf nodded, she was ready. "Alright. Grelf?" Dalen prepared for time to start flowing again. He pointed to where the Chaos Dragon was about to emerge and asked, "Have you met the Chaos Dragon?"

Time started moving forward again and the ground began to rise as if a new hill were being formed but then it ruptured, and the dragon began to emerge from underneath.

Christoph balled himself up and then stretched out wide, and as he did giant dragon wings spread out from his back, and scales formed over most of his visible skin. He leaped into the air and with a flap of his wings he was airborne and beginning to climb.

Grelf turned into stardust and twinkled out of existence then reappeared the same way on the tip of the Chaos Dragon's head and held on to one of its horns as the dragon pulled herself out of the rock face and began to stand up.

As the Chaos Dragon rose it created a void in the cliffs that it used to create itself. The ground gave way quickly and began to fall. Becky put one of the handles from her blades under her butt and clicked it into position, and then used the other to stabilize herself as the ground fell away from them. Master Peace leaped out as the last piece of ground fell from under him and flew through the air, landing by Grelf's side.

The ground dropped directly under Sir Adam. He dropped straight down into the cavernous void. Dalen watched as Maddicus leaped in after him, Dalen just smiled and shook his head. He remembered that he had to catch the city, but he decided that trying to hold up that whole thing was a huge waste of effort.

Dalen reached out with the Mind Sphere and connected to Aiden who was scared and glad to hear from him. *I am going to need your help son.*

Aiden opened his mind and power to his father. *What do you need me to do?*

Dalen began to move himself along the ground as the city fell toward the sea. *Allow me to connect with you and your abilities. I have to bend time and space at the same time.*

Aiden relented and connected his powers to Dalen's who positioned himself at sea level, nearly side by side with the Chaos Dragon.

Toomba was surprised to see him as Dalen appeared on Toomba's boat. He was too far away to make out the details of his face but recognized Dalen's garb and armor from where he was. He looked up and gave thanks to the Goddess of the Sea. "What the bibitz, man!" Toomba pointed at the Chaos Dragon and said, "Biggest dragon I have ever seen, man."

Dalen was standing on the bow of Toomba's ship. "It's good you are here. You want to help me save Venger?"

"That's why I came, man!" Toomba got to the wheel and called out. "What do you need from me?"

"Try to keep the boat steady!" Dalen called out.

Toomba closed his eyes and said aloud, "I have always been faithful, and not once have I strayed from the path you have given me and my people. I need you with me now. This I pray to you. Goddess of the Sea. "Give this vessel peace."

The ship was far enough out of the way to keep from being stepped on, but the water was choppy, and with every step, the Chaos Dragon caused large waves in every direction, although the waves beat against its hull, Toomba's ship stood perfectly still upon the water.

The Chaos Dragon was busy with Christoph as he flew around her and dodged her attacks. Dalen watched as the cave-in happened sending out a ripple of destruction that changed the landscape permanently. When the ripple hit the ground that Venger was on, it began to fall. Dalen opened the Quantum sphere just by thinking of it. No one had ever considered attempting what he was going to do, but any thought that even sounded like doubt had been banished from his heart and mind. He had already had his lesson about size having no bearing when it came to his abilities, and he was well past listening to the rules of reality, reminding himself that only he could impose limitations on what he could do.

Ready son? Dalen asked, but he could already feel that

Aiden was ready to lend his abilities to bend not just time but space to his father. Dalen closed one eye and put out his hand so that it looked like Venger was in the palm of his hand. He closed both eyes and made a wish. When he opened them again Dalen was holding Venger City in the palm of his hand, and now that it was there, he simply moved his hand away from the cliff face and brought it close to him to keep it safe. Having Venger City in the palm of his hand gave him the opportunity to thoroughly examine it from above and see the beauty of it.

The Chaos Dragon roared with pain and Dalen looked over as she caught Christoph in midflight. She held him close to her face and then dropped him as Grelf planted the Horn of the Unicorn into her head.

Dalen knew what was coming next and knew he had to move as he watched the dragon throw Grelf to the ground. He opened his dimensional pocket and placed the City of Venger inside it and quickly closed it. He knew he was going to have to move quickly if he was going to be where this timeline needed him to be. He turned to Toomba and gave him a quick bow and said thank you. Toomba barely heard him, he was staring up at the Chaos Dragon from a much closer angle than he ever wanted to be.

The Chaos Dragon brought her foot down and then quickly stepped back and roared with pain and frustration. Dalen flew toward where he knew Grelf was going to be and stopped short to avoid the blast. He watched as Becky bamphed out of the way and although Grelf was broken and dying she smiled. Dalen slowed time down and watched in slow motion as she put her right arm up to protect herself as the blast came in. The first thing the blast touched was the phoenix feather which ignited as the energy hit her.

"No!" Christoph, Maddicus, and Sir Adam crash-landed moments after Grelf was vaporized. Christoph dropped to his knees in the ash and sobbed. "No."

All of a sudden Grelf sat up naked from the ash with a scream that surprised everyone except for Dalen.

Christoph was by her side and helping her up. "Leave it to you to go down in the history books facing the Chaos Dragon nude."

The Chaos Dragon was furious, so it decided to end everything by destroying Venger City, but it was nowhere to be found. *I will kill you all for this!* She screamed into everyone's mind.

Grelf grabbed the Horn of the Unicorn and transformed. She was wearing the attire of the Fire Princess, but her body was made of obsidian. Her eyes matched her hair which was ablaze with fire and light.

Master Peace spoke to everyone over the Vengerian Pin. ‹I am still in position. Maybe we can still kill this thing.›

Dalen stood in front of Christoph and Grelf. "Hey, check this out, everyone is still alive. One more step and this is over, but you are going to have to act as one."

Maddicus put something in Sir Adam's hand and kissed him.

"Because you would try to stop me." She kissed him once more and then she got back on her board and shot off towards the Chaos Dragon. "I'll keep her busy."

Sir Adam tried to stop her, but she was too fast. He looked in his hand and found she had placed her Vengerian Pin in his hand. He couldn't contact her and tell her to come back. She flew out and directly into the Chaos Dragon's line of sight. As Maddicus came in, the Chaos Dragon reached for her. Maddicus leaped off her board and ran the length of the dragon's arm toward her neck. The Bodite laughed and yelled out "Missed me!" as she leaped off the dragon's shoulder and caught her board as it came under the Chaos Dragon's arm.

It had worked. The Chaos Dragon was now swatting at the Bodite, but Maddicus continued to outmaneuver each attack with an aerial cabaret of the most breathtaking stunts of skill and mastery.

"Hey guys?" Sir Adam's voice was calm but urgent. "I know that my girlfriend is amazing."

"Girlfriend?" asked Master Peace.

"Yeah."

"Nice"

"Yeah. Later." Sir Adam cleared his throat. "I know that my girlfriend is amazing, and I understand that after everything we have been through in the last some odd days, we are pretty numb to all of this, and so it's awesome to just sit here and watch her go, but she did it so you guys can form Voltron, or do whatever it

is you guys are supposed to do... so, maybe we should, you know..."
Sir Adam gestured with his hand like he couldn't find the words.
"Whatever?"

Sir Adam's words sunk deep into all of them. It had been
years for Dalen, and Master Peace, and all of it in temples of
meditation or prayer. They had been seekers of peace and truth.
But the last few weeks, for all of them, had been a radical set of
events that had literally changed them. Elemental forces. Dragons.
Unicorns. Gods. It had become commonplace, and they had become
numb to it.

"Right." Christoph gripped the Eye of the Dragon and
refocused his mind. As he did, Christoph felt the presence of both
dragons. His mind opened like an iris to the understanding of the
universe as he himself became the embodiment of both of them.
The All-Seeing...The All-Knowing Dragon. His wings lit up for
a moment and when they dimmed his wing was no longer broken,
and his eyes lit up gold and blue. "I am ready to do what must
be done."

Grelf gave Dalen a nod. "Good call, about the feather."
Dalen smiled and shrugged. "I'm ready." She focused the power
that was surging inside her and harmonized it to the frequency of
the Horn of the Unicorn, and then let go. It happened between the
frames of time so; it was only Dalen who got to witness it. To all
else, it was a flash of light that was too bright to look into, but to
Dalen, he watched as Grelf became The Unicorn. Kargen and Pipim
together brought forth a new unicorn into the world, but this one
would be a gateway between their worlds.

They were not the last of the unicorns, they were the last to stay. They had been captured and put into servitude, but the other unicorns had left because they believed that there was none left, who was worthy. Pipim and Kargen had found worthy heroes, and this was their queen. She would serve as a bridge and if ever needed, the unicorns would stand with the fate of Venger.

Grelf stood before them changed. She had the form of a woman in a silver celestium full plate armor with a complete bodysuit of white celestium that gave off moonlight. Her skin was white as was her hair, and in the center of her forehead grew a real unicorn horn.

"Okay." Christoph took a long, hard slow look and Grelf. "I know that we are supposed to be focusing, but... Damn."

Grelf smiled and whispered, "Hush you." Both refocused and then looked to Dalen for their next step.

"Right. That would be me." Dalen opened his third eye, now known as the Eye of Time, and looked forward into the future. He looked through the Quantum Field at all the ways that this could go and found the one where they were victorious. He looked at it until that frame of time became real. Then he watched the memory backward in time until he saw how it happened. "Okay, that's pretty beautiful" The Eye of Time closed, and Dalen gestured to Christoph to stand close to Grelf. "Stand directly behind her." Christoph did as he was told and put his left arm around her waist. She leaned into him and rested her head against his chest and then focused on the moment. "The Horn of the Unicorn is a physical blade representing the body and heart. The Eye of the Dragon is a formless spirit blade of the mind and soul. They must become one." Dalen looked at them both. "And with them, so must you."

"It makes sense." Christoph held Grelf close. "If there is anybody in this world that can defeat the Chaos Dragon. It's you and me together."

"I love you." Grelf began to glow.

"I love you too." Christoph closed his wings around them, as he placed the Eye of the Dragon into the Horn of the Unicorn, and they phased together and became one.

Dalen took the white stone from his being. He no longer needed it and could surpass anything that it offered. He let go of the stone and it flew to the center of the two becoming one, and light erupted from Christoph's wings.

The light faded and they spread their wings. Their wings were still like a dragon's, with scales of silver celestium with white sails and they had a single horn made of white celestium. They looked down at themselves and found that they had the form of a biped made of celestium with a masculine physique but obvious feminine features, creating something that could not be defined either way. In their hand they held the blade, Dorn's Promise. A blade that could stop even a god. It was so powerful it cut through time and space with fire as it moved, and their arm began to burn. The pain was tremendous, but there were pressing matters, and pain would have to wait its turn.

Dalen reached out with the Mind Sphere and sent a message directly to Maddicus. *We need this bitch to look up.*

Maddicus yelped as he entered her mind but was able to maintain her flight. She dodged under the Chaos Dragon's arm and flew directly at her midsection. She pulled up just as she got there and began to climb as the Chaos Dragon began to slap her own body again and again trying to squash her. Maddicus flew right past the mouth and just out of reach, she leaped off her board into a backward summersault.

The Chaos Dragon looked up and opened her mouth to catch her on the way down. This was their moment, and they leaped from the ground and with blinding speed flew at the unsuspecting Chaos Dragon.

Dalen slowed down time for Maddicus so she could watch in slow motion as she spun upside down. The Chaos Dragon was directly underneath Maddicus with her jaws wide open as a streak made of white light came ripping through the universe. It was flying straight at the Chaos Dragon but tilted upward and went through the bottom of the Chaos Dragon's throat. From her angle, she could see them as they moved through the Chaos Dragon's gullet and watched as they continued their trajectory through the soft tissue of the throat and into the Chaos Dragon's skull. Maddicus could see a moment of shock and panic on the Chaos Dragon's face before her head erupted into a ball of light large enough to encompass her entire head. Maddicus reached out, reactivated her board, sat on it, and cheered as she watched the Chaos Dragon disintegrate into a ball of light.

As did everyone who watched the Chaos Dragon and her threat fade into nothing. Everyone continued to cheer until

Christoph and Grelf returned. Once they landed, they separated and Grelf and Christoph lay there exhausted surrounded by the four Elemental Blades. They looked at each other and began to laugh. They kissed each other and collapsed back into laughter.

Dalen looked on as his friends piled onto the both of them. I stood next to him, watching as well. "You should join them," I said as I placed a brotherly hand on his shoulder. "You earned it."

"You know, don't you?"

"Of course, I do."

"Have you always known?"

I smiled. "I had a strong belief, but I knew it would always come down to you." I patted him on the back and said, "Now that you have ascended, I think we should talk soon."

"Ascended?"

"Yes, you are now the Master of Time, and many will consider Dalen Pax the God of Time." Dalen looked back at me with a look of surprise. "That's why we should talk. For now, I want to remind you that you have a city to put back, and I just wanted to remind you to check your pocket."

Dalen opened his dimensional pocket and removed the city. He closed one eye, tilted his head to get the right angle with the landscape, and placed his arm the right distance away from his eye. Then he blinked and let go and Venger, now a coastal city, was nestled along the shoreline.

Dalen was just about to close his pocket when he noticed

that there was something in there that he didn't remember putting in. It was a cup and a notebook. There was a scrap of paper being used as a bookmark and Dalen opened it and read what it said. Dalen knew what this meant, and he yelled to get everyone's attention.

"Hey guys!" They all looked up from their cuddle puddle of victory and Dalen read aloud. "If this works, none of you will remember me, but if you are reading this it means that we were victorious, and I was right about Dalen's pocket dimension protecting these artifacts when I was pulled from time. More importantly, it means destroying the Time Stone was worth it." Dalen choked up as he read the last lines that were written. "I love you all... Travis."

34

DALEN'S BROTHER

Dalen stood next to me in the doorway of the healing temple of the Brotherhood of Light. Everything that he had done and gone through since David had been cursed with the Soul Freezer had been done so this moment could happen. He smiled as he watched Master Love use her abilities to connect to the Divine Field of the universe and channel it through her soul into David's. She knew that there was nothing to be done, but that had never stopped Master Love before.

She felt Dalen's presence and finished her healing. "I have

asked for the impossible. Tell me that I have not placed my faith in the wrong hands."

"As you wish." Dalen floated off the ground, glided over to them both, and knelt beside his brother. "I know how to wake him. It turns out that there is no other way to wake him, except by the creator of the blade that cut him. They can wake him at will." Dalen smirked with a shrug as he reached out with his right hand and the sapphire blade known as Soul Freezer appeared in his hand. "Turns out I am the original creator of this accursed thing."

Master Love stared at the blade with doubt and concern. "I thought it was created by the mad genie DeSalvo."

"Decades ago, I was." Dalen made the blade vanish. "I'm still trying to come to grips with it, but I will tell you this, Master Peace has been instrumental in getting me through the truth of it."

She raised Dalen's chin and looked him in the eyes with tears in hers. "Master... Peace?"

"Yes." Dalen gave her a wink. "He sends his best."

"Oh, Ben... I'm so proud of you." Her heart produced a ripple that could be felt for miles in every direction.

"If it wasn't for him. I could have just lost myself in the realization of the monster I used to be." Dalen was kneeling but gave Master Love a bow. "He has been teaching me how to heal. Not only outward but inward."

Master Love glanced over at David. "May I make a suggestion?" Before you wake up David, you might want to consider that you are wearing the face of the man who attacked him. It might be jarring as he wakes."

Dalen raised an eyebrow as he considered the truth of her suggestion. "You have a good point."

Dalen slid a magic ring onto David's finger, much like the ones he had made for his friends when they had first arrived. It granted the wearer a sight that would supersede their eye's natural vision. It would draw in the things their mind was not ready to accept. So, when Dalen removed the curse from David, he saw Dalen the way that he had seen him last.

Dalen used his ability to read the fabric of magic and located the curse inside David. He took a deep breath and placed his hand on David's chest. He pressed his fingertips firmly against his sternum and connected to the Body Sphere, he slowly pulled his fingertips inward and up, drawing with it the dark magic that had stolen David's life.

"I am guessing you granted my wish and kicked that guy's butt?" David set up and looked around at the walls of the Temple of Light's healing room. "I remember that guy had a knife to my throat." David rubbed his neck. "Is this some sort of a hospital?"

"Yes and no." Dalen was playing his role well, allowing David time to acclimate to his surroundings. "There is so much to tell you." Dalen walked around, behind Master Love, and put his hands on her shoulders. "This is Master Love, and she is going to give you one more check-up before they release you." Then he came over and gave me a side hug. "This guy is the greatest storyteller ever, I must admit, even better than you, but just barely. He is a friend and a brother. I need to go talk to the guy who runs this place about checking you out, but I want you to listen to what this man is going to tell you."

David turned to me and shook my hand. "Any brother of Dalen's is a brother of mine." He let Master Love put her hands on his back along his spine in a few places. "So, what do I call you?"

"You can call me Will of Grey, and I have a story to tell you."

"Hit me."

"Let's go back to the last thing you remember..."

Dalen walked out of the healer's quarter and made his way to the only place that mattered to him at the moment. When he walked out onto the stone terrace courtyard the Grand Master of the Temple of Light was waiting for him. They stood together and watched the sun come up over a new world.

Dalen chuckled at a memory. "When I first met you, I asked you if you were a ghost."

Master Truth smiled and said, "If you remember correctly, I asked you the same."

"I guess we were both right." Dalen pulled out his cup and allowed it to fill.

Grand Master Truth turned the coin over in his mind and said, "Or we were both wrong."

"Ha." Dalen nodded. "Indeed." And then took a sip of his cup. They sat there in silence for a moment and just reveled in being in the moment they were in...together. After each of them took a few more sips Dalen asked, "Where are you in all of this?"

"After a lifetime of adventures and eons with the Continuum, I stood with them and watched as this world finally came to its conclusion, and for once it was not by my hand, I went back to the dawn of time, and I built this temple and retired."

"Retired?"

"Well, being Master Truth, Master Ki, and the other Gods of the Temple of Light, keep me busy. Ever notice that Master Ki and I were never there at the same time?" He took another sip from his cup. "Diem. Between them and being the God of Time, I can't really call it a retirement, but here is where I find myself and recharge. I have always loved it here, far from the constant struggles of good and evil."

"You know all those things I am about to say about how much you mean to me and all that?"

"I do."

"Yeah. All that."

Master Truth nodded and rubbed one of his eyes with his thumb, and then reached out and clinked his cup against Dalen's.

"Are you going to tell me what's coming?" Dalen asked as a joke to lighten the mood.

"That's up to you, but if I had to guess, you'll end up

here." He smiled and took another sip from his cup. "Having this conversation, or at least that's how I remember it."

Dalen frowned and nodded. "Fair."

"I will tell you one thing about the future."

Dalen took a sip off his cup and asked, "Yeah, and what's that?"

"David in three... Two... One..."

"You're a freaking jinn?" David came out to the stone courtyard and stopped in his tracks long enough to look around and stare at the wonderment of where he was, but it was only for a moment, and then he blinked a few times and shook the view from his mind and power walked over to Dalen who was standing alone at the far end of the courtyard. "A freaking jinn?"

"Technically, 'We' are freaking jinn." Dalen took a sip from his cup and looked back over the courtyard railing and watched the sun finish cresting over the waterfall to the east.

"Right. Let's start one page before that." David hugged Dalen with great force. He wept and Dalen held him. "If I were to ever pick who I could have to be a brother, I would so pick you." Dalen matched his strength and for the first time, they embraced each other as brothers.

"Two long lost brothers..." Dalen said, referring to an old joke that they had with each other because they had the same mismatched blue and violet eyes.

"That found each other in the foster system." They

said together.

"And what!?" David ran his hands through his hair nervously. "Ms. Warren is our actual mother?"

"And a jinn."

"Right. Earth Jinn. Heartstone. That was crazy."

"Right?"

"Okay... I have to see it. I know this isn't you. I'm all good. I want to see it. I need to make it real in my mind." David was almost giddy.

Dalen looked back at his friend and brother and said, "If you are truly ready to know me for who I am, all you need do, is remove the ring that is creating this more familiar image of me."

David didn't hesitate. He removed the ring and stared at Dalen Pax. The Master of Time. Balanced and in harmony with himself and everyone he had ever been. David openly wept as the truth set his mind free, and in that moment, he knew that anything was possible. He hugged his brother again and then pulled back with tears rolling down his cheeks. "I am so proud of you."

"Wait until you see everyone else. There have been a lot of changes since you decided to take a nap." Dalen was truly happy to have David back, and he knew that after everything, his friends could really use David's return. "Would you like to go see them? They miss you like crazy."

David took a deep breath in and smiled with a nod. "Yes please." David looked out over the view. "Shame we have to go, this place is beautiful."

Dalen looked out over the canyon and agreed. "In all of the world, this is where I call home." Dalen tugged on David's shirt. "Come on. I'll tell you what. After we meet up with everyone and you say hello, we will wait for everyone to go to bed and we will come back and sleep here tonight, under the stars."

David liked the sound of that and couldn't wait to see his friends. Now that Dalen had full knowledge of his abilities, he prepared himself for the journey and took David's hand. Their friends were still a couple of thousand years in the past so together they traveled back through time and appeared next to the white tree. Dalen could have moved himself closer, but he wanted David to have the experience of this view. It was midday, and the sun was glistening on the waves. The ground had been turned and folded over on itself, and much of the landscape was more dirt than grass and wildflowers, but Dalen knew that it would grow back and soon this entire area would be alive again.

"That's quite a view." David looked out over the amphitheater-shaped valley, and at its bottom sat the City of Venger, nestled down into the valley between two mountainous cliffs.

Dalen nodded and floated over to him. "You want to see something amazing?"

"Dalen," David smirked. "Your ability to ask questions that only crest the edge of being rhetorical is astounding."

"The moment I stopped time, Becky was staring at the end

of the world." Dalen began to shift back and forth and from left to right, trying to find the exact location. "She was staring at it so fiercely that when time began to move backward the final frame was..." Dalen struggled for the right word. "Imprinted?"

Dalen looked out over the view of the valley and asked me, through the continuum, "Imprinted?"

I reciprocated his use of the Grey Continuum and sent him back the understanding that the word 'imprinted' was as good a term as any other.

"Yes, imprinted," David asked who he was talking to, and Dalen told him that he and I were telepathically connected. Dalen found the exact spot where Becky was standing. "Ah, there we go," Dalen instructed David to stand exactly where he was. "It's not the actual frame of time, I checked, but it is the image that was imprinted in the eyes of Becky as she stood here."

As David adjusted for height and got his eyes exactly where Becky's had been he could see the battlefield as it was and the Chaos Dragon breathing its attack onto Venger. It caught David off guard at first and he fell back.

"I know. Right?" Dalen helped David to his feet and helped him find the spot again.

"Oh damn!" David flinched but found the spot again quickly. Dalen let David look at it for as long as the novelty held and when David was ready Dalen took David's hand again and bamphed them directly outside of Dorn's. Dalen walked in first to see who was there.

Master Peace and Becky were sitting across the table from Sir Adam and Maddicus at a booth having lunch. They didn't notice Dalen as he walked in, so he quickly ushered David in, and they moved together along the wall to get out of sight. The booth was an alcove built into the wall so once they made it in, they were out of sight and could move within feet of their friends and they wouldn't be able to see him.

Dalen walked up to the table directly. "Good morning. How is everyone?"

Maddicus, Master Peace, and Adam said that they were all right, but Becky was still broken up about everything. She had been reading Travis's notebook since they had found it the day before.

"I am at such a loss." Becky turned a page in the notebook and stared at the writing without reading it. "I have read this three times now. Back to front. I was hoping that reading it would jog my memory, but no matter how hard I try, I can't remember him." She began to cry. "He loved me. I loved him. I gave him my virginity... from everything I read he was the love of my life, and I can't remember him."

Dalen scooted into the booth right next to her and held her while she cried. After a few moments, she took her napkin, wiped her eyes, and apologized. Dalen squeezed her and said, "No need. I think what you are feeling is right on the money, and you have nothing to be sorry for." She nodded and thanked him. "It's all good. Now, I am the bearer of good news. Would it be alright if I help get you in the right mind frame to appreciate it?"

Becky agreed to it, so Dalen used his free hand to touch his throat chakra. In doing so he activated the Arcane Element within him and with the arm that was around Becky, he reached up and touched her forehead, directly over her third eye, activating the observer within her so that she would truly take in what he was about to say.

Relax. That was all that he said. But it moved through him and deeply touched her mind. It was a skill he learned while he was DeSalvo. Back then he used it to entrap the mind and the soul through emotions, but Dalen understood that there was more than one truth and that nothing is either good or evil until it is given a field of intent. He had asked her, and she was aware of what was happening. The Fire Jinn had done it to him when they first met. She was still aware of the situation and her pain was not diminished. He hadn't removed the truth, all he did was redirect her mind, body, and soul from responding to the trauma with stress but instead responding with peace and clarity.

"Thank you." She hugged him. "You didn't take it from me."

"What good would that have done?" He hugged her back. "Fair warning. That will only last as long as you let it." She understood and nodded. "Alright, the first bit of good news... finding our friend is what we are doing next. After I give you the rest of the good news, we are going to do everything we can to find Travis."

She hugged Dalen again and said, "Thank you. Thank you so much."

"It's like I said, Becky. It's not that we don't care, we care a great deal." Dalen rubbed her shoulder and then let her go so he could scoot out of the booth. "We were just dealing with end-of-the-world, time-sensitive events. There is no one here who is not ready to devote our complete attention to it." Dalen smiled. "All six of us."

"Master Peace nodded and said, "That was my guess for the other good news."

Sir Adam visibly counted everyone at the table.

"Six?" asked Becky.

"Yeah." Dalen raised an eyebrow and grinned. "All five of us, and..."

David popped his head from around the corner and said, "Hello everyone. Having adventures without me?"

Becky squealed with delight. She reached over and turned the crystal cone in the center of the table and as the table retracted and their mugs began to fall, Master Peace, Maddicus, and Sir Adam caught them on the way down. Becky had thought that she was all out of tears because she had cried all night, but these were tears of joy and Becky's body relented to her relief and wept once more.

Sir Adam joined in the hug and then Master Peace. David took it all in. Cherish these moments. Dalen's thoughts flowed like water in David's mind. When I look back at the moments that really mattered, they were not the moments when we fought dragons and fears. It was when we had moments to just be who we truly are.

A family.

It was time to get down to business and they all moved over to the bar so that they could introduce Dorn's to him properly. Dorn was working at the bar and welcomed David. "So, you are the one that this group is willing to risk life and limb, travel through time, and then help bring peace to this world for, and all of it so you could be standing with us now. It's nice to meet you. I'm Dorn. I uh... run everything you see here."

"It's nice to meet you." David blushed and seemed nervous. "Will of Grey brought me up to speed. It's an honor to meet you."

Dorn smiled. "That Bard's been telling stories about me again? I swear one day I will have to pay him as a publicist. I have no doubt he has exaggerated greatly." Dorn put both hands on the bar and leaned in. "Today, I just run this tavern. So, what can I get you?"

"He's not kidding around. Think super amazing magic tavern. He can get you anything you want." Sir Adam said with glee.

David closed his eyes for a moment, and Dalen watched his brother accept all of it as true. "Anything?"

Dorn had a devilish grin on his face. He stared at David and said, "Push me."

"When I was ten, I was placed in a foster home for five months. It was one of the nicest people I ever got to live with. I stayed with them through winter and every Thursday night the lady who was my foster mom made us hot cocoa. It was one of the only times during my time in foster care, besides Ms. Warren's, that I felt happy. I mean truly happy. I want that hot cocoa."

Dorn softened and sincerely looked at David. "Now that is a good order." He reached below the bar and took the mug by the handle. When he brought it up, it was a white porcelain mug that had Dorn's logo on it.

It had toasted marshmallows on top with whipped cream, and everyone could smell the fresh ground cinnamon. David took a sip and just stared at it. He took another sip and as he did, he closed his eyes and tears fell from both of them. "I'm going to need a minute guys." He looked up at Dorn and asked, "How did you do that?"

Dorn smiled and gave him a wink. "Magic."

"Okay." Sir Adam sat at the bar next to David. "Now I want one too."

They all sat at the bar and shared one of David's happiest memories with him. It was the conversation about memories that sparked Dalen's next thoughts. He explained that although as Dalen, he couldn't find Travis anywhere on the timeline, DeSalvo had memories of Travis from his.

Becky got excited for a moment. "Dalen, you said I could have a wish. I wish for you to go back to that memory and get him and bring him back here."

"That would be a fantastic wish, but the truth is, that the memories are from a timeline that is completely destroyed." Dalen shrugged. "I can start trying to figure out how to move between the timelines, but it is not an ability I have at this time."

"You would need a Jinn of Dimension for that. Not time."
Dorn rubbed his chin. "Well, actually you would need a Jinn of
Dimension and a Jinn of Time to even consider it. You want to
go back in time to an old memory, but even then, that wouldn't
even begin to cover the whole problem. That would work for a
dimensional jump to an active timeline. The problem here is that
the entire timeline was destroyed."

"Okay." Becky shrugged. "Then I wish for you to make a
duplicate of him from that memory."

"It wouldn't be real." Dalen shook his head. "It would be a
facsimile based on a memory. But not even a full memory, but one
from another lifetime ago and from secondhand knowledge. I didn't
know his mind and heart. His thoughts and feelings."

"Then I wish that he never broke the Time Stone!" she
demanded and then stopped herself. "No. I can't." She flipped
through Travis's notebook and found a page. "It explains right
here. He knew that it had to be done, and he understood why.
This was our only chance to defeat the Chaos Dragon just as she
emerged." She flipped to another section. "Here. Here is where
we all told each other our secrets. When he told me I came up
with some reason not to listen to him. I just closed off and said
it was impossible." She was letting it get to her again and the
pain began to grow. "He tried. He tried to tell me, but I wouldn't
listen. I told him that it was impossible because there was a statue
of him in the Savior's Garden. A statue that none of us remember
and so somehow, we didn't create the future that was supposed
to happen."

"Not yet," David said simply.

It stopped Becky in her tracks and Oubliette whispered, "Please. Go on."

"If we find him tomorrow, then when they make the statues six months from now, Travis will have already been returned and remembered." David took a long pull off his cocoa and then said, "If you are going to make a wish, if you can't bring him back, you should at least have him be remembered."

Becky allowed hope to grant her one more tear. "Alright." She didn't speak directly to Dalen for her wish, instead, she just spoke it into the air like an open invitation. "What is killing me is the loss of memory. I can't even properly mourn his loss. None of us can. I wish that instead of there being a loss that creates sadness and pain, I wish we all could remember him and that the memory of him brought joy and peace."

"That can be arranged." Aiden's voice surprised everyone as if he had just appeared from nowhere and started talking. Which he had. He walked around behind the bar and set down the tray of cups he'd gathered from around the tavern. "I make it a point to be able to provide for folk who order from the bar. I think this is what you wanted." Aiden reached from behind the bar and pulled out a stick of chalk and handed it to Becky. "I suggest you drink to his memory."

"What am I supposed to do with this?" Becky asked as she looked at the chalk.

"Drink to his memory," Aiden said like that should have

made sense. "You have his cup, correct?" Becky pulled it out. "Where would you like to put it?" Becky looked at the chalk and figured since it was chalk it wouldn't matter and drew a circle near where she was sitting at the end of the bar. Aiden nodded. "And where will you be when you make this toast?"

Becky looked at Dorn asking for confirmation from him. He just shrugged and said this was her wish. She got out of her seat and drew a large enough circle to stand in comfortably, and once she did, she stood inside it. "Right here."

Aiden nodded. "You have a cup. You have your place. You have our attention. So, fulfill your own wish, and make a toast to the memory of your friend."

Becky sat the chalk down and picked up Travis's cup. She activated it and it filled with Travis's favorite drink. Becky smelled it and recognized it as cranberry grape juice. She raised it and said, "Here is to Travis. He was brilliant and answered questions before any of us knew to ask them. He was the only one who knew what was coming and the only one to always understand what was needed. He was kind and sentimental. He won our friendship, and he won my heart. I loved him so much..." She began to weep again but pulled it together to finish the toast. "I loved him so much that even though I cannot remember him I can feel him and the loss of him in my soul. So, here's to the memory of our friend. The man who is like a brother to you and the man who earned my heart. We love you." She took a sip of his cup, and the wish was complete.

Memories and feelings began to fill our minds. I was chatting with Toomba and the King and Queen. We watched as all of Becky's memories began to unlock in her mind and heart. As they played out, we relived them with her as she remembered. Then the waves of emotion and memories from everyone began to hit all of us. Everyone in the room could feel the collective loss of the Vengerian Guardians, and all of us together as a whole felt the heartache, but then it was washed away as the memories of Travis and a montage of Travis's greatest moments began to fill our heads and hearts. First came the memories of Sir Adam and Travis as they grew up together. Followed by David's memory of their friendship and how Travis had always been so clever in their games. And then from Dalen how he had always just accepted him when most people could only see how different he was. Master Peace's memories filled our minds as we remembered together how Travis saved his life. Then Becky's memories began to seep in, and we watched with great anticipation as we saw their relationship grow and blossom. Then came a collage of memories from each of us as we remembered how Travis had been through the adventure. We remembered the fifth statue. We remembered the speech that he gave just before we stormed the Shadow Army to free Venger.

All of us laughed and cried as we all remembered his smile and his brilliance. We all felt comradery and connection. Then we felt what had been building slowly beneath it. Love. A pure love of friendship, that bloomed like a fountain into brotherhood, and then our hearts burst as the love became whole and we knew how much Becky had always loved him back. Everyone just held each other as it washed over us. None of us moved. We just reveled in it for as long as we could. We looked around at the others in the room and we knew that together we had shared something extraordinary.

Dorn sent out his staff with a free round of whatever the patrons were drinking, but we only wanted one thing at that moment, and it was whatever Becky had drank from his cup. Dorn decided then and there that if anyone ever used the circle again, he would make it a tradition to share a drink with all who were there to witness the event.

What was more important than anything else was that each of us could remember Travis completely. Dalen moved back through his timeline to a memory of Travis with the intent to bring him here, but when actually in the moment, he was met with a hole in time. The same way he had tried to see him before but could only see a hole that his mind screamed at him to look away from, and that had only been a memory of what he was now experiencing. Being in the moment directly was far more potent and the hole began to try and take him, he had no choice but to return to his own time or be ripped from it himself. He reappeared in the frame seconds after he had originally left and fell to the floor. Master Peace was farthest from him when he appeared but was at his side and caught him before he hit the ground.

"I tried." was all that Dalen could get out. Master Peace could feel he was not alright and healed him, and after a few moments, Dalen patted Master Peace's hand. "I'm alright. Thank you." Dalen got back up and began to hover as he often did. "Now that I remember him from my timeline, I was hoping I could pull him from time."

Master Peace's tone was still that of concern. "Whatever you did, it almost killed you."

"Worth the risk. He would have tried for me." Dalen replied.

"So. What's the next step to get my brother back?" Sir Adam had a look in his eyes, and Dalen knew that now that he could remember Travis, there was going to be nothing stopping them from finding a way to rescue him. They all did.

"Well, let's ask the Fountain of Truth." Dalen closed his eyes and took a deep breath in. He pulled out his cup and activated it. He took a sip and then opened his eyes again. "Tomorrow morning, we are taking a journey. I'm not sure why." He took another sip from his cup. "When DeSalvo got the Time Stone, he plucked it from the hole that had been used by the Chaos Dragon when she originally ripped through the universe and destroyed the City of Dreams."

"You are talking about the Breath of Time, aren't you?" asked Becky. She flipped through Travis's notebook. She found the page and showed it to Dalen. Everyone leaned in and read:

Breath of Time. Good name.

Folds into infinite possibility and unlimited time.

Once I am lost, this may be an answer.

"Travis is lost in time, and we would need a one-in-a-trillion chance to find him." Becky looked hopeful for the first time in a day. "This sounds like a good place to start."

Sir Adam put up his hand and said, "All in favor?"

It was a unanimous decision. They were going to rest tonight, even Becky, and get up at first light, for tomorrow they were going to set off for the ancient City of Dreams, and they weren't going to stop until they saved Travis.

They had a few good hours of light left so they made their plans, figured out the path they would take, and the provisions they would need. Christoph and Grelf both agreed that this mission was important for two reasons. Getting to Travis was the main quest but closing the Breath of Time was a priority as well. If left unchecked, it would become a doorway for other things to push themselves into this world and it needed to be closed.

Dalen mentioned that he had the fragments of the original Time Stone. He had picked them up from the bottom of the well before he left to awaken David, and he believed that with a little research, he could find a way to repair it or make another. He said he knew a couple of places, like the Brotherhood of Light's library where he might be able to find some information. He turned to Dorn and asked, "May I have a key to one of the rooms upstairs? I am going to take David with me, and if we are going to..." He glanced at David. "Do all of the research needed and still be back here in the morning, I think it would be helpful to use one of your rooms for the night."

Dorn looked at David and said, "Your brother wants to use one of my rooms so that a lot can be done in a short period of time. He wants to take you with him, because one, he has missed you, but two, I believe he wishes to take time to help you catch up a little more before you head out. Listen close and be careful of what you ask for at this bar. Do you wish a key?"

"Yes, please," David said, knowing what he had just done

held weight. "I would like a little more time to catch up."

Dorn smiled and said, "As you wish." He reached under the bar and retrieved a key. It had the number two etched on it. The brothers said goodnight and that they would see them in the morning.

• • •

As they walked through the door, which was another portal, they stepped outside, back at the Brotherhood of Light, David smiled and said, "I love this. This is way awesome."

When David and Dalen returned to the stone courtyard of the Brotherhood of Light, David wanted a few minutes to take in everything that had just happened. Dalen let him have his moment, and when he had gathered himself, Dalen said he had two gifts for him. The first was David's twenty-sided die. "I picked it up for you when everyone left to go to school that last day. I knew that you wouldn't be able to come back for it, so I decided to take it with me."

"Hey, my lucky die." As soon as David had it in his hand, he somehow felt like a piece of him that had been missing had been returned. "You know, I kinda missed this."

"It's more than that." Dalen took a long sip of his cup, and although the visions that confirmed his thoughts raced through him, he slowed down time and went through all of it like he was learning a spell, until he understood the truth of what was being shown. It happened every time he took a sip, that swift and intense rush of truth, but it had been a long time since it caused him any harm. He was the Master of Truth as well as the Master of Time and although he endured this process every time he sipped from the Fountain of Truth, the intensity of the rush was never perceived by those around him. "The same way that the silver figure was my item, that die is yours."

"Heard, but what does that mean?" David held it close to his heart. "I believe you. I just want to understand."

Dalen took a deep breath in. "We, by our nature, are incorporeal beings. Our natural state is something that can be either corporeal or incorporeal, but what we are is jinn. Divine beings. The object is an anchor to connect us to this corporeal plane, so when we do things like sleep, we don't wink out of existence. "The Mad Genie DeSalvo's object worked like the proverbial genie's lamp. Whoever had control of it, had control of his power on the corporeal physical plane. That's how genies work, but the true form of it is what you have in your hand. It can give your avatar peace in times of stress. It can help them be brave in moments of weakness."

David looked at it closely. "Wow."

"It's a focus. A talisman if you will. Keep it close. You will need it before all of this is done."

"What do you mean?" David asked with a hint of concern.

"Think of that as a talisman of yourself." Dalen let him reinspect it. "Mine looked like a silver figure of the man you see before you now. It literally was a figure of me."

"Why is mine a twenty-sided die?" David rolled it in his

hand, and it landed on twenty.

"I am a time jinn. Mine had to do with who I would be within time. I would guess that yours has to do with it being something like that. Just like every aspect of this, it will relent and take the shape of what is needed. So, chances are it will have something directly to do..."

"With chance." Dalen smiled as David came to the right conclusion. He always knew how smart he was. "So." David rolled the die in his hand again and it landed on a ten. "How does someone train in chance?"

"We are going to work on that together, and when you feel you are ready, I will bring you back to Dorn's tomorrow morning. They won't even notice you were gone."

David smiled and looked at the die in his hands. "So, what am I supposed to do with this?"

I used mine to empower the Heartstone that Mother gave me. It was the object that brought me into my power. My guess is it will do the same for you." That is when Dalen presented David with his second gift. "With this."

Dalen retrieved from his pocket the crystal ball that was etched with all the Elements of Reality. He handed it to David who recognized it from the story I had told him.

"This is the thing that Mother gave you, for me?" David looked at it closely and inspected all the runes that were on it.

"Yeah. It has the exact symbols of my casting circle etched

into it and I believe that it is your piece of Mother's Heartstone. Once you are ready and you have the ability to combine the two into one, you will be ready to take your next form."

"How long will it take?" David asked with excitement about what was to come.

Dalen took a sip from his cup and smirked. "As long as you make it take." They both laughed at the simple logic of it. "I'll tell you what, and if you can listen to me it will help. When you are with me time has no relevance in your training. We got here by stepping through a room at Dorn's. Aiden made it so that I could study at the Temple of All Faith for twenty years, and when I finished no time had passed. So do not fret about things like time and how long it takes. We will work on this together. Brothers, until you are ready, and only you can decide when that is, but... and this is the part you need to hear, there is no such thing as a rush."

"From the story that Will told me, I think I have a basic concept of what's before me, but I do have one favor." David gave a basic bow of the brotherhood. "I would like to take the name Brother Chance."

Dalen took another sip from his cup and grinned. "As you wish."

THE END

Thank you to my wife Rhiannon. You have always been my muse and inspiration, but you are also my editor and co-conspirator. This is not just mine. It's ours, my love. Thank you for everything Darlin'.

What is Dyslexie Font?

Each letter is given its own identity making it easier for people with dyslexia
to be more successful at reading.

The Dyslexie font:
1 Makes letters easier to distinguish
2 Offers more ease, regularity and joy in reading
3 Enables you to read with less effort
4 Gives your self-esteem a boost
5 Can be used anywhere, anytime and on (almost) every device
6 Does not require additional software or programs
7 Offers the simplest and most effective reading support

The Dyslexie font is specially designed for people with dyslexia, in order
to make reading easier – and more fun. During the design process, all
basic typography rules and standards were ignored. Readability and
specific characteristics of dyslexia are used as guidelines for the design.

Graphic designer Christian Boer created a dyslexic-friendly font to make reading easier for people
with dyslexia, like himself.

"Traditional fonts are designed solely from an aesthetic point of view," Boer writes on his website,
"which means they often have characteristics that make characters difficult to recognize for people
with dyslexia. Oftentimes, the letters of a word are confused, turned around or jumbled up because
they look too similar."

Designed to make reading clearer and more enjoyable for people with dyslexia, Dyslexie uses heavy
base lines, alternating stick and tail lengths, larger openings, and semicursive slants to ensure that
each character has a unique and more easily recognizable form.

Our books are not just for children to enjoy, they are also for adults
who have dyslexia who want the experience of reading
to the children in their lives.

Learn more and get the font for your digital devices at
www.dyslexiefont.com

Buy More Books in Dyslexic Font @ m-cpublishing.org

www.ingramcontent.com/pod-product-compliance
Ingram Content Group UK Ltd.
Pitfield, Milton Keynes, MK11 3LW, UK
UKHW030839180225
455237UK00005B/29

9 781643 721408